The Collected Works
of Phillis Wheatley

THE SCHOMBURG LIBRARY OF
NINETEENTH-CENTURY BLACK WOMEN WRITERS

General Editor, Henry Louis Gates, Jr.

Titles are listed chronologically; collections that include works published over a span of years are listed according to the publication date of their initial work.

Phillis Wheatley, *The Collected Works of Phillis Wheatley*

Six Women's Slave Narratives: M. Prince; Old Elizabeth; M. J. Jackson; L. A. Delaney; K. Drumgoold; A. L. Burton

Spiritual Narratives: M. W. Stewart; J. Lee; J. A. J. Foote; V. W. Broughton

Ann Plato, *Essays*

Collected Black Women's Narratives: N. Prince; L. Picquet; B. Veney; S. K. Taylor

Frances E. W. Harper, *Complete Poems of Frances E. W. Harper*

Charlotte Forten Grimké, *The Journals of Charlotte Forten Grimké*

Mary Seacole, *Wonderful Adventures of Mrs. Seacole in Many Lands*

Harriet Jacobs, *Incidents in the Life of a Slave Girl*

Collected Black Women's Poetry, Volumes 1–4: M. E. Tucker; A. I. Menken; M. W. Fordham; P. J. Thompson; C. A. Thompson; H. C. Ray; L. A. J. Moorer; J. D. Heard; E. Bibb; M. P. Johnson; Mrs. H. Linden

Elizabeth Keckley, *Behind the Scenes. Or, Thirty Years a Slave, and Four Years in the White House*

C. W. Larison, M.D., *Silvia Dubois, A Biografy of the Slav Who Whipt Her Mistres and Gand Her Fredom*

Mrs. A. E. Johnson, *Clarence and Corinne; or, God's Way*

Octavia V. Rogers Albert, *The House of Bondage: or Charlotte Brooks and Other Slaves*

Emma Dunham Kelley, *Megda*

Anna Julia Cooper, *A Voice From the South*

Frances E. W. Harper, *Iola Leroy, or Shadows Uplifted*

Amanda Smith, *An Autobiography: The Story of the Lord's Dealings with Mrs. Amanda Smith the Colored Evangelist*

Mrs. A. E. Johnson, *The Hazeley Family*

Mrs. N. F. Mossell, *The Work of the Afro-American Woman*

Alice Dunbar-Nelson, *The Works of Alice Dunbar-Nelson*, Volumes 1–3

Emma D. Kelley-Hawkins, *Four Girls at Cottage City*

Pauline E. Hopkins, *Contending Forces: A Romance Illustrative of Negro Life North and South*

Pauline Hopkins, *The Magazine Novels of Pauline Hopkins*

Hallie Q. Brown, *Homespun Heroines and Other Women of Distinction*

The Collected Works

of

Phillis Wheatley

Edited with an Essay by
JOHN C. SHIELDS

New York   Oxford
OXFORD UNIVERSITY PRESS

Oxford University Press

Oxford   New York   Toronto
Delhi   Bombay   Calcutta   Madras   Karachi
Petaling Jaya   Singapore   Hong Kong   Tokyo
Nairobi   Dar es Salaam   Cape Town
Melbourne   Auckland

and associated companies in
Berlin   Ibadan

Library of Congress Cataloging-in-Publication Data

Wheatley, Phillis, 1753–1784.
The collected works of Phillis Wheatley.
(The Schomburg library of nineteenth-century black
women writers)
Bibliography: p.
1. Wheatley, Phillis, 1753–1784—Correspondence.
2. Poets, American—18th century—Correspondence.
I. Shields, John C., 1944–   . II. Title.   III. Series
PS866.W5   1988   811'.1   87-12498
ISBN 0-19-505241-2
ISBN 0-19-505267-6 (set)
ISBN 0-19-506085-7 (pbk)

4 6 8 10 9 7 5 3

Printed in the United States of America

The
Schomburg Library
of
Nineteenth-Century
Black Women Writers
is
Dedicated
in Memory
of
PAULINE AUGUSTA COLEMAN GATES

1916–1987

PUBLISHER'S NOTE

FOREWORD
In Her Own Write

Henry Louis Gates, Jr.

One muffled strain in the Silent South, a jarring chord and a vague and uncomprehended cadenza has been and still is the Negro. And of that muffled chord, the one mute and voiceless note has been the sadly expectant Black Woman, ...

The "other side" has not been represented by one who "lives there." And not many can more sensibly realize and more accurately tell the weight and the fret of the "long dull pain" than the open-eyed but hitherto voiceless Black Woman of America.

. . . as our Caucasian barristers are not to blame if they cannot *quite* put themselves in the dark man's place, neither should the dark man be wholly expected fully and adequately to reproduce the exact Voice of the Black Woman.

—ANNA JULIA COOPER, *A Voice From the South* (1892)

The birth of the Afro-American literary tradition occurred in 1773, when Phillis Wheatley published a book of poetry. Despite the fact that her book garnered for her a remarkable amount of attention, Wheatley's journey to the printer had been a most arduous one. Sometime in 1772, a young African girl walked demurely into a room in Boston to undergo an oral examination, the results of which would determine the direction of her life and work. Perhaps she was shocked upon entering the appointed room. For there, perhaps gathered in a semicircle, sat eighteen of Boston's most notable citizens. Among them were John Erving, a prominent Boston merchant; the Reverend Charles Chauncy, pastor of the Tenth Congregational Church; and John Hancock, who would later gain fame for his signature on the Declaration of Independence. At the center of this group was His Excellency, Thomas Hutchinson, governor of Massachusetts, with Andrew Oliver, his lieutenant governor, close by his side.

Why had this august group been assembled? Why had it seen fit to summon this young African girl, scarcely eighteen years old, before it? This group of "the most respectable Characters in *Boston*," as it would later define itself, had assembled to question closely the African adolescent on the slender sheaf of poems that she claimed to have "written by herself." We can only speculate on the nature of the questions posed to the fledgling poet. Perhaps they asked her to identify and explain—for all to hear—exactly who were the Greek and Latin gods and poets alluded to so frequently in her work. Perhaps they asked her to conjugate a verb in Latin or even to translate randomly selected passages from the Latin, which she and her master, John Wheatley, claimed that she "had made some Progress in." Or perhaps they asked her to recite from memory key passages from the texts of John Milton and Alexander Pope, the two poets by whom the African claimed to be most directly influenced. We do not know.

We do know, however, that the African poet's responses were more than sufficient to prompt the eighteen august gentlemen to compose, sign, and publish a two-paragraph "Attestation," an open letter "To the Publick" that prefaces Phillis Wheatley's book and that reads in part:

> We whose Names are under-written, do assure the World, that the Poems specified in the following Page, were (as we

verily believe) written by Phillis, a young Negro Girl, who
was but a few Years since, brought an uncultivated Barbarian
from *Africa*, and has ever since been, and now is, under the
Disadvantage of serving as a Slave in a Family in this Town.
She has been examined by some of the best Judges, and is
thought qualified to write them.

So important was this document in securing a publisher for
Wheatley's poems that it forms the signal element in the
prefatory matter preceding her *Poems on Various Subjects, Religious and Moral*, published in London in 1773.

Without the published "Attestation," Wheatley's publisher
claimed, few would believe that an African could possibly
have written poetry all by herself. As the eighteen put the
matter clearly in their letter, "Numbers would be ready to
suspect they were not really the Writings of Phillis." Wheatley and her master, John Wheatley, had attempted to publish
a similar volume in 1772 in Boston, but Boston publishers
had been incredulous. One year later, "Attestation" in hand,
Phillis Wheatley and her master's son, Nathaniel Wheatley,
sailed for England, where they completed arrangements for
the publication of a volume of her poems with the aid of the
Countess of Huntington and the Earl of Dartmouth.

This curious anecdote, surely one of the oddest oral ex-
aminations on record, is only a tiny part of a larger, and
even more curious, episode in the Enlightenment. Since the
beginning of the sixteenth century, Europeans had won-
dered aloud whether or not the African "species of men," as
they were most commonly called, *could* ever create formal
literature, could ever master "the arts and sciences." If they
could, the argument ran, then the African variety of humanity was fundamentally related to the European variety. If not,
then it seemed clear that the African was destined by nature

to be a slave. This was the burden shouldered by Phillis Wheatley when she successfully defended herself and the authorship of her book against counterclaims and doubts.

Indeed, with her successful defense, Wheatley launched two traditions at once—the black American literary tradition *and* the black woman's literary tradition. If it is extraordinary that not just one but both of these traditions were founded simultaneously by a black woman—certainly an event unique in the history of literature—it is also ironic that this important fact of common, coterminous literary origins seems to have escaped most scholars.

That the progenitor of the black literary tradition was a woman means, in the most strictly literal sense, that all subsequent black writers have evolved in a matrilinear line of descent, and that each, consciously or unconsciously, has extended and revised a canon whose foundation was the poetry of a black woman. Early black writers seem to have been keenly aware of Wheatley's founding role, even if most of her white reviewers were more concerned with the implications of her race than her gender. Jupiter Hammon, for example, whose 1760 broadside "An Evening Thought. Salvation by Christ, With Penitential Cries" was the first individual poem published by a black American, acknowledged Wheatley's influence by selecting her as the subject of his second broadside, "An Address to Miss Phillis Wheatly [*sic*], Ethiopian Poetess, in Boston," which was published at Hartford in 1778. And George Moses Horton, the second Afro-American to publish a book of poetry in English (1829), brought out in 1838 an edition of his *Poems By A Slave* bound together with Wheatley's work. Indeed, for fifty-six years, between 1773 and 1829, when Horton published *The Hope of Liberty*, Wheatley was the *only* black person to have published a book of imaginative literature in English. So central was this black woman's role in the shaping of the Afro-American literary tradition that, as one historian has maintained, the history of the reception of Phillis Wheatley's poetry *is* the history of Afro-American literary criticism. Well into the nineteenth century, Wheatley and the black literary tradition were the same entity.

But Wheatley is not the only black woman writer who stands as a pioneering figure in Afro-American literature. Just as Wheatley gave birth to the genre of black poetry, Ann Plato was the first Afro-American to publish a book of essays (1841) and Harriet E. Wilson was the first black person to publish a novel in the United States (1859).

Despite this pioneering role of black women in the tradition, however, many of their contributions before this century have been all but lost or unrecognized. As Hortense Spillers observed as recently as 1983,

> With the exception of a handful of autobiographical narratives from the nineteenth century, the black woman's realities are virtually suppressed until the period of the Harlem Renaissance and later. Essentially the black woman as artist, as intellectual spokesperson for her own cultural apprenticeship, has not existed before, for anyone. At the source of [their] own symbol-making task, [the community of black women writers] confronts, therefore, a tradition of work that is quite recent, its continuities, broken and sporadic.

Until now, it has been extraordinarily difficult to establish the formal connections between early black women's writing and that of the present, precisely because our knowledge of their work has been broken and sporadic. Phillis Wheatley, for example, while certainly the most reprinted and discussed poet in the tradition, is also one of the least understood. Ann Plato's seminal work, *Essays* (which includes biographies and poems), has not been reprinted since it was published a century and a half ago. And Harriet Wilson's *Our Nig*, her compelling novel of a black woman's expanding consciousness in a racist Northern antebellum environment, never received even *one* review or comment at a time when virtually *all* works written by black people were heralded by abolitionists as salient arguments against the existence of human slavery. Many of the books reprinted in this set experienced a similar fate, the most dreadful fate for an author: that of being ignored then relegated to the obscurity of the rare book section of a university library. We can only wonder how many other texts in the black woman's tradition have been lost to this generation of readers or remain unclassified or uncatalogued and, hence, unread.

This was not always so, however. Black women writers dominated the final decade of the nineteenth century, perhaps spurred to publish by an 1886 essay entitled "The Coming American Novelist," which was published in *Lippincott's Monthly Magazine* and written by "A Lady From Philadelphia." This pseudonymous essay argued that the "Great American Novel" would be written by a black person. Her argument is so curious that it deserves to be repeated:

> When we come to formulate our demands of the Coming American Novelist, we will agree that he must be native-born. His ancestors may come from where they will, but we must give him a birthplace and have the raising of him. Still, the longer his family has been here the better he will represent us. Suppose he should have no country but ours, no traditions but those he has learned here, no longings apart from us, no future except in our future—the orphan of the world, he finds with us his home. And with all this, suppose he refuses to be fused into that grand conglomerate we call the "American type." With us, he is not of us. He is original, he has humor, he is tender, he is passive and fiery, he has been

taught what we call justice, and he has his own opinion about it. He has suffered everything a poet, a dramatist, a novelist need suffer before he comes to have his lips anointed. And with it all he is in one sense a spectator, a little out of the race. How would these conditions go towards forming an original development? In a word, suppose the coming novelist is of African origin? When one comes to consider the subject, there is no improbability in it. One thing is certain,—our great novel will not be written by the typical American.

An atypical American, indeed. Not only would the great American novel be written by an African-American, it would be written by an African-American *woman:*

> Yet farther: I have used the generic masculine pronoun because it is convenient; but Fate keeps revenge in store. It was a woman who, taking the wrongs of the African as her theme, wrote the novel that awakened the world to their reality, and why should not the coming novelist be a woman as well as an African? She—the woman of that race—has some claims on Fate which are not yet paid up.

It is these claims on fate that we seek to pay by publishing The Schomburg Library of Nineteenth-Century Black Women Writers.

This theme would be repeated by several black women authors, most notably by Anna Julia Cooper, a prototypical black feminist whose 1892 *A Voice From the South* can be considered to be one of the original texts of the black feminist movement. It was Cooper who first analyzed the fallacy of referring to "the Black man" when speaking of black people and who argued that just as white men cannot speak through the consciousness of black men, neither can black *men* "fully and adequately . . . reproduce the exact Voice of the Black Woman." Gender and race, she argues, cannot be conflated, except in the instance of a black woman's voice, and it is this voice which must be uttered and to which we must listen. As Cooper puts the matter so compellingly:

> It is not the intelligent woman vs. the ignorant woman; nor the white woman vs. the black, the brown, and the red,—it is not even the cause of woman vs. man. Nay, 'tis woman's strongest vindication for speaking that *the world needs to hear her voice*. It would be subversive of every human interest that the cry of one-half the human family be stifled. Woman in stepping from the pedestal of statue-like inactivity in the domestic shrine, and daring to think and move and speak,— to undertake to help shape, mold, and direct the thought of her age, is merely completing the circle of the world's vision. Hers is every interest that has lacked an interpreter and a defender. Her cause is linked with that of every agony that has been dumb—every wrong that needs a voice.
>
> It is no fault of man's that he has not been able to see truth from her standpoint. It does credit both to his head and heart that no greater mistakes have been committed or even wrongs perpetrated while she sat making tatting and snipping paper flowers. Man's own innate chivalry and the mutual interdependence of their interests have insured his treating her cause, in the main at least, as his own. And he is pardonably surprised and even a little chagrined, perhaps, to find his legislation not considered "perfectly lovely" in every respect. But in any case his work is only impoverished by her remaining dumb. The world has had to limp along with the wobbling gait and one-sided hesitancy of a man with one eye. Suddenly the bandage is removed from the other eye and the whole body is filled with light. It sees a circle where before it saw a segment. The darkened eye restored, every member rejoices with it.

The myopic sight of the darkened eye can only be restored when the full range of the black woman's voice, with its own special timbres and shadings, remains mute no longer.

Similarly, Victoria Earle Matthews, an author of short stories and essays, and a cofounder in 1896 of the National Association of Colored Women, wrote in her stunning essay, "The Value of Race Literature" (1895), that "when the literature of our race is developed, it will of necessity be different in all essential points of greatness, true heroism and real Christianity from what we may at the present time, for convenience, call American literature." Matthews argued that this great tradition of Afro-American literature would be the textual outlet "for the unnaturally suppressed inner lives which our people have been compelled to lead." Once these "unnaturally suppressed inner lives" of black people are unveiled, no "grander diffusion of mental light" will shine more brightly, she concludes, than that of the articulate Afro-American woman:

> And now comes the question, What part shall we women play in the Race Literature of the future? . . . within the compass of one small journal ["Woman's Era"] we have struck out a new line of departure—a journal, a record of Race interests gathered from all parts of the United States, carefully selected, moistened, winnowed and garnered by the ablest intellects of educated colored women, shrinking at no lofty theme, shirking no serious duty, aiming at every possible excellence, and determined to do their part in the future uplifting of the race.
>
> If twenty women, by their concentrated efforts in one literary movement, can meet with such success as has engendered, planned out, and so successfully consummated this convention, what much more glorious results, what wider spread success, what grander diffusion of mental light will not come forth at the bidding of the enlarged hosts of women writers, already called into being by the stimulus of your efforts?
>
> And here let me speak one word for my journalistic sisters

who have already entered the broad arena of journalism. Before the "Woman's Era" had come into existence, no one except themselves can appreciate the bitter experience and sore disappointments under which they have at all times been compelled to pursue their chosen vocations.

If their brothers of the press have had their difficulties to contend with, I am here as a sister journalist to state, from the fullness of knowledge, that their task has been an easy one compared with that of the colored woman in journalism.

Woman's part in Race Literature, as in Race building, is the most important part and has been so in all ages. . . . All through the most remote epochs she has done her share in literature. . . .

One of the most important aspects of this set is the republication of the salient texts from 1890 to 1910, which literary historians could well call "The Black Woman's Era." In addition to Mary Helen Washington's definitive edition of Cooper's *A Voice From the South,* we have reprinted two novels by Amelia Johnson, Frances Harper's *Iola Leroy,* two novels by Emma Dunham Kelley, Alice Dunbar-Nelson's two impressive collections of short stories, and Pauline Hopkins's three serialized novels as well as her monumental novel, *Contending Forces*—all published between 1890 and 1910. Indeed, black women published more works of fiction in these two decades than black men had published in the previous half century. Nevertheless, this great achievement has been ignored.

Moreover, the writings of nineteenth-century Afro-American women in general have remained buried in obscurity, accessible only in research libraries or in overpriced and poorly edited reprints. Many of these books have never been reprinted at all; in some instances only one or two copies are extant. In these works of fiction, poetry, autobiography, biography, essays, and journalism resides the mind of the nineteenth-century Afro-American woman. Until these works are made readily available to teachers and their students, a significant segment of the black tradition will remain silent.

Oxford University Press, in collaboration with the Schomburg Center for Research in Black Culture, is publishing thirty volumes of these compelling works, each of which contains an introduction by an expert in the field. The set includes such rare texts as Johnson's *The Hazeley Family* and *Clarence and Corinne*, Plato's *Essays*, the most complete edition of Phillis Wheatley's poems and letters, Emma Dunham Kelley's pioneering novel *Megda*, several previously unpublished stories and a novel by Alice Dunbar-Nelson, and the first collected volumes of Pauline Hopkins's three serialized novels and Frances Harper's poetry. We also present four volumes of poetry by such women as Mary Eliza Tucker Lambert, Adah Menken, Josephine Heard, and Maggie Johnson. Numerous slave and spiritual narratives, a newly discovered novel—*Four Girls at Cottage City*—by Emma Dunham Kelley (-Hawkins), and the first American edition of *Wonderful Adventures of Mrs. Seacole in Many Lands* are also among the texts included.

In addition to resurrecting the works of black women authors, it is our hope that this set will facilitate the resurrection of the Afro-American woman's literary tradition itself by unearthing its nineteenth-century roots. In the works of Nella Larsen and Jessie Fauset, Zora Neale Hurston and Ann Petry, Lorraine Hansberry and Gwendolyn Brooks, Paule Marshall and Toni Cade Bambara, Audre Lorde and Rita Dove, Toni Morrison and Alice Walker, Gloria Naylor and Jamaica Kincaid, these roots have branched luxuriantly. The eighteenth- and nineteenth-century authors whose works are presented in this set founded and nurtured the black women's literary tradition, which must be revived, explicated, analyzed, and debated before we can understand more completely the formal shaping of this tradition within a tradition, a coded literary universe through which, regrettably, we are only just beginning to navigate our way. As Anna Cooper said nearly one hundred years ago, we have been blinded by the loss of sight in one eye and have therefore been unable to detect the full *shape* of the Afro-American literary tradition.

Literary works configure into a tradition not because of some mystical collective unconscious determined by the biology of race or gender, but because writers read other writers and *ground* their representations of experience in models of language provided largely by other writers to whom they feel akin. It is through this mode of literary revision, amply evident in the *texts* themselves—in formal echoes, recast metaphors, even in parody—that a "tradition" emerges and defines itself.

This is formal bonding, and it is only through formal bonding that we can know a literary tradition. The collective publication of these works by black women now, for the first time, makes it possible for scholars and critics, male and female, black and white, to *demonstrate* that black women writers read, and revised, other black women writers. To demonstrate this set of formal literary relations is to demonstrate that sexuality, race, and gender are both the condition and the basis of *tradition*—but tradition as found in discrete acts of language use.

A word is in order about the history of this set. For the past decade, I have taught a course, first at Yale and then at Cornell, entitled "Black Women and Their Fictions," a course that I inherited from Toni Morrison, who developed it in the mid-1970s for Yale's Program in Afro-American Studies. Although the course was inspired by the remarkable accomplishments of black women novelists since 1970, I gradually extended its beginning date to the late nineteenth century, studying Frances Harper's *Iola Leroy* and Anna Julia Cooper's *A Voice From the South,* both published in 1892. With the discovery of Harriet E. Wilson's seminal novel, *Our Nig* (1859), and Jean Yellin's authentication of Harriet Jacobs's brilliant slave narrative, *Incidents in the Life of a Slave Girl* (1861), a survey course spanning over a century and a quarter emerged.

But the discovery of *Our Nig,* as well as the interest in nineteenth-century black women's writing that this discovery generated, convinced me that even the most curious and diligent scholars knew very little of the extensive history of the creative writings of Afro-American women before 1900. Indeed, most scholars of Afro-American literature had never even read most of the books published by black women, simply because these books—of poetry, novels, short stories, essays, and autobiography—were mostly accessible only in rare book sections of university libraries. For reasons unclear to me even today, few of these marvelous renderings of the Afro-American woman's consciousness were reprinted in the late 1960s and early 1970s, when so many other texts of the Afro-American literary tradition were resurrected from the dark and silent graveyard of the out-of-print and were reissued in facsimile editions aimed at the hungry readership for canonical texts in the nascent field of black studies.

So, with the help of several superb research assistants—including David Curtis, Nicola Shilliam, Wendy Jones, Sam Otter, Janadas Devan, Suvir Kaul, Cynthia Bond, Elizabeth Alexander, and Adele Alexander—and with the expert advice of scholars such as William Robinson, William Andrews, Mary Helen Washington, Maryemma Graham, Jean Yellin, Houston A. Baker, Jr., Richard Yarborough, Hazel Carby, Joan R. Sherman, Frances Foster, and William French, dozens of bibliographies were used to compile a list of books written or narrated by black women mostly before 1910. Without the assistance provided through this shared experience of scholarship, the scholar's true legacy, this project could not have been conceived. As the list grew, I was struck by how very many of these titles that I, for example, had never even heard of, let alone read, such as Ann Plato's *Essays,* Louisa Picquet's slave narrative, or Amelia Johnson's two novels, *Clarence and Corinne* and *The Hazeley Family.* Through our research with the Black Periodical Fiction and Poetry Project (funded by NEH and the Ford Foundation), I also realized that several novels by black women, including three works of fiction by Pauline Hopkins, had been serialized in black periodicals, but had never been collected and published as books. Nor had the several books of poetry published by black women, such as the prolific Frances E. W. Harper, been collected and edited. When I discovered still another "lost" novel by an Afro-American woman (*Four Girls at Cottage City,* published in 1898 by Emma Dunham Kelley-Hawkins), I decided to attempt to edit a collection of reprints of these works and to publish them as a "library" of black women's writings, in part so that I could read them myself.

Convincing university and trade publishers to undertake this project proved to be a difficult task. Despite the commercial success of *Our Nig* and of the several reprint series of women's works (such as Virago, the Beacon Black Women Writers Series, and Rutgers' American Women Writers Series), several presses rejected the project as "too large," "too limited," or as "commercially unviable." Only two publishers recognized the viability and the import of the project and, of these, Oxford's commitment to publish the titles simultaneously as a set made the press's offer irresistible.

While attempting to locate original copies of these exceedingly rare books, I discovered that most of the texts were housed at the Schomburg Center for Research in Black Culture, a branch of The New York Public Library, under the direction of Howard Dodson. Dodson's infectious enthusiasm for the project and his generous collaboration, as well as that of his stellar staff (especially Diana Lachatanere, Sharon Howard, Ellis Haizip, Richard Newman, and Betty Gubert), led to a joint publishing initiative that produced this set as part of the Schomburg's major fund-raising campaign. Without Dodson's foresight and generosity of spirit, the set would not have materialized. Without William P. Sisler's masterful editorship at Oxford and his staff's careful attention to detail, the set would have remained just another grand idea that tends to languish in a scholar's file cabinet.

I would also like to thank Dr. Michael Winston and Dr. Thomas C. Battle, Vice-President of Academic Affairs and the Director of the Moorland-Spingarn Research Center (respectively) at Howard University, for their unending encouragement, support, and collaboration in this project, and Esme E. Bhan at Howard for her meticulous research and bibliographical skills. In addition, I would like to acknowledge the aid of the staff at the libraries of Duke University, Cornell University (especially Tom Weissinger and Donald Eddy), the Boston Public Library, the Western Reserve Historical Society, the Library of Congress, and Yale University. Linda Robbins, Marion Osmun, Sarah Flanagan, and Gerard Case, all members of the staff at Oxford, were extraordinarily effective at coordinating, editing, and producing the various segments of each text in the set. Candy Ruck, Nina de Tar, and Phillis Molock expertly typed reams of correspondence and manuscripts connected to the project.

I would also like to express my gratitude to my colleagues who edited and introduced the individual titles in the set. Without their attention to detail, their willingness to meet strict deadlines, and their sheer enthusiasm for this project, the set could not have been published. But finally and ultimately, I would hope that the publication of the set would help to generate even more scholarly interest in the black women authors whose work is presented here. Struggling against the seemingly insurmountable barriers of racism *and* sexism, while often raising families and fulfilling full-time professional obligations, these women managed nevertheless to record their thoughts and feelings and to *testify* to all who dare read them that the will to harness the power of collective endurance and survival is the will to write.

The Schomburg Library of Nineteenth-Century Black Women Writers is dedicated in memory of Pauline Augusta Coleman Gates, who died in the spring of 1987. It was she who inspired in me the love of learning and the love of literature. I have encountered in the books of this set no will more determined, no courage more noble, no mind more sublime, no self more celebratory of the achievements of all Afro-American women, and indeed of life itself, than her own.

A NOTE FROM
THE SCHOMBURG CENTER

Howard Dodson

The Schomburg Center for Research in Black Culture, The New York Public Library, is pleased to join with Dr. Henry Louis Gates and Oxford University Press in presenting The Schomburg Library of Nineteenth-Century Black Women Writers. This thirty-volume set includes the work of a generation of black women whose writing has only been available previously in rare book collections. The materials reprinted in twenty-four of the thirty volumes are drawn from the unique holdings of the Schomburg Center.

A research unit of The New York Public Library, the Schomburg Center has been in the forefront of those institutions dedicated to collecting, preserving, and providing access to the records of the black past. In the course of its two generations of acquisition and conservation activity, the Center has amassed collections totaling more than 5 million items. They include over 100,000 bound volumes, 85,000 reels and sets of microforms, 300 manuscript collections containing some 3.5 million items, 300,000 photographs and extensive holdings of prints, sound recordings, film and videotape, newspapers, artworks, artifacts, and other book and nonbook materials. Together they vividly document the history and cultural heritages of people of African descent worldwide.

Though established some sixty-two years ago, the Center's book collections date from the sixteenth century. Its oldest item, an Ethiopian Coptic Tunic, dates from the eighth or ninth century. Rare materials, however, are most available

for the nineteenth-century African-American experience. It is
from these holdings that the majority of the titles selected for
inclusion in this set are drawn.

The nineteenth century was a formative period in African-
American literary and cultural history. Prior to the Civil
War, the majority of black Americans living in the United
States were held in bondage. Law and practice forbade teaching them to read or write. Even after the war, many of the
impediments to learning and literary productivity remained.
Nevertheless, black men and women of the nineteenth century
persevered in both areas. Moreover, more African-Americans
than we yet realize turned their observations, feelings, social
viewpoints, and creative impulses into published works. In
time, this nineteenth-century printed record included poetry,
short stories, histories, novels, autobiographies, social criticism, and theology, as well as economic and philosophical
treatises. Unfortunately, much of this body of literature
remained, until very recently, relatively inaccessible to twentieth-
century scholars, teachers, creative artists, and others interested in black life. Prior to the late 1960s, most Americans
(black as well as white) had never heard of these nineteenth-
century authors, much less read their works.

The civil rights and black power movements created un-
precedented interest in the thought, behavior, and achievements of black people. Publishers responded by revising
traditional texts, introducing the American public to a new
generation of African-American writers, publishing a variety
of thematic anthologies, and reprinting a plethora of "classic
texts" in African-American history, literature, and art. The
reprints usually appeared as individual titles or in a series of
bound volumes or microform formats.

The Schomburg Center, which has a long history of supporting publishing that deals with the history and culture of Africans in diaspora, became an active participant in many of the reprint revivals of the 1960s. Since hard copies of original printed works are the preferred formats for producing facsimile reproductions, publishers frequently turned to the Schomburg Center for copies of these original titles. In addition to providing such material, Schomburg Center staff members offered advice and consultation, wrote introductions, and occasionally entered into formal copublishing arrangements in some projects.

Most of the nineteenth-century titles reprinted during the 1960s, however, were by and about black men. A few black women were included in the longer series, but works by lesser known black women were generally overlooked. The Schomburg Library of Nineteenth-Century Black Women Writers is both a corrective to these previous omissions and an important contribution to Afro-American literary history in its own right. Through this collection of volumes, the thoughts, perspectives, and creative abilities of nineteenth-century African-American women, as captured in books and pamphlets published in large part before 1910, are again being made available to the general public. The Schomburg Center is pleased to be a part of this historic endeavor.

I would like to thank Professor Gates for initiating this project. Thanks are due both to him and Mr. William P. Sisler of Oxford University Press for giving the Schomburg Center an opportunity to play such a prominent role in the set. Thanks are also due to my colleagues at The New York Public Library and the Schomburg Center, especially Dr. Vartan Gregorian, Richard De Gennaro, Paul Fasana, Betsy

Pinover, Richard Newman, Diana Lachatanere, Glenderlyn Johnson, and Harold Anderson for their assistance and support. I can think of no better way of demonstrating than in this set the role the Schomburg Center plays in assuring that the black heritage will be available for future generations.

PREFACE

John C. Shields

I first became acquainted with Phillis Wheatley in January of 1977 when, as a graduate teaching assistant, I was given the assignment I had requested the previous term—a section of the popular Black American Literature Survey. As this occasion marked my own introduction to this field, and especially since I was given the assignment only one day before the first class was to meet, I discovered Wheatley was the first author on the already prepared syllabus. After picking up a copy of G. Herbert Renfro's *Life and Works of Phillis Wheatley* (1916; reprint Miami, Fla.: Mnemosyne Press, 1969), I busied myself (somewhat panic-stricken) with the task of examining this poet's works. Almost immediately, however, task became delight. From the very first reading of Wheatley's work, I found her poetry particularly charming and fresh. I saw quite soon that I would not be able to leave her after a single class period, so for the second class on Wheatley I investigated the critical response to her work. Already feeling as if I had been robbed because I had not been allowed to meet Wheatley at an earlier opportunity, I was bewildered by the tenor of what I soon unearthed of the meager commentary about her.

Virtually all opinions I encountered while preparing for this second class disclosed primarily two positions in regard to Wheatley's writings. The first found her work subsumed in some socioanthropological argument whose tenets justified or challenged the grievously erroneous notion of racial supremacy. In the case of the other, more recent position, she and her works were (and continue to be) viewed as typical of eighteenth-century blacks who sold their blackness for a pottage of white acceptability. Practically all commentators quoted a few lines from Wheatley's poetry (while ignoring her letters), but hardly a one indicated that he or she ever took seriously the content of her words. It is my objective in this volume to do what I can to provoke serious interest in reading the fine poetry and prose of this harshly underrated black American poet.

Readers confronting Wheatley's works for the first time may well be confounded by what appears to be a remote idiom—the rhetoric of eighteenth-century neoclassicism. This poet preferred to render her lines in heroic couplets (though she does not always choose this form), and she often uses such expressions as "feathery race" (for birds) and "gentle zephyr" (for a warm, pleasant breeze)—examples of what Wordsworth, the British romantic, would later censure as poetic diction (expressions not descriptive of ordinary people or natural events). When appropriate, I have tried to assist, but not direct, Wheatley's readers by undertaking the sometimes difficult task of reclaiming as much of Wheatley's literary and cultural milieu as is comfortably feasible; perhaps it will appear that I have overloaded the notes for specialists.

I have tried to make this poet's writing accessible to contemporary readers. In carrying out this resolve, I have concentrated heavily on what I think are her most important poems. I have not pursued this objective from the point of view of one who is in search of peculiar patterns of thought which may or may not align her with some socioanthropological argument. Quite the contrary, I have tried ever to keep in mind the critical perspective of one whose primary concern with these poems has been aesthetic. In addition, the attentive reader should be warned that a plethora of invalid generalities have been hurled at this poet's work, such as the notion that she is a derivative imitator of Alexander Pope. If she is supposed to be such an imitator, then where, specifically, does she display this imitation? The only cases of conscious borrowing from Pope that I have managed to locate occur in her introductory poem to the 1773 *Poems*, "To Maecenas." I do not at all mean to suggest, however, that the striding cadences of her couplets do not owe a debt to Pope's insistence that the artist must control the sounds of his or her words; indeed, most other British and American poets of the later eighteenth century (and later times) share the same indebtedness.

I do intend to suggest that, after satisfying her thirst for knowledge of words by reading virtually all the British and American poets of her century, this poet discovered for herself her own idiom. This determination to be individual (or original) led Wheatley to construct poems in which one may perceive a palpable tension between form and content. The stubborn, horizontal rhythm of her usually regular (but not always) iambic pentameter lines is offset by the vertical thrust of the content of these same lines. That is, while she adopts the almost complacent regularity of the heroic couplet—a mode which invites one to hear echoed the eighteenth century's faith in the certainty of a mechanical universe—her primary subject, freedom, prompts the reader to focus on the soaring, ascending activity of contemplating a boundless state, one never "oppressed with woes a painful, endless train."

What Wheatley essentially does, then, is to decide that this world, which allows slavery to remain legitimate, is unsatisfactory to her; so she manipulates the conventions of neoclassicism to build in her poems another, acceptable world. This

use of poetry as a means to achieve freedom constitutes a
poetics of liberation (see my forthcoming *Phillis Wheatley's
Poetics of Liberation*). Though such a process has always been
potentially present in the practice of meditation (e.g., see the
poetry of John Donne and Edward Taylor), few poets before
Wheatley use the medium of poetry in so self-conscious a
manner—though the romantics who followed her most assuredly do. For a more thorough introduction to the works
of this poet, please consult the essay, "Phillis Wheatley's
Struggle for Freedom in Her Poetry and Prose," which immediately follows the texts of Wheatley's works and variants
in this volume.

What I know about Wheatley I have accumulated from a ten-
year journey, beginning that fateful evening in January 1977
and lasting until the present. In this journey I have encountered many who encouraged and promoted my interest. The
first to do so was Mary P. Richards, then Assistant Professor
of English at the University of Tennessee, Knoxville, and
now Associate Dean of Liberal Arts at that university. The
second to motivate me was R. Baxter Miller, Chairman of
Black Studies at the University of Tennessee; he would eventually consent to direct my doctoral dissertation on the subject
of Phillis Wheatley. Additionally, I am indebted to the other
members of my doctoral committee—Percy G. Adams, Bain
T. Stewart, John A. Hansen, and James E. Shelton—for
their tireless efforts in supervising the evolution of the dissertation. I owe Professor Shelton a special note of thanks for
unselfishly and eagerly sharing with me through the years his
extensive and substantial knowledge of ancient classicism.

  For the inspiration of their example, I salute my friends
and fellow Wheatley scholars William H. Robinson, Julian

D. Mason, Jr., Mukhtar Ali Isani, Erlene Stetson, Sondra O'Neale, Richard K. Barksdale, William W. Cook, and James A. Levernier. For his tireless efforts given to proofing this book, I hail my honored friend and colleague, Russell Rutter. This collection would never have materialized were it not for Henry Louis Gates's unflagging faith in my work; it was he who offered me the opportunity to contribute *The Collected Works of Phillis Wheatley* to this worthy series, The Schomburg Library of Nineteenth-Century Black Women Writers. I would be remiss indeed if I did not acknowledge the kind attention and intelligent counsel of Oxford University Press's William P. Sisler, Linda Robbins, Marion Osmun (a special bow to you, Ms. Osmun), Wendy Warren Keebler, and Stephanie Sakson-Ford. Diana Lachatanere of The New York Public Library's Schomburg Center for Research in Black Culture was particularly helpful, as were the library staffs of Illinois State University's Milner Library (especially Joan Winters, my friend and colleague), the University of Illinois Library (particularly the late Hugh Atkinson, who served as University Librarian, Frederick Nash, Head Librarian of the Rare Book Collection, and Vera Mitchell, Librarian of the Afro-American and African Studies Collections), Cornell University's Olin Library, and the University of California Library at Berkeley. Finally, I must express a special debt of gratitude to my typist, Sherry Sharp, who makes me look good. And to my family, Ruth Ann and Melanie, whose loyalty and consideration have remained constant, I give my fondest thanks.

For permission to publish portions of Wheatley's verse and prose, I am grateful to the following individuals and/or agencies: William H. Robinson; Julian D. Mason, Jr., and the University of North Carolina Press; Kenneth Silverman; *The Journal of Negro History;* William C. Brown Company Publishers; Mukhtar Ali Isani; *The South Atlantic Bulletin; American Literature; Modern Philology; The New England Quarterly; Early American Literature;* G. K. Hall (for a few lines from my essay "Phillis Wheatley and the Sublime," in *Critical Essays on Phillis Wheatley,* William H. Robinson, ed., 1982); the Massachusetts Historical Society; and the Schomburg Center for Research in Black Culture, a division of The New York Public Library.

CONTENTS

A Note on the Texts   xl

POEMS ON VARIOUS SUBJECTS,
RELIGIOUS AND MORAL
(As originally appeared in 1773 edition
published by A. Bell, London)   1

To Maecenas   9
On Virtue   13
To the University of Cambridge,
    in New-England   15
To the King's Most Excellent Majesty. 1768.   17
On Being Brought from Africa to America   18
On the Death of the Rev. Dr. Sewell. 1769.   19
On the Death of the Rev. Mr. George
    Whitefield. 1770.   22
On the Death of a Young Lady of
    Five Years of Age   25
On the Death of a Young Gentleman   27
To a Lady on the Death of Her Husband   29
Goliath of Gath   31
Thoughts on the Works of Providence   43
To a Lady on the Death of Three Relations   51
To a Clergyman on the Death of His Lady   53
An Hymn to the Morning   56
An Hymn to the Evening   58
Isaiah LXIII. 1–8.   60
On Recollection   62

On Imagination   65

A Funeral Poem on the Death of C. E. an
     Infant of Twelve Months   69

To Captain H———d, of the 65th Regiment   72

To the Right Honourable William, Earl of
     Dartmouth, His Majesty's Principal Secretary
     of State for North America, &c.   73

Ode to Neptune. On Mrs. W———'s Voyage to
     England   76

To a Lady on Her Coming to North America with
     Her Son, for the Recovery of Her Health   78

To a Lady on Her Remarkable Preservation in an
     Hurricane in North-Carolina   80

To a Lady and Her Children, on the Death of
     Her Son and Their Brother   82

To a Gentleman and Lady on the Death of the
     Lady's Brother and Sister, and a Child of the
     Name Avis, Aged One Year   84

On the Death of Dr. Samuel Marshall. 1771.   86

To a Gentleman on His Voyage to Great-Britain
     for the Recovery of His Health   88

To the Rev. Dr. Thomas Amory on Reading His
     Sermons on Daily Devotion, in Which That
     Duty Is Recommended and Assisted   90

On the Death of J.C. an Infant   92

An Hymn to Humanity. To S.P.G. Esq.   95

To the Honourable T.H. Esq; on the Death of
     His Daughter   98

Niobe in Distress for Her Children Slain by
     Apollo, from Ovid's *Metamorphoses*, Book

VI. And from a View of the Painting of Mr.
    Richard Wilson 101
To S.M. a Young African Painter, on Seeing His
    Works 114
To His Honour the Lieutenant-Governor, on the
    Death of His Lady. March 24, 1773. 116
A Farewel to America. To Mrs. S.W. 119
A Rebus, by I.B. 123
An Answer to the Rebus, by the Author of These
    Poems 124

EXTANT POEMS NOT INCLUDED
IN THE 1773 *POEMS* 129

Atheism 129
An Address to the Deist 131
On Messrs. Hussey and Coffin 133
America 134
To the Honble. Commodore Hood on His
    Pardoning a Deserter 135
On Friendship 136
On the Death of Mr. Snider Murder'd by
    Richardson 136
An Elegy to Miss Mary Moorhead, On the Death
    of Her Father, the Rev. Mr. John Moorhead 137
To a Gentleman of the Navy 140
The Answer [By the Gentleman of the Navy] 141
Phillis's Reply to the Answer 143
To His Excellency General Washington 145
On the Capture of General Lee 146
On the Death of General Wooster 149

To Mr. and Mrs. ——, on the Death of Their
  Infant Son   150
An Elegy Sacred to the Memory of That Great
  Divine, the Reverend and Learned Dr.
  Samuel Cooper   152
Liberty and Peace   154
An Elegy on Leaving ——   156

                      PROSE   158

Letters   162
  To the Rt. Hon'ble the Countess of Huntingdon
    (October 25, 1770)   162
  Madam [to Abigail May?] (November or
    December 1771)   162
  Hon'd Sir [John Thornton] (April 21, 1772)   163
  To Abour Tanner, in Newport (May 19, 1772)   164
  To Arbour Tanner, in Newport (July 19, 1772)   165
  My Lord [Earl of Dartmouth] (October 10,
    1772)   166
  Madam [the Countess of Huntingdon] (June
    27, 1773)   167
  Madam [the Countess of Huntingdon] (July
    17, 1773)   168
  Sir [David Wooster] (October 18, 1773)   169
  To Obour Tanner, in New Port (October 30,
    1773)   171
  Hon'd Sir [John Thornton] (December 1,
    1773)   172
  [To the Rev. Samuel Hopkins] (February 9,
    1774)   175

Reverend and Honoured Sir [To Samson
   Occom] (February 11, 1774)   176
To Miss Obour Tanner, Newport (March 21,
   1774)   177
Much Honoured Sir [John Thornton] (March
   29, 1774)   178
To Miss Obour Tanner, New Port, Rhode
   Island (May 6, 1774)   181
Rev'd Sir [Samuel Hopkins] (May 6, 1774)   181
Much Hon'd Sir [John Thornton] (October
   30, 1774)   182
Sir [George Washington] (October 26, 1775)   185
Miss Obour Tanner, Worcester (May 29,
   1778)   185
Madam [Mary Wooster] (July 15, 1778)   186
Miss Obour Tanner, Worcester (May 10,
   1779)   186
Proposals for Volumes   188
Proposals for Printing by Subscription
   (February 29, 1772)   188
Proposals (October 30, 1779)   190
Wheatley's Final Proposal (September 1784)   192

Prayer: Sabbath—June 13, 1779   194

       VARIANT POEMS AND LETTERS   195
Poems   196
To the University of Cambridge, Wrote in
   1767   196
On Atheism [Variant I]   197
On Atheism [Variant II]   199

Deism   201
To the King's Most Excellent Majesty on His
    Repealing the American Stamp Act   202
On the Death of the Rev'd Dr. Sewall, 1769   203
To Mrs. Leonard, on the Death of Her
    Husband   205
An Elegiac Poem, on the Death of . . . George
    Whitefield [Variant I]   206
An Ode of Verses on the Much-Lamented
    Death of the Rev. Mr. George Whitefield
    [Variant II]   209
On the Death of Doctor Samuel Marshall   211
Recollection, to Miss A——, M——   212
To the Rev. Mr. Pitkin, on the Death of His
    Lady   214
To the Hon'ble Thomas Hubbard, Esq; On the
    Death of Mrs. Thankfull Leonard   216
To the Right Honourable William Legge, Earl
    of Dartmouth   217
To the Empire of America, Beneath the
    Western Hemisphere. Farewell to America.
    To Mrs. S.W. [Variant I]   219
Farewell to America [Variant II]   221
An Elegy Sacred to the Memory of the Rev'd
    Samuel Cooper, D.D.   223
On the Death of J.C. an Infant   225

Letters   226
Most Noble Lady [the Countess of
    Huntingdon] (October 25, 1770)   226
My Lord [Dartmouth] (June 3, 1773)   227

PHILLIS WHEATLEY'S STRUGGLE FOR
FREEDOM IN HER POETRY AND PROSE

by John C. Shields   229

NOTES   271

Abbreviations   271
Poems on Various Subjects, Religious and Moral (1773)   272
Extant Poems Not Included in the 1773 *Poems*   297
Prose   310
  Letters   310
  Proposals for Volumes   317
  Prayer   318

Variant Poems and Letters   318
  Poems   318
  Letters   323

Phillis Wheatley's Struggle for Freedom in
  Her Poetry and Prose   324

CHRONOLOGY   337

A NOTE ON THE TEXTS

The entire text of *Poems on Various Subjects, Religious and Moral* is reproduced from my personal copy of Wheatley's first 1773 edition. Under the circumstances, I am enjoined to make a clean breast of things—which is to say I had absolutely nothing to do with the worm which has munched and undulated his own avenue through this text. He had done his worst long before the book came to me. This text is readable, however, and not too severely damaged to be useful.

As for the remainder of Wheatley's extant texts, I have quite simply selected what I judged to be the best among the available versions. I alone am responsible for all errors contained within these texts and within all other portions of this volume authored by me—but, alas, I will not accept responsibility for that infernal worm!

J.C.S.

The Collected Works
of Phillis Wheatley

PHILLIS WHEATLEY, NEGRO SERVANT to Mr JOHN WHEATLEY, of BOSTON.

Publiſhed according to Act of Parliament, Septr. 1, 1773 by Archd. Bell,
Bookſeller No. 8 near the Saracens Head Aldgate.

P O E M S

O N

VARIOUS SUBJECTS,

RELIGIOUS AND MORAL.

B Y

PHILLIS WHEATLEY,

Negro Servant to Mr. John Wheatley,
of Boston, in New England.

———————————————

L O N D O N:

Printed for A. Bell, Bookseller, Aldgate; and sold by
Messrs. Cox and Berry, King-Street, *BOSTON.*

M DCC LXXIII.

DEDICATION.

To the Right Honourable the

COUNTESS of HUNTINGDON,

THE FOLLOWING

P   O   E   M   S

Are moft refpectfully

Infcribed,

By her much obliged,

Very humble,

And devoted Servant,

Phillis Wheatley.

Bofton, June 12,
1773.

PREFACE.

THE following POEMS were written originally for the Amusement of the Author, as they were the Products of her leisure Moments. She had no Intention ever to have published them; nor would they now have made their Appearance, but at the Importunity of many of her best, and most generous Friends; to whom she considers herself, as under the greatest Obligations.

As her Attempts in Poetry are now sent into the World, it is hoped the Critic will not severely censure their Defects; and we presume they have too much Merit

to

to be caſt aſide with Contempt, as worthleſs and trifling Effuſions.

As to the Diſadvantages ſhe has laboured under, with Regard to Learning, nothing needs to be offered, as her Maſter's Letter in the following Page will ſufficiently ſhew the Difficulties in this Reſpect ſhe had to encounter.

With all their Imperfections, the Poems are now humbly ſubmitted to the Peruſal of the Public.

The

The following is a Copy of a LETTER sent by the Author's Master to the Publisher.

PHILLIS was brought from *Africa* to *America*, in the Year 1761, between Seven and Eight Years of Age. Without any Assistance from School Education, and by only what she was taught in the Family, she, in sixteen Months Time from her Arrival, attained the English Language, to which she was an utter Stranger before, to such a Degree, as to read any, the most difficult Parts of the Sacred Writings, to the great Astonishment of all who heard her.

As to her WRITING, her own Curiosity led her to it; and this she learnt in so short a Time, that in the Year 1765, she wrote a Letter to the Rev. Mr. Occom, the *Indian* Minister, while in *England*.

She has a great Inclination to learn the Latin Tongue, and has made some Progress in it. This Relation is given by her Master who bought her, and with whom she now lives.

JOHN WHEATLEY.

Boston, Nov. 14, 1772.

To the PUBLICK.

AS it has been repeatedly suggested to the Publisher, by Persons, who have seen the Manuscript, that Numbers would be ready to suspect they were not really the Writings of PHILLIS, he has procured the following Attestation, from the most respectable Characters in *Boston*, that none might have the least Ground for disputing their original.

WE whose Names are under-written, do assure the World, that the POEMS specified in the following Page, * were (as we verily believe) written by PHILLIS, a young Negro Girl, who was but a few Years since, brought an uncultivated Barbarian from *Africa*, and has ever since been, and now is, under the Disadvantage of serving as a Slave in a Family in this Town. She has been examined by some of the best Judges, and is thought qualified to write them.

His Excel'ency THOMAS HUTCINSON, *Governor,*

The Hon. ANDREW OLIVER, *Lieutenant-Governor.*

The Hon. Thomas Hubbard,	*The Rev.* Charles Cheuney, D. D.
The Hon. John Erving,	*The Rev.* Mather Byles, D. D.
The Hon. James Pitts,	*The Rev.* Ed. Pemberton, D. D.
The Hon. Harrison Gray,	*The Rev.* Andrew Elliot, D. D.
The Hon. James Bowdoin,	*The Rev.* Samuel Cooper, D. D.
John Hancock, *Esq;*	*The Rev. Mr.* Samuel Mather,
Joseph Green, *Esq;*	*The Rev. Mr.* John Moorhead,
Richard Carey, *Esq;*	*Mr.* John Wheatley, *her Master.*

N. B. The original Attestation, signed by the above Gentlemen, may be seen by applying to *Archibald Bell* Bookseller, No. 8, *Aldgate-Street.*

---

* The Words "*following Page,*" allude to the Contents of the Manuscript Copy, which are wrote at the Back of the above Attestation.

P O E M S

VARIOUS SUBJECTS.

To MÆCENAS.

MÆCENAS, you, beneath the myrtle
  shade,
Read o'er what poets sung, and shepherds play'd.
What felt those poets but you feel the same?
Does not your soul possess the sacred flame?
Their noble strains your equal genius shares
In softer language, and diviner airs.

While *Homer* paints lo! circumfus'd in air,
Celestial Gods in mortal forms appear;

B

Swift

Swift as they move hear each recefs rebound,
Heav'n quakes, earth trembles, and the fhores re-
    found.   10
Great Sire of verfe, before my mortal eyes,
The lightnings blaze acrofs the vaulted fkies,
And, as the thunder fhakes the heav'nly plains,
A deep-felt horror thrills through all my veins.
When gentler ftrains demand thy graceful fong, 15
The length'ning line moves languifhing along.
When great *Patroclus* courts *Achilles*' aid,
The grateful tribute of my tears is paid ;
Prone on the fhore he feels the pangs of love,
And ftern *Pelides* tend'reft paffions move.   20

    Great *Maro's* ftrain in heav'nly numbers flows,
The *Nine* infpire, and all the bofom glows.
O could I rival thine and *Virgil's* page,
Or claim the *Mufes* with the *Mantuan* Sage ;
Soon the fame beauties fhould my mind adorn, 25
And the fame ardors in my foul fhould burn :
Then fhould my fong in bolder notes arife,
And all my numbers pleafingly furprize ;

                                            But

But here I fit, and mourn a grov'ling mind.
That fain would mount and ride upon the wind.

Not you, my friend, thefe plaintive ftrains be-
  come,
Not you, whofe bofom is the *Mufes* home;
When they from tow'ring *Helicon* retire,
They fan in you the bright immortal fire,
But I lefs happy, cannot raife the fong,   35
The fault'ring mufic dies upon my tongue.

The happier *Terence* * all the choir infpir'd,
His foul replenifh'd, and his bofom fir'd;
But fay, ye *Mufes*, why this partial grace,
To one alone of *Afric*'s fable race;   40
From age to age tranfmitting thus his name
With the firft glory in the rolls of fame?

Thy virtues, great *Mæcenas !* fhall be fung
In praife of him, from whom thofe virtues fprung:

* He was an *African* by birth.

While blooming wreaths around thy temples
    spread,   45
I'll snatch a laurel from thine honour'd head,
While you indulgent smile upon the deed.

As long as *Thames* in streams majestic flows,
Or *Naiads* in their oozy beds repose,
While *Phœbus* reigns above the starry train,   50
While bright *Aurora* purples o'er the main,
So long, great Sir, the muse thy praise shall sing,
So long thy praise shall make *Parnassus* ring :
Then grant, *Mœcenas*, thy paternal rays,
Hear me propitious, and defend my lays.   55

On

On VIRTUE.

O Thou bright jewel in my aim I ſtrive
   To comprehend thee. Thine own words
     declare
Wiſdom is higher than a fool can reach.
I ceaſe to wonder, and no more attempt
Thine height t' explore, or fathom thy profound. 5
But, O my ſoul, ſink not into deſpair,
Virtue is near thee, and with gentle hand
Would now embrace thee, hovers o'er thine head.
Fain would the heav'n born ſoul with her converſe,
Then ſeek, then court her for her promis'd bliſs.

Auſpicious queen, thine heav'nly pinions ſpread,
And lead celeſtial *Chaſtity* along ;
Lo ! now her ſacred retinue deſcends,
Array'd in glory from the orbs above.
Attend me, *Virtue*, thro' my youthful years ! 15
O leave me not to the falſe joys of time !
But guide my ſteps to endleſs life and bliſs.

               Greatneſs,

Greatneſs, or *Goodneſs,* ſay what l ſhall call thee,
To give an higher appellation ſtill,
Teach me a better ſtrain, a nobler lay,　　　　20
O thou, enthron'd with Cherubs in the realms of
　　　day !

To

To the University of CAMBRIDGE, in NEW-ENGLAND.

WHILE an intrinſic ardor prompts to write,
  The muſes promiſe to aſſiſt my pen;
'Twas not long ſince I left my native ſhore
The land of errors, and *Egyptian* gloom:
Father of mercy, 'twas thy gracious hand   5
Brought me in ſafety from thoſe dark abodes.

  Students, to you 'tis giv'n to ſcan the heights
Above, to traverſe the ethereal ſpace,
And mark the ſyſtems of revolving worlds.
Still more, ye ſons of ſcience ye receive   10
The bliſsful news by meſſengers from heav'n,
How *Jeſus'* blood for your redemption flows.
See him with hands out-ſtretcht upon the croſs;
Immenſe compaſſion in his boſom glows;
He hears revilers, nor reſents their ſcorn: 15
What matchleſs mercy in the Son of God!
When the whole human race by ſin had fall'n,
                                        He

He deign'd to die that they might rife again,
And fhare with him in the fublimeft fkies,
Life without death, and glory without end.   20

Improve your privileges while they ftay,
Ye pupils, and each hour redeem, that bears
Or good or bad report of you to heav'n.
Let fin, that baneful evil to the foul,
By you be fhunn'd, nor once remit your guard;   25
Supprefs the deadly ferpent in its egg.
Ye blooming plants of human race divine,
An *Ethiop* tells you 'tis your greateft foe;
Its tranfient fweetnefs turns to endlefs pain,
And in immenfe perdition finks the foul.   30

To

To the K I N G's Moſt Excellent Majeſty.
1768.

Y OUR ſubjects hope, dread Sire——
   The crown upon your brows may flouriſh
    long,
And that your arm may in your God be ſtrong !
O may your ſceptre num'rous nations ſway,
And all with love and readineſs obey !

But how ſhall we the *Britiſh* king reward !   5
Rule thou in peace, our father, and our lord !
Midſt the remembrance of thy favours paſt,
The meaneſt peaſants moſt admire the laſt. *
May *George*, belov'd by all the nations round,
Live with heav'ns choiceſt conſtant bleſſings
   crown'd !   10
Great God, direct, and guard him from on high
And from his head let ev'ry evil fly !
And may each clime with equal gladneſs ſee
A monarch's ſmile can ſet his ſubjects free !

    * The Repeal of the Stamp Act.

C   On

On being brought from A F R I C A to A M E R I C A.

'TWAS mercy brought me from my *Pagan*
    land,
Taught my benighted foul to underftand
That there's a God, that there's a *Saviour* too:
Once I redemption neither fought nor knew.
Some view our fable race with fcornful eye,   5
" Their colour is a diabolic die."
Remember, *Chriftians*, *Negros*, black as *Cain*,
May be refin'd, and join th' angelic train.

On the Death of the Rev. Dr. SEWELL.
1769.

ERE yet the morn its lovely blushes spread,
See *Sewell* number'd with the happy dead.
Hail, holy man, arriv'd th' immortal shore,
Though we shall hear thy warning voice no more.
Come, let us all behold with wishful eyes   5
The saint ascending to his native skies;
From hence the prophet wing'd his rapt'rous way
To the blest mansions in eternal day.
Then begging for the Spirit of our God,
And panting eager for the same abode,   10
Come, let us all with the same vigour rise,
And take a prospect of the blissful skies;
While on our minds *Christ's* image is imprest,
And the dear Saviour glows in ev'ry breast.
Thrice happy saint! to find thy heav'n at last, 15
What compensation for the evils past!

C 2   Great

Great God, incomprehenfible, unknown
By fenfe, we bow at thine exalted throne.
O, while we beg thine excellence to feel,
Thy facred Spirit to our hearts reveal,   20
And give us of that mercy to partake,
Which thou haft promis'd for the *Saviour's* fake!

" *Sewell* is dead."   Swift-pinion'd *Fame* thus
        cry'd.
" Is *Sewell* dead," my trembling tongue reply'd,
O what a blefling in his flight deny'd !   25
How oft for us the holy prophet pray'd !
How oft to us the Word of Life convey'd !
By duty urg'd my mournful verfe to clofe,
I for his tomb this epitaph compofe.

" Lo, here a man, redeem'd by *Jefus'* blood,   30
" A finner once, but now a faint with God;
" Behold ye rich, ye poor, ye fools, ye wife,
" Nor let his monument your heart furprize;
" 'Twill tell you what this holy man has done,
" Which gives him brighter luftre than the fun.
                              " Liften,

" Liften, ye happy, from your feats above.
" I fpeak fincerely, while I fpeak and love,
" He fought the paths of piety and truth,
" By thefe made happy from his early youth !
" In blooming years that grace divine he felt,   40
" Which refcues finners from the chains of guilt.
" Mourn him, ye indigent, whom he has fed,
" And henceforth feek, like him, for living bread ;
" Ev'n *Chrift*, the bread defcending from above,
" And afk an int'reft in his faving love.   45
" Mourn him, ye youth, to whom he oft has told
" God's gracious wonders from the times of old.
" I, too have caufe this mighty lofs to mourn,
" For he my monitor will not return.
" O when fhall we to his bleft ftate arrive ?   50
" When the fame graces in our bofoms thrive."

On

On the Death of the Rev. Mr. G E O R G E W H I T E F I E L D. 1770.

HAIL, happy faint, on thine immortal throne,
Poffeft of glory, life, and blifs unknown;
We hear no more the mufic of thy tongue,
Thy wonted auditories ceafe to throng.
Thy fermons in unequall'd accents flow'd,   5
And ev'ry bofom with devotion glow'd;
Thou didft in ftrains of eloquence refin'd
Inflame the heart, and captivate the mind.
Unhappy we the fetting fun deplore,
So glorious once, but ah! it fhines no more.   10

Behold the prophet in his tow'ring flight!
He leaves the earth for heav'n's unmeafur'd
     height,
And worlds unknown receive him from our fight.
There *Whitefield* wings with rapid courfe his way,
And fails to *Zion* through vaft feas of day.   15
Thy pray'rs, great faint, and thine inceffant cries
Have pierc'd the bofom of thy native fkies.

                                        Thou

Thou moon haſt ſeen, and all the ſtars of light,
How he has wreſtled with his God by night.
He pray'd that grace in ev'ry heart might dwell, 20
He long'd to ſee *America* excel;
He charg'd its youth that ev'ry grace divine
Should with full luſtre in their conduct ſhine;
That Saviour, which his ſoul did firſt receive,
The greateſt gift that ev'n a God can give, 25
He freely offer'd to the num'rous throng,
That on his lips with liſt'ning pleaſure hung.

" Take him, ye wretched, for your only good,
" Take him ye ſtarving ſinners, for your food;
" Ye thirſty, come to this life-giving ſtream, 30
" Ye preachers, take him for your joyful theme;
" Take him my dear *Americans*, he ſaid,
" Be your complaints on his kind boſom laid :
" Take him, ye *Africans*, he longs for you,
" *Impartial Saviour* is his title due : 35
" Waſh'd in the fountain of redeeming blood,
" You ſhall be ſons, and kings, and prieſts to God."

Great

Great *Countess*, * we *Americans* revere
Thy name, and mingle in thy grief sincere;
New England deeply feels, the *Orphans* mourn, 40
Their more than father will no more return.

But, though arrested by the hand of death,
Whitefield no more exerts his lab'ring breath,
Yet let us view him in th' eternal skies,
Let ev'ry heart to this bright vision rise;   45
While the tomb safe retains its sacred trust,
Till life divine re-animates his dust.

* The Countess of *Huntingdon*, to whom Mr. *Whitefield*
was Chaplain.

On

On the Death of a young Lady of Five Years
of Age.

FROM dark abodes to fair etherial light
　　Th' enraptur'd innocent has wing'd her flight;
On the kind bofom of eternal love
She finds unknown beatitude above.
This know, ye parents, nor her lofs deplore,　　5
She feels the iron hand of pain no more;
The difpenfations of unerring grace,
Should turn your forrows into grateful praife;
Let then no tears for her henceforward flow,
No more diftrefs'd in our dark vale below.　　10

Her morning fun, which rofe divinely bright,
Was quickly mantled with the gloom of night;
But hear in heav'n's bleft bow'rs your *Nancy* fair,
And learn to imitate her language there.
" Thou, Lord, whom I behold with glory crown'd,
" By what fweet name, and in what tuneful found

　　　　　D　　　　　　　　" Wilt

" Wilt thou be prais'd ? Seraphic pow'rs are faint
" Infinite love and majesty to paint.
" To thee let all their grateful voices raise,
" And faints and angels join their songs of
　　　" praise."　　　　　　　　　　　　20

Perfect in bliss she from her heav'nly home
Looks down, and smiling beckons you to come;
Why then, fond parents, why these fruitless groans ?
Restrain your tears, and cease your plaintive moans.
Freed from a world of sin, and snares, and pain, 25
Why would you wish your daughter back again ?
No—bow resign'd.　Let hope your grief control,
And check the rising tumult of the soul.
Calm in the prosperous, and adverse day,
Adore the God who gives and takes away;　　30
Eye him in all, his holy name revere,
Upright your actions, and your hearts sincere,
Till having sail'd through life's tempestuous sea,
And from its rocks, and boist'rous billows free,
Yourselves, safe landed on the blissful shore,　35
Shall join your happy babe to part no more.

On

On the Death of a young Gentleman.

WHO taught thee conflict with the pow'rs
    of night,
To vanquiſh Satan in the fields of fight?
Who ſtrung thy feeble arms with might unknown,
How great thy conqueſt, and how bright thy
    crown!
War with each princedom, throne, and pow'r
    is o'er,   5
The ſcene is ended to return no more.
O could my muſe thy feat on high behold,
How deckt with laurel, how enrich'd with gold!
O could ſhe hear what praiſe thine harp em-
    ploys,
How ſweet thine anthems, how divine thy joys! 10
What heav'nly grandeur ſhould exalt her ſtrain!
What holy raptures in her numbers reign!
To ſooth the troubles of the mind to peace,
To ſtill the tumult of life's toſſing ſeas,

                 To

To eafe the anguifh of the parents heart,   15
What fhall my fympathizing verfe impart?
Where is the balm to heal fo deep a wound?
Where fhall a fov'reign remedy be found?
Look, gracious Spirit, from thine heav'nly bow'r,
And thy full joys into their bofoms pour;   20
The raging tempeft of their grief control,
And fpread the dawn of glory through the foul,
To eye the path the faint departed trod,
And trace him to the bofom of his God.

To

To a Lady on the Death of her Husband.

GRIM monarch! see, depriv'd of vital breath,
   A young physician in the dust of death:
Dost thou go on incessant to destroy,
Our griefs to double, and lay waste our joy?
Enough thou never yet wast known to say,   5
Though millions die, the vassals of thy sway:
Nor youth, nor science, nor the ties of love,
Nor aught on earth thy flinty heart can move.
The friend, the spouse from his dire dart to save,
In vain we ask the sovereign of the grave.   10
Fair mourner, there see thy lov'd *Leonard* laid,
And o'er him spread the deep impervious shade;
Clos'd are his eyes, and heavy fetters keep
His senses bound in never-waking sleep,
Till time shall cease, till many a starry world   15
Shall fall from heav'n, in dire confusion hurl'd,
Till nature in her final wreck shall lie,
And her last groan shall rend the azure sky:

                               Not

Not, not till then his active soul shall claim
His body, a divine immortal frame.   20

But see the softly-stealing tears apace
Pursue each other down the mourner's face:
But cease thy tears, bid ev'ry sigh depart,
And cast the load of anguish from thine heart:
From the cold shell of his great soul arise,   25
And look beyond, thou native of the skies;
There fix thy view, where fleeter than the wind
Thy *Leonard* mounts, and leaves the earth behind.
Thyself prepare to pass the vale of night
To join for ever on the hills of light: 30
To thine embrace his joyful spirit moves
To thee, the partner of his earthly loves;
He welcomes thee to pleasures more refin'd,
And better suited to th' immortal mind.

GOLI-

GOLIATH of GATH.
1 SAM. Chap. xvii.

YE martial pow'rs, and all ye tuneful nine,
    Infpire my fong, and aid my high defign.
The dreadful fcenes and toils of war I write,
The ardent warriors, and the fields of fight:
You beft remember, and you beft can fing   5
The acts of heroes to the vocal ftring:
Refume the lays with which your facred lyre,
Did then the poet and the fage infpire.

    Now front to front the armies were difplay'd,
Here *Ifrael* rang'd, and there the foes array'd; 10
The hofts on two oppofing mountains ftood,
Thick as the foliage of the waving wood;
Between them an extenfive valley lay,
O'er which the gleaming armour pour'd the day,
When from the camp of the *Philiftine* foes, 15
Dreadful to view, a mighty warrior rofe;
In the dire deeds of bleeding battle fkill'd,
The monfter ftalks the terror of the field.

                      From

From *Gath* he fprung, *Goliath* was his name,
Of fierce deportment, and gigantic frame :   20
A brazen helmet on his head was plac'd,
A coat of mail his form terrific grac'd,
The greaves his legs, the targe his fhoulders preft :
Dreadful in arms high-tow'ring o'er the reft
A fpear he proudly wav'd, whofe iron head,   25
Strange to relate, fix hundred fhekels weigh'd ;
He ftrode along, and fhook the ample field,
While *Phœbus* blaz'd refulgent on his fhield :
Through *Jacob's* race a chilling horror ran,
When thus the huge, enormous chief began :   30

    " Say, what the caufe that in this proud array
" You fet your battle in the face of day ?
" One hero find in all your vaunting train,
" Then fee who lofes, and who wins the plain ;
" For he who wins, in triumph may demand   35
" Perpetual fervice from the vanquifh'd land :
" Your armies I defy, your force defpife,
" By far inferior in *Philiftia's* eyes :

                       " Produce

" Produce a man, and let us try the fight,
" Decide the conteft, and the victor's right." 40

Thus challeng'd he: all *Ifrael* ftood amaz'd,
And ev'ry chief in confternation gaz'd;
But *Jeffe's* fon in youthful bloom appears,
And warlike courage far beyond his years:
He left the folds, he left the flow'ry meads, 45
And foft receffes of the fylvan fhades.
Now *Ifrael's* monarch, and his troops arife,
With peals of fhouts afcending to the fkies;
In *Elah's* vale the fcene of combat lies.

When the fair morning blufh'd with orient
    red,   50
What *David's* fire enjoin'd the fon obey'd,
And fwift of foot towards the trench he came,
Where glow'd each bofom with the martial flame,
He leaves his carriage to another's care,
And runs to greet his brethren of the war. 55
While yet they fpake the giant-chief arofe,
Repeats the challenge, and infults his foes:

Struck

Struck with the found, and trembling at the view,
Affrighted *Ifrael* from its poft withdrew.
" Obferve ye this tremerdous foe, they cry'd, 60
" Who in proud vaunts our armies hath defy'd:
" Whoever lays him proftrate on the plain,
" Freedom in *Ifrael* for his houfe fhall gain ;
" And on him wealth unknown the king will pour,
" And give his royal daughter for his dow'r." 65

    Then *Jeffe's* youngeft hope : " My brethren
      " fay,
" What fhall be done for him who takes away
" Reproach from *Jacob*, who deftroys the chief,
" And puts a period to his country's grief.
" He vaunts the honours of his arms abroad, 70
" And fcorns the armies of the living God."

    Thus fpoke the youth, th' attentive people ey'd
The wond'rous hero, and again reply'd :
" Such the rewards our monarch will beftow,
" On him who conquers, and deftroys his foe." 75

                          Eliab

Eliab heard, and kindled into ire
To hear his shepherd-brother thus inquire,
And thus begun? " What errand brought thee ?
   " say
" Who keeps thy flock ? or does it go astray ?
" I know the base ambition of thine heart,   **80**
" But back in safety from the field depart."

Eliab thus to *Jesse's* youngest heir,
Express'd his wrath in accents most severe.
When to his brother mildly he reply'd,
" What have I done ? or what the cause to
   " chide?"   **85**

The words were told before the king, who sent
For the young hero to his royal tent :
Before the monarch dauntless he began,
" For this *Philistine* fail no heart of man :
" I'll take the vale, and with the giant fight: **90**
" I dread not all his boasts, nor all his might."

When thus the king : " Dar'ft thou a ftripling go,

" And venture combat with fo great a foe ?

" Who all his days has been inur'd to fight,

" And made its deeds his ftudy and delight :   95

" Battles and bloodfhed brought the monfter forth,

" And clouds and whirlwinds ufher'd in his birth."

When *David* thus : " I kept the fleecy care,

" And out there rufh'd a lion and a bear ;

" A tender lamb the hungry lion took,   100

" And with no other weapon than my crook

" Bold I purfu'd, and chas'd him o'er the field,

" The prey deliver'd, and the felon kill'd :

" As thus the lion and the bear I flew,

" So fhall *Goliath* fall, and all his crew :   105

" The God, who fav'd me from thefe beafts of
        " prey,

" By me this monfter in the duft fhall lay."

So *David* fpoke.   The wond'ring king reply'd ;

" Go thou with heav'n and victory on thy fide :

" This coat of mail, this fword gird on," he
        faid,   110

And plac'd a mighty helmet on his head :

                                        The

The coat, the ſword, the helm he laid aſide,
Nor choſe to venture with thoſe arms untry'd,
Then took his ſtaff, and to the neighb'ring
   brook
Inſtant he ran, and thence five pebbles took. 115
Mean time deſcended to *Philiſtia's* ſon
A radiant cherub, and he thus begun :
" Goliath, well thou know'ſt thou haſt defy'd
" Yon Hebrew armies, and their God deny'd :
" Rebellious   wretch !   audacious worm ! for-
   " bear,   120
" Nor tempt the vengeance of their God too far :
" Them, who with his omnipotence contend,
" No eye ſhall pity, and no arm defend :
" Proud as thou art, in ſhort liv'd glory great,
" I come to tell thee thine approaching fate. 125
" Regard my words.   The judge of all the gods,
" Beneath whoſe ſteps the tow'ring mountain nods,
" Will give thine armies to the ſavage brood,
" That cut the liquid air, or range the wood.
" Thee too a well-aim'd pebble ſhall deſtroy, 130
" And thou ſhalt periſh by a beardleſs boy :
                                    " Such

" Such is the mandate from the realms above,
" And fhould I try the vengeance to remove,
" Myfelf a rebel to my king would prove.
" *Goliath* fay, fhall grace to him be fhown,   135
" Who dares heav'ns monarch, and infults his
    " throne ?"

" Your words are loft on me," the giant
    cries,
While fear and wrath contended in his eyes,
When thus the meffenger from heav'n replies :
" Provoke no more *Jehovah's* awful hand   140
" To hurl its vengeance on thy guilty land :
" He grafps the thunder, and, he wings the
    " ftorm,
" Servants their fov'reign's orders to perform."

  The angel fpoke, and turn'd his eyes away,
Adding new radiance to the rifing day.   145

  Now *David* comes : the fatal ftones demand
His left, the ftaff engag'd his better hand

                The

The giant mov'd, and from his tow'ring height
Survey'd the ftripling, and difdain'd the fight,
And thus began : " Am I a dog with thee ?   150
" Bring'ft thou no armour, but a ftaff to me ?
" The gods on thee their vollied curfes pour,
" And beafts and birds of prey thy flefh de-
    " vour."

    David undaunted thus, " Thy fpear and fhield
" Shall no protection to thy body yield :   155
" *Jehovah's* name ——— no other arms I bear,
" I ask no other in this glorious war.
" To-day the Lord of Hofts to me will give
" Vict'ry, to-day thy doom thou fhalt receive ;
" The fate you threaten fhall your own be-
    " come,   160
" And beafts fhall be your animated tomb,
" That all the earth's inhabitants may know
" That there's a God, who governs all below
" This great affembly too fhall witnefs ftand,
" That needs nor fword, nor fpear, th' Almighty's
    hand :   165
                         " The

" The battle his, the conquest he bestows,
" And to our pow'r consigns our hated foes."

Thus *David* spoke ; *Goliath* heard and came
To meet the hero in the field of fame.
Ah! fatal meeting to thy troops and thee.   170
But thou wast deaf to the divine decree ;
Young *David* meets thee, meets thee not in vain;
'Tis thine to perish on th' ensanguin'd plain.

And now the youth the forceful pebble flung,
Philistia trembled as it whizz'd along :   175
In his dread forehead, where the helmet ends,
Just o'er the brows the well-aim'd stone descends,
It pierc'd the skull, and shatter'd all the brain,
Prone on his face he tumbled to the plain :
Goliath's fall no smaller terror yields   180
Than riving thunders in aerial fields :
The soul still ling'red in its lov'd abode,
Till conq'ring *David* o'er the giant strode :
Goliath's sword then laid its master dead,
And from the body hew'd the ghastly head ;   185
                                        The

The blood in gushing torrents drench'd the plains,
The soul found passage through the spouting
    veins.

    And now aloud th' illustrious victor said,
" Where are your boastings now your cham-
    " pion's dead ?"
Scarce had he spoke, when the *Philistines* fled :
But fled in vain; the conqu'ror swift pursu'd :
What scenes of slaughter ! and what seas of blood !
There *Saul* thy thousands grasp'd th' impurpled
    sand
In pangs of death the conquest of thine hand;
And *David* there were thy ten thousands laid: 195
Thus *Israel's* damsels musically play'd.

    Near *Gath* and *Ekron* many an hero lay,
Breath'd out their souls, and curs'd the light of
    day :
Their fury, quench'd by death, no longer burns,
And *David* with *Goliath's* head returns;   200
To *Salem* brought, but in his tent he plac'd
The load of armour which the giant grac'd.

        F   His

His monarch saw him coming from the war,
And thus demanded of the son of *Ner*.
" Say, who is this amazing youth ?" he cry'd, 205
When thus the leader of the host reply'd;
" As lives thy soul I know not whence he sprung,
" So great in prowess though in years so young :"
" Inquire whose son is he," the sov'reign said,
" Before whose conq'ring arm *Philistia* fled." 210
Before the king behold the stripling stand,
Goliath's head depending from his hand :
To him the king : " Say of what martial line
" Art thou, young hero, and what sire was thine ?"
He humbly thus; " the son of *Jesse* I : 215
" I came the glories of the field to try.
" Small is my tribe, but valiant in the fight;
" Small is my city, but thy royal right."
" Then take the promis'd gifts," the monarch
    cry'd,
Conferring riches and the royal bride : 220
" Knit to my soul for ever thou remain
" With me, nor quit my regal roof again."

Thoughts

Thoughts on the WORKS of PROVIDENCE,

ARISE, my foul, on wings enraptur'd, rife
To praife the monarch of the earth and
fkies,
Whofe goodnefs and beneficence appear
As round its centre moves the rolling year,
Or when the morning glows with rofy charms, 5
Or the fun flumbers in the ocean's arms :
Of light divine be a rich portion lent
To guide my foul, and favour my intent,
Celeftial mufe, my arduous flight fuftain,
And raife my mind to a feraphic ftrain !   10

Ador'd for ever be the God unfeen,
Which round the fun revolves this vaft machine,
Though to his eye its mafs a point appears :
Ador'd the God that whirls furrounding fpheres,
Which firft ordain'd that mighty *Sol* fhould
reign   15
The peerlefs monarch of th' ethereal train :

Of

Of miles twice forty millions is his height,
And yet his radiance dazzles mortal fight
So far beneath—from him th' extended earth
Vigour derives, and ev'ry flow'ry birth :   20
Vaft through her orb fhe moves with eafy grace
Around her *Phœbus* in unbounded fpace ;
True to her courfe th' impetuous ftorm derides.
Triumphant o'er the winds, and furging tides.

Almighty, in thefe wond'rous works of thine, 25
What *Pow'r*, what *Wifdcm*, and what *Goodnef*
    fhine ?
And are thy wonders, Lord, by men explor'd,
And yet creating glory unador'd !

Creation fmiles in various beauty gay,
While day to night, and night fucceeds to day : 30
That *Wifdom*, which attends *Jehovah's* ways,
Shines moft confpicuous in the folar rays :
Without them, deititute of heat and light,
This world would be the reign of endlefs
    night :

In

In their excefs how would our race complain, 35
Abhorring life ! how hate its length'ned chain !
From air aduft what num'rous ills would rife ?
What dire contagion taint the burning fkies ?
What peftilential vapours, fraught with death,
Would rife, and overfpread the lands beneath ? 40

Hail, fmiling morn, that from the orient main
Afcending doft adorn the heav'nly plain !
So rich, fo various are thy beauteous dies,
That fpread through all the circuit of the fkies,
That, full of thee, my foul in rapture foars, 45
And thy great God, the caufe of all adores.

O'er beings infinite his love extends,
His *Wifdom* rules them, and his *Pow'r* defends.
When tafks diurnal tire the human frame,
The fpirits faint, and dim the vital flame, 50
Then too that ever active bounty fhines,
Which not infinity of fpace confines.
The fable veil, that *Night* in filence draws,
Conceals effects, but fhews th' *Almighty Caufe*;

Night

Night seals in sleep the wide creation fair, 55
And all is peaceful but the brow of care.
Again, gay *Phœbus*, as the day before,
Wakes ev'ry eye, but what shall wake no more;
Again the face of nature is renew'd,
Which still appears harmonious, fair, and good. 60
May grateful strains salute the smiling morn,
Before its beams the eastern hills adorn!

Shall day to day and night to night conspire
To show the goodness of the Almighty Sire?
This mental voice shall man regardless hear, 65
And never, never raise the filial pray'r?
To-day, O hearken, nor your folly mourn
For time mispent, that never will return.

But see the sons of vegetation rise,
And spread their leafy banners to the skies. 70
All-wise Almighty Providence we trace
In trees, and plants, and all the flow'ry race;
As clear as in the nobler frame of man,
All lovely copies of the Maker's plan.

The

The pow'r the fame that forms a ray of light, 75
That call'd creation from eternal night.
" Let there be light," he faid : from his profound
Old *Chaos* heard, and trembled at the found :
Swift as the word, infpir'd by pow'r divine,
Behold the light around its maker fhine, 80
The firft fair product of th' omnific God,
And now through all his works diffus'd abroad.

As reafon's pow'rs by day our God difclofe,
So we may trace him in the night's repofe :
Say what is fleep ? and dreams how paffing
    ftrange ! 85
When action ceafes, and ideas range
Licentious and unbounded o'er the plains,
Where *Fancy's* queen in giddy triumph reigns,
Hear in foft ftrains the dreaming lover figh
To a kind fair, or rave in jealoufy ; 90
On pleafure now, and now on vengeance bent,
The lab'ring paffions ftruggle for a vent.
What pow'r, O man ! thy *reafon* then reftores,
So long fufpended in nocturnal hours ?

What

What secret hand returns the mental train,   95
And gives improv'd thine active pow'rs again?
From thee, O man, what gratitude should rise!
And, when from balmy sleep thou op'st thine
    eyes,
Let thy first thoughts be praises to the skies.
How merciful our God who thus imparts   100
O'erflowing tides of joy to human hearts,
When wants and woes might be our righteous lot,
Our God forgetting, by our God forgot!

Among the mental pow'rs a question rose,
" What most the image of th' Eternal shows?"
When thus to *Reason* (so let *Fancy* rove)
Her great companion spoke immortal *Love*.

" Say, mighty pow'r, how long shall strife pre-
    vail,
" And with its murmurs load the whisp'ring
    " gale?
" Refer the cause to *Recollection's* shrine,   110
" Who loud proclaims my origin divine,

    " The

" The caufe whence heav'n and earth began to be,
" And is not man immortaliz'd by me ?
" *Reafon* let this moft caufelefs ftrife fubfide."
Thus *Love* pronounc'd, and *Reafon* thus re-
    ply'd.   115

    " Thy birth, celeftial queen ! 'tis mine to own,
" In thee refplendent is the Godhead fhown ;
" Thy words perfuade, my foul enraptur'd feels
" Refiftlefs beauty which thy fmile reveals."
Ardent fhe fpoke, and, kindling at her
    charms,   120
She clafp'd the blooming goddefs in her arms.

    Infinite *Love* where'er we turn our eyes
Appears : this ev'ry creature's wants fupplies ;
This moft is heard in *Nature's* conftant voice,
This makes the morn, and this the eve re-
    joice ;   125
This bids the foft'ring rains and dews defcend
To nourifh all, to ferve one gen'ral end,

G   The

The good of man: yet man ungrateful pays
But little homage, and but little praife.
To him, whofe works array'd with mercy
    fhine   130
What fongs fhould rife, how conftant, how di-
    vine!

To a Lady on the Death of Three Relations.

WE trace the pow'r of Death from tomb to
    tomb,
And his are all the ages yet to come.
'Tis his to call the planets from on high,
To blacken *Phœbus*, and diffolve the fky;
His too, when all in his dark realms are hurl'd, 5
From its firm bafe to fhake the folid world;
His fatal fceptre rules the fpacious whole,
And trembling nature rocks from pole to pole.

Awful he moves, and wide his wings are fpread:
Behold thy brother number'd with the dead!   10
From bondage freed, the exulting fpirit flies
Beyond *Olympus*, and thefe ftarry fkies.
Loft in our woe for thee, bleft fhade, we mourn
In vain; to earth thou nevcr muft retu.n?
Thy fifters too, fair mourner, feel the dart   15
Of Death, and with frefh torture rend thine heart.

        Weep

Weep not for them, who wiſh thine happy mind
To riſe with them, and leave the world behind.

 As a young plant by hurricanes up torn, 20
So near its parent lies the newly born —
But 'midſt the bright ethereal train behold
It ſhines ſuperior on a throne of gold :
Then, mourner, ceaſe ; let hope thy tears reſtrain,
Smile on the tomb, and ſooth the raging pain. 25
On yon bleſt regions fix thy longing view,
Mindleſs of ſublunary ſcenes below ;
Aſcend the ſacred mount, in thought ariſe,
And ſeek ſubſtantial, and immortal joys ;
Where hope receives, where faith to viſion
 ſprings,   30
And raptur'd ſeraphs tune th' immortal ſtrings
To ſtrains extatic. Thou the chorus join,
And to thy father tune the praiſe divine.

To

To a Clergyman on the Death of his Lady.

WHERE contemplation finds her sacred
   spring,
Where heav'nly music makes the arches ring,
Where virtue reigns unsully'd and divine,
Where wisdom thron'd, and all the graces shine,
There sits thy spouse amidst the radiant throng, 5
While praise eternal warbles from her tongue;
There choirs angelic shout her welcome round,
With perfect bliss, and peerless glory crown'd.

While thy dear mate, to flesh no more confin'd,
Exults a blest, an heav'n-ascended mind,   10
Say in thy breast shall floods of sorrow rise?
Say shall its torrents overwhelm thine eyes?
Amid the seats of heav'n a place is free,
And angels ope their bright ranks for thee;
For thee they wait, and with expectant eye   15
Thy spouse leans downward from th' empyreal
  sky:
        " O come

" O come away, her longing spirit cries,

" And share with me the raptures of the skies.

" Our bliss divine to mortals is unknown;

" Immortal life and glory are our own.　　20

" There too may the dear pledges of our love

" Arrive, and taste with us the joys above;

" Attune the harp to more than mortal lays,

" And join with us the tribute of their praise

" To him, who dy'd stern justice to atone,　　25

" And make eternal glory all our own.

" He in his death slew ours, and, as he rose,

" He crush'd the dire dominion of our foes;

" Vain were their hopes to put the God to flight,

" Chain us to hell, and bar the gates of light."　30

She spoke, and turn'd from mortal scenes her eyes,
Which beam'd celestial radiance o'er the skies.

Then thou, dear man, no more with grief re-
　　tire,
Let grief no longer damp devotion's fire,
But rise sublime, to equal bliss aspire.　　35

Thy

Thy ſighs no more be wafted by the wind,
No more complain, but be to heav'n reſign'd.
'Twas thine t' unfold the oracles divine,
To ſooth our woes the taſk was alſo thine;
Now ſorrow is incumbent on thy heart,   40
Permit the muſe a cordial to impart;
Who can to thee their tend'reſt aid refuſe?
To dry thy tears how longs the heav'nly muſe!

An

An H Y M N to the Morning.

ATTEND my lays, ye ever honour'd nine,
      Affift my labours, and my ftrains refine;
In fmootheft numbers pour the notes along,
For bright *Aurora* now demands my fong.

Aurora hail, and all the thoufands dies,   5
Which deck thy progrefs through the vaulted
      fkies:
The morn awakes, and wide extends her rays,
On ev'ry leaf the gentle zephyr plays;
Harmonious lays the feather'd race refume,
Dart the bright eye, and fhake the painted
      plume.   10

Ye fhady groves, your verdant gloom difplay
To fhield your poet from the burning day:
Calliope awake the facred lyre,
While thy fair fifters fan the pleafing fire:

                                    The

The bow'rs, the gales, the variegated ſkies   15
In all their pleaſures in my boſom riſe.

See in the eaſt th' illuſtrious king of day!
His riſing radiance drives the ſhades away—
But Oh! I feel his fervid beams too ſtrong,
And ſcarce begun, concludes th' abortive ſong. 20

H   **An**

An H Y M N to the Evening.

S O O N as the fun forfook the eaftern main
   The pealing thunder fhook the heav'nly
      plain;
Majeftic grandeur! From the zephyr's wing,
Exhales the incenfe of the blooming fpring.
Soft purl the ftreams, the birds renew their
     notes,   5
And through the air their mingled mufic floats.

Through all the heav'ns what beauteous dies are
     fpread!
But the weft glories in the deepeft red:
So may our breafts with ev'ry virtue glow,
The living temples of our God below!   10

Fill'd with the praife of him who gives the
     light,
And draws the fable curtains of the night,

                         Let

Let placid ſlumbers ſooth each weary mind,
At morn to wake more heav'nly, more refin'd,
So ſhall the labours of the day begin   15
More pure, more guarded from the ſnares of ſin.

   Night's leaden ſceptre ſeals my drowſy eyes,
Then ceaſe, my ſong, till fair *Aurora* riſe.

Isaiah lxiii. 1—8.

SAY, heav'nly mufe, what king, or mighty
      God,
That moves fublime from *Idumea's* road?
In *Bozrah's* dies, with martial glories join'd,
His purple vefture waves upon the wind.
Why thus enrob'd delights he to appear   5
In the dread image of the *Pow'r* of war?

Comprefs'd in wrath the fwelling wine-prefs
        groan'd,
It bled, and pour'd the gufhing purple round.

"Mine was the act," th' Almighty Saviour
        faid,
And fhook the dazzling glories of his head,   10
"When all forfook I trod the prefs alone,
"And conquer'd by omnipotence my own;
"For man's releafe fuftain'd the pond'rous load,
"For man the wrath of an immortal God:

"To

" To execute th' Eternal's dread command   15
" My foul I facrific'd with willing hand ;
" Sinlefs I ftood before the avenging frown,
" Atoning thus for vices not my own."

His eye the ample field of battle round
Survey'd, but no created fuccours found;   20
His own omnipotence fuftain'd the fight,
His vengeance funk the haughty foes in night;
Beneath his feet the proftrate troops were fpread,
And round him lay the dying, and the dead.

Great God, what light'ning flafhes from thine
        eyes ?   25
What pow'r withftands if thou indignant rife ?

Againft thy *Zion* though her foes may rage,
And all their cunning, all their ftrength engage,
Yet fhe ferenely on thy bofom lies,
Smiles at their arts, and all their force defies.   30

On

On Recollection.

MNEME begin. Inſpire, ye ſacred nine,
    Your vent'rous *Afric* in her great deſign.
Mneme, immortal pow'r, I trace thy ſpring :
Aſſiſt my ſtrains, while I thy glories ſing :
The acts of long departed years, by thee   5
Recover'd, in due order rang'd we ſee :
Thy pow'r the long-forgotten calls from night,
That ſweetly plays before the *fancy's* ſight.

  Mneme in our nocturnal viſions pours
The ample treaſure of her ſecret ſtores ;   10
Swift from above ſhe wings her ſilent flight
Through *Phœbe's* realms, fair regent of the
       night ;
And, in her pomp of images diſplay'd,
To the high-raptur'd poet gives her aid,
Through the unbounded regions of the mind, 15
Diffuſing light celeſtial and refin'd.

                     The

The heav'nly *phantom* paints the actions done
By ev'ry tribe beneath the rolling fun.

Mneme, enthron'd within the human breaft,
Has vice condemn'd, and ev'ry virtue bleft.   20
How fweet the found when we her plaudit hear?
Sweeter than mufic to the ravifh'd ear,
Sweeter than *Maro's* entertaining ftrains
Refounding through the groves, and hills, and
     plains.
But how is *Mneme* dreaded by the race,   25
Who fcorn her warnings, and defpife her grace?
By her unveil'd each horrid crime appears,
Her awful hand a cup of wormwood bears.
Days, years mifpent, O what a hell of woe!
Hers the worft tortures that our fouls can know.   30

Now eighteen years their deftin'd courfe have
     run,
In faft fucceffion round the central fun.
How did the follies of that period pafs
Unnotic'd, but behold them writ in brafs!

                                        In

In Recollection fee them frefh return,   35
And fure 'tis mine to be afham'd, and mourn.

O *Virtue*, fmiling in immortal green,
Do thou exert thy pow'r, and change the fcene;
Be thine employ to guide my future days,
And mine to pay the tribute of my praife.   40

Of *Recollection* fuch the pow'r enthron'd
In ev'ry breaft, and thus her pow'r is own'd.
The wretch, who dar'd the vengeance of the fkies,
At laft awakes in horror and furprize,
By her alarm'd, he fees impending fate,   45
He howls in anguifh, and repents too late.
But O! what peace, what joys are hers t' impart
To ev'ry holy, ev'ry upright heart!
Thrice bleft the man, who, in her facred fhrine,
Feels himfelf fhelter'd from the wrath divine! 50

On

On IMAGINATION.

THY various works, imperial queen, we see,
   How bright their forms! how deck'd with
     pomp by thee!
Thy wond'rous acts in beauteous order stand,
And all attest how potent is thine hand.

  From *Helicon's* refulgent heights attend,   5
Ye sacred choir, and my attempts befriend:
To tell her glories with a faithful tongue,
Ye blooming graces, triumph in my song.

  Now here, now there, the roving *Fancy* flies,
Till some lov'd object strikes her wand'ring
    eyes,   10
Whose silken fetters all the senses bind,
And soft captivity involves the mind.

Imagination! who can fing thy force?
Or who defcribe the fwiftnefs of thy courfe?
Soaring through air to find the bright abode,   15
Th' empyreal palace of the thund'ring God,
We on thy pinions can furpafs the wind,
And leave the rolling univerfe behind :
From ftar to ftar the mental optics rove,
Meafure   the   fkies,   and   range   the   realms
        above.   20
There in one view we grafp the mighty whole,
Or with new worlds amaze th' unbounded foul.

'Though *Winter* frowns to *Fancy's* raptur'd
        eyes
The fields may flourifh, and gay fcenes arife ;
The frozen deeps may break their iron bands, 25
And bid their waters murmur o'er the fands.
Fair *Flora* may refume her fragrant reign,
And with her flow'ry riches deck the plain ;
Sylvanus may diffufe his honours round,
And all the foreft may with leaves be crown'd : 30
                            Show'rs

Show'rs may defcend, and dews their gems difclofe,
And nectar fparkle on the blooming rofe.

Such is thy pow'r, nor are thine orders vain,
O thou the leader of the mental train :
In full perfection all thy works are wrought,   35
And thine the fceptre o'er the realms of thought.
Before thy throne the fubject-paffions bow,
Of fubject-paffions fov'reign ruler Thou ;
At thy command joy rufhes on the heart,
And through the glowing veins the fpirits dart. 40

Fancy might now her filken pinions try
To rife from earth, and fweep th' expanfe on
   high ;
From *Tithon's* bed now might *Aurora* rife,
Her cheeks all glowing with celeftial dies,
While a pure ftream of light o'erflows the
   fkies.   45
The monarch of the day I might behold,
And all the mountains tipt with radiant gold,

             But

But I reluctant leave the pleasing views,
Which *Fancy* dresses to delight the *Muse*;
Winter austere forbids me to aspire,   50
And northern tempests damp the rising fire;
They chill the tides of *Fancy's* flowing sea,
Cease then, my song, cease the unequal lay.

A Fu-

A Funeral POEM on the Death of C. E.
an Infant of Twelve Months.

THROUGH airy roads he wings his inſtant
flight
To purer regions of celeſtial light;
Enlarg'd he ſees unnumber'd ſyſtems roll,
Beneath him ſees the univerſal whole,
Planets on planets run their deſtin'd round,   5
And circling wonders fill the vaſt profound.
Th' ethercal now, and now th' empyreal ſkies
With growing ſplendors ſtrike his wond'ring eyes:
The angels view him with delight unknown,
Preſs his ſoft hand, and ſeat him on his throne;
Then ſmiling thus.   " To this divine abode,
" The ſeat of ſaints, of ſeraphs, and of God,
" Thrice welcome thou." The raptur'd babe
replies,
" Thanks to my God, who ſnatch'd me to the
" ſkies,

                    " E'er

" E'er vice triumphant had poſſeſs'd my heart, 15
" E'er yet the tempter had beguil'd my heart,
" E'er yet on ſin's baſe actions I was bent,
" E'er yet I knew temptation's diɾe intent ;
" E'er yet the laſh for horrid crimes I felt,
" E'er vanity had led my way to guilt,   20
" But, ſoon arriv'd at my celeſtial goal,
" Full glories ruſh on my expanding ſoul."
Joyful he ſpoke : exulting cherubs round
Clapt their glad wings, the heav'nly vaults reſound.

Say, parents, why this unavailing moan ?   25
Why heave your penſive boſoms with the groan ?
To *Charles*, the happy ſubject of my ſong,
A brighter world, and nobler ſtrains belong.
Say would you tear him from the realms above
By thoughtleſs wiſhes, and prepoſt'rous love ? 30
Doth his felicity increaſe your pain ?
Or could you welcome to this world again
The heir of bliſs ? with a ſuperior air
Methinks he anſwers with a ſmile ſevere,
" Thrones and dominions cannot tempt me
      " there."   35

But

But ftill you cry, " Can we the figh forbear,
" And ftill and ftill muft we not pour the tear ?
" Our only hope, more dear than vital breath,
" Twelve moons revolv'd, becomes the prey of
   " death ;
" Delightful infant, nightly vifions give   40
" Thee to our arms, and we with joy receive,
" We fain would clafp the *Phantom* to our breaft,
" The *Phantom* flies, and leaves the foul unbleft."

To yon bright regions let your faith afcend,
Prepare to join your deareft infant friend
In pleafures without meafure, without end.

To Captain H——D, of the 65th Regiment.

S A Y, mufe divine, can hoftile fcenes delight
    The warrior's bofom in the fields of fight?
Lo! here the chriftian, and the hero join
With mutual grace to form the man divine.
In H——D fee with pleafure and furprize,   5
Where *valour* kindles, and where *virtue* lies:
Go, hero brave, ftill grace the poft of fame,
And add new glories to thine honour'd name,
Still to the field, and ftill to virtue true:
Britannia glories in no fon like you.   10

To the Right Honourable WILLIAM, Earl
of DARTMOUTH, His Majesty's Principal Secretary of State for North America, &c.

HAIL, happy day, when, smiling like the
morn,
Fair *Freedom* rose *New-England* to adorn:
The northern clime beneath her genial ray,
Dartmouth, congratulates thy blissful sway:
Elate with hope her race no longer mourns, 5
Each soul expands, each grateful bosom burns,
While in thine hand with pleasure we behold
The silken reins, and *Freedom's* charms unfold.
Long lost to realms beneath the northern skies
She shines supreme, while hated *faction* dies: 10
Soon as appear'd the *Goddess* long desir'd,
Sick at the view, she languish'd and expir'd;
Thus from the splendors of the morning light
The owl in sadness seeks the caves of night.

K

No

No more, *America*, in mournful ftrain   15 ⎫
Of wrongs, and grievance unredrefs'd complain,   ⎬
No longer fhall thou dread the iron chain,   ⎭
Which wanton *Tyranny* with lawlefs hand
Had made, and with it meant t' enflave the land.

Should you, my lord, while you perufe my
  fong,   20
Wonder from whence my love of *Freedom* fprung,
Whence flow thefe wifhes for the common good,
By feeling hearts alone beft underftood,
I, young in life, by feeming cruel fate
Was fnatch d from *Afric's* fancy'd happy feat: 25
What pangs excruciating muft moleft,
What forrows labour in my parent's breaft?
Steel'd was that foul and by no mifery mov'd
That from a father feiz'd his babe belov'd:
Such, fuch my cafe.   And can I then but
  pray   30
Others may never feel tyrannic fway?

        For

For favours paſt, great Sir, our thanks are due,
And thee we aſk thy favours to renew,
Since in thy pow'r, as in thy will before,
To ſooth the griefs, which thou did'ſt once de-
    plore.   35
May heav'nly grace the ſacred ſanction give
To all thy works, and thou for ever live
Not only on the wings of fleeting *Fame*,
Though praiſe immortal crowns the patriot's
    name,
But to conduct to heav'ns refulgent fane,   40
May fiery courſers ſweep th' ethereal plain,
And bear thee upwards to that bleſt abode,
Where, like the prophet, thou ſhalt find thy God.

O D E to N E P T U N E.

On Mrs. W—'s Voyage to England.

I.

WHILE raging tempefts fhake the fhore,
 While *Æ'lus'* thunders round us roar,
And fweep impetuous o'er the plain
Be ftill, O tyrant of the main;
Nor let thy brow contracted frowns betray, 5
While my *Sufannah* fkims the wat'ry way.

II.

The *Pow'r* propitious hears the lay,
The blue-ey'd daughters of the fea
With fweeter cadence glide along,
And *Thames* refponfive joins the fong. 10
Pleas'd with their notes *Sol* fheds benign his ray,
And double radiance decks the face of day.

III. To

III.

To court thee to *Britannia's* arms
  Serene the climes and mild the ſky,
Her region boaſts unnumber'd charms,   15
  Thy welcome ſmiles in ev'ry eye.
Thy promiſe, *Neptune* keep, record my pray'r,
Nor give my wiſhes to the empty air.

               Boſton, October 10, 1772.

To

To a LADY on her coming to North-America
with her Son, for the Recovery of her Health.

INdulgent muſe! my grov'ling mind inſpire,
   And fill my boſom with celeſtial fire.

  See from *Jamaica's* fervid ſhore ſhe moves,
Like the fair mother of the blooming loves,
When from above the *Goddeſs* with her hand   5
Fans the ſoft breeze, and lights upon the land;
Thus ſhe on *Neptune's* wat'ry realm reclin'd
Appear'd, and thus invites the ling'ring wind.

  " Ariſe, ye winds, *America* explore,
" Waft me, ye gales, from this malignant
   " ſhore;   10
" The *Northern* milder climes I long to greet,
" There hope that health will my arrival meet."
Soon as ſhe ſpoke in my ideal view
The winds aſſented, and the veſſel flew.

                                    Madam,

Madam, your spouse bereft of wife and son, 15
In the grove's dark recesses pours his moan ;
Each branch, wide-spreading to the ambient sky,
Forgets its verdure, and submits to die.

From thence I turn, and leave the sultry plain,
And swift pursue thy passage o'er the main : 20
The ship arrives before the fav'ring wind,
And makes the *Philadelphian* port assign'd,
Thence I attend you to *Bostonia's* arms,
Where gen'rous friendship ev'ry bosom warms :
Thrice welcome here ! may health revive again, 25
Bloom on thy cheek, and bound in ev'ry vein !
Then back return to gladden ev'ry heart,
And give your spouse his soul's far dearer part,
Receiv'd again with what a sweet surprize,
The tear in transport starting from his eyes ! 30
While his attendant son with blooming grace
Springs to his father's ever dear embrace.
With shouts of joy *Jamaica's* rocks resound,
With shouts of joy the country rings around.

To

To a Lady on her remarkable Preservation
in an Hurricane in *North-Carolina*.

THOUGH thou did'st hear the tempest from
  afar,
And felt'st the horrors of the wat'ry war,
To me unknown, yet on this peaceful shore
Methinks I hear the storm tumultuous roar,
And how stern *Boreas* with impetuous hand 5
Compell'd the *Nereids* to usurp the land.
Reluctant rose the daughters of the main,
And slow ascending glided o'er the plain,
Till *Æolus* in his rapid chariot drove
In gloomy grandeur from the vault above: 10
Furious he comes. His winged sons obey
Their frantic sire, and madden all the sea
The billows rave, the wind's fierce tyrant roars,
And with his thund'ring terrors shakes the shores.
Broken by waves the vessel's frame is rent, 15
And strows with planks the wat'ry element.

          But

But thee, *Maria*, a kind *Nereid's* fhield
Preferv'd from finking, and thy form upheld :
And fure fome heav'nly oracle defign'd
At that dread crifis to inftruct thy mind   20
Things of eternal confequence to weigh,
And to thine heart juft feelings to convey
Of things above, and of the future doom,
And what the births of the dread world to come.

From toffing feas I welcome thee to land.   25
" Refign her, *Nereid*," 'twas thy God's command.
Thy fpoufe late buried, as thy fears conceiv'd,
Again returns, thy fears are all reliev'd :
Thy daughter blooming with fuperior grace
Again thou fee'ft, again thine arms embrace ;   30
O come, and joyful fhow thy fpoufe his heir,
And what the bleffings of maternal care !

L   To

To a Lady and her Children, on the Death
of her Son and their Brother.

OErwhelming sorrow now demánds my song:
   From death the overwhelming sorrow sprung.
What flowing tears ? What hearts with grief op-
   preſt ?
What sighs on sighs heave the fond parent's
   breaſt ?
The brother weeps, the hapleſs siſters join   5
Th' increaſing woe, and ſwell the cryſtal brine;
The poor, who once his gen'rous bounty fed,
Droop, and bewail their benefactor dead.
In death the friend, the kind companion lies,
And in one death what various comfort dies ! 10

   Th' unhappy mother ſees the ſanguine rill
Forget to flow, and nature's wheels ſtand ſtill,
But ſee from ea-th his ſpirit far remov'd,
And know no grief recals your beſt-belov'd:
                        He.

He, upon pinions fwifter than the wind,   15
Has left mortality's fad fcenes behind
For joys to this terreftrial ftate unknown,
And glories richer than the monarch's crown.
Of virtue's fteady courfe the prize behold!
What blifsful wonders to his mind unfold!   20
But of celeftial joys I fing in vain:
Attempt not, mufe, the too advent'rous ftrain.

No more in briny fhow'rs, ye friends around,
Or bathe his clay, or wafte them on the ground:
Still do you weep, ftill wifh for his return?   25
How cruel thus to wifh, and thus to mourn?
No more for him the ftreams of forrow pour,
But hafte to join him on the heav'nly fhore,
On harps of gold to tune immortal lays,
And to your God immortal anthems raife.   30

To

To a GENTLEMAN and LADY on the Death of
   the Lady's Brother and Sifter, and a Child
   of the Name *Avis*, aged one Year.

ON *Death's* domain intent I fix my eyes,
    Where human nature in vaft ruin lies ;
With penfive mind I fearch the drear abode,
Where the great conqu'ror has his fpoils beftow'd ;
There there the offspring of fix thoufand years 5
In endlefs numbers to my view appears :
Whole kingdoms in his gloomy den are thruft,
And nations mix with their primeval duft :
Infatiate ftill he gluts the ample tomb ;
His is the prefent, his the age to come   10
See here a brother, here a fifter fpread,
And a fweet daughter mingled with the dead.

   But, *Madam*, let your grief be laid afide,
And let the fountain of your tears be dry'd,
In vain they flow to wet the dufty plain,   15
Your fighs are wafted to the fkies in vain,

                  Your

Your pains they witnefs, but they can no more,
While *Death* reigns tyrant o'er this mortal fhore.

The glowing ftars and filver queen of light
At laft muft perifh in the gloom of night : 20
Refign thy friends to that Almighty hand,
Which gave them life, and bow to his command;
Thine *Avis* give without a murm'ring heart,
Though half thy foul be fated to depart.
To fhining guards confign thine infant care 25
To waft triumphant through the feas of air :
Her foul enlarg'd to heav'nly pleafure fprings,
She feeds on truth and uncreated things.
Methinks I hear her in the realms above,
And leaning forward with a filial love, 30
Invite you there to fhare immortal blifs
Unknown, untafted in a ftate like this.
With tow'ring hopes, and growing grace arife,
And feek beatitude beyond the fkies.

On

On the Death of Dr. SAMUEL MARSHALL.
1771.

THROUGH thickeſt glooms look back,
  immortal ſhade,
On that confuſion which thy death has made;
Or from *Olympus'* height look down, and ſee
A *Town* involv'd in grief bereft of thee.
Thy *Lucy* ſees thee mingle with the dead,   5
And rends the graceful treſſes from her head,
Wild in her woe, with grief unknown oppreſt
Sigh follows ſigh deep heaving from her breaſt.

 Too quickly fled, ah! whither art thou gone?
Ah! loſt for ever to thy wife and ſon!   10
The hapleſs child, thine only hope and heir,
Clings round his mother's neck, and weeps his
  ſorrows there.
The loſs of thee on *Tyler's* ſoul returns,
And *Boſton* for her dear phyſician mourns.

        When

When ſickneſs call'd for *Marſhall's* healing
    hand,   15
With what compaſſion did his ſoul expand?
In him we found the father and the friend:
In life how lov'd! how honour'd in his end!

    And muſt not then our *Æſculapius* ſtay
To bring his ling'ring infant into day?   20
The babe unborn in the dark womb is toſt,
And ſeems in anguiſh for its father loſt.

    Gone is *Apollo* from his houſe of earth,
But leaves the ſweet memorials of his worth:
The common parent, whom we all deplore,   25
From yonder world unſeen muſt come no more,
Yet 'midſt our woes immortal hopes attend
The ſpouſe, the ſire, the univerſal friend.

To

To a Gentleman on his Voyage to *Great-Britain*
for the Recovery of his Health.

WHILE others chant of gay *Elysian* scenes,
　　Of balmy zephyrs, and of flow'ry plains,
My song more happy speaks a greater name,
Feels higher motives and a nobler flame.
For thee, O R—, the muse attunes her strings, 5
And mounts sublime above inferior things.

　I sing not now of green embow'ring woods,
I sing not now the daughters of the floods,
I sing not of the storms o'er ocean driv'n,
And how they howl'd along the waste of heav'n, 10
But I to R— would paint the *British* shore,
And vast *Atlantic*, not untry'd before :
Thy life impair'd commands thee to arise,
Leave these bleak regions, and inclement skies,
Where chilling winds return the winter past, 15
And nature shudders at the furious blast.

O thou

O thou ſtupendous, earth-encloſing main
Exert thy wonders to the world again!
If ere thy pow'r prolong'd the fleeting breath,
Turn'd back the ſhafts, and mock'd the gates of
    death,   20
If ere thine air diſpens'd an healing pow'r,
Or ſnatch'd the victim from the fatal hour,
This equal caſe demands thine equal care,
And equal wonders may this patient ſhare.
But unavailing, frantic is the dream   25
To hope thine aid without the aid of him
Who gave thee birth, and taught thee where to
    flow,
And in thy waves his various bleſſings ſhow.

May R— return to view his native ſhore
Replete with vigour not his own before,   30
Then ſhall we ſee with pleaſure and ſurprize,
And own thy work, great Ruler of the ſkies!

            M   To

To the Rev. Dr. THOMAS AMORY
on reading his Sermons on DAILY DEVOTION,
in which that Duty is recommended and affifted.

To cultivate in ev'ry noble mind
    Habitual grace, and fentiments refin'd,
Thus while you ftrive to mend the human heart,
Thus while the heav'nly precepts you impart,
O may each bofom catch the facred fire,   5
And youthful minds to *Virtue's* throne afpire!

When God's eternal ways you fet in fight,
And *Virtue* fhines in all her native light,
In vain would *Vice* her works in night conceal,
For *Wifdom's* eye pervades the fable veil.   10

Artifts may paint the fun's effulgent rays,
But *Amory's* pen the brighter God difplays:
While his great works in *Amory's* pages fhine,
And while he proves his effence all divine,

                            The

The Atheist sure no more can boast aloud   15
Of chance, or nature, and exclude the God;
As if the clay without the potter's aid
Should rise in various forms, and shapes self-made,
Or worlds above with orb o'er orb profound
Self-mov'd could run the everlasting round.   20
It cannot be   unerring *Wisdom* guides
With eye propitious, and o'er all presides.

    Still prosper, *Amory!* still may'st thou receive
The warmest blessings which a muse can give,
And when this transitory state is o'er,   25
When kingdoms fall, and fleeting *Fame's* no more,
May *Amory* triumph in immortal fame,
A nobler title, and superior name!

On

On the Death of J. C. an Infant.

NO more the flow'ry scenes of pleasure rise,
  Nor charming prospects greet the mental
    eyes,
No more with joy we view that lovely face
Smiling, disportive, flush'd with ev'ry grace.

The tear of sorrow flows from ev'ry eye,   5
Groans answer groans, and sighs to sighs reply;
What sudden pangs shot thro' each aching heart,
When, *Death*, thy messenger dispatch'd his dart?
Thy dread attendants, all-destroying *Pow'r*,
Hurried the infant to his mortal hour.   10
Could'st thou unpitying close those radiant
    eyes?
Or fail'd his artless beauties to surprize?
Could not his innocence thy stroke controul,
Thy purpose shake, and soften all thy soul?

The

The blooming babe, with fhades of *Death* o'er-
     fpread,   15
No more fhall fmile, no more fhall raife its
    head,
But, like a branch that from the tree is torn,
Falls proftrate, wither'd, languid, and forlorn.
" Where flies my *James?*" 'tis thus I feem to
    hear
The parent afk, " Some angel tell me where 20
" He wings his paffage thro' the yielding air ?"
Methinks a cherub bending from the fkies
Obferves the queftion, and ferene replies,
" In heav'ns high palaces your babe appears :
" Prepare to meet him, and difmifs your tears." 25
Shall not th' intelligence your grief reftrain,
And turn the mournful to the chearful ftrain ?
Ceafe your complaints, fufpend each rifing figh,
Ceafe to accufe the Ruler of the fky.
Parents, no more indulge the falling tear :   30
Let *Faith* to heav'n's refulgent domes repair,
There fee your infant, like a feraph glow :
What charms celeftial in his numbers flow

                  Melodious,

Melodious, while the soul-enchanting strain
Dwells on his tongue. and fills th' ethereal plain? 35
Enough— for ever cease your murm'ring breath ;
Not as a foe, but friend converse with *Death*,
Since to the port of happiness unknown
He brought that treasure which you call your own.
The gift of heav'n intrusted to your hand   40
Chearful resign at the divine command :
Not at your bar must sov'reign *Wisdom* stand.

An

An H Y M N to HUMANITY.
To S. P. G. Efq;

I.

LO! for this dark terreftrial ball
Forfakes his azure-paved hall
  A prince of heav'nly birth!
Divine *Humanity* behold.
What wonders rife, what charms unfold   5
  At his defcent to earth!

II.

The bofoms of the great and good
With wonder and delight he view'd,
  And fix'd his empire there:
Him, clofe compreffing to his breaft,   10
The fire of gods and men addrefs'd,
  " My fon, my heav'nly fair!

III. " Defcend

III.

" Defcend to earth, there place thy throne;
" To fuccour man's afflicted fon
    " Each human heart infpire :   15
" To act in bounties unconfin'd
" Enlarge the clofe contracted mind,
    " And fill it with thy fire."

IV.

Quick as the word, with fwift career
He wings his courfe from ftar to ftar,   20
    And leaves the bright abode.
The *Virtue* did his charms impart;
Their G——y ! then thy raptur'd heart
    Perceiv'd the rufhing God :

V.

For when thy pitying eye did fee   25
The languid mufe in low degree,
    Then, then at thy defire
Defcended the celeftial nine ;
O'er me methought they deign'd to fhine,
    And deign'd to ftring my lyre.   30

VI. Can

VI.

Can *Afric's* mufe forgetful prove ?
Or can fuch friendfhip fail to move
    A tender human heart ?
Immortal *Friendfhip* laurel-crown'd
The fmiling *Graces* all furround   **35**
    With ev'ry heav'nly *Art.*

To the Honourable T. H. Efq; on the Death
of his Daughter.

WHILE deep you mourn beneath the
cyprefs-fhade
The hand of Death, and your dear daughter laid
In duft, whofe abfence gives your tears to flow,
And racks your bofom with inceffant woe,
Let *Recollection* take a tender part,   5
Affuage the raging tortures of your heart,
Still the wild tempeft of tumultuous grief,
And pour the heav'nly nectar of relief:
Sufpend the figh, dear Sir, and check the groan,
Divinely bright your daughter's *Virtues* fhone: 10
How free from fcornful pride her gentle mind,
Which ne'er its aid to indigence declin'd!
Expanding free, it fought the means to prove
Unfailing charity, unbounded love!

    She unreluctant flies to fee no more   15
Her dear-lov'd parents on earth's dufky fhore:
                              Impatient

Impatient heav'n's refplendent goal to gain,
She with fwift progrefs cuts the azure plain,
Where grief fubfides, where changes are no more,
And life's tumultuous billows ceafe to roar;   20
She leaves her earthly manfion for the fkies,
Where new creations feaft her wond'ring eyes.

To heav'n's high mandate chearfully refign'd
She mounts, and leaves the rolling globe behind ;
She, who late wifh'd that *Leonard* might return, 25
Has ceas'd to languifh, and forgot to mourn ;
To the fame high empyreal manfions come,
She joins her fpoufe, and fmiles upon the tomb :
And thus I hear her from the realms above :
" Lo ! this the kingdom of celeftial love!   30
" Could ye, fond parents, fee our prefent blifs,
" How foon would you each figh, each fear dif-
     " mifs ?
" Amidft unutter'd pleafures whilft I play
" In the fair funfhine of celeftial day,
" As far as grief affects an happy foul   35
" So far doth grief my better mind controul,

" To fee on earth my aged parents mourn,

" And fecret wifh for T——l to return :

" Let brighter fcenes your ev'ning-hours em-
    " ploy :

" Converfe with heav'n, and tafte the promis'd
    " joy."   40

NIOBE

NIOBE in Diſtreſs for her Children ſlain by
    APOLLO, from *Ovid's* Metamorphoſes, Book VI.
    and from a view of the Painting of Mr. *Richard*
    Wilſon.

APOLLO's wrath to man the dreadful
    ſpring
Of ills innum'rous, tuneful goddeſs, ſing!
Thou who did'ſt firſt th' ideal pencil give,
And taught'ſt the painter in his works to live,
Inſpire with glowing energy of thought,   5
What *Wilſon* painted, and what *Ovid* wrote.
Muſe! lend thy aid, nor let me ſue in vain,
Tho' laſt and meaneſt of the rhyming train!
O guide my pen in lofty ſtrains to ſhow
The *Phrygian* queen, all beautiful in woe.   10

   'Twas where *Mæonia* ſpreads her wide domain
Niobe dwelt, and held her potent reign:
See in her hand the regal ſceptre ſhine,
The wealthy heir of *Tantalus* divine,

He

He moſt diſtinguiſh'd by *Dodonean Jove*,   15.
To approach the tables of the gods above :
Her grandſire *Atlas*, who with mighty pains
Th' ethereal axis on his neck ſuſtains :
Her other gran ſire on the throne on high
Rolls the loud-pealing thunder thro' the ſky.   20

Her ſpouſe, *Anphion*, who from *Jove* too ſprings,
Divinely taught to ſweep the ſounding ſtrings.

Seven ſprightly ſons the royal bed adorn,
Seven daughters beauteous as the op'ning morn,
As when *Aurora* fills the raviſh'd ſight,   25
And decks the orient realms with roſy light
From their bright eyes the living ſplendors play,
Nor can beholders bear the flaſhing ray.

Wherever, *Niobe*, thou turn'ſt thine eyes,
New beauties kindle, and new joys ariſe !   30
But thou had'ſt far the happier mother prov'd,
If this fair offspring had been leſs belov'd :

                                        What

What if their charms exceed *Aurora's* teint,
No words could tell them, and no pencil paint,
Thy love too vehement haftens to deftroy   35
Each blooming maid, and each celeftial boy.

Now *Manto* comes, endu'd with mighty fkill,
The paft to explore, the future to reveal.
Thro' *Thebes'* wide ftreets *Tirefia's* daughter came,
Divine *Latona's* mandate to proclaim: 40
The Theban maids to hear the orders ran,
When thus *Mæonia's* prophetefs began:

" Go, *Thebans!* great *Latona's* will obey,
" And pious tribute at her altars pay:
" With rights divine, the goddefs be implor'd,   45
" Nor be her facred offspring unador'd."
Thus *Manto* fpoke.   The *Theban* maids obey,
And pious tribute to the goddefs pay.
The rich perfumes afcend in waving fpires,
And altars blaze with confecrated fires;   50
The fair affembly moves with graceful air,
And leaves of laurel bind the flowing hair.

                                      Niobe

Niobe comes with all her royal race,
With charms unnumber'd, and superior grace:
Her *Phrygian* garments of delightful hue,   55
Inwove with gold, refulgent to the view,
Beyond description beautiful she moves
Like heav'nly *Venus*, 'midst her smiles and loves:
She views around the supplicating train,
And shakes her graceful head with stern dif-
      dain,   60
Proudly she turns around her lofty eyes,
And thus reviles celestial deities:
" What madness drives the *Theban* ladies fair
" To give their incense to surrounding air?
" Say why this new sprung deity preferr'd?   65
" Why vainly fancy your petitions heard?
" Or say why *Cœus*' offspring is obey'd,
" While to my goddeship no tribute's paid?
" For me no altars blaze with living fires,
" No bullock bleeds, no frankincense transpires, 70
" Tho' *Cadmus*' palace, not unknown to fame,
" And *Phrygian* nations all revere my name.
                              " Where'er

" Where'er I turn my eyes vaft wealth I find.

" Lo! here an emprefs with a goddefs join'd.

" What, fhall a *Titanefs* be deify'd,   75

" To whom the fpacious earth a couch deny'd?

" Nor heav'n, nor earth, nor fea receiv'd your
   " queen,

" 'Till pitying *Delos* took the wand'rer in.

" Round me what a large progeny is fpread!

" No frowns of fortune has my foul to dread. 80

" What if indignant fhe decreafe my train

" More than *Latona's* number will remain?

" Then hence, ye *Theban* dames, hence hafte
   " away,

" Nor longer off'rings to *Latona* pay?

" Regard the orders of *Amphion's* fpoufe,   85

" And take the leaves of laurel from your brows."

Niobe fpoke. The *Theban* maids obey'd,

Their brows unbound, and left the rights un-
   paid.

The angry goddefs heard, then filence broke

On *Cynthus'* fummit, and indignant fpoke;   90

     O   " *Phœbus!*

" *Phœbus!* behold, thy mother in difgrace,

" Who to no goddefs yields the prior place

" Except to *Juno's* felf, who reigns above,

" The fpoufe and fifter of the thund'ring *Jove.*

" *Niobe* fprung from *Tantalus* infpires   95

" Each *Theban* bofom with rebellious fires;

" No reafon her imperious temper quells,

" But all her father in her tongue rebels;

" Wrap her own fons for her blafpheming breath,

" *Apollo!* wrap them in the fhades of death." 100

Latona ceas'd, and ardent thus replies,

The God, whofe glory decks th' expanded fkies:

" Ceafe thy complaints, mine be the tafk af-
          " fign'd

" To punifh pride, and fcourge the rebel mind."

This *Phœbe* join'd.—They wing their inftant
          flight;   105

Thebes trembled as th' immortal pow'rs alight.

With clouds incompafs'd glorious *Phœbus*
          ftands;

The feather'd vengeance quiv'ring in his hands.

                                        Near

Near *Cadmus*' walls a plain extended lay,
Where *Thebes*' young princes pafs'd in fport the
    day :   110
There the bold courfers bounded o'er the plains,
While their great mafters held the golden reins.
Ifmenus firft the racing paftime led,
And rul'd the fury of his flying fteed.
" Ah me," he fudden cries, with fhrieking
    breath,   115
While in his breaft he feels the fhaft of death ;
He dropʳ the bridle on his courfer's mane,
Before his eyes in fhadows fwims the plain,
He, the firft-born of great *Amphion's* bed,
Was ftruck the firft, firft mingled with the
    dead.   120

Then didft thou, *Sipylus*, the language hear
Of fate portentous whiftling in the air :
As when th' impending ftorm the failor fees
He fpreads his canvas to the fav'ring breeze,

So to thine horse thou gav'ft the golden reins, 125
Gav'ft him to rufh impetuous o'er the plains:
But ah! a fatal fhaft from *Phœbus'* hand
Smites through thy neck, and finks thee on the
  fand.

 Two other brothers were at *wreftling* found,
And in their paftime clafpt each other round: 130
A fhaft that inftant from *Apollo's* hand
Transfixt them both, and ftretcht them on the
  fand:
Together they their cruel fate bemoan'd,
Together languifh'd, and together groan'd:
Together too th' unbodied fpirits fled, 135
And fought the gloomy manfions of the dead.

 Alphenor faw, and trembling at the view,
Beat his torn breaft, that chang'd its fnowy hue.
He flies to raife them in a kind embrace;
A brother's fondnefs triumphs in his face: 140
Alphenor fails in this fraternal deed,
A dart difpatch'd him (fo the fates decreed:)
         Soon

Soon as the arrow left the deadly wound,
His iffuing entrails fmoak'd upon the ground.

What woes on blooming *Damafichon* wait!   145
His fighs portend his near impending fate.
Juft where the well-made leg begins to be,
And the foft finews form the fupple knee,
The youth fore wounded by the *Delian* god
Attempts t' extract the crime-avenging rod,   150
But, whilft he ftrives the will of fate t' avert,
Divine *Apollo* fends a fecond dart;
Swift thro' his throat the feather'd mifchief flies,
Bereft of fenfe, he drops his head, and dies.

Young *Ilioneus*, the laft, directs his pray'r,   155
And cries, " My life, ye gods celeftial! fpare."
Apollo heard, and pity touch'd his heart,
But ah! too late, for he had fent the dart:
Thou too, O *Ilioneus*, are doom'd to fall,
The fates refufe that arrow to rical.   160

On

On the fwift wings of ever-flying *Fame*
To *Cadmus*' palace foon the tidings came:
Niobe heard, and with indignant eyes
She thus exprefs'd her anger and furprize:
" Why is fuch privilege to them allow'd?   165
" Why thus infulted by the *Delian* god?
" Dwells there fuch mifchief in the pow'rs above?
" Why fleeps the vengeance of immortal *Jove?*"
For now *Amphion* too, with grief opprefs'd,
Had plung'd the deadly dagger in his breaft. 170
Niobe now, lefs haughty than before,
With lofty head directs her fteps no more.
She, who late told her pedigree divine,
And drove the *Thebans* from *Latona's* fhrine,
How ftrangely chang'd!——yet beautiful in
        woe,   175
She weeps, nor weeps unpity'd by the foe.
On each pale corfe the wretched mother fpread
Lay overwhelm'd with grief, and kifs'd her dead.
Then rais'd her arms, and thus, in accents flow,
" Be fated cruel *Goddefs!* with my woe;   180
                                        " If

" If I've offended, let thefe ftreaming eyes,
" And let this fev'nfold funeral fuffice :
" Ah ! take this wretched life you deign'd to fave,
" With them I too am carried to the grave.
" Rejoice triumphant, my victorious foe,   185
" But fhow the caufe from whence your triumphs
   " flow ?
" Tho' I unhappy mourn thefe children flain,
" Yet greater numbers to my lot remain."
She ceas'd, the bow-ftring twang'd with awful
   found,
Which ftruck with terror all th' affembly round,
Except the queen, who ftood unmov'd alone,
By her diftreffes more prefumptuous grown.
Near the pale corfes ftood their fifters fair
In fable veftures and difhevell'd hair ;
One, while fhe draws the fatal fhaft away,   195
Faints, falls, and fickens at the light of day.
To footh her mother, lo ! another flies,
And blames the fury of inclement fkies,
And, while her words a filial pity fhow,
Struck   dumb———indignant   feeks   the   fhades
   below.   200
                                       Now

Now from the fatal place another flies,
Falls in her flight, and languishes, and dies.
Another on her sister drops in death ;
A fifth in trembling terrors yields her breath ;
While the sixth seeks some gloomy cave in
        vain,   205
Struck with the rest, and mingl'd with the slain.

One only daughter lives, and she the least ;
The queen close clasp'd the daughter to her breast :
" Ye heav'nly pow'rs, ah spare me one," she cry'd,
" Ah ! spare me one," the vocal hills reply'd : 210
In vain she begs, the Fates her suit deny,
In her embrace she sees her daughter die.

  * " The queen of all her family bereft,
" Without or husband, son, or daughter left,
" Grew stupid at the shock.   The passing air 215
" Made no impression on her stiff'ning hair.

* This Verse to the End is the Work of another Hand.

                                    " The

" The blood forfook her face : amidft the flood
" Pour'd from her cheeks, quite fix'd her eye-balls
    " ftood.
" Her tongue, her palate both obdurate grew,
" Her curdled veins no longer motion knew ; 220
" The ufe of neck, and arms, and feet was gone,
" And ev'n her bowels hard'ned into ftone :
" A marble ftatue now the queen appears,
" But from the marble fteal the filent tears."

P   To

To S. M. a young *African* Painter, on feeing his Works.

TO fhow the lab'ring bofom's deep intent,
　　And thought in living characters to paint,
When firft thy pencil did thofe beauties give,
And breathing figures learnt from thee to live,
How did thofe profpects give my foul delight,　5
A new creation rufhing on my fight?
Still, wond'rous youth! each noble path purfue,
On deathlefs glories fix thine ardent view:
Still may the painter's and the poet's fire
To aid thy pencil, and thy verfe confpire!　10
And may the charms of each feraphic theme
Conduct thy footfteps to immortal fame!
High to the blifsful wonders of the fkies
Elate thy foul, and raife thy wifhful eyes.
Thrice happy, when exalted to furvey　15
That fplendid city, crown'd with endlefs day,
Whofe twice fix gates on radiant hinges ring:
Celeftial *Salem* blooms in endlefs fpring.

Calm

Calm and ferene thy moments glide along,
And may the mufe infpire each future fong !   20
Still, with the fweets of contemplation blefs'd,
May peace with balmy wings your foul inveft !
But when thefe fhades of time are chas'd away,
And darknefs ends in everlafting day,
On what feraphic pinions fhall we move,   25
And view the landfcapes in the realms above ?
There fhall thy tongue in heav'nly murmurs flow,
And there my mufe with heav'nly tranfport glow :
No more to tell of *Damon's* tender fighs,
Or rifing radiance of *Aurora's* eyes,   30
For nobler themes demand a nobler ftrain,
And purer language on th' ethereal plain.
Ceafe, gentle mufe ! the folemn gloom of night
Now feals the fair creation from my fight.

To His Honour the Lieutenant-Governor, on the
    Death of his Lady.   *March* 24, 1773.

ALL-conquering Death! by thy refiftlefs
        pow'r,
Hope's tow'ring plumage falls to rife no more!
Of fcenes terreftrial how the glories fly,
Forget their fplendors, and fubmit to die!
Who erc efcap'd thee, but the faint * of old   5
Beyond the flood in facred annals told,
And the great fage, † whom fiery courfes drew
To heav'n's bright portals from *Elifha's* view;
Wond'ring he gaz'd at the refulgent car,
Then fnatch'd the mantle floating on the air.   10
From *Death* thefe only could exemption boaft,
And without dying gain'd th' immortal coaft.
Not falling millions fate the tyrant's mind,
Nor can the victor's progrefs be confin'd.
But ceafe thy ftrife with *Death*, fond *Nature,*
    ceafe: 15
He leads the *virtuous* to the realms of peace;

* Enoch.   † Elijah.

His

His to conduct to the immortal plains,
Where heav'n's Supreme in bliss and glory reigns.

There sits, illustrious Sir, thy beauteous spouse;
A gem-blaz'd circle beaming on her brows.   20
Hail'd with acclaim among the heav'nly choirs,
Her soul new-kindling with seraphic fires,
To notes divine she tunes the vocal strings,
While heav'n's high concave with the music rings.
Virtue's rewards can mortal pencil paint?   25
No—all descriptive arts, and eloquence are faint;
Nor canst thou, *Oliver*, assent refuse
To heav'nly tidings from the *Afric* muse.

As soon may change thy laws, eternal *fate*,
As the saint miss the glories I relate;   30
Or her *Benevolence* forgotten lie,
Which wip'd the trick'ling tear from *Mis'ry's* eye.
Whene'er the adverse winds were known to blow,
When loss to loss * ensu'd, and woe to woe,

* Three amiable Daughters who died when just arrived to
Womens Estate.

Calm

Calm and ſerene beneath her father's hand   35
She ſat reſign'd to the divine command.

No longer then, great Sir, her death deplore,
And let us hear the mournful ſigh no more,
Reſtrain the ſorrow ſtreaming from thine eye,
Be all thy future moments crown'd with joy !   40
Nor let thy wiſhes be to earth confin'd,
But ſoaring high purſue th' unbodied mind.
Forgive the muſe, forgive th' advent'rous lays,
That fain thy ſoul to heav'nly ſcenes would raiſe.

A Farewel

A Farewel to AMERICA. To Mrs. S. W.

I.

ADIEU, *New-England's* smiling meads,
   Adieu, the flow'ry plain :
I leave thine op'ning charms, O spring,
   And tempt the roaring main.

II.

In vain for me the flow'rets rise,   5
   And boast their gaudy pride,
While here beneath the northern skies
   I mourn for *health* deny'd.

III.

Celestial maid of rosy hue,
   O let me feel thy reign !   10
I languish till thy face I view,
   Thy vanish'd joys regain.

IV. *Susannah*

IV.

Susannah mourns, nor can I bear
 To see the cryſtal ſhow'r,
Or mark the tender falling tear   15
 At ſad departure's hour;

V.

Not unregarding can I ſee
 Her ſoul with grief oppreſt:
But let no ſighs, no groans for me,
 Steal from her penſive breaſt.   20

VI.

In vain the feather'd warblers ſing,
 In vain the garden blooms,
And on the boſom of the ſpring
 Breathes out her ſweet perfumes,

VII.

While for *Britannia's* diſtant ſhore   25
 We ſweep the liquid plain,
And with aſtoniſh'd eyes explore
 The wide-extended main.

         VIII. Lo!

VIII.

Lo! *Health* appears! celeftial dame!
   Complacent and ferene,
With *Hebe*'s mantle o'er her Frame,   30
   With foul-delighting mein.

IX.

To mark the vale where *London* lies
   With mifty vapours crown'd,
Which cloud *Aurora's* thoufand dyes,   35
   And veil her charms around,

X.

Why, *Phœbus*, moves thy car fo flow?
   So flow thy rifing ray?
Give us the famous town to view,
   Thou glorious king of day!   40

XI.

For thee, *Britannia*, I refign
   New-England's fmiling fields;
To view again her charms divine,
   What joy the profpect yields!

Q   XII. But

XII.

But thou! Temptation hence away,   45
   With all thy fatal train
Nor once feduce my foul away,
   By thine enchanting ftrain.

XIII.

Thrice happy they, whofe heav'nly fhield
   Secures their fouls from harms,   50
And fell *Temptation* on the field
   Of all its pow'r difarms!

Bofton, May 7, 1773.

A REBUS,

A REBUS, by *I. B.*

I.

A BIRD delicious to the taſte,
   On which an army once did feaſt,
  Sent by an hand unſeen;
A creature of the horned race,
Which *Britain's* royal ſtandards grace;   5
  A gem of vivid green;

II.

A town of gaiety and ſport,
Where beaux and beauteous nymphs reſort,
  And gallantry doth reign;
A *Dardan* hero fam'd of old   10
For youth and beauty, as we're told,
  And by a monarch ſlain;

III.

A peer of popular applauſe,
Who doth our violated laws,
  And grievances proclaim.   15
Th' initials ſhow a vanquiſh'd town,
That adds freſh glory and renown
  To old *Britannia's* fame.

An ANSWER to the *Rebus*, by the Author of these
P O E M S.

THE poet asks, and *Phillis* can't refuse
To shew th'obedience of the Infant muse.
She knows the *Quail* of most inviting taste
Fed *Israel's* army in the dreary waste;
And what's on *Britain's* royal standard borne,   5
But the tall, graceful, rampant *Unicorn*?
The *Emerald* with a vivid verdure glows
Among the gems which regal crowns compose;
Boston's a town, polite and debonair,
To which the beaux and beauteous nymphs repair,
Each *Helen* strikes the mind with sweet surprise,
While living lightning flashes from her eyes.
See young *Euphorbus* of the *Dardan* line
By *Menelaus'* hand to death resign :
The well known peer of popular applause
Is *C—m* zealous to support our laws.
   Quebec now vanquish'd must obey,
   She too must annual tribute pay
   To *Britain* of immortal fame,
   And add new glory to her name.   20

F I N I S.

CONTENTS.

	Page
TO Mæcenas	9
On Virtue	13
To the Univerſity of Cambridge, in New-England	15
To the King's Moſt Excellent Majeſty	17
On being brought from Africa	18
On the Rev. Dr. Sewell	19
On the Rev. Mr. George Whitefield	22
On the Death of a young Lady of five Years of Age	25
On the Death of a young Gentleman	27
To a Lady on the Death of her Huſband	29
Goliath of Gath	31
Thoughts on the Works of Providence	43
To a Lady on the Death of three Relations	51
To a Clergyman on the Death of his Lady	53
An Hymn to the Morning	56
An Hymn to the Evening	58
On	

CONTENTS.

On Isaiah lxiii. 1—8   60

On Recollection   62

On Imagination   65

A Funeral Poem on the Death of an Infant
    aged twelve Months   69

To Captain H. D. of the 65th Regiment   72

To the Rt. Hon. William, Earl of Dartmouth   73

Ode to Neptune   76

To a Lady on her coming to North America
    with her Son, for the Recovery of her Health   78

To a Lady on her remarkable Preservation in
    a Hurricane in North Carolina   80

To a Lady and her Children on the Death of
    her Son, and their Brother   82

To a Gentleman and Lady on the Death of the
    Lady's Brother and Sister, and a Child of
    the Name of *Avis*, aged one Year   84

On the Death of Dr. Samuel Marshall   86

To a Gentleman on his Voyage to Great-Britain,
    for the Recovery of his Health   88

To the Rev. Dr. Thomas Amory on reading his
    Sermons on Daily Devotion, in which that
    Duty is recommended and assisted   90

On

CONTENTS.

On the Death of J. C. an Infant   92

An Hymn to Humanity   95

To the Hon. T. H. Efq; on the Death of his
    Daughter   98

Niobe in Diftrefs for her Children flain by
    Apollo, from *Ovid's* Metamorphofes, Book
    VI. and from a View of the Painting of
    Mr. *Richard Wilfon*   101

To S. M. a young African Painter, on feeing
    his Works   114

To his Honour the Lieutenant-Governor, on
    the Death of his Lady   116

A Farewel to America   119

A Rebus by I. B.   123

An Anfwer to ditto, by *Phillis Wheatley*   124

EXTANT POEMS NOT INCLUDED
IN THE 1773 *POEMS*

According to the titles listed in her first and last proposals for volumes (see the discussion prefacing the section "Prose"), Wheatley composed at least eighty-eight poems. The 1773 Poems *contains thirty-eight by her. Of the fifty poems not included in the 1773 volume, Wheatley scholars such as William H. Robinson, Mukhtar Ali Isani, Robert Kuncio, and Julian Mason have uncovered seventeen, bringing to fifty-five the total number of her extant poems. The last of this group, "An Elegy on Leaving ————," surfaced just shortly before* The Collected Works *went to press. Hence at least thirty-three additional poems are known to have been written but have yet to appear. As new poems continue to be discovered, allowing new details about her poetic praxis to be adduced, both the Wheatley canon and the body of critical commentary will demand revision.*

ATHEISM

Where now shall I begin this Spacious Field
To tell what curses unbelief doth yield
Thou that dost daily feel his hand and rod
And dare deny the essence of a god
If there's no god from whence did all things spring   5
He made the greatest and minutest thing
If there's no heaven whither wilt thou go

Make thy Elysium in the Shades below
With great astonishment any soul is struck
O rashness great hast thou thy sense forsook   10
Hast thou forgot the preterperfect days
They are recorded in the Book of praise
If twas not written by the hand of God
Why was it sealed with Immanuel's blood
Tho 'tis a second point thou dost deny   15
Unmeasur'd vengeance Scarlet sins do cry
Turn now I pray thee from the dangerous road
Rise from the dust and seek the mighty God
By whose great mercy we do move and live
Whose Loving kindness doth our sins forgive   20
Tis Beelzebub our adversary great
Withholds from us the kingdom and the seat
Bliss weeping waits us in her arms to fly
To the vast regions of Felicity
Perhaps thy Ignorance will ask us where   25
Go to the corner stone it will declare
Thy heart in unbelief will harder grow
Altho thou hidest it for pleasure now
Thou takst unusual means, the path forbear
Unkind to Others to thyself severe   30
Methinks I see the consequence thou art blind
Thy unbelief disturbs the peaceful mind
The endless Scene too far for me to tread
Too great to Accomplish from so weak a head
If men such wise inventions then should know   35
In the high Firmament who made the bow
That covenant was made for to ensure
Made to establish lasting to endure
Who made the heavens and earth a lasting spring
Of Admiration, to whom dost thou bring   40
Thy thanks, and tribute, Adoration pay,
To heathen Gods, can wise Apollo say

Tis I that saves thee from the deepest hell
Minerva teach thee all thy days to tell
Doth Pluto tell thee thou shalt see the shade   45
Of fell perdition for thy learning made
Doth Cupid in thy breast that warmth inspire
To Love thy brother which is Gods desire
Look thou above and see who made the sky
Nothing more Lucid to an Atheist's eye   50
Look thou beneath, behold each purling stream
It surely cannot a Delusion Seem
Mark rising Pheobus when he spreads his ray
And his commission for to guide the day
At night keep watch, and see a Cynthia bright   55
And her commission for to guide the night
See how the stars when they do sing his praise
Witness his essence in celestial Lays

[1767]

AN ADDRESS TO THE DEIST

Must Ethiopians be employ'd for you?
Much I rejoice if any good I do.
I ask O unbeliever, Satan's child
Hath not thy Saviour been too much revil'd
Th' auspicious rays that round his temples shine   5
Do still declare him to be Christ divine.
Doth not the great *Eternal* call him Son
Is he not pleas'd with his beloved One—?
How canst thou thus divide the Trinity
The blest the Holy the eternal three   10
Tis Satan's snares are fluttering in the wind
Whereby he doth ensnare thy foolish mind
God, the Eternal Orders this to be

Sees thy vain arg'ments to divide the three
Cans't thou not see the Consequence in store?   15
Begin th' Almighty monarch to adore?
Attend to Reason whispering in thine ear
Seek the Eternal while he is so near.
Full in thy view I point each path I know
Lest to the vale of black dispair I go   20
At the last day where wilt thou hide thy face
That Day approaching is no time for Grace
Too late perceive thyself undone and lost
To late own Father, Son, and Holy Ghost.
Who trod the wine-press of Jehovah's wrath?   25
Who taught us prayer, and promis'd grace and faith?
Who but the Son, who reigns supremely blest
Ever, and ever, in immortal rest?
The vilest prodigal who comes to God
Is not cast out but bro't by Jesus's blood   30
When to the faithless Jews he oft did cry
Some own'd their teacher some made him a lye
He came to you in mean apparel clad
He came to save us from our sins, and had
Compassion more than language can express.   35
Pains his companions, and his friends distress
Immanuel on the cross those pains did bear
Will the eternal our petitions hear?
Ah! wond'rous Destiny his life he laid
"Father forgive them," thus the Saviour pray'd   40
Nail'd was king Jesus on the cross for us
For our transgressions he sustain'd the Curse.

[1767]

ON MESSRS. HUSSEY AND COFFIN

DID Fear and Danger so perplex your Mind,
As made you fearful of the whistling Wind?
Was it not Boreas knit his angry Brow
Against you? or did Consideration bow?
To lend you Aid, did not his Winds combine?   5
To stop your Passage with a churlish Line,
Did haughty Eolus with Contempt look down
With Aspect windy, and a study'd Frown?
Regard them not;—the Great Supreme, the Wise,
Intends for something hidden from our Eyes.   10
Suppose the groundless Gulph had snatch'd away
Hussey and Coffin to the raging Sea;
Where wou'd they go? where wou'd be their Abode?
With the supreme and independent God,
Or made their Beds down in the Shades below,   15
Where neither Pleasure nor Content can stow.
To Heaven their Souls with eager Raptures soar,
Enjoy the Bliss of him they wou'd adore.
Had the soft gliding Streams of Grace been near,
Some favourite Hope their fainting Hearts to cheer,   20
Doubtless the Fear of Danger far had fled:
No more repeated Victory crown their Heads.

   Had I the Tongue of a Seraphim, how would I exalt thy
Praise; thy Name as Incense to the Heavens should fly, and the
Remembrance of thy Goodness to the shoreless Ocean of
      Beatitude!—   25
Then should the Earth glow with seraphick Ardour.
Blest Soul, which sees the Day while Light doth shine,
To guide his Steps to trace the Mark divine.

[*Newport Mercury*, December 21, 1767]

AMERICA

New England first a wilderness was found
Till for a continent 'twas destin'd round
From feild to feild the savage monsters run
E'r yet Brittania had her work begun
Thy Power, O Liberty, makes strong the weak   5
And (wond'rous instinct) Ethiopians speak
Sometimes by Simile, a victory's won
A certain lady had an only son
He grew up daily virtuous as he grew
Fearing his Strength which she undoubted knew   10
She laid some taxes on her darling son
And would have laid another act there on
Amend your manners I'll the taxes remove
Was said with seeming Sympathy and Love
By many Scourges she his goodness try'd   15
Untill at length the Best of Infants cry'd
He wept, Brittania turn'd a senseless ear
At last awaken'd by maternal fear
Why weeps americus why weeps my Child
Thus spake Brittania, thus benign and mild   20
My dear mama said he shall I repeat—
Then Prostrate fell, at her maternal feet
What ails the rebel, great Brittania Cry'd
Indeed said he you have no cause to Chide
You see each day my fluent tears my food.   25
Without regard, what no more English blood?
Was length of time drove from our English veins.
The kindred he to Great Brittania deigns?
Tis thus with thee O Brittain keeping down
New English force, thou fear'st his Tyranny and thou didst
     frown   30
He weeps afresh to feel this Iron chain

Turn, O Brittania claim thy child again
Riccho Love drive by thy powerful charms
Indolence Slumbering in forgetful arms
See Agenoria diligent imploys   35
Her sons, and thus with rapture she replys
Arise my sons with one consent arise
Lest distant continents with vult'ring eyes
Should charge America with Negligence
They praise Industry but no pride commence   40
To raise their own Profusion, O Britain See
By this New England will increase like thee

[1768]

TO THE HONBLE.
COMMODORE HOOD
ON HIS PARDONING A DESERTER

It was thy noble soul and high desert
That caus'd these breathings of my grateful heart
You sav'd a soul from pluto's dreary shore
You sav'd his body and he asks no more
This generous act Immortal wreaths shall bring   5
To thee for meritorious was the Spring
From whence from whence, this candid ardor flow'd
To grace thy name, and Glorify thy God
The Eatherial spirits in the realms above
Rejoice to see thee exercise thy Love   10
Hail Commodore may heaven delighted pour
Its blessings plenteous in a silent shower
The voice of pardon did resound on high
While heaven consented, and he must not die

On thee fair victor be the Blessing shed   15
And rest forever on thy matchless Head

[1769]

ON FRIENDSHIP

Lest Amicitia in her ample reign
Extend her notes to a celestial strain,
Benevolent, far more divinely bright;
Amor, like me, doth triumph at the sight
When to my thoughts in gratitude employ;   5
Mental imaginations give me joy;
Now let my thoughts in contemplation steer
The footsteps of the superlative fair.

[Boston, July 15, 1769]

ON THE DEATH OF MR. SNIDER
MURDER'D BY RICHARDSON

In heavens eternal court it was decreed
Thou the first martyr for the common good
Long hid before, a vile infernal here
Prevents Achilles in his mid career
Where'er this fury darts his Poisonous breath   5
All are endanger'd to the shafts of death
The generous Sires beheld the fatal wound
Saw their young champion gasping on the ground
They rais'd him up but to each present ear
What martial glories did his tongue declare   10
The wretch appal'd no longer can despise

But from the Striking victim turns his eyes—
When this young martial genius did appear
The Tory chief no longer could forbear.
Ripe for destruction, see the wretches doom   15
He waits the curses of the age to come
In vain he flies, by Justice Swiftly chaced
With unexpected infamy disgraced
Be Richardson for ever banish'd here
The grand Usurpers bravely vaunted Heir.   20
We bring the body from the watry bower
To lodge it where it shall remove no more
Snider behold with what Majestic Love
The Illustrious retinue begins to move
With Secret rage fair freedom's foes beneath   25
See in thy corse ev'n Majesty in Death

[Late February or early March 1770]

AN ELEGY
TO MISS MARY MOORHEAD,
ON THE DEATH OF HER FATHER,
THE REV. MR. JOHN MOORHEAD

Involv'd in Clouds of Wo, *Maria* Mourns,
And various Anguish wracks her Soul by turns;
See thy lov'd Parent languishing in Death,
His Exit watch, and catch his flying Breath;
"Stay happy Shade," distress'd *Maria* cries;   5
"Stay happy Shade," the hapless Church replies;
"Suspend a while, suspend thy rapid flight,
"Still with thy Friendship, chear our sullen Night;
"The sullen Night of Error, Sin, and Pain;
"See Earth astonish'd at the Loss, complain";   10

Thine, and the Church's Sorrows I deplore;
Moorhead is dead, and Friendship is no more;
From Earth she flies, nor mingles with our Wo,
Since cold the Breast, where once she deign'd to glow;
Here shone the heavenly Virtue, there confess'd,   15
Celestial Love, reign'd joyous in his Breast;
Till Death grown jealous for his drear Domain,
Sent his dread Offspring, unrelenting Pain.
With hasty Wing, the Son of Terror flies,
Lest *Moorhead* find the Portal of the Skies;   20
Without a Passage through the Shades below,
Like great *Elijah*, Death's triumphant Foe;
Death follows soon nor leaves the Prophet long,
His Eyes are seal'd, and every Nerve unstrung;
Forever silent is the stiff'ning Clay,   25
While the rapt Soul, explores the Realms of Day.
Oft has he strove to raise the Soul from Earth,
Oft has he travail'd in the heavenly Birth;
Till JESUS took possession of the Soul,
Till the new Creatur liv'd throughout the whole.   30

   When the fierce conviction seiz'd the Sinner's Mind,
The Law-loud thundering he to Death consign'd;
JEHOVAH'S Wrath revolving, he surveys,
The Fancy's terror, and the Soul's amaze.
Say, what is Death? The Gloom of endless Night,   35
Which from the Sinner, bars the Gates of Light:
Say, what is Hell? In Horrors passing strange;
His Vengeance views, who seals his final Change;
The winged Hours, the final Judgment brings,
Decides his fate, and that of Gods and Kings;   40
Tremendous Doom! And dreadful to be told,
To dwell in Tophet 'stead of shrines of Gold.
"Gods! Ye shall die like Men," the Herald cries,
"And stil'd no more the Children of the Skies."

Trembling he sees the horrid Gulf appear,   45
Creation quakes, and no Deliverer near;
With Heart relenting to his Feelings kind,
See *Moorhead* hasten to relieve his Mind.
See him the Gospel's healing Balm impart,
To sooth the Anguish of his tortur'd Heart.   50
He points the trembling Mountain, and the Tree,
Which bent beneath th' incarnate Deity,
How God descended, wonderous to relate,
To bear our Crimes, a dread enormous Weight;
Seraphic Strains too feeble to repeat,   55
Half the dread Punishment the GOD-HEAD meet.
Suspended there, (till Heaven was reconcil'd,)
Like MOSES' Serpent in the Desert wild.
The Mind appeas'd what new Devotion glows,
With Joy unknown, the raptur'd Soul o'erflows;   60
While on his GOD-like Savior's Glory bent,
His Life proves witness of his Heart's intent.
Lament ye indigent the Friendly Mind,
Which oft relented, to your Mis'ry kind.

With humble Gratitude he render'd Praise,   65
To Him whose Spirit had inspir'd his Lays;
To Him whose Guidance gave his Words to flow,
Divine instruction, and the Balm of Wo:
To you his Offspring, and his Church, be given,
A triple Portion of his Thirst for Heaven;   70
Such was the Prophet; we the Stroke deplore,
Which let's us hear his warning Voice no more.
But cease complaining, hush each murm'ring Tongue,
Pursue the Example in your Conduct shine;
Own the afflicting Providence, divine;   75
So shall bright Periods grace your joyful Days,
And heavenly Anthems swell your songs of Praise.

[Boston, December 15, 1773]

TO A GENTLEMAN OF THE NAVY

Celestial muse! for sweetness fam'd inspire
My wondrous theme with true poetic fire,
Rochfort, for thee! And Greaves deserve my lays
The sacred tribute of ingenuous praise.
For here, true merit shuns the glare of light,   5
She loves oblivion, and evades the sight.
At sight of her, see dawning genius rise
And stretch her pinions to her native skies.

Paris, for Helen's bright resistless charms,
Made Illion bleed and set the world in arms.   10
Had you appear'd on the Achaian shore
Troy now had stood, and Helen charm'd no more.
The Phrygian hero had resign'd the dame
For purer joys in friendship's sacred flame,
The noblest gift, and of immortal kind,   15
That brightens, dignifies the manly mind.

Calliope, half gracious to my prayer,
Grants but the half and scatters half in air.

Far in the space where ancient Albion keeps
Amidst the roarings of the sacred deeps,   20
Where willing forests leave their native plain,
Descend, and instant, plough the wat'ry main.
Strange to relate! with canvas wings they speed
To distant worlds; of distant worlds the dread.
The trembling natives of the peaceful plain,   25
Astonish'd view the heroes of the main,
Wond'ring to see two chiefs of matchless grace,
Of generous bosom, and ingenuous face,
From ocean sprung, like ocean foes to rest,
The thirst of glory burns each youthful breast.   30

In virtue's cause, the muse implores for grace,

These blooming sons of Neptune's royal race;
Cerulean youths! your joint assent declare,
Virtue to rev'rence, more than mortal fair,
A crown of glory, which the muse will twine,   35
Immortal trophy! Rochfort shall be thine!
Thine too O Greaves! for virtue's offspring share,
Celestial friendship and the muse's care.
Yours is the song, and your's the honest praise,
Lo! Rochfort smiles, and Greaves approves my lays.   40

[*Royal American Magazine*, Boston, October 30, 1774]

THE ANSWER [BY THE
GENTLEMAN OF THE NAVY]

Celestial muse! sublimest of the nine,
Assist my song, and dictate every line:
Inspire me once, nor with imperfect lays,
To sing this great, this lovely virgins praise;
But yet, alas! what tribute can I bring,   5
WH-TL-Y but smiles, whilst I thus faintly sing,

Behold with reverence, and with joy adore;
The lovely daughter of the Affric shore,
Where every grace, and every virtue join,
That kindles friendship and makes love divine;   10
In hue as diff'rent as in souls above;
The rest of mortals who in vain have strove,
Th'immortal wreathe, the muse's gift to share,
Which heav'n reserv'd for this angelic fair.

Blest be the guilded shore, the happy land,   15
Where spring and autumn gently hand in hand;
O'er shady forests that scare know a bound,
In vivid blaze alternately dance round:

Where cancers torrid heat the soul inspires;
With strains divine and true poetic fires;   20
(Far from the reach of Hudson's chilly bay)
Where cheerful phoebus makes all nature gay;
Where sweet refreshing breezes gently fan;
The flow'ry path, the ever verdent lawn,
The artless grottos, and the soft retreats;   25
"At once the lover and thee muse's seats."
Where nature taught, (tho' strange it is to tell,)
Her flowing pencil Europe to excell.
Britania's glory long hath fill'd the skies;
Whilst other nations, tho' with envious eyes,   30
Have view'd her growing greatness, and the rules,
That's long been taught in her untainted schools:
Where great Sir Isaac! whose immortal name;
Still shines the brightest on the seat of fame;
By ways and methods never known before;   35
The sacred depth of nature did explore:
And like a God, on philosophic wings;
Rode with the planets thro' their circling rings:
Surveying nature with a curious eye,
And viewing other systems in the sky.   40

    Where nature's bard with true poetic lays,
The pristine state of paradise displays,
And with a genius that's but very rare
Describes the first the only happy pair
That in terrestial mansions ever reign'd,   45
View'd happiness now lost, and now regain'd,
Unravel'd all the battles of the Gods,
And view'd old night below the antipodes.
On his imperious throne, with awful sway,
Commanding regions yet unknown today,   50

    Or where those lofty bards have dwelt so long,
That ravish'd Europe with their heavenly song,

But now this blissful clime, this happy land,
That all the neighbouring nations did command;
Whose royal navy neptunes waves did sweep,   55
Reign'd Prince alone, and sov'reign of the deep:
No more can boast, but of the power to kill,
By force of arms, or diabolic skill.
For softer strains we quickly must repair
To Wheatly's song, for Wheatly is the fair;   60
That has the art, which art could ne'er acquire:
To dress each sentence with seraphic fire.

Her wondrous virtues I could ne'er express!
To paint her charms, would only make them less.

[*Royal American Magazine*, Boston, December 2, 1774]

PHILLIS'S REPLY TO THE ANSWER

For one bright moment, heavenly goddess! shine,
Inspire my song and form the lays divine.
Rochford, attend. Beloved of Phoebus! hear,
A truer sentence never reach'd thine ear;
Struck with thy song, each vain conceit resign'd   5
A soft affection seiz'd my grateful mind,
While I each golden sentiment admire
In thee, the muse's bright celestial fire.
The generous plaudit 'tis not mine to claim,
A muse untutor'd, and unknown to fame.   10

The heavenly sisters pour thy notes along
And crown their bard with every grace of song.
My pen, least favour'd by the tuneful nine,
Can never rival, never equal thine;
Then fix the humble Afric muse's seat   15
At British Homer's and Sir Isaac's feet.

Those bards whose fame in deathless strains arise
Creation's boast, and fav'rites of the skies.

   In fair description are thy powers display'd
In artless grottos, and the sylvan shade;   20
Charm'd with thy painting, how my bosom burns!
And pleasing Gambia on my soul returns,
With native grace in spring's luxuriant reign,
Smiles the gay mead, and Eden blooms again,
The various bower, the tuneful flowing stream,   25
The soft retreats, the lovers golden dream,
Her soil spontaneous, yields exhaustless stores;
For phoebus revels on her verdant shores.
Whose flowery births, a fragrant train appear,
And crown the youth throughout the smiling year,   30

   There, as in Britain's favour'd isle, behold
The bending harvest ripen into gold!
Just are thy views of Afric's blissful plain,
On the warm limits of the land and main.

   Pleas'd with the theme, see sportive fancy play,   35
In realms devoted to the God of day!

   Europa's bard, who the great depth explor'd,
Of nature, and thro'boundless systems soar'd,
Thro' earth, thro' heaven, and hell's profound domain,
Where night eternal holds her awful reign.   40
But, lo! in him Britania's prophet dies,
And whence, ah! whence, shall other Newton's rise?
Muse, bid they Rochford's matchless pen display
The charms of friendship on the sprightly lay.
Queen of his song, thro' all his numbers shine,   45
And plausive glories, goddess! shall be thine.
With partial grace thou mak'st his verse excel,
And his glory to describe so well.

Cerulean bard! to thee these strains belong,
The Muse's darling and the prince of song,   50

[*Royal American Magazine*, Boston, December 5, 1774]

TO HIS EXCELLENCY
GENERAL WASHINGTON

Celestial choir! enthron'd in realms of light,
  Columbia's scenes of glorious toils I write.
While freedom's cause her anxious breast alarms,
She flashes dreadful in refulgent arms.
See mother earth her offspring's fate bemoan,   5
And nations gaze at scenes before unknown!
See the bright beams of heaven's revolving light
Involved in sorrows and veil of night!

  The goddess comes, she moves divinely fair,
Olive and laurel bind her golden hair: 10
Wherever shines this native of the skies,
Unnumber'd charms and recent graces rise.

  Muse! bow propitious while my pen relates
How pour her armies through a thousand gates,
As when Eolus heaven's fair face deforms,   15
Enwrapp'd in tempest and a night of storms;
Astonish'd ocean feels the wild uproar,
The refluent surges beat the sounding shore;
Or thick as leaves in Autumn's golden reign,
Such, and so many, moves the warrior's train.   20
In bright array they seek the work of war,
Where high unfurl'd the ensign waves in air.
Shall I to Washington their praise recite?

Enough thou know'st them in the fields of fight.
Thee, first in peace and honours,—we demand 25
The grace and glory of thy martial band.
Fam'd for thy valour, for thy virtues more,
Hear every tongue thy guardian aid implore!

One century scarce perform'd its destined round,
When Gallic powers Columbia's fury found; 30
And so may you, whoever dares disgrace
The land of freedom's heaven-defended race!
Fix'd are the eyes of nations on the scales,
For in their hopes Columbia's arm prevails.
Anon Britannia droops the pensive head, 35
While round increase the rising hills of dead.
Ah! cruel blindness to Columbia's state!
Lament thy thirst of boundless power too late.

Proceed, great chief, with virtue on thy side,
Thy ev'ry action let the goddess guide. 40
A crown, a mansion, and a throne that shine,
With gold unfading, WASHINGTON! be thine.

[Providence, October 26, 1775]

ON THE CAPTURE
OF GENERAL LEE

The deed perfidious, and the Hero's fate,
In tender strains, celestial Muse! relate.
The latent foe to friendship makes pretence,
The name assumes without the sacred sense!
He, with a rapture well dissembl'd, press'd 5
The hero's hand, and, fraudful, thus address'd,

"O friend belov'd! may heaven its aid afford,
And spread yon troops beneath thy conquering sword!

Grant to America's united prayer
A glorious conquest on the field of war!   10
But thou indulgent to my warm request,
Vouchsafe thy presence as my honour'd guest:
From martial cares a space unbend thy soul
In social banquet, and the sprightly bowl,"
Thus spoke the foe; and warlike LEE reply'd,   15
"Ill fits it me, who such an army guide,
To whom his conduct each brave soldier owes,
To waste an hour in banquets or repose:
This day important, with loud voice demands
Our wisest Counsels, and our bravest hands."   20
Thus having said, he heav'd a boding sigh;
The hour approach'd that damps Columbia's Joy.
Inform'd, conducted by the treach'rous friend,
With winged speed the adverse train attend,
Ascend the Dome, and seize with frantic air   25
The self surrender'd glorious prize of war!
On sixty coursers, swifter than the wind,
They fly, and reach the British camp assign'd.
Arriv'd, what transport touch'd their leader's breast!
Who thus deriding, the brave Chief address'd.   30
"Say, art thou he, beneath whose vengeful hands
Our best of heroes grasp'd in death the sands?
One fierce regard of thine indignant eye
Turn'd Britain pale, and made her armies fly:
But Oh! how chang'd! a prisoner in our arms   35
Till martial honour, dreadful in her charms,
Shall grace Britannia at her sons' return,
And widow'd thousands in our triumphs mourn."
While thus he spoke, the hero of renown
Survey'd the boaster with a gloomy frown,   40
And stern reply'd: "Oh arrogance of tongue!
And wild ambition, ever prone to wrong!
Believ'st thou chief, that armies such as thine

Can stretch in dust that heaven-defended line?
In vain allies may swarm from distant lands,   45
And demons aid in formidable bands.
Great as thou art, thou shun'st the field of fame,
Disgrace to Britain, and the British name!
When offer'd combat by the noble foe,
(Foe to mis-rule,) why did thy sword forego   50
The easy conquest of the rebel-land?
Perhaps too easy for thy martial hand.
What various causes to the field invite!
For plunder you, and we for freedom fight.
Her cause divine with generous ardor fires,   55
And every bosom glows as she inspires!
Already, thousands of your troops are fled
To the drear mansions of the silent dead:
Columbia too, beholds with streaming eyes
Her heroes fall—'tis freedom's sacrifice!   60
So wills the Power who with convulsive storms
Shakes impious realms, and nature's face deforms;
Yet those brave troops innum'rous as the sands
One soul inspires, one General Chief commands.
Find in your train of boasted heroes, one   65
To match the praise of Godlike Washington.
Thrice happy Chief! in whom the virtues join,
And heaven-taught prudence speaks the man divine!"

    He ceas'd. Amazement struck the warrior-train,
    And doubt of conquest, on the hostile plain.   70

[Boston, December 30, 1776]

ON THE DEATH OF
GENERAL WOOSTER

From this the Muse rich consolation draws
He nobly perish'd in his Country's cause
His Country's Cause that ever fir'd his mind
Where martial flames, and Christian virtues join'd.
How shall my pen his warlike deeds proclaim   5
Or paint them fairer on the list of Fame—
Enough, great Chief-now wrapt in Shades around,
Thy grateful Country shall thy praise resound—
Tho not with mortals' empty praise elate
That vainest vapour to th' immortal State   10
Inly serene the expiring hero lies
And thus (while heav'nward roll his swimming eyes):

     "Permit, great power, while yet my fleeting breath
And Spirits wander to the verge of Death—
Permit me yet to point fair freedom's charms   15
For her the Continent shines bright in arms,
By thy high will, celestial prize she came—
For her we combat on the field of fame
Without her presence vice maintains full sway
And social love and virtue wing their way   20
O still propitious be thy guardian care
And lead Columbia thro' the toils of war.
With thine own hand conduct them and defend
And bring the dreadful contest to an end—
For ever grateful let them live to thee   25
And keep them ever Virtuous, brave, and free—
But how, presumptuous shall we hope to find
Divine acceptance with th' Almighty mind—
While yet (O deed Ungenerous!) they disgrace
And hold in bondage Afric's blameless race?   30
Let Virtue reign—And thou accord our prayers

Be victory our's, and generous freedom theirs."
The hero pray'd—the wond'ring spirits fled
And sought the unknown regions of the dead—
Tis thine, fair partner of his life, to find   35
His virtuous path and follow close behind—
A little moment steals him from thy sight
He waits thy coming to the realms of light
Freed from his labours in the ethereal Skies
Where in succession endless pleasures rise!   40

[July 1778]

TO MR. AND MRS. ———, ON THE DEATH OF THEIR INFANT SON

O DEATH! whose sceptre, trembling realms obey,
And weeping millions mourn thy savage sway;
Say, shall we call thee by the name of friend,
Who blasts our joys, and bids our glories end?
Behold, a child who rivals op'ning morn,   5
When its first beams the eastern hills adorn;
So sweetly blooming once that lovely boy,
His father's hope, his mother's only joy,
Nor charms nor innocence prevail to save,
From the grim monarch of the gloomy grave!   10
Two moons revolve when lo! among the dead
The beauteous infant lays his weary head:
For long he strove the tyrant to withstand,
And the dread terrors of his iron hand;
Vain was his strife, with the relentless power,   15
His efforts weak; and this his mortal hour;
He sings—he dies—celestial muse, relate,
His spirit's entrance at the sacred gate.

Methinks I hear the heav'nly courts resound,
The recent theme inspires the choirs around.   20
His guardian angel with delight unknown,
Hails his bless'd charge on his immortal throne;
His heart expands at scenes unknown before,
Dominions praise, and prostrate throngs adore;
Before the Eternal's feet their crowns are laid,   25
The glowing seraph vails his sacred head.
Spirits redeem'd, that more than angels shine,
For nobler praises tune their harps divine:
These saw his entrance; his soft hand they press'd,
Sat on his throne, and smiling thus address'd,   30
"Hail: thou! thrice welcome to this happy shore,
Born to new life where changes are no more;
Glad heaven receives thee, and thy God bestows,
Immortal youth exempt from pain and woes.
Sorrow and sin, those foes to human rest,   35
Forever banish'd from thy happy breast."
Gazing they spoke, and raptur'd thus replies,
The beauteous stranger in the etherial skies,
"Thus safe conducted to your bless'd abodes,
With sweet surprize I mix among the Gods;   40
The vast profound of this amazing grace,
Beyond your search, immortal powers, I praise;
Great Sire, I sing thy boundless love divine,
Mine is the bliss, but all the glory thine."
All heav'n rejoices as your ———— sings,   45
To heavenly airs he tunes the sounding strings;
Mean time on earth the hapless parents mourn,
"Too quickly fled, ah! never to return."
Thee, the vain visions of the night restore,
Illusive fancy paints the phantom o'er;   50
Fain would we clasp him, but he wings his flight;
Deceives our arms, and mixes with the night;
But oh! suppress the clouds of grief that roll,

Invading peace, and dark'ning all the soul.
Should heaven restore him to your arms again,   55
Oppress'd with woes, a painful endless train,
How would your prayers, your ardent wishes, rise,
Safe to repose him in his native skies.

[1779 or earlier]

AN ELEGY
SACRED TO THE MEMORY OF THAT
GREAT DIVINE,
THE REVEREND AND LEARNED
DR. SAMUEL COOPER

O THOU whose exit wraps in boundless woe,
  For Thee the tears of various Nations flow:
For Thee the floods of various sorrows rise
From the full heart and burst from streaming eyes,
Far from our view to Heaven's eternal height,   5
The Seat of bliss divine, and glory bright;
Far from the restless turbulence of life,
The war of factions, and impassion'd strife.
From every ill mortality endur'd,
Safe in celestial *Salem's* walls secur'd.   10

  E'ER yet from this terrestrial state retir'd,
The Virtuous lov'd Thee, and the Wife admir'd.
The gay approv'd Thee, and the grave rever'd;
And all thy words with rapt attention heard!
The Sons of Learning on thy lessons hung,   15
While soft persuasion mov'd th' illit'rate throng.
Who, drawn by rhetoric's commanding laws,

Comply'd obedient, nor conceiv'd the cause.
Thy every sentence was with grace inspir'd,
And every period with devotion fir'd;   20
Bright Truth thy guide without a dark disguise,
And penetration's all-discerning eyes.

THY COUNTRY mourns th' afflicting Hand divine
That now forbids thy radiant lamp to shine,
Which, like the sun, resplendent source of light.   25
Diffus'd its beams, and chear'd our gloom of night.

WHAT deep-felt sorrow in each *Kindred* breast
With keen sensation rends the heart distress'd!
Fraternal love sustains a tenderer part,
And mourns a BROTHER with a BROTHER's heart.   30

THY CHURCH laments her faithful PASTOR fled
To the cold mansions of the silent dead.
There hush'd forever, cease the heavenly strain,
That wak'd the soul, but here resounds in vain.
Still live thy merits, where thy name is known,   35
As the sweet Rose, its blooming beauty gone
Retains its fragrance with a long perfume:
Thus COOPER! thus thy death-less name shall bloom
Unfading, in thy *Church* and *Country's* love,
While winter frowns, or spring renews the grove.   40
The hapless Muse, her loss in COOPER mourns,
And as she sits, she writes, and weeps, by turns;
A Friend sincere, whose mild indulgent grace
Encourag'd oft, and oft approv'd her lays.

WITH all their charms, terrestrial objects strove,   45
But vain their pleasures to attract his love.
Such COOPER was—at Heaven's high call he flies,
His task well finish'd, to his native skies.
Yet to his fate reluctant we resign,

Tho' our's to copy conduct such as thine: 50
Such was thy wish, th' observant Muse survey'd
Thy latest breath, and this advice convey'd.

[Boston, January 1784]

LIBERTY AND PEACE

LO! Freedom comes. Th' prescient Muse foretold,
   All Eyes th' accomplish'd Prophecy behold:
Her Port describ'd, *"She moves divinely fair,*
"Olive and Laurel bind her golden Hair."
She, the bright Progeny of Heaven, descends,   5
And every Grace her sovereign Step attends;
For now kind Heaven, indulgent to our Prayer,
In smiling *Peace* resolves the Din of *War*.
Fix'd in *Columbia* her illustrious Line,
And bids in thee her future Councils shine.   10
To every Realm her Portals open'd wide,
Receives from each the full commercial Tide.
Each Art and Science now with rising Charms
Th' expanding Heart with Emulation warms.
E'en great *Britannia* sees with dread Surprize,   15
And from the dazzl'ing Splendor turns her Eyes!
Britain, whose Navies swept th' *Atlantic* o'er,
And Thunder sent to every distant Shore;
E'en thou, in Manners cruel as thou art,
The Sword resign'd, resume the friendly Part!   20
For *Galia's* Power espous'd *Columbia's* Cause,
And new-born *Rome* shall give *Britannia* Law,
Nor unremember'd in the grateful Strain,
Shall princely *Louis'* friendly Deeds remain;
The generous Prince th' impending Vengeance eye's,   25
Sees the fierce Wrong, and to the rescue flies.

Perish that Thirst of boundless Power, that drew
On *Albion's* Head the Curse to Tyrants due.
But thou appeas'd submit to Heaven's decree,
That bids this Realm of Freedom rival thee!   30
Now sheathe the Sword that bade the Brave attone
With guiltless Blood for Madness not their own.
Sent from th' Enjoyment of their native Shore
Ill-fated—never to behold her more!
From every Kingdom on *Europa's* Coast   35
Throng'd various Troops, their Glory, Strength and Boast.
With heart-felt pity fair *Hibernia* saw
Columbia menac'd by the Tyrant's Law:
On hostile Fields fraternal Arms engage,
And mutual Deaths, all dealt with mutual Rage;   40
The Muse's Ear hears mother Earth deplore
Her ample Surface smoak with kindred Gore:
The hostile Field destroys the social Ties,
And every-lasting Slumber seals their Eyes.
Columbia mourns, the haughty Foes deride,   45
Her Treasures plunder'd, and her Towns destroy'd:
Witness how *Charlestown's* curling Smoaks arise,
In sable Columns to the clouded Skies!
The ample Dome, high-wrought with curious Toil,
In one sad Hour the savage Troops despoil.   50
Descending *Peace* and Power of War confounds;
From every Tongue celestial *Peace* resounds:
As for the East th' illustrious King of Day,
With rising Radiance drives the Shades away,
So Freedom comes array'd with Charms divine,   55
And in her Train Commerce and Plenty shine.
Britannia owns her Independent Reign,
Hibernia, *Scotia*, and the Realms of *Spain;*
And great *Germania's* ample Coast admires
The generous Spirit that *Columbia* fires.   60
Auspicious Heaven shall fill with fav'ring Gales,

Where e'er *Columbia* spreads her swelling Sails:
To every Realm shall *Peace* her Charms display,
And Heavenly *Freedom* spread her golden Ray.

[1784]

AN ELEGY ON LEAVING ———

FAREWEL! ye friendly bow'rs, ye streams adieu,
    I leave with sorrow each sequester'd seat:
The lawns, where oft I swept the morning dew,
    The groves, from noon-tide rays a kind retreat.

Yon wood-crown'd hill, whose far projecting shade,   5
    Inverted trembles in the limpid lake:
Where wrapt in thought I pensively have stray'd,
    For crowds and noise, reluctant, I forsake.

The solemn pines, that, winding through the vale,
    In grateful rows attract the wand'ring eye,   10
Where the soft ring-dove pours her soothing tale,
    No more must veil me from the fervid sky.

Beneath yon aged oak's protecting arms,
    Oft-times beside the pebbl'd brook I lay;
Where, pleas'd with simple Nature's various charms,   15
    I pass'd in grateful solitude the day.

Rapt with the melody of Cynthio's strain,
    There first my bosom felt poetic flame;
Mute was the bleating language of the plain,
    And with his lays the wanton fawns grew tame.   20

But, ah! those pleasing hours are ever flown;
    Ye scenes of transport from my thoughts retire;
Those rural joys no more the day shall crown,
    No more my hand shall wake the warbling lyre.

But come, sweet Hope, from thy divine retreat,   **25**
   Come to my breast, and chase my cares away,
Bring calm Content to gild my gloomy seat,
   And cheer my bosom with her heav'nly ray.

[July 1784]

PROSE

Judging from the thirteen letters Wheatley named for inclusion in her proposed volume for 1779, she consciously cultivated the epistolary genre as belles lettres. Certain of her letters to the Earl of Dartmouth and to the Countess of Huntingdon have come to light during this century (we can only speculate that these letters are the same ones she lists in the 1779 "Proposals"—there may well be still others to discover), but those to Benjamin Rush, Susanna Wheatley, and others have not yet been reclaimed.

Of the twenty-two extant letters composed by Wheatley (I have not herein included those dictated to her by others), the three she lists in the 1779 "Proposals" may be the same three found and published by Sarah Dunlap Jackson in "Letters of Phillis Wheatley and Susanna Wheatley," Journal of Negro History *57, no. 2 (April 1972): 211–15; the one letter she lists as being to the Earl of Dartmouth may well be that found and published by Julian Mason in his 1966 edition of Wheatley's works (Mason, pp. 110–11). In addition, Wheatley is known to have written a letter in 1765 to the Mohegan Indian minister Samson Occom (cited by John Wheatley regarding the poet's authenticity as a writer in his testimonial which is included in the prefatory material to her 1773* Poems*); however, this letter is not now extant. In all, then, Wheatley is known to have written at least thirty-two letters, leaving some ten others not yet re-*

*covered. In an age of letter writing, such a slender produc-
tion is virtually unthinkable. Surely the coming years will
witness the discovery both of letters Wheatley is known to
have composed and of others as yet unknown.*

*Wheatley's first proposals for a volume of poetry were
made in the early months of 1772 in Boston. They failed
to attract sufficient subscribers and were unsuccessful in elic-
iting the financial backing necessary for the volume's publication. William H. Robinson has deduced, with good
reason, that this first attempt was rejected largely on racist
grounds (see his persuasive argument presented in* Black
New England Letters *[Boston: Boston Public Library,
1977], pp. 46–57). Of the twenty-eight titles listed in
this first set of Wheatley proposals, probably only fifteen,
some slightly altered (names of Bostonians unlikely to be
known in London were dropped), recur in the 1773* Poems.
*Wheatley included thirty-eight poems in the 1773 volume,
for a total of twenty-three poems not named in the 1772
"Proposals." One may well conclude that the volume of
1772, had it been published, and that of 1773 were two
quite different books. For example, while the American book
was to have numbered among its pages several poems chronicling events in the growing colonial resistance, such as "On
America," "On the Affray in King-Street, on the Evening
of the 5th of March" (i.e., the Boston Massacre), and "To*
Samuel Quincy, Esq.; a Panegyrick" *(Quincy, the
Wheatleys' lawyer, defended the colonial survivors of the
massacre; see "Samuel Quincy of Massachusetts," in* Dictionary of Literary Biography: American Colonial

Writers, 1735–1781 *[Detroit: Bruccoli Clark, 1984],
pp. 209–11), the 1773* Poems *which appeared in London
dropped these potentially inflammatory pieces. It should not
go unremarked, however, that the twenty-three new poems
of the 1773 volume strongly suggest that the period from
February 1772 through July 1773 must have been the most
productive of Wheatley's poetic career. Such poems as "To
Maecenas," "Thoughts on the Works of Providence," "To
S.M. a Young African Painter," "On Recollection," "An
Hymn to the Morning," "An Hymn to the Evening," "Niobe
in Distress," and "On Imagination" may have been composed during this period; it is certain that Wheatley polished final versions of them for the press. These very poems
represent Wheatley's most mature, sophisticated, and creative productions.*

*The 1779 "Proposals" name thirty-three poems, none of
which appeared either in the 1772 "Proposals" or in the
1773* Poems. *Since the "Proposals" of October 30, 1779,
Wheatley is known to have published only four poems: "An
Elegy, Sacred to the Memory of . . . Samuel Cooper" in
January 1784, "Liberty and Peace" in the same year, the
recently recovered "An Elegy on Leaving————" in July
1784, and "To Mr. and Mrs.————, on the Death of
Their Infant Son" in September 1784, just two months
before Wheatley died on December 5, 1784. If this last
poem, which was published as a "Specimen of her Work"
along with her last proposal for a new volume, is the same
poem named in the 1779 "Proposals" and titled there "To
P.N.S. & Lady on the Death of Their Infant Son" (fol-*

*lowing her former practice of dropping identifying details),
then Wheatley may have composed as few as three poems
between the 1779 "Proposals" and her death in December
1784; we can acknowledge with certainty, however regrettably, that after 1779 she composed only "An Elegy
[on] Samuel Cooper," "Liberty and Peace," and "An Elegy on Leaving————." As for the possibility that her
decline in fortune and her consequent assumption of an im-
poverished condition permitted her to compose additional
poems, we can only speculate at this stage in our limited
knowledge of her affairs during this period. It is certain
nonetheless that counting the total known output of poems
from Wheatley's pen, we find the twenty-eight titles in the
1772 "Proposals," the twenty-three new titles in the 1773*
Poems, *the thirty-three new poems given in the 1779
"Proposals," and the three additional poems composed after
1779, for a total of at least eighty-seven poems definitely
composed by Wheatley. Only fifty-five are known to exist
at the present time, leaving a remainder of at least thirty-
two yet to be located.*

*The Wheatley canon to date, then, comprises fifty-five
poems, twenty-two letters, and one prose prayer. In arriv-
ing at this count, I have excluded all known variants of
the letters and poems. It is crucial to recognize that the
letters and poems, which have surfaced only during the last
twenty years or so, must be read along with the older portions of the canon before one can make any just and fair
assessment of this significant poet's works.*

LETTERS

To the Rt. Hon'ble the Countess of Huntingdon

Most noble Lady,

 The Occasion of my addressing your Ladiship will I hope, apologize for this my boldness in doing it. it is to enclose a few lines on the decease of your worthy chaplain, the Rev'd Mr. Whitefield, in the loss of whom I sincerely sympathize with your Ladiship; but your great loss which is his Greater gain, will, I hope, meet with infinite reparation, in the presence of God, the Divine Benefactor whose image you bear by filial imitation.

 The Tongues of the Learned are insufficient, much less the pen of an untutor'd African, to paint in lively character, the excellencies of this Citizen of Zion! I beg an Interest in your Ladiship's Prayer and am,

With great humility
your Ladiship's most
obedient Humble Servant
Phillis Wheatley

Boston Octr. 25th 1770

Madam [to Abigail May?],

 Agreeable to your proposing Recollection as a subject proper for me to write upon, I enclose these few thoughts upon it; and, as you was the first person who mentioned it, I thought none more proper to dedicate it to; and, if it meets with your

approbation, the poem is honoured, and the authoress satisfied. I am, Madam,

Your very humble servant,
Phillis

[November or December 1771]

Boston April 21st 1772

Hon'd Sir [John Thornton],

I rec'd your instructive favr. of Feb. 29. for which, return you ten thousand thanks. I did not flatter myself with
the tho'ts of your honouring me with an Answer to my letter,
I thank you for recommending the Bible to be my cheif study,
I find and acknowledge it the best of Books, it contains an
endless treasure of wisdom and knowledge. O that my eyes
were more open'd to see the real worth, and true excellence
of the word of truth, my flinty heart soften'd with the grateful dew of divine grace and the stubborn will, and affections,
bent on God alone their proper object, and the vitiated palate
may be corrected to relish heav'nly things. It has pleas'd God
to lay me on a bed of sickness, and I knew not but my death
bed, but he has been graciously pleas'd to restore me in a
great measure. I beg your prayers, that I may be made thankful
for his paternal corrections, and that I may make proper use
of them to the glory of his grace. I am still very weak & the
Physicians, seem to think there is danger of a consumpsion.
And O that when my flesh and my heart fail me God would
be my strength and portion for ever, that I might put my
whole trust and Confidence in him, who has promis'd never
to forsake those who seek him with the whole heart. you

could not, I am sure have express *[sic]* greater tenderness and affection for me, than by being a welwisher to my soul, the friends of souls bear/some/resemblance to the father of spirits and are made partakers of his divine Nature.

I am affraid I have entruded on your patient, but if I had not thot it ungrateful/to omit writing in answer to your favour/should not have troubl'd you, but I can't expect you to answer this,

> I am sir with greatest respect,
> Your very hum. sert.
> Phillis Wheatley

To Abour Tanner, in Newport

Boston, May 19th 1772

Dear Sister,—I rec'd your favour of February 6th for which I give you my sincere thanks. I greatly rejoice with you in that realizing view, and I hope experience, of the saving change which you so emphatically describe. Happy were it for us if we could arrive to that evangelical Repentance, and the true holiness of heart which you mention. Inexpressibly happy should we be could we have a due sense of beauties and excellence of the crucified Saviour. In his Crucifixion may be seen marvellous displays of Grace and Love, sufficient to draw and invite us to the rich and endless treasures of his mercy; let us rejoice in and adore the wonders of God's infinite Love in bringing us from a land semblant of darkness itself, and where the divine light of revelation (being obscur'd) is as darkness. Here the knowledge of the true God and eternal life are made manifest; but there, profound ignorance overshadows the land. Your observation is true, namely, that there was nothing in us to recommend us to God. Many of our fellow creatures are pass'd by, when the bowels of divine love expanded towards us. May this goodness & long suffering of God lead us to unfeign'd repentance.

It gives me very great pleasure to hear of so many of my nation, seeking with eagerness the way to true felicity. O may we all meet at length in that happy mansion. I hope the correspondence between us will continue, (my being much indispos'd this winter past, was the reason of my not answering yours before now) which correspondence I hope may have the happy effect of improving our mutual friendship. Till we meet in the regions of consummate blessedness, let us endeavor by the assistance of divine grace, to live the life, and we shall die the death of the Righteous. May this be our happy case, and of those who are travelling to the region of Felicity, is the earnest request of your affectionate

Friend & humble servant, Phillis Wheatley

To Arbour Tanner, in Newport
To the care of Mr. Pease's Servant   Rhode Island

Boston, July 19th 1772

Dear Friend,—I rec'd your kind epistle a few days ago; much disappointed to hear that you had not rec'd my answer to your first letter. I have been in a very poor state of health all the past winter and spring, and now reside in the country for the benefit of its more wholesome air. I came to town this morning to spend the Sabbath with my master and mistress. Let me be interested in your prayers that God would please to bless to me the means us'd for my recovery, if agreeable to his holy will. While my outward man languishes under weakness and pa[in], may the inward be refresh'd and strengthen'd more abundantly by him who declar'd from heaven that his strength was made perfect in weakness! May he correct our vitiated taste, that the meditation of him may be delightful to us. No longer to be so excessively charm'd with fleeting vanities: but pressing forward to the fix'd mark for the prize. How happy that man who is prepar'd for that night wherein no man can work! Let us be mindful of our high calling, continually on our guard, lest our treacherous hearts should give the adversary an advantage over us. O! who can think without horror of the snares of the Devil. Let us, by frequent meditation on the eternal Judgment, prepare for it. May the Lord bless to us these thoughts, and teach us by his Spirit to live to him alone, and when we leave this world may we be his. That this may be our happy case, is the sincere desire

of, your affectionate friend, & humble serv't,
Phillis Wheatley

I sent the letter to Mr. Whitwell's who said he wou'd forward it.

My Lord [Earl of Dartmouth],
The Joyful occacion which has given me this Confidence in Addressing your Lordship in the inclosed peice will, I hope sufficiently apologize for this freedom in an African who with the now happy America exults with equal transport in the view of one of its greatest advocates presiding with the Special tenderness of a Fatherly Heart over that Department.

Nor can they my Lord be insensible of the Friendship so much exemplified in your Endeavours in their behalf during the late unhappy Disturbances.

I sincerely wish your Lordship all possible success in your Undertaking for the Interest of north America

That the united blessings of Heaven & Earth may attend you here and the endless Felicity of the invisible State in the presence of the divine ["divine" is inserted above the line and indicated with a caret] Benefactor may be your portion hereafter is the hearty Desire of

My Lord
Your Lordships
Most Obedient
H'ble Servant

Boston N.E. Octo. 10th 1772   Phillis Wheatley

London
June 27, 1773

Madam [the Countess of Huntingdon],

It is with pleasure I acquaint your Ladyship of my safe arrival in London after a fine passage of 5 weeks in the Ship London with my young master (advised by my physician for my Health) have Brought a letter from Richd. Carey Esqr. but was Disappointed by your absence of the honour of waiting upon your Ladyship with it. I would have inclosed it, but was doubtful of the Safety of the conveyance.

I should think my self very happy in seeing your Ladyship, and if you was so desirous of the Image of the Author as to propose it for a Frontispiece I flatter myself that you would accept the Reality.

I conclude with thanking your Ladyship for permitting the dedication of my poems to you; and am not insinsible, that under the patronage of your Ladyship, not more eminent in the Station of Life than in your exemplary piety and virtues, my feeble efforts will be shielded from the severe trials of uppity Criticism and, being encourage'd by your Ladyship'd Indulgence, I the more feebly resign to the world these Juvenile productions, and am Madam, with greatest humility, your Dutiful Huml Ser't,

Phillis Wheatley

Madam [the Countess of Huntingdon],

I rec'd with mixed sensations of pleasure & disappointment your Ladiship's message favored by Mr. Rien acquainting us with your pleasure that my Master & I should wait upon you in So. Wales, delighted with your Ladiship Condescention to me so unworthy of it. Am sorry to acquaint your Ladiship that the Ship is certainly to Sail next Thursday (on) which I must return to America. I long to see my Friend there. (I am) extremely reluctant to go without having first seen your Ladiship. It gives me very great satisfaction to hear of an African so worthy to be honored with your Ladiship's approbation & Friendship as him whom you call your Brother. I rejoice with your Ladiship in that Friend of Mental Felicity which you cannot but be possessed of, in the consideration of your exceeding great reward. My great opinion of your Ladiship's goodness, leads to believe, I have an interest in, your most happy hours of communion, with your most indulgent Father and our great & common Benifactor

With greatest humility I am
most dutifully
Your Ladiship's obed't Sevt
Phillis Wheatley

London July 17
    1773

The Right Honble
  The Countess
  of Huntingdon
My master is yet undetermind about
going home, and sends his dutiful
respects to your Ladiship.

Sir [David Wooster],

Having an opportunity by a Servant of Mr. Badcock's who lives near you, I am glad to learn you and your Family are well. I take the Freedom to transmit to you, a short Sketch of my voyage and return from London where I went for the recovery of my health as advis'd by my Physician. I was receiv'd in England with such kindness[,] Complaisance, and so many marks of esteem and real Friendship as astonishes me on the reflection, for I was no more than 6 weeks there. Was introduced to Lord Dartmouth and had near half an hour's conversation with his Lordship, with whom was Alderman Kirkman. Then to Lord Lincoln, who visited me at my own Lodgings with the famous Dr. Solander who accompany'd Mr. Banks in his late expedition round the World. Then to Lady Cavendish, and Lady Carteret Webb, Mrs. Palmer a Poetess, an accomplished Lady. [To] Dr. Thos. Gibbons, Rhetoric Professor. To Israel Mauduit Esqr. [,] Benjamin Franklin Esqr. F.R.S., Greenville Sharp Esqr. who attended me to the Tower & show'd the Lions, Panthers, Tigers, &c. the Horse Armoury, Small Armoury, the

Crowns, Sceptres, Diadems, the Fount for christening the
Royal Family. Saw Westminster Abbey, British Museum[,]
Coxe's Museum, Saddler's wells, Greenwich Hospital, Park
and Chapel, the royal Observatory at Greenwich, &c. &c.
too many things and places to trouble you with in a Letter.
The Earl of Dartmouth made me a Compliment of 5 guineas, and desired me to get the whole of Mr. Pope's Works,
as the best he could recommend to my perusal, this I did,
also got Hudibrass, Don Quixot, & Gay's Fables[.] Was
presented with a Folio Edition of Milton's Paradise Lost,
printed on a Silver Type (so call'd from its elegance, I suppose) by Mr. Brook Watson Mercht, whose Coat of Arms
is prefix'd. Since my return to America my Master, has at
the desire of my friends in England given me my freedom.
The Instrument is drawn, so as to secure me and my prop-
erty from the hands of Executvs.[,] administrators, &c. of
my master, and secure whatsoever should be given me as my
Own. A Copy is sent to Isra. Mauduit Esqr. F.R.S.

I expect my Books which are publish'd in London in Capt.
Hall, who will be here I believe in 8 or 10 days. I beg the
favour that you would honour the enclos'd Proposals, & use
your interest with Gentlemen & Ladies of your acquaintance
to subscribe also, for the more subscribers there are, the more
it will be for my advantage as I am to have half the Sale of
the Books. This I am the more solicitous for, as I am now
upon my own footing and whatever I get by this is entirely
mine, & it is the Chief I have to depend upon. I must also
request you would desire the Printers in New Haven, not to
reprint that Book, as it will be a great hurt to me, preventing
any further Benefit that I might receive from the Sale of my
Copies from England. The price is 2/6d [two pounds six
pence] Bound or 2/Sterling Sewed. If any should be so ungenerous as to reprint them the genuine Copy may be known,

for it is sign'd in my own handwriting. My dutiful respects
attend your Lady and Children and I am

ever respectfully your oblig'd Huml. sert.

Phillis Wheatley

Boston October
18th 1773
I found my mistress very sick on my return But she is somewhat better. We wish we could depend on it. She gives her
compliments to you & your Lady.

To Obour Tanner, in New Port

Boston Oct. 30, 1773

Dear Obour,—I rec'd your most kind epistles of Augt.
27th, & Oct. 13th, by a young man of your acquaintance,
for which I am oblig'd to you. I hear of your welfare with
pleasure; but this acquaints you that I am at present indispos'd by a cold, & since my arrival have been visited by the
asthma.

Your observations on our dependence on the Deity, & your
hopes that my wants will be supply'd from his fulness which
is in Christ Jesus, is truly worthy of your self. I can't say
but my voyage to England has conduced to the recovery (in
a great measure) of my health. The friends I found there
among the nobility and gentry, their benevolent conduct towards me, the unexpected and unmerited civility and complaisance with which I was treated by all, fills me with astonishment. I can scarcely realize it. This I humbly hope has
the happy effect of lessening me in my own esteem. Your
reflections on the sufferings of the Son of God, & the inestimable price of our immortal souls, plainly demonstrate the
sensations of a soul united to Jesus. What you observe of

Esau is true of all mankind, who, (left to themselves) would sell their heavenly birth rights for a few moments of sensual pleasure, whose wages at last (dreadful wages!) is eternal condemnation. Dear Obour, let us not sell our birthright for a thousand worlds, which indeed would be as dust upon the balance. The God of the seas and dry land, has graciously brought me home in safety. Join with me in thanks to him for so great a mercy, & that it may excite me to praise him with cheerfulness, to persevere in Grace & Faith, & in the knowledge of our Creator and Redeemer,—that my heart may be fill'd with gratitude. I should have been pleas'd greatly to see Miss West, as I imagine she knew you. I have been very busy ever since my arrival, or should have now wrote a more particular account of my voyage, but must submit that satisfaction to some other opportunity. I am Dear friend,

Most affectionately ever yours,
Phillis Wheatley

My mistress has been very sick above 14 weeks, & confined to her bed the whole time, but is I hope somewhat better, now.

The young man by whom this is handed you seems to me to be a very clever man, knows you very well, & is very complaisant and agreeable.

I enclose Proposals for my book, and beg you'd use your interest to get subscriptions, as it is for my benefit.

Hon'd Sir [John Thornton],

It is with great satisfaction, I acquaint you with my experience of the goodness of God in safely conducting my passage over the mighty waters, and returning me in safety to my American Friends. I presume you will join with them and me in praise to God for so distinguishing a favour, it was amazing Mercy, altogether unmerited by me: and if possible it is augmented by the consideration of the bitter reverse, which is the deserved wages of my evil doings. The Apostle Paul, tells us, that the wages of sin is death. I don't imagine he excepted any sin whatsoever, being equally hateful in its nature in the sight of God, who is essential Purity.

Should we not sink hon'd sir, under this sentence of Death, pronounced on every sin, from the comparatively least to the greatest, were not this blessed Contrast annexed to it. "But the Gift of God is eternal Life, through Jesus Christ our Lord." It is his Gift, O let us be thankful for it! What a load is taken from the sinner's shoulder, when he thinks, what Jesus has done that work for him which he could never have done, and suffer'd, that punishment of his imputed Rebellions, for which a long Eternity of Torments could not have made sufficient expiation. O that I could meditate continually on this work of wonder in Deity itself. This, which Kings & Prophets have desir'd to see, & have not seen[.] This, which Angels are continually exploring, yet are not equal to the search.—Millions of Ages shall roll away, and they may try in vain to find out to perfection, the sublime mysteries of Christ's Incarnation. Nor will this desire to look into the deep things of God, cease, in the Breasts of glorified saints & Angels. It's duration will be coeval with Eternity. This Eternity how dreadful, how delightful! Delightful to those who have an interest in the Crucified saviour, who has dignified our Nature, by seating it at the Right Hand of the divine Majesty.—They alone who are thus interested, have Cause to rejoice even on the brink of that Bottomless Profound: and I doubt not (without the least Adulation) that you are one of that happy number, O pray that I may be one also, who shall join with you in songs of praise at the Throne of him, who is no respecter of Persons, being equally the

great Maker of all:—Therefor disdain not to be called the
Father of Humble Africans and Indians; though despised on
earth on account of our colour, we have this Consolation, if
he enables us to deserve it. "That God dwells in the humble
& contrite heart." O that I were more & more possess'd of
this inestimable blessing: to be directed by the immediate
influence of the divine spirit in my daily walk & Conversation.

Do you, my hon'd sir, who have abundant Reason to be
thankful for the great share you possess of it, be always mindful
in your Closet, of those who want it, of me in particular.—

When I first arrived at home my mistress was so bad as
not to be expected to live above two or three days, but through
the goodness of God she is still alive but remains in a very
weak & languishing Condition. She begs a continued interest
in your most earnest prayers, that she may be duly prepar'd
for that great Change which she is likely soon to undergo;
she intreats you, as her son is still in England, that you would
take all opportunities to advise & counsel him; /she says she
is going to leave him & desires you [a few letters blotted: to
be?] a spiritual Father to him./ She will take it very kind.
She thanks you heartily for the kind notice you took of me
while in England. please to give my best Respects to Mrs.
& miss Thorton, and masters Henry and Robert who held
with me a long conversation on many subjects which Mrs.
Drinkwater knows very well. I hope she is in better Health
than when I left her. Please to remember me to your whole
family & I thank them for their kindness to me, begging
still an interest in your best hours
I am Hon'd sir

most respectfully your Humble servt.

Boston Dec. 1, 1773   Phillis Wheatley

I have written to Mrs. Wilberforce, sometime since please to give my duty to her; since writing the above the Rev'd Mr. Moorhead has made his Exit from this world, in whom we lament the loss of the Zealous Pious & true christian.

[To the Rev. Samuel Hopkins]

Boston, Feb. 9, 1774

Rev'd Sir,—I take with pleasure the opportunity by the Post, to acquaint you with the arrival of my books from London. I have sealed up a package containing 17 for you, and 2 for Mr. Tanner, and one for Mrs. Mason, and only wait for you to appoint some proper person, by whom I may convey them to you. I received some time ago 20s sterling upon them, by the hands of your son, in a letter from Abour Tanner. I received at the same time a paper, by which I understand there are two negro men, who are desirous of returning to their native country. to preach the Gospel, but being much indisposed by the return of my asthmatic complaint, besides the sickness of my mistress, who has been long confined to her bed, and is not expected to live a great while; all these things render it impracticable for me to do anything at present with regard to that paper, but what I can do in influencing my Christian friends and acquaintances, to promote this laudable design, shall not be wanting. Methinks, Rev. Sir, this is the beginning of that happy period foretold by the Prophets, when all shall know the Lord from the least to the greatest, and that without the assistance of human Art of Eloquence. My heart expands with sympathetic joy to see at distant time the thick cloud of ignorance dispersing from the face of my benighted country. Europe and America have long been fed with the heavenly provision, and I fear they loath it, while Africa is perishing with a spiritual Famine. O that they could partake of the crumbs, the precious crumbs, which fall from the table of these distinguished children of the kingdom.

Their minds are unprejudiced against the truth, therefore 'tis to be hoped they would receive it with their whole heart. I hope that which the divine royal Psalmist says by inspiration is now on the point of being accomplished, namely, Ethiopia shall soon stretch forth her hands unto God. Of this, Abour Tanner, and I trust many others within your knowledge, are living witnesses. Please to give my love to her, and I intend to write her soon. My best respects attend every kind inquiry after your obliged Humble servant,

Phillis Wheatley

Reverend and Honoured Sir [Samson Occom],

I have this Day received your obliging kind Epistle, and am greatly satisfied with your Reasons respecting the Negroes, and think highly reasonable what you offer in Vindication of their natural Rights: Those that invade them cannot be insensible that the divine Light is chasing away the thick Darkness which broods over the Land of Africa; and the Chaos which has reigned so long, is converting into beautiful Order, and reveals more and more clearly, the glorious Dispensation of civil and religious Liberty, which are so inseparably united, that there is little or no Enjoyment of one without the other: Otherwise, perhaps, the Israelites had been less solicitous for their Freedom from Egyptian Slavery; I do not say they would have been contented without it, by no Means, for in every human Breast, God has implanted a Principle, which we call Love of Freedom; it is impatient of Oppression, and pants for Deliverance; and by the Leave of our Modern Egyptians I will assert, that the same Principle lives in us. God grant Deliverance in his own way and Time, and get him honor upon all those whose Avarice impels them to countenance and help forward the Calamities of their Fellow Creatures. This I desire not for their Hurt, but to convince them of the strange Absurdity of their Conduct whose Words and Actions are so diametrically opposite. How well the Cry for Liberty, and the reverse Disposition for the Exercise of oppressive Power over others agree,—I humbly think it does not require the Penetration of a Philosopher to determine.

[February 11, 1774]

To Miss Obour Tanner, Newport

Boston, March 21, 1774

Dear Obour,—I rec'd your obliging letter, enclos'd in your revd Pastor's & handed me by his son. I have lately met with a great trial in the death of my mistress; let us imagine the loss of a parent, sister, or brother, the tenderness of all these were united in her. I was a poor little outcast & a stranger when she took me in: not only into her house, but I presently became a sharer in her most tender affections. I was treated by her more like her child than her servant; no opportunity was left unimproved of giving me the best of advice; but in terms how tender! how engaging! This I hope ever to keep in remembrance. Her exemplary life was a greater monitor than all her precepts and instruction; thus we may observe of how much greater force example is than instruction. To alleviate our sorrows we had the satisfaction to see her depart in inexpressible raptures, earnest longings, & impatient thirstings for the upper courts of the Lord. Do, my dear friend, remember me & this family in your closet, that this afflicting dispensation may be sanctify'd to us. I am very sorry to hear that you are indispos'd, but hope this will find you in better health. I have been unwell the greater part of the winter, but am much better as the spring approaches. Pray excuse my not writing to you so long before, for I have been so busy lately that I could not find leisure. I shall send the 5 books you wrote for, the first convenient opportunity; if you want more, they shall be ready for you. I am very affectionately your friend,

Phillis Wheatley

Much Honoured Sir [John Thornton],

I should not so soon have troubled you with the 2d. Letter, but the mournful Occasion will sufficiently Apologize. It is the death of Mrs. Wheatley. She has been labouring under a languishing illness for many months past and has at length took her flight from hence to those blissful regions, which need not the light of any, but the sun of Righteousness. O could you have been present, to see how she long'd to drop the tabernacle of Clay, and to be freed from the cumbrous shackles of a mortal Body, which had so many Times retarded her desires when soaring upward. She has often told me how your Letters have quicken'd her in her spiritual Course: when she has been in darkness of mind they have rais'd and enliven'd her insomuch, that she went on, with chearfulness, and alacrity in the path of her duty. She did truely, run with patience the race that was set before her, and hath, at length obtained the celestial Goal. She is now sure, that the afflictions of this present time, were not worthy to be compared to the Glory, which is now, revealed in her, seeing they have wrought out for her, a far more exceeding and eternal weight of Glory. This, sure, is sufficient encouragement under the bitterest sufferings, which we can endure.—About half an hour before her Death, she spoke with a more audible voice, than she had for 3 months before. She call'd her friends & relations around her, and charg'd them not to have their great work undone till that hour, but to fear God, and keep his Commandments, being ask'd if her faith faild her she answer'd, No. Then [word unclear] out her arms crying come! come quickly! come, come! O pray for an easy and quick Passage! She eagerly longed to depart to be with Christ. She retain'd her senses till the very last moment when "fare well, fare well" with a very low voice, were the last words she utter'd. I sat the whole time by her bed side, and saw with Grief and Wonder the Effects of sin on the human race. Had not Christ taken away the envenom'd sting, where had been our hopes? what might we not have fear'd, what might we not/have/expect/d/ from the dreadful King of Terrors? But this is matter of endless praise, to the King eternal immortal, invisible, that, it is finished. I hope her son will be interested in your Closet duties, & that the prayers which she was continually putting up & w'ch are recorded before God in the Book of his remembrance for her son & for me may be answer'd. I can scarcely think that an Object of so many prayers, will fail of the Blessings implor'd for him ever since he was born. I intreat the same Interest in your best thoughts for my self, that her prayers, in my behalf, may be favour'd with an Answer of Peace. We received and forwarded your Letter to the rev'd Mr. Occom, but first took the freedom to peruse it, and are exceeding glad, that you have order'd him to draw immediately for £25, for I really think he is in absolute necessity for that and as much more, he is so loth to run in debt for fear he shall not be able to repay, that he has not the least shelter for his Creatures/to defend them/from the inclemencies of the weather, and he has lost some already for want of it. His hay is quite as defenceless, thus the former are in a fair way of being lost, and the latter to be wasted; It were to be wished that his *dwelling house* was like the Ark, with apartments, to contain the beasts and their provision; He said Mrs. Wheatley and the rev'd Mr. Moorhead were his best friends in Boston. But alass! they are gone. I trust/gone/to receive the rewards promis'd to those, who Offer a Cup of cold water in the name/& for the sake/of Jesus—They have both been very [instrumental? this and the next word or two torn] the wants of that child of God, Mr. Occom—but I fear your [patience? this and the next word torn] exhausted, it remains only that we thank you for your kind Letter to my Mistress it came above a fortnight after her Death.—Hoping for an interest in your prayers for these sanctificiation *[sic]* of this bereaving Providence. I am hon'd sir with dutiful respect ever your obliged

and devoted Humble servant Phillis Wheatley

Boston
    N England March 29th
        1774
    John Thornton Esqr.

To Miss Obour Tanner, New Port, Rhode Island
favd by Mr. Pemberton

Dear Obour,—I rec'd last evening your kind & friendly
letter and am not a little animated thereby. I hope ever to
follow your good advices and be resigned to the afflicting
hand of a seemingly frowning Providence. I have rec'd the
money you sent for the 5 books & 2/6 [2 pounds six pence]
more for another, which I now send & wish safe to hand.
Your tenderness for my welfare demands my gratitude. Assist me, dear Obour! to praise our great benefactor, for the
innumerable benefits continually pour'd upon me, that while
he strikes one comfort dead he raises up another. But O that
I could dwell on & delight in him alone above every other
object! While the world hangs loose about us we shall not be
in painful anxiety in giving up to God that which he first
gave to us. Your letter came by Mr. Pemberton who brings
you the book you write for. I shall wait upon Mr. Whitwell
with your letter and am

Dear sister, ever affectionately, your
Phillis Wheatley

I have rec'd by some of the last ships 300 more of my
Poems. Boston May 6, 1774

Rev'd Sir [Samuel Hopkins],

I received your kind letter last Evening by Mr. Pemberton, by whom also this is to be handed you. I have also rec'd
the Money for the 5 books I sent Obour, & 2/6 more for
another. She has wrote me, but the date is 29 April. I am
very sorry to hear, that Philip Quaque has very little or no
apparent Success in his mission. Yet, I wish that what you

hear respecting him, may be only a misrepresentation. Let us not be discouraged, but still hope, that God will bring about his great work, tho' Philip may not be the instrument in the Divine Hand, to perform this work of wonder, turning the African "from darkness to light." Possibly, if Philip would introduce himself properly to them, (I don't know the reverse) he might be more Successful, and in setting a good example which is more powerfully winning than Instruction. I Observe your Reference to the Maps of Guinea & Salmon's Gazetteer, and shall consult them. I have rec'd in some of the last ships from London 300 more copies of my Poems, and wish to dispose of them as soon as Possible. If you know of any being wanted I flatter myself you will be pleas'd to let me know it, which will be adding one more to the many Obligations already confer'd on her, who is, with a due Sense of your kindness,

> Your most humble,
> And Obedient servant
> Phillis Wheatley

Boston
May 6, 1774
The revd S. Hopkins

Much Hon'd Sir [John Thornton],

I have the honour of your Obliging favour of August 1st by Mr. Wheatley who arriv'd not before the 27th. Ultimo after a tedious passage of near two months; the obligations I am under to the family I desire to retain a grateful sense of and consequently rejoice in the bountiful dealings of providence towards him—

By the great loss I have sustain'd of my best friend, I feel like One forsaken by her parent in a desolate wilderness, for such the world appears to me, wandring thus without/ my/friendly guide. I fear lest every step should lead me into error and confusion. She gave me many precepts and instructions; which I hope I shall never forget. Hon'd sir, pardon me if after the retrospect of such uncommon tenderness for thirteen years from my earliest youth—such unwearied diligence to instruct me in the principles of the true Religion, this in some degree Justifies me while I deplore my misery— /If/I readily join with you in wishing that you could in these respects supply her place, but this does not seem probable from the great distance of your residence. However I will endeavour to compensate it by a strict Observance of hers and your good advice from time/to/time, which you have given me encouragement to hope for—What a Blessed source of consolation that our greatest friend is an immortal God whose friendship is invariable! from whom I have all that is/ *in me*/praise worthy in/mental/possession. This consideration humbles me much under ecomiums on the gifts of God, the fear that I should not improve them to his glory and the good of mankind, it almost hinders a commendable self estimation (at times) but quite beats down the boldness of presumption. The world is a severe schoolmaster, for its frowns are less dang'rous than its smiles and flatteries, and it is a difficult task to keep in the path of Wisdom. I attended, and find exactly true your thoughts on the behaviour of those who seem'd to respect me while under my mistresses patronage: you said right, for some of those have already put on a reserve; but I submit while God rules; who never forsakes any till they have ungratefully forsaken him—. My old master's generous behaviour in granting me my freedom, and still so kind to me I delight to acknowledge my great obligations to him, this he did about 3 months before the death of my dear mistress & at her desire, as well as his own humanity,/of w'ch/I hope ever to retain a grateful sense, and treat/him/ with that respect which is ever due to a paternal friendship— If this had not been the Case, yet I hope I should willingly submit to servitude to be free in Christ.—But since it is thus—Let me be a *servant of Christ* and that is the most perfect freedom.—

You propose my returning to Africa with Bristol Yamma and John Quamine if either of them upon strict enquiry is such, as I dare give my heart and hand to, I believe they are either of them good enough if not too good for me, or they would not be fit for Missionaries; but why do you hon'd sir, wish those poor men so much trouble as to carry me so long a voyage? Upon my arrival, how like a Barbarian shou'd I look to the Natives; I can promise that my tongue shall be quiet/for a strong reason indeed/being an utter stranger to the language of Anamaboe. Now to be serious, this undertaking appears too hazardous, and not sufficiently Eligible, to go—and leave my British & American Friends—I am also unacquainted with those Missionaries in Person. The reverend gentleman who under [ta]kes their Education has repeatedly inform'd me by Letters of their prospect in Learning also an account of John Quamine's family and [Kingdom? letter torn] But be that as it will I resign it all to God's all wise governance; I thank you heartily for your generous Offer With sincerity—

I am hon'd sir
most gratefully your Devoted serv't
Phillis Wheatley

Boston October 30th 1774

Sir [George Washington],

I Have taken the freedom to address your Excellency in the enclosed poem, and entreat your acceptance, though I am not insensible of its inaccuracies. Your being appointed by the Grand Continental Congress to be Generalissimo of the armies of North America, together with the fame of your virtues, excite sensations not easy to suppress. Your generosity, therefore, I presume, will pardon the attempt. Wishing your Excellency all possible success in the great cause you are so generously engaged in. I am,

> Your Excellency's most obedient humble servant,
> Phillis Wheatley

[October 26, 1775]

Miss Obour Tanner, Worcester

> Boston May 29th '78

Dear Obour,—I am exceedingly glad to hear from you by Mrs. Tanner, and wish you had timely notice of her departure, so as to have wrote me; next to that is the pleasure of hearing that you are well. The vast variety of scenes that have pass'd before us these 3 years past, will to a reasonable mind serve to convince us of the uncertain duration of all things temporal, and the proper result of such a consideration is an ardent desire of, & preparation for, a state and enjoyments which are more suitable to the immortal mind. You will do me a great favour if you'll write me by every opportunity. Direct your letters under cover to Mr. John Peters in Queen Street. I have but half an hour's notice; and must apologize for this hasty scrawl. I am most affectionately, My dear Obour, your sincere friend

> Phillis Wheatley

Madam [Mary Wooster],

I recd your favour by Mr. Dennison inclosing a paper containing the Character of the truely worthy General Wooster. It was with the most sensible regret that I heard of his fall in battle: but the pain of so afflicting a dispensation of Providence must be greatly alleviated to you and all his friends in the consideration that he fell a martyr in the Cause of Freedom—you will do me a great favour by returning to me by the first oppy [opportunity] those books that remain unsold and remitting the money for those that are sold—I can easily dispose of them here for 12/Lmo [lawful money, an extremely inflated sum] each—I am greatly obliged to you for the care you show me, and your condescention in taking so much pains for my Interest—I am extremely sorry not to have been honour'd with a personal acquaintance with you— if the foregoing lines meet with your acceptance and approbation I shall think them highly honour'd. I hope you will pardon the length of my letter, when reason is apparent— fondness of the subject & the highest respect for the deceas'd—I sincerely sympathize with you in the great loss you and your family sustain and am Sincerely

Your friend & very humble Sert
Phillis Wheatley

Queenstreet
Boston July—
15th 1778

Miss Obour Tanner, Worcester
favd by Cumberland

Boston May 10, 1779

Dr. Obour,—By this opportunity I have the pleasure to inform you that I am well and hope you are so; tho' I have been silent, I have not been unmindful of you, but a variety of hindrances was the cause of my not writing to you. But in time to come I hope our correspondence will revive—and revive in better times—pray write me soon, for I long to hear from you—you may depend on constant replies—I wish you much happiness, and am

Dr. Obour, your friend & sister
Phillis Peters

PROPOSALS FOR VOLUMES

Proposals for Printing by Subscription

A Collection of POEMS, wrote at several times, and upon various occasions, by PHILLIS, a Negro Girl, from the strength of her own Genius, it being but a few Years since she came to this Town an uncultivated Barbarian from Africa. The Poems having been seen and read by the best judges, who think them well worthy of the Publick View; and upon critical examination, they find that the declared Author was capable of writing them. The Order in which they were penned, together with the Occasion, are as follows;

[1] On the Death of the Rev. Dr. Sewell, when sick, 1765—;
[2] On virtue, 66—;
[3] On two Friends, who were cast away, do.—;
[4] To the University of Cambridge, 1767—;
[5] An Address to the Atheist, do.—;
[6] An Address to the Deist, do.—;
[7] On America, 1768—;
[8] On the King, do.—;
[9] On Friendship, do.—;
[10] Thoughts on being brought from Africa to America, do.—;
[11] On the Nuptials of Mr. Spence to Miss Hooper, do.—;
[12] On the Hon. Commodore Hood, on his pardoning a Deserter, 1769—;
[13] On the Death of Reverend Dr. Sewell, do.—;
[14] On the Death of Master Seider, who was killed by Ebenezer Richardson, 1770.—;
[15] On the Death of the Rev. George Whitefield, do.—;

[16] On the Death of a young Miss, aged 5 years, do—;

[17] On the Arrival of the Ships of War, and landing of the Troops. [no date]—;

[18] On the Affray in King-Street, on the Evening of the 5th of March. [no date]—;

[19] On the death of a young Gentleman. [no date]—;

[20] To Samuel Quincy, Esq; a Panegyrick. [no date]—;

[21] To a Lady on her coming to America for her Health. [no date]—;

[22] To Mrs. Leonard, on the Death of her Husband. [no date]—;

[23] To Mrs. Boylston and Children on the Death of her Son and their Brother. [no date]—;

[24] To a Gentleman and Lady on the Death of their Son, aged 9 Months. [no date]—;

[25] To a Lady on her remarkable Deliverance in a Hurricane. [no date]—;

[26] To James Sullivan, Esq; and Lady on the Death of her Brother and Sister, and a child Avis, aged 12 Months. [no date]—;

[27] Goliah [*sic* for Goliath] of Gath. [no date]—;

[28] On the Death of Dr. Samuel Marshall. [no date]—;

It is supposed they will make one small Octavo Volume, and will contain about 200 Pages. They will be printed on Demy Paper, and beautiful Types. The Price to Subscribers, handsomely bound and lettered, will be Four Shillings. — Stitched in blue, Three Shillings. It is hoped Encouragement will be given to this Publication, as a reward to a very uncommon Genius, at present a Slave. This Work will be put to the Press as soon as three Hundred Copies are subscribed for, and shall be published with all Speed. Subscriptions are taken in by E. Russell, in Marlborough Street.
[February 29, 1772]

Proposals

For printing by subscription a volume of Poems & Letters
on various subjects, dedicated to the Right Hon. Benjamin
Franklin Esq: One of the Ambassadors of the United States
at the Court of France,

By Phillis Peters

Poems
Thoughts on the Times.
On the Capture of General Lee, to I.B. Esq.
To his Excellency General Washington.
On the death of General Wooster.
An Address to Dr —— ——.
To Lieut R—— of the Royal Navy.
To the same.
To T.M. Esq. of Granada.
To Sophia of South Carolina.
To Mr. A.M'B—— of the Navy.
To Lieut R—— D—— of the Navy.
Ocean.
The choice and advantages of a Friend; to Mr. T—— M——.
Farewell to England 1773.
To Mrs. W——ms on Anna Eliza.
To Mr. A McB——d.
Epithalamium to Mrs. H—— ——.
To P.N.S. & Lady on the death of their infant son.
To Mr. El——y on the death of his Lady.
On the death of Lieut. L——ds.
To Penelope.
To Mr. & Mrs. L—— on the death of their daughter.
A Complaint.
To Mr. A.I.M. on Virtue.
To Dr. L——d and Lady on the death of their son aged 5 years.

To Mr. L——g on the death of his son.
To Capt. F——r on the death of his granddaughter.
To Philandra an Elegy.
Niagara.
Chloe to Calliope.
To Musidora on Florello.
To Sir E.L—— Esq.
To the Hon. John Montague Esq. Rear Admiral of the Blue.

Letters
1. To the Right Hon. Wm E. of Dartmouth, Sec. of State of N. America.
2. To the Rev. Mr. T.P. Framington.
3. To Mr. T.W.—Dartmouth College.
4. To the Hon. T.H. Esq.
5. To Dr. B. Rush, Phila.
6. To the Rev. Dr. Thomas, London.
7. To the Right Hon. Countess of H——.
8. To I.M— Esq. London.
9. To Mrs. W——e in the County of Surrey.
10. To Mr. T.M. Homerton, near London.
11. To Mrs. S. W——.
12. To the Rt. Hon. the Countess of H——.
13. To the same.

Messieurs Printers,—The above collection of Poems and Letters was put into my hands by the desire of the ingenious author, in order to be introduced to public View.

The subjects are various and curious, and the author a female African, whose lot it was to fall into the hands of a generous master and great benefactor.

The learned and ingenuous, as well as those who are pleased with novelty, are invited to incourage the publication by a generous subscription—the former that they may fan the sacred fire which is self-enkindled in the breast of this young

African—The ingenuous that they may by reading this collection have a large play for their imaginations, and be excited to please and benefit mankind by some brilliant production of their own pens.—Those who are always in search of some new thing, that they may obtain a sight of this rara avis in terra—And every one that the ingenious author may be encouraged to improve her own mind, benefit and please mankind.

CONDITIONS

They will be printed on good paper and a neat Type, and will contain about 300 Pages in Octavo.

The price to Subscribers will be Twelve Pounds, neatly Bound & Lettered, and Nine Pounds sew'd in blue paper, one Half to be paid on Subscribing, the other Half on delivery of the Books.

The Work will be put to the Press as soon as a sufficient Number of Encouragers offer.

Those who subscribe for Six Books will have a Seventh Gratis.

Subscriptions are taken by White and Adams, the Publishers, in School-Street, Boston.

[October 30, 1779]

Wheatley's Final Proposal

The Poem, in page 488, of this Number, was selected from a manuscript Volume of Poems, written by PHILLIS PETERS, formerly PHILLIS WHEATLEY—and is inserted as a Specimen of her Work; should this gain the approbation of the Publick and sufficient encouragement be given, a Volume will be shortly Published, by the Printers hereof, who received subscriptions for said Work.

[September 1784]

PRAYER

Sabbath—June 13, 1779

Oh my Gracious Preserver!
hitehero thou hast brot [me,]
be pleased when thou bringest
to the birth to give [me] strength
to bring forth living & perfect a
being who shall be greatly instrumental in promoting thy [glory]
Tho conceived in Sin & brot forth
in iniquity yet thy infinite wisdom
can bring a clean thing out of an
unclean, a vesse[l] of Honor filled
for thy glory—grant me
to live a life of gratitude to thee
for the innumerable benefits—
O Lord my God! instruct my ignorance
& enlighten my Darkness
Thou art my King, take [thou]
the entire possession of [all] my
powers & faculties & let me be
no longer under the dominion
of sin—Give me a sincere &
hearty repentance for all my
[grievous?] offences & strengthen
by thy grace my resolutions
on amendment & circumspection
for the time to come—Grant me
[also] the spirit of Prayer & Suppli[cation]
according to thy own
most gracious Promises.

VARIANT POEMS
AND LETTERS

While most variant versions of Wheatley's poems published after her death on December 5, 1784, indicate editorial tampering and/or emending, certainly her manuscript versions of poems subsequently printed, as well as some pointedly distinct variants of poems published during her lifetime, demand serious attention. Such attention reveals at least two interesting observations which describe this poet's modus operandi. *First, although she had a reputation for spontaneity and agility of expression, she was also most concerned to revise and improve her poems; and, second, she sometimes altered her texts (i.e., composed alternative versions of certain poems) so as not to ruffle the feathers of her overwhelmingly white and, at first, often British audience.*

For example, in one of the two broadside versions of "On the Death of the Rev. Mr. George Whitefield," which were published in London, there appear the following lines supposedly recalled from one of Whitefield's pulpit performances: "Take him, ye Africans, *he longs for you,/ Impartial Saviour is his Title due./ If you will walk in Grace's heavenly Road,/* He'll make you free *[emphasis added], and Kings, and Priests to God." None of the other versions of this elegy makes this bold case for the freedom of black people; the sentiment is conspicuously absent from the American versions of this elegy. Regarding Wheatley's concern for careful revision, her first published version of "On Rec-*

ollection" *(March 1772) describes the power of Mnemo-syne, mother of the Muses, in terms of imprecise referents: "Calm, in the visions of the night he pours/ Th' exhaustless treasures of his secret stores." By the time of the later version, revised for the 1773* Poems, *Wheatley has corrected these errors (which could have largely been those of her printer), yielding this deft couplet: "Mneme in our nocturnal visions pours/ The ample treasure of her secret stores" (p. 62, ll. 9–10).*

Variant letters by Wheatley are rare. The two given here illustrate that extant variant letters are not nearly as crucial to Wheatley studies as are the variant poems. Perhaps other variants—not by the hands of others, as is the case here, but by her own hand—will come to light and provide further insight into her thought and poetic development.

TO THE UNIVERSITY OF CAMBRIDGE, WROTE IN 1767

While an intrinsic ardor bids me write
The muse doth promise to assist my pen.
'Twas but e'en now I left my native shore
The sable Land of error's darkest night.
There, sacred Nine! for you no place was found.   5
Parent of mercy, 'twas thy Powerful hand
Brought me in safety from the dark abode.

   To you, Bright youths! he points the height of Heav'n.
To you, the knowledge of the depths profound.

Above, contemplate the ethereal space   10
And glorious Systems of revolving worlds.

    Still more, ye sons of Science! you've receiv'd
The pleasing sound by messengers from heav'n,
The saviour's blood, for your redemption flows.
See Him, with hands stretched out upon the Cross!   15
Divine compassion in his bosom glows.
He hears revilers with oblique regard.
What Condescention in the Son of God!
When the whole human race by Sin had fal'n;
He deign'd to die, that they might rise again,   20
To live with him beyond the starry sky
Life without death, and Glory without End.—

    Improve your privileges while they stay;
Caress, redeem each moment, which with haste
Bears on its rapid wing Eternal bliss.   25
Let hateful vice so baneful to the Soul,
Be still avoided with becoming care;
Suppress the sable monster in its growth,
Ye blooming plants of human race, divine
An Ethiop tells you, tis your greatest foe   30
Its transient sweetness turns to endless pain,
And brings eternal ruin on the Soul.

ON ATHEISM [VARIANT I]

Where now Shall I begin this Spacious feild
To Tell what Curses,—Unbeleif doth Yeild,
Thou That Doest, daily, feel his hand & rod,
And dar'st deny the Essence of a God,
If There's No God,—from Whence, did all things Spring,   5
He Made the Greatest, & Minutest Thing,
If There's No heaven,—whither wilt Thou go,

Make thy Elysium—in the Shades below,
With great Astonishment my Soul is Struck,
O Weakness great,—hast Thou thy sense forsook?   10
Hast Thou forgot thy Preterperfect days,
They are recorded, in the Book of Praise,
If Tis not written with the hand of God,
Why is it Seal'd With dear Immanuel's blood,
Now Turn, I pray Thee, from ye dang'rous road,   15
Rise from ye Dust,—& See the Mighty God;
'Tis by his Mercy, we do move & live,
His Loving kindness doth our Sin's forgive,
'Tis Satan's power, (our Adversary great)
With holds us, from the kingdom & ye State,   20
Bliss weeping, wants us, in her Arm's to fly,
To the vast Regions of felicity,
Perhaps Thy Ignorance will ask us, where?
Go to The Cornerstone, it will declare,
Thy heart in Unbelief will harder grow,   25
Altho' thou hidest it, for Pleasure Now,
Thou Takes Unusual means, the Path forbear,
Unkind to Other's, to thyself Severe,
Methinks I see the Consequence,—thou'rt blind,
Thy Unbelief, distroys Thy Peace of Mind,   30
If Men Such Wise inventions then Coud know,
In The high firmament, who made the Bow,
Which Covenant was made, for to insure,
Made to Establish, Lasting to endure,
Who Made The Heaven's & Earth, a lasting spring   35
Of Admiration,—To whom doest Thou bring,
Thy Thanks & Tribute,—Thy adoration pay,
To heathen God's, & own their fabled Sway,
Doth Pluto Tell thee thou Shall see ye Shades,
Of fell Perdition for thy learning Made   40
Doth Cupid in thy breast that warmth inspire,
To Love thy Brother which is God's desire,

Look thou above & see who made ye Sky
Nothing More Lucid To An Atheist's eye,
Look Thou beneath, & see each Purlingstream,   45
It surely Canot all Delusion Seem
Mark rising Phebus, when he spreads his ray,
And his Comission is to Rule ye day,
At Night keep watch,—& see a Cynthia bright,
And her Commission is,—to rule the Night.   50

[c. 1767]

ON ATHEISM [VARIANT II]

Where now shall I begin this Spacious field
To Tell what Curses,—Unbelief doth Yield,
Thou that Doest, daily, feel his hand & rod,
And dar'st deny the Essence of a God,
If there's no heaven—whither wilt Thou go,   5
Make thy Elysium—in the shades below,
If there's no God—from whence did all things spring,
He made the Greatest, & minutest Thing
With great astonishment my soul is struck
O weakness great?—hast Thou thy sense forsook?   10
Hast Thou forgot thy Preterperfect days
They are recorded, in the book of praise
If 'Tis not written with the hand of God,
Why is it seal'd with dear Imanuel's blood,
Now Turn, I pray Thee, from ye dang'rous road   15
Rise from ye Dust,—& see the Mighty God;
Tis by his Mercy, we do move & live
His loving kindness doth our Sin's forgive,
Tis Satan's power, (our Adversary great)
With holds us, from the kingdom & ye state,   20

Bliss weeping, wants us, in her arms to fly,
To the vast Regions of felicity,
Perhaps Thy Ignorance, will ask us, where?
Go to the Cornerstone, it will declare,
Thy heart in Unbelief will harder grow,   25
Altho' thou hidest it, for Pleasure Now,
Thou Takes Unusual means, the Path forbear,
Unkind to others, to thyself severe?
Methinks I see the Consequence,—thou'rt blind,
Thy Unbelief destroys thy Peace of Mind,   30
If Men such wise inventions then coud know,
In the high firmament, who made the Bow,
Which Covenant was made, for to insure,
Made to Establish, Lasting to endure,
Who made the Heaven's & Earth, a lasting spring   35
Of Admiration,—To whom doest Thou bring
Thy Thanks & Tribute,—Thy adoration pay,
To heathen God's, & own their fabled sway,
Doth Pluto Tell thee thou shall see ye Shades,
Of fell Perdition,—for thy learning made   40
Doth Cupid in thy breast that warmth inspire,
To Love thy B *[sic]* Brother which is God's desire,
Look thou above, & see who made ye sky
Nothing more Lucid, to an Atheist's eye,
Look Thou beneath & see each Purling stream,   45
It surely canot all Delusion seem.
Mark rising Phebus, when he spreads his ray,
And his Comission is—to Rule ye day,
At Night keep watch—& see a Cynthia bright
And her Comission is,—to rule the Night.   50

                                                              Africania

[c. 1767]

DEISM

Must Ethiopians be imploy'd for you
Greatly rejoice if any good I do
I ask O unbeliever satan's child
Has not thy saviour been to meek [&] mild
The auspicious rays that round his head do shine   5
Do still declare him to be christ divine
Doth not the Omnipotent call him son?
And is well pleas'd with his beloved One
How canst thou thus divide the trinity
What can'st thou take up for to make the three   10
Tis satans snares a Fluttering in the wind
Whereby he hath ensnar'd thy Foolish mind
God the eternal Orders this to be
Sees thy vain Arg'ments to divide the three
Canst thou not see the consequence in store   15
Begin the Omnipotent to adore
Arise the pinions of Persuasion's here
Seek the Eternal while he is so near
At the last day where wilt thou hide thy face
The day approaching is no time for grace   20
Then wilt thou cry thyself undone and lost
Proclaiming Father, Son, and Holy Ghost
Who trod the wine press of Jehovahs wrath
Who taught us prayer and gave us grace and faith
Who but the great and the Supreme who bless'd   25
Ever and ever in immortal rest
The meanest prodigal that comes to God
Is not cast off, but bought by Jesus Blood
When to the faithless Jews he oft did cry
One call'd him Teacher some made him a lye   30
He came to you in mean apparell clad
He came to save you from your sins and had
Far more Compassion than I can express

Pains his companions, and his Friends Distress
Immanuel God with us these pains did bear   35
Must the Eternal our petitions hear?
Ah! cruel distiny his life he laid
Father Forgive them thus the saviour said
They nail'd King Jesus to the cross for us
For our Transgressions he did bear the curse.   40

  May I O Eternal salute aurora to begin thy
Praise, shall mortal dust do that which Immortals scarcely
can comprehend, then O omnipotent I will humbly ask,
    after
imploring thy pardon for this presumpsion, when we shall
approach thy majestys presence, crown'd with celestial
    Dignities   45
When shall we see the resting place of the great Supreme
When shall we behold thee, O redeemer in all the
    resplendent
Graces of a Suffering God,

  ye wise men sent from the Orient [clime?]   50
  Now led by seraphs to the bless'd abode

[1767]

TO THE KING'S MOST EXCELLENT
MAJESTY ON HIS REPEALING
THE AMERICAN STAMP ACT

Your Subjects hope
The crown upon your head may flourish long
And in great wars your royal arms be strong
May your Sceptre many nations sway
Resent it on them that dislike Obey   5

But how shall we exalt the British king
Who ruleth france Possessing every thing
The sweet remembrance of whose favours past
The meanest peasants bless the great the last
May George belov'd of all the nations round   10
Live and by earths and heavens blessings crownd
May heaven protect and Guard him from on high
And at his presence every evil fly
Thus every clime with equal gladness See
When kings do smile it sets their subjects free   15
When wars came on the proudest rebel fled
God thunder'd fury on their guilty head

[1768]

ON THE DEATH OF THE
REV'D DR. SEWALL, 1769

E'er yet the morning heav'd its Orient head
Behold him praising with the happy dead.
Hail! happy Saint, on the immortal shore.
We hear thy warnings and advice no more;
Then let each one behold with wishful eyes   5
The saint ascending to his native skies,
From hence the Prophet wing'd his rapturous way
To mansions pure, to fair celestial day.—

   Then begging for the spirit of his God
And panting eager for the bless'd abode,   10
Let every one, with the same vigour soar
To bliss, and happiness, unseen before.
Then be Christ's image on our minds impress'd
And plant a saviour in each glowing Breast.

Thrice happy thou, arriv'd to glory at last,   15
What compensation for the evil past!

   Thou Lord, incomprehensible, unknown,
To Sense, we bow, at thy exalted Throne!
While thus we beg thy excellence to feel
Thy sacred spirit, in our hearts reveal   20
And make each one of us, that grace partake
Which thus we ask for the Redeemer's sake.

   "Sewall is dead," swift pinion'd fame thus cry'd. ⎫
"Is Sewall dead?" my trembling heart reply'd.   ⎬
O what a blessing in thy flight deny'd!   ⎭   25
But when our Jesus had ascended high,
With Captive bands he led Captivity;
And gifts receiv'd for such as knew not God.
Lord! find a Pastor, for thy Churche's
O ruin'd world! bereft of thee, we cry'd,   30
(The rocks responsive to the voice, reply'd.)
How oft for us this holy Prophet pray'd;
But ah! behold him in his Clay-cold bed.
By duty urg'd, my weeping verse to close,
I'll on his Tomb, an Epitaph compose.   35

   Lo! here, a man bought with Christ's precious blood
Once a poor Sinner, now a Saint with God.—
Behold ye rich and poor, and fools and wise;
Nor let this monittor your hearts surprize!
I'll tell you all, what this great Saint has done   40
Which makes him Brighter than the Glorious Sun.—
Listen ye happy from your seats above
I speak sincerely and with truth and Love.
He sought the Paths of virtue and of Truth
Twas this which made him happy in his Youth.   45
In Blooming years he found that grace divine
Which gives admittance to the sacred shrine.

Mourn him, ye Indigent, Whom he has fed,
Seek yet more earnest for the living Bread:
E'en Christ your Bread, who cometh from above   50
Implore his pity and his grace and Love.
Mourn him ye youth, whom he hath often told
God's bounteous Mercy from the times of Old.
I too, have cause this mighty loss to mourn
For this my monitor will not return.   55

Now this faint semblance of his life complete, ⎫
He is, thro' Jesus, made divinely great   ⎬
And left a glorious pattern to repeat.   ⎭

But when shall we, to this bless'd state arrive!
When the same graces in our hearts do thrive.   60

TO MRS. LEONARD, ON
THE DEATH OF HER HUSBAND

Grim Monarch! see depriv'd of vital breath,
A young Physician in the dust of death!
Dost thou go on incessant to destroy:
The grief to double, and impair the joy?
Enough thou never yet wast known to say,   5
Tho' millions die thy mandate to obey.
Nor youth, nor science nor the charms of love,
Nor aught on earth thy rocky heart can move.
The friend, the spouse, from his dark realm to save,
In vain we ask the tyrant of the grave.   10

Fair mourner, there see thy own LEONARD spread,
Lies undistinguish'd from the vulgar dead;
Clos'd are his eyes, eternal slumbers keep,
His senses bound in never-waking sleep,

Till time shall cease; till many a shining world,   15
Shall fall from Heav'n, in dire confusion hurl'd:
Till dying Nature in wild torture lies;
Till her last groans shall rend the brazen skies!
And not till then, his active Soul shall claim,
Its body, now, of more than mortal frame.   20
But ah! methinks the rolling tears apace,
Pursue each other down the alter'd face.
Ah! cease ye sighs, nor rend the mourner's heart:
Cease thy complaints, no more thy griefs impart.
From the cold shell of his great soul arise!   25
And look above, thou native of the skies!
There fix thy view, where fleeter than the wind
Thy LEONARD flies, and leaves the earth behind.

Thyself prepare to pass the gloomy night,
To join forever in the fields of light;   30
To thy embrace, his joyful spirit moves,
To thee the partner of his earthly loves;
He welcomes thee to pleasures more refin'd
And better suited to the deathless mind.

[June 1771]

AN ELEGIAC POEM, ON THE DEATH OF THAT CELEBRATED DIVINE, AND EMINENT SERVANT OF JESUS CHRIST, THE LATE REVEREND, AND PIOUS GEORGE WHITEFIELD [VARIANT I]

Hail happy Saint on thy immortal throne!
To thee complaints of grievance are unknown;

We hear no more the music of thy tongue,
Thy wonted auditories cease to throng.
Thy lessons in unequal'd accents flow'd!   5
While emulation in each bosom glow'd;
Thou didst, in strains of eloquence refin'd,
Inflame the soul, and captivate the mind.
Unhappy we, the setting Sun deplore!
Which once was splendid, but it shines no more;   10
He leaves this earth for Heaven's unmeasur'd height:
And worlds unknown, receive him from our sight;
There WHITEFIELD wings, with rapid course his way,
And sails to Zion, through vast seas of day.

When his AMERICANS were burden'd sore,   15
When streets were crimson'd with their guiltless gore!
Unrival'd friendship in his breast now strove:
The fruit thereof was charity and love.
Towards *America*—couldst thou do more
Than leave thy native home, the *British* shore,   20
To cross the great Atlantic's wat'ry road,
To see *America's* distress'd abode?
Thy prayers, great Saint, and thy incessant cries,
Have pierc'd the bosom of thy native skies!
Thou moon hast seen, and ye bright stars of light   25
Have witness been of his requests by night!
He pray'd that grace in every heart might dwell:
He long'd to see *America* excell;
He charg'd its youth to let the grace divine
Arise, and in their future actions shine;   30
He offer'd THAT he did himself receive,
A greater gift not GOD himself can give:
He urg'd the need of HIM to every one;
It was no less than GOD's co-equal SON!
Take HIM ye wretched for your only good,   35
Take HIM ye starving souls to be your food.
Ye thirsty, come to his life giving stream:

Ye Preachers, take him for your joyful theme:
Take HIM, "my dear AMERICANS," he said,
Be your complaints in his kind bosom laid: 40
Take HIM ye *Africans*, he longs for you;
Impartial SAVIOUR, is his title due;
If you will chuse to walk in grace's road,
You shall be sons, and kings, and priests to GOD.

  Great COUNTESS! we *Americans* revere   45
Thy name, and thus condole thy grief sincere:
We mourn with thee, that TOMB obscurely plac'd,
In which thy Chaplain undisturb'd doth rest.
New-England sure, doth feel the ORPHAN's smart;
Reveals the true sensations of his heart: 50
Since this fair Sun, withdraws his golden rays,
No more to brighten these distressful days!
His lonely *Tabernacle*, sees no more
A WHITEFIELD landing on the *British* shore:
Then let us view him in yon azure skies: 55
Let every mind with this lov'd object rise.
No more can he exert his lab'ring breath,
Seiz'd by the cruel messenger of death.
What can his dear AMERICA return?
But drop a tear upon his happy urn,   60
Thou tomb, shalt safe retain thy sacred trust,
Till life divine re-animate his dust.

[October 1770]

AN ODE OF VERSES
ON THE MUCH-LAMENTED
DEATH OF THE
REV. MR. GEORGE WHITEFIELD
[VARIANT II]

HAIL Happy Saint, on thy Immortal Throne!
  To thee Complaints of Grievance are unknown.
We hear no more the Music of thy Tongue,
Thy wonted Auditories cease to throng.
Thy Lessons in unequal'd Accents flow'd,   5
While Emulation in each Bosom glow'd.
Thou didst, in Strains of Eloquence refin'd,
Inflame the Soul, and captivate the Mind.
Unhappy we thy setting Sun deplore,
Which once was splendid, but it shines no more.   10
He leaves the Earth for Heaven's unmeasur'd Height,
And Worlds unknown receive him out of Sight.
There *Whitefield* wings with rapid Course his Way,
And sails to *Zion* thro' vast Seas of Day.
When his *Americans* were burthen'd sore,   15
When Streets were crimson'd with their guiltless Gore,
Wond'rous Compassion in his Breast now strove,
The Fruit thereof was Charity and Love.
Towards *America* what could be more!
Than leave his native Home, the *British* Shore,   20
To croœ the Great *Atlantick* wat'ry Road,
To see *New England's* much-distress'd Abode.
Thy Prayers, great Saint, and thy incessant Cries,
Have often pierc'd the Bosom of the Skies.
Thou, Moon, has seen, and thou, bright Star of Light.   25
Hast Witness been of his Requests by Night.
He pray'd for Grace in ev'ry Heart to dwell,
He long'd to see *America* excel.

He charg'd its Youth to let the Grace Divine
Arise, and in their future Actions shine.   30
He offer'd that he did himself receive:
A greater Gift not God himself could give.
He urg'd the Need of Him to ev'ry one,
It was no less than God's co-equal Son.
Take him, ye Wretched, for your only Good;   35
Take him, ye hungry Souls, to be your Food;
Take him, ye Thirsty, for your cooling Stream;
Ye Preachers, take him for your joyful Theme;
Take him, my dear *Americans,* he said,
Be your Complaints in his kind Bosom laid;   40
Take him, ye *Africans,* he longs for you,
Impartial Saviour is his Title due.
If you will walk in Grace's heavenly Road,
He'll make you free, and Kings, and Priests to God.
No more can he exert his lab'ring Breath,   45
Seiz'd by the cruel Messenger of Death.
What can his dear *America* return,
But drop a Tear upon his happy Urn.
Thou, Tomb, shalt safe retain thy sacred Trust,
Till Life Divine reanimate his Dust.   50

Our *Whitefield* the Haven has gain'd,
   Outflying the Tempest and Wind;
His Rest he has sooner obtain'd,
   And left his Companions behind.

With Songs let us follow his Flight,   55
   And mount with his Spirit above;
Escap'd to the Mansions of Light,
   And lodg'd in the *Eden* of Love.

THE CONCLUSION

May *Whitefield's* Virtues flourish with his Fame,
And Ages yet unborn record his Name.   60

All Praise and Glory be to God on High,
Whose dread Command is, That we all must die.
To live to Life eternal, may we emulate
The worthy Man that's gone, e'er tis too late.

[October 1770]

ON THE DEATH OF
DOCTOR SAMUEL MARSHALL

Thro' thickest glooms, look back, immortal Shade!
On that confusion which thy flight has made.
Or from Olympus' height look down, and see
A Town involv'd in grief for thee:
His Lucy sees him mix among the dead. 5
And rends the graceful tresses from her head:
Frantic with woe, with griefs unknown, oppres'd,
Sigh follows sigh, and heaves the downy breast.
Too quickly fled, ah! whither art thou gone:
Ah! lost for ever to thy Wife and Son! 10
The hapless child, thy only hope and heir,
Clings round her neck, and weeps his sorrows there.
The loss of thee on Tyler's soul returns,
And Boston too, for her Physician mourns.
When sickness call'd for Marshall's kindly hand, 15
Lo! how with pity would his heart expand!
The sire, the friend, in him we oft have found,
With gen'rous friendship did his soul abound.
Could Esculapius then no longer stay?
To bring his ling'ring infant into day! 20
The babe unborn, in dark confines is toss'd.
And seems in anguish for its father lost.
Gone, is Apollo! from his house of earth,
And leaves the sweet memorials of his worth.

From yonder world unseen, he comes no more,   25
The common parent, whom we thus deplore:
Yet, in our hopes, immortal joys attend
The Sire, the Spouse, the universal Friend.

[*Boston Evening-Post*, October 14, 1771]

RECOLLECTION,
TO MISS A——, M——

MNEME, begin; inpire, ye sacred Nine!
Your vent'rous *Afric* in the deep design.
Do ye rekindle the celestial fire,
Ye god-like powers! the glowing thoughts inspire,
Immortal Pow'r! I trace thy sacred spring,   5
Assist my strains, while I *thy* glories sing.
By *thee*, past acts of many thousand years,
Rang'd in due order, to the mind appears;
The *long-forgot* thy gentle hand conveys,
Returns, and soft upon the fancy plays.   10
Calm, in the visions of the night he pours
Th' exhaustless treasures of his secret stores.
Swift from above he wings his downy flight
Thro' *Phoebe*'s realm, fair regent of the night.
Thence to the raptur'd poet gives his aid,   15
Dwells in his heart, or hovers round his head;
To give instruction to the lab'ring mind,
Diffusing light coelestial and refin'd.
Still he pursues, unweary'd in the race,
And wraps his senses in the pleasing maze.   20
The Heav'nly Phantom *points* the actions done
In the past worlds, and tribes beneath the sun.
He, from his throne in ev'ry human breast,

Has *vice* condemn'd, and ev'ry *virtue* bless'd.
Sweet are the sounds in which thy words we hear,   **25**
Coelestial musick to the ravish'd ear.
We hear thy voice, resounding o'er the plains,
Excelling Maro's sweet Menellian strains.
But awful *Thou!* to that perfidious race,
Who scorn thy warnings, nor the good embrace;   **30**
By *Thee* unveil'd, the horrid crime appears,
Thy mighty hand redoubled fury bears;
The time mis-spent augments their hell of woes,
While through each breast the dire contagion flows.
Now turn and leave the rude ungraceful scene,   **35**
And paint fair Virtue in immortal green.
For ever flourish in the glowing veins,
For ever flourish in poetick strains.
Be *Thy* employ to guide my early days,
And *Thine* the tribute of my youthful lays.   **40**

    Now eighteen years [i.e., her age] their destin'd course
      have run,
In due succession, round the central sun;
How did each folly unregarded pass!
But sure 'tis graven on eternal brass!
To *recollect*, inglorious I return;   **45**
'Tis mine past follies and past crimes to mourn.
The *virtue*, ah! unequal to the vice,
Will scarce afford small reason to rejoice.

    Such, RECOLLECTION! is thy pow'r, high-thron'd
In ev'ry breast of mortals, ever own'd.   **50**
The wretch, who dar'd the vengeance of the skies,
At last awakes with horror and surprise.
By *Thee* alarm'd, he sees impending fate,
He howls in anguish, and repents too late.
But oft *thy* kindness moves with timely fear   **55**

The furious rebel in his mad career.
Thrice bless'd the man, who in *thy* sacred shrine
Improves the REFUGE from the wrath divine.

[*The London Magazine: Or Gentleman's Monthly
Intelligencer*, March 1772]

TO THE REV. MR. PITKIN, ON THE DEATH OF HIS LADY

WHERE Contemplation finds her sacred Spring;
  Where heav'nly Music makes the Centre ring;
  Where Virtue reigns unsulled [*sic*], and divine;
  Where Wisdom thron'd, and all the Graces shine;
There sits thy Spouse, amid the glitt'ring Throng;   5
There central Beauty feasts the ravish'd Tongue;
With recent Powers, with recent glories crown'd,
The Choirs angelic shout her Welcome round.

  The virtuous Dead, demand a grateful Tear—
But cease thy Grief a-while, thy Tears forbear,   10
Nor thine alone, the Sorrow I relate,
Thy blooming Off-spring feel the mighty Weight;
Thus, from the Bosom of the tender Vine,
The Branches torn, fall, wither, sink supine.

  Now flies the Soul, thro' Aether unconfin'd.   15
Thrice happy State of the immortal Mind!
Still in thy Breast tumultuous Passions rise,
And urge the lucent Torrent from thine Eyes.
Amidst the Seats of Heaven, a Place is free
Among those bright angelic Ranks for thee.   20
For thee, they wait—and with expectant Eye,
Thus in my Hearing, "Come away," she cries,
"Partake the sacred Raptures of the Skies!

"Our Bliss divine, to Mortals is unknown,
"And endless Scenes of Happiness our own; 25
"May the dear Off-spring of our earthly Love,
"Receive Admittance to the Joys above!
"Attune the Harp to more than mortal Lays,
"And pay with us, the Tribute of their Praise
"To Him, who died, dread Justice to appease, 30
"Which reconcil'd, holds Mercy in Embrace;
"Creation too, her MAKER'S Death bemoan'd,
"Retir'd the Sun, and deep the Centre groan'd.
"He in his Death slew ours, and as he rose,
"He crush'd the Empire of our hated Foes. 35
"How vain their Hopes to put the God to flight,
"And render Vengeance to the Sons of Light!"

  Thus having spoke she turn'd away her Eyes,
Which beam'd celestial Radiance o'er the skies.
Let Grief no longer damp the sacred Fire, 40
But rise sublime, to equal Bliss aspire;
Thy sighs no more be wafted by the Wind,
Complain no more, but be to Heav'n resign'd.
'Twas thine to shew those Treasures all divine,
To sooth our Woes, the Task was also thine. 45
Now Sorrow is recumbent on thy Heart,
Permit the Muse that healing to impart,
Nor can the World, a pitying tear refuse,
They weep, and with them, ev'ry heavenly Muse.

[Boston, June 16, 1772]

TO THE HON'BLE
THOMAS HUBBARD, ESQ;
ON THE DEATH
OF MRS. THANKFULL LEONARD

WHILE thus you mourn beneath the Cypress shade
That hand of Death, a kind conductor made
To her whose flight commands your tears to flow
And wracks your bosom with a scene of wo:
Let Recollection bear a tender part   5
To sooth and calm the tortures of your heart;
To still the tempest of tumultous grief;
To give the heav'nly Nectar of relief
Ah! cease, no more her unknown bliss bemoan!
Suspend the sigh, and check the rising groan.   10
Her virtues shone with rays divinely bright,
But ah! soon clouded with the shades of night.
How free from tow'ring pride, that gentle mind!
Which ne'er the hapless indigent declin'd,
Expanding free, it sought the means to prove   15
Unfailing Charity, unbounded Love!

    She unreluctant flies, to see no more
Her much lov'd Parents on Earth's dusky shore,
'Till dark mortality shall be withdrawn,
And your bless'd eyes salute the op'ning morn
[i.e., the Resurrection].   20
Impatient heav'n's resplendent goal to gain
She with swift progress scours the azure plain,
Where grief subsides, where passion is no more
And life's tumultous billows cease to roar,
She leaves her earthly mansions for the skies   25
Where new creations feast her won'dring eyes.
To heav'n's high mandate chearfully resign'd

She mounts, she flies, and leaves the rolling Globe behind.
She who late sigh'd for LEONARD to return
Has ceas'd to languish, and forgot to mourn.   30
Since to the same divine dominions come
She joins her Spouse, and smiles upon the Tomb;
And thus addresses;—(let Idea rove)—
Lo! this the Kingdom of celestial Love!
Could our fond Parents view our endless Joy,   35
Soon would the fountain of their sorrows dry;
Then would delightful retrospect inspire,
Their kindling bosoms with the sacred fire!
Amidst unutter'd pleasures, whilst I play,
In the fair sunshine of celestial day: 40
As far as grief affects a deathless Soul,
So far doth grief my better mind controul:
To see on Earth, my aged Parents mourn,
And secret, wish for THANKFULL to return!
Let not such thought their latest hours employ   45
But as advancing fast, prepare for equal Joy.

[Boston, January 2, 1773]

TO THE RIGHT HONOURABLE
WILLIAM LEGGE,
EARL OF DARTMOUTH . . .

HAIL, happy Day! when smiling like the Morn,
Fair *Freedom* rose, New England to adorn:
The Northern Clime beneath her genial Ray
Beholds, exulting, thy paternal Sway;
For, big with Hopes, her Race no longer mourns;   5
Each Soul expands, and every Bosom burns:

While in thy Hand, with Pleasure we behold,
The silken Reins, and *Freedom's* Charms unfold!
Long lost to Realms beneath the Northern skies,
She shines supreme; while hated *Faction* dies: 10
Soon as appear'd the Triumph long desir'd,
Sick at the View, he languish'd and expir'd.

  No more, of Grievance unredress'd complain,
Or injur'd Rights, or groan beneath the Chain,
Which wanton Tyranny, with lawless Hand,   15
Made to enslave, O *Liberty!* thy Land.—
My Soul rekindles, at thy glorious Name,
Thy Beams, essential to the vital Flame.—
The Patriot's Breast, what Heavenly Virtue warms,
And adds new Lustre to his mental Charms!   20
While in thy Speech, the Graces all combine,
Apollo's too, with Sons of Thunder join.
Then shall the Race of injur'd Freedom bless,
The Sire, the Friend, and Messenger of Peace.

  While you, my Lord, read o'er the advent'rous Song   25
And wonder, whence such daring Boldness sprung;
Whence flow my Wishes for the common Good,
By feeling Hearts alone best understood?
From native Clime, when seeming cruel Fate
Me snatch'd from Afric's fancy'd happy Seat,   30
Impetuous—Ah! what bitter Pangs molest,
What Sorrows labour'd in the Parent Breast?
That, more than Stone, ne'er soft Compassion mov'd,
Who from its Father seiz'd his much belov'd.
Such once my Case—Thus I deplore the Day,   35
When Britons weep beneath Tyrannick Sway.
To thee our Thanks for Favours past are due;
To thee we still solicit for the new:
Since in thy Pow'r, as in thy will before,
To sooth the Griefs which thou di[d]st then deplore;   40

May Heav'nly Grace the sacred Sanction give,
To all thy Works, and thou for ever live;
Not only on the Wing of fleeting Fame,
(Immortal Honours Grace the Patriot's Name,)
Thee to conduct to Heaven's refulgent Fane;   45
May fiery Courses sweep the ethereal Plain,
There, like the Prophet, find the bright Abode,
Where dwells thy Sire, the Everlasting GOD.

[Boston, October 10, 1772; *New-York Journal* for June 3,
1773]

TO THE EMPIRE OF AMERICA, BENEATH THE WESTERN HEMISPHERE. FAREWELL TO AMERICA. TO MRS. S.W. [VARIANT I]

ADIEU, NEW ENGLAND'S smiling Meads,
   Adieu, the flow'ry Plain:
I leave thy op'ning Charms, O Spring!
   To try the azure Reign.—

In vain for me, the Flowrets rise,   5
   And show their guady *[sic]* Pride,
While here beneath the Northern Skies
   I mourn for Health deny'd.

Thee, charming Maid, while I pursue,
   In thy luxuriant Reign,   10
And sigh, and languish thee to view,
   Thy Pleasures to regain:—

SUSANNA mourns, nor can I bear
   To see the Christal Show'r

Fast falling,—the indulgent Tear,   15
    In sad Departure's Hour!

Not unregarding, lo! I see
    Thy soul with Grief oppress'd:
Ah! curb the rising Groan for me,
    Nor Sighs Disturb thy Breast!   20

In vain the feather'd Songsters sing,
    In vain the Garden blooms,
And on the Bosom of the Spring
    Breathes out her sweet Perfumes;—

While for Britannia's distant Shore   25
    We sweep the liquid Plain,
'Till Aura to the Armes restore,
    Of this belov'd Domain.

Lo, Health appears, coelestial Dame!
    Complacent and serene,   30
With Hebe's Mantle o'er her Frame,
    With Soul-delighting Mien.

Deep in a Vale, where London lies,
    With misty Vapours crown'd;
Which cloud Aurora's thousand Dyes,   35
    And veil her Charms around.

Why, P[h]oebus, moves thy Car so slow,
    So slow thy rising Ray;—
Nor give the mantl'd Town to View
    Thee, glorious King of Day?   40

But late from Orient Skies behold,
    He shines benignly bright,
He decks his native Plains with Gold,
    With chearing Rays of Light.

For thee, Britannia, I resign 45
  New England's smiling Face,
To view again her Charms divine,
  One short reluctant Space.

But thou, Temptation, hence away,
  With all thy hated Train 50
Of Ills,—nor tempt my Mind astray
  From Virtue's sacred Strain.

Most happy! who with Sword and Shield
  Is screen'd from dire Alarms,
And fell Temptation on the Field 55
  Of fatal Pow'r disarms.

But cease thy Lays; my Lute forbear;
  Nor frown, my gentle Muse,
To see the secret, falling Tear,
  Nor pitying look refuse. 60

[May 7, 1773; first published May 10, 1773; *The
Massachusetts Gazette and Boston Post-Boy* version]

FAREWELL TO AMERICA
[VARIANT II]

ADIEU New England's smiling Meads;
  Adieu the flow'ry Plain,
I leave thy opening Charms, O Spring!
  To try the Azure Reign.

In vain for me the Flow'rets rise 5
  And show their gawdy Pride,
While here beneath the Northern Skies
  I mourn for Health deny'd.

Thee, charming Maid! while I pursue
   In thy luxuriant Reign;   10
And sigh and languish, thee to view,
   Thy Pleasures to regain.

Susanna mourns, nor can I bear
   To see the Christal Show'r
Fast falling—the indulgent Tear   15
   In sad Departure's Hour.

Not unregarding lo! I see
   Thy Soul with Grief oppress'd;
Ah! curb the rising Groan for me,
   Nor Sighs disturb thy Breast.   20

In vain the feather'd Songsters sing,
   In vain the Garden Blooms,
And on the Bosom of the Spring,
   Breaths out her sweet Perfumes.

While for Britannia's distant Shore,   25
   We sweep the liquid Plain,
Till Aura to the Arms restore
   Of this belov'd Domain.

Lo! Health appears! Celestial dame,
   Complacent and serene,   30
With Hebe's Mantle o'er her Frame,
   With Soul-delighting Mein [*sic*].

Deep in a Vale where London lies,
   With misty Vapours crown'd,
Which cloud Aurora's thousand Dyes,   35
   And Veil her Charms around.

Why Phoebus! moves thy Car so slow,
   So slow thy rising Ray;
Nor gives the mantled Town to View
   Thee glorious King of Day!   40

But late from Orient Skies, behold!
  He Shines benignly bright,
He decks his native Plains with Gold,
  With chearing Rays of Light.

For thee Britannia! I resign   45
  New England's smiling Face,
To view again her Charms divine,
  One short reluctant Space.

But thou Temptation! hence, away,
  With all thy hated Train   50
Of Ills—nor tempt my Mind astray
  From Virtue's sacred Strain.

Most happy! who with Sword and Shield
  Is screen'd from dire Alarms,
And fell Temptation, on the Field,   55
  Of fatal Power disarms.

But cease thy Lays, my Lute forbear
  Nor frown my gentle Muse,
To see the secret falling Tear,
  Nor pitying look refuse.   60

[*The Massachusetts Gazette and Boston Weekly News Letter*,
May 13, 1773]

AN ELEGY SACRED
TO THE MEMORY
OF THE
REV'D SAMUEL COOPER, D.D.

O Thou whose exit wraps in boundless woe,
For thee the tears of various Nations flow

For thee the floods of virtuous sorrows rise
From the full heart and burst from streaming eyes,
Far from our view to heaven's eternal height   5
The seat of bliss divine and glory bright;
Far from the restless turbulence of life,
The war of factions, and impassion'd strife.
From every ill mortality indured
Safe in Celestial Salem's walls secured.   10

E'er yet from this terrestrial state retir'd,
The Virtuous lov'd Thee and the wise admir'd.
The gay approv'd Thee, and the grave rever'd.
And all thy words with rapt attention heard!
The Sons of learning on thy lessons hung,   15
While soft persuasion mov'd the illit'rate throng.
Who, drawn by rhetoric's commanding laws,
Comply'd obedient nor conceived the cause.
Thy every sentence was with grace inspir'd,
And every period with devotion fir'd,   20
Bright Truth thy guide without disguise,
And penetration's all discerning eyes.

Thy Country mourns th' afflicting hand divine
That now forbids thy radient lamp to shine,
Which, like the sun, resplendent source of light   25
Diffus'd its beams, and chear'd our gloom of night.

What deep felt sorrow in each *kindred* breast
With keen sensations rends the heart distress't!
Fraternal love sustains a tenderer part
And mourns a Brother with a Brother's heart.   30

Thy Church laments her faithfull Pastor fled
To the cold mansions of the silent dead
There hush'd forever, cease the heavenly strain
That wak'd the soul but here resounds in vain.
Still live thy merits, where thy name is known,   35

As the sweet Rose, its blooming beauty gone
Retains its fragrance with a long perfume:
Thus Cooper! thus thy deathless name shall bloom
Unfading, in thy *Church* and *Country's* love,
While Winter frowns or Spring renews the grave.   40
The hapless Muse, her loss in Cooper mourns,
And as she sits, she writes, and weeps by turns;
A Friend sincere, whose mild indulgent rays
Encouraged oft, and oft approv'd her lays.

With all their charms terrestrial objects strove,   45
But vain their pleasures to attract his love.
Such Cooper was—at Heaven's high call he flies,
His task well finished, to his native skies.
Yet to his fate reluctant we resign,
Tho' ours to copy conduct such as thine: 50
Such was thy wish, th' observant Muse survey'd
Thy latest breath, and this advice convey'd.

[December 30 or 31, 1783]

ON THE DEATH OF J.C. AN INFANT

No more the flow'ry scenes of pleasure rise,
No charming prospects greet the mental eyes,
No more with joy we view that lovely face,
Smiling, disportive, flush'd with ev'ry grace.

The tear of sorrow flows from ev'ry eye,   5
Groans answer groans, and sighs respond to sigh;
What sudden pangs shot through each aching heart,
When ruthless death dispatch'd his mortal dart?

"Where flies my James?" ('tis thus I seem to hear ⎫
The parent ask) "some angel tell me where   ⎬   10
He wings his passage through the yielding air?" ⎭

Methinks a cherub, bending from the skies,
Observes the question, and serene replies,
"Before his Saviour's face, your babe appears:
Prepare to meet him, and dismiss your tears.   15

"There, there behold him, like a seraph glow:
While sounds celestial in his numbers flow:
Melodious, while the soul-enchanting strain
Dwells on his tongue, and fills th' ethereal plain."

Enough—for ever cease your murmuring breath;   20
Not as a foe, but friend, converse with death,
Since to the parts of happiness unknown
Is gone the treasure which you call your own.

[*Methodist Magazine*, September 1797]

LETTERS

Most Noble Lady [the Countess of Huntingdon],

The occasion of my addressing your Ladiship will, I hope,
apoligize for this my boldness in doing it; it is to inclose a
few lines on the decease of your worthy Chaplain The Reverend Mr. Whitefield, in the loss of whom, I sincerely sympathize with your Ladiship; but your great loss, which is his
greater gain, will I hope, meet with infinite reparation in the
presence of God the divine benefactor, whose image you are
by filial imitation. The tongues of the learned are insufficient

much less the pen of an untutor'd African, to paint in lively Characters, the excellencies of this citizen of Zion—

I am with great humility your Ladiship's
Most Obedient humble Servant,
Phillis Wheatley

I beg an interest in your Ladiship's Prayers
Boston Octo 25th 1770

My Lord [Dartmouth],

The joyful Occasion which has given me this Confidence in addressing your Lordship in the inclos'd Piece, will I hope sufficiently apologize for this Freedom in an African, who, with the now happy America, exults with equal Transport, in the View of one of its greatest Advocates, presiding with equal Tenderness of a fatherly Heart over that Department.

Nor can they, my Lord, be insensible of the Friendship so much exemplified in your Endeavours in their Behalf, during the late unhappy Disturbances,—I sincerely wish your Lordship all possible Success in your Undertakings, for the Interest of North America.—That the united Blessings of Heaven and Earth may attend you here; and that the endless Felicity of the invisible State, in the Presence of the divine Benefactor, may be your Portion hereafter, is the hearty Desire of,

My LORD,
Your Lordship's
Most obedient humble Servant,
Phillis Wheatley

[*New-York Journal*, June 3, 1773]

PHILLIS WHEATLEY'S
STRUGGLE FOR FREEDOM IN
HER POETRY AND PROSE

John C. Shields

Phillis Wheatley was the first black American to publish a book, and for a time she enjoyed international fame. In her "adoptive" Boston, she was celebrated for her learning and talent by such notable civil servants as Thomas Hutchinson, then governor of Massachusetts Bay; James Bowdoin, later a founder of Bowdoin College; and John Hancock, signer of the Declaration of Independence; and by such renowned divines as Charles Chauncy and Mather Byles. All of these gentlemen and many others signed the letter "To the Publick" which prefaced Wheatley's 1773 volume of poetry, testifying that after rigorous examination of her intellectual powers, they believed her to be the indisputable author of *Poems on Various Subjects, Religious and Moral*.

Despite this attestation, Wheatley found Boston's publishers unwilling to publish her book. England, however, was more receptive. While visiting the mother country in the summer of 1773 and seeing her *Poems* through the press, she received the attention of some of England's most illustrious citizenry. Sir Brook Watson, a wealthy London merchant who would by 1796 become Lord Mayor of London, presented her with a folio edition of Milton's *Paradise Lost*. William Legge, Earl of Dartmouth, secretary of state for the colonies, and president of the Board of Trade and Foreign Plantations, gave her a copy of Smollet's translation of *Don Quixote* and five shillings to purchase Pope's *Works*. Benjamin Franklin, to whom she would later propose to inscribe her second book of poetry (never published), called on her during a diplomatic visit to London. Selina Hastings, Countess of Huntingdon, to whom Wheatley dedicated her *Poems* and who was one of the leading benefactors of the Methodist evangelical movement in England and the colonies, offered financial support for the young poet's publication venture. During the Revolution, Wheatley wrote a poem honoring George Washington's appointment as commander-in-chief of the Continental Army which prompted an actual meeting between Washington and the black poet and which Thomas Paine subsequently published in *The Pennsylvania Magazine;* and she stirred the interest of John Paul Jones, who requested in a letter to one of the *Ranger*'s officers that he secure for him a copy of her *Poems.*

Yet Wheatley, who wrote most of her extant verse by the age of twenty, has been censured for her alleged dependence on and imitation of neoclassical conventions and poetics, and she has been denigrated for lack of sympathy with her people's struggle for freedom.[1] An investigation of her poems and letters proves these charges false. In a letter treating the slavery issue written in February 1774 and addressed to Samson Occom, the American Indian missionary, Wheatley forcefully and eloquently states, "in every human Breast, God has implanted a Principle, which we call Love of Freedom; it is impatient of Oppression, and pants for Deliverance" (p. 177). She made this statement some four months after her own manumission.[2] Not only was Wheatley vitally concerned for the plight of her enslaved brothers and sisters, but she fervently sought her own freedom, both in this world and in the next. So complete was her absorption in the struggle for freedom that this endeavor governed her conception of poetry, causing her to be no more imitative than any other good student and writer of literature.

Wheatley articulates the theme of freedom in four ways. The first may be surprising, especially from the pen of a black slave: she sometimes uttered passionate political statements supporting the American colonial quest for freedom from Great Britain. Although not as readily observable, the second way is much more prevalent. Wheatley displays numerous examples of what Jung called the mandala archetype, a circular image pattern closely associated with a psychological attempt to discover freedom from chaos. The persistence of this pattern suggests Wheatley's discontent with her enslavement and indicates a means by which she adapted to it.

One conscious poetic escape from slavery was the writing of contemplative elegies; this was the third means by which Wheatley achieved freedom, not in this world but in the next. So enthusiastically does she celebrate death and its rewards in her numerous elegies that she becomes more clearly aligned with the thanatos-eros motif of nineteenth-century romantics than with her eighteenth-century contemporaries. Her poetics of the imagination and the sublime, comprising the fourth representation of freedom, even more strongly attests her romantic alignment. This young poet's intense longing for the spiritual world motivated her to use her poetry as a means of escaping an unsatisfactory, temporal world. The imagination and the sublime become tools by which she accomplishes her short-lived escape. She presents so sophisticated a grasp of these two eighteenth-century aesthetic ideas, which emphatically heralded the romantic movement, that their consideration deserves extended attention.

I

Wheatley's political poetry has been ignored for too long. From her birth about 1753 and her sale into the Boston family of John Wheatley in 1761, until her death in 1784, Wheatley witnessed the American struggle for independence. Her own poetry documents major incidents of that temporal battle for freedom. In 1768, she composed "To the King's Most Excellent Majesty on His Repealing the American Stamp Act" (of 1766; p. 202). When it appeared much revised in the 1773 volume, *Poems on Various Subjects, Religious and Moral*, the poet politically deleted the last two lines of the original, which read, "When wars came on [against George] the proudest rebel fled/ God thunder'd fury on their guilty head" (p. 203). Five years later, the threat of the king's retaliation did not seem so forbidding, nor did the injustice of rebels against him seem so grave.

"America," probably written just after "To the King's Most Excellent Majesty" but published only recently (pp. 134–35),[3] admonishes Britain to treat "americus," the British child, with more careful deference. According to the poem, the child, now a growing seat of "Liberty," is no longer a mere adorer of an overwhelming "Majesty" but has acquired strength of his own: "Fearing his Strength which she [Britain] undoubted knew/ She laid some taxes on her darling son." Recognizing her mistake, "great Brittania" promised to lift the burden, but the promise proved only "seeming Sympathy and Love." Now the child "weeps afresh to feel this Iron chain" (p. 134). The urge to draw an analogy here between the poem's "Iron chain" and Wheatley's own predicament is irresistible; while America longs for its independence, the poet doubtlessly yearns for her own.

The year 1770 marked the beginning of armed resistance against British oppression. Wheatley chronicles this resistance in two poems, the second of which is now lost. The first, "On the Death of Mr. Snider Murder'd by Richardson," appeared initially along with "America."[4] This poem relates how Ebenezer Richardson, an informer on American colonial traders involved in circumventing British taxation, found his home surrounded on the evening of February 22, 1770, by an angry mob of colonial sympathizers. Taking fright, Richardson emerged from his house armed with a musket and fired indiscriminately into the mob, killing the eleven- or twelve-year-old son of Snider, a poor German colonist. Wheatley calls young Christopher Snider, of whose death Richardson was later judged guilty in a trial by jury, "the first martyr for the common good" (p. 136). She identifies young Snider—rather than those men killed less than two weeks later in the Boston Massacre—as the first martyr of the Revolution. The poem's fine closing couplet suggests that even those not in sympathy with the quest for freedom can grasp the nobility of that quest and are made indignant by its sacrifice: "With Secret rage fair freedom's foes beneath/ See in thy [corpse] ev'n Majesty in Death" (p. 137).[5]

Wheatley does not, however, ignore the Boston Massacre. In a proposal for a volume which was to have been published in Boston in 1772, she lists among twenty-eight titles of poems (the 1773 volume had thirty-eight) "On the Affray in King Street, on the Evening of the 5th of March."[6] This title, which names the time and place of the massacre, suggests the probability that the poet celebrated the martyrdom of Crispus Attucks, the first black to lose his life in the American struggle for freedom, along with the deaths of two other whites.[7] At that time, Wheatley was still residing with the Wheatley family in their mansion on the corner of King Street and Mackerel Lane; it is probable that she was an eyewitness of this momentous event of the American Revolution. It is regrettable that the poem recording the event has not yet been recovered. Even so, the title alone confirms Wheatley's continued chronicling of America's freedom struggle. This concern shifted in tone from obedient praise to supplicatory admonition and then to guarded defiance. Having finally found a willing publisher not in Boston but in London,[8] she prudently omitted "America" and the poems about Christopher Snider and the Boston Massacre from her 1773 volume.

Wheatley nevertheless chose to include a poem dedicated to the Earl of Dartmouth, who was appointed secretary of state for the colonies in August 1772. In "To the Right Honourable William, Earl of Dartmouth, His Majesty's Principal Secretary of State for North America," she gives the earl extravagant praise as one whom she supposes to be the scion of "Fair *Freedom*" who will lay to rest "hated *faction*" (p. 73). She knew of the earl's reputation as a humanitarian through the London contacts of her mistress, Susanna Wheatley.[9] When the earl proved to be loyal to British oppressive policies, the poet's expectations were not realized; within four years of the poem's date, October 10, 1772, America had declared its independence. Her optimism undaunted by foreknowledge, Wheatley wrote a poem which was even more laudatory than "To the King's Most Excellent Majesty." Perhaps she was not totally convinced, however; the poem contains some unusually bold passages for a colonist who was also a woman and a slave.

For example, Wheatley remarks that, with Dartmouth as secretary, America need no longer "dread the iron chain,/ Which wanton *Tyranny* with lawless hand/ Had made, and with it meant t'enslave the land" (p. 74). Once again Wheatley uses the slave metaphor of the iron chain. But quite clearly she also accuses the crown of "wanton *Tyranny*," which it had wielded illegally and with the basest of motives—to reduce the colonies to the inhuman condition of slave states. Here rebellious defiance, no longer guarded, becomes unmistakable; the tone matches that of the Declaration of Independence. It is a mystery how these lines could have gone unnoticed in the London reviews, all of them positive, of Wheatley's 1773 volume.[10] Perhaps the reviewers, as most of her critics and commentators have been, were too bedazzled by the "improbability" that a black woman could produce such a volume to take the content of her poetry seriously.

In this poem, Wheatley also presents a rare autobiographical portrait describing the manner by which she was taken from her native Africa. Because the manuscript version of this passage is more spontaneous and direct than the formal and correct one printed in the 1773 volume, and because it may be thought, consequently, more closely to approximate the poet's true feeling, I quote now from the earlier version. Conscious of her biting candor, she acknowledges to Dartmouth that "you, my Lord [may well] . . . wonder, whence such daring Boldness sprung" (p. 218). Then she explains by affirming that her desire for freedom proceeds from the breast of a patriot concerned "for the common Good" (p. 218). This phrase also appeared in the poem about Snider's martyrdom and reflects Wheatley's knowledge of and sympathy for the rhetoric which preceded the Revolution.

It was "seeming cruel Fate" which snatched Wheatley "from Afric's fancy'd happy Seat" (p. 218). Fate here is only apparently cruel because her capture has enabled her to become a Christian; the young poet's piety resounds throughout her poetry and letters, especially during this early period. Her days in her native land were nevertheless happy ones, but her abduction at the hands of ruthless slavers doubtless left behind unconsolable parents:

> Ah! what bitter Pangs molest,
> What Sorrows labour'd in the Parent Breast?
> *That*, more than Stone, ne'er soft Compassion mov'd,
> Who from its Father seiz'd his much belov'd. (p. 218)

Such background fully qualifies her to "deplore the Day/ When Britons weep beneath Tyrannick Sway" (p. 218); the later version reads, "And can I then but pray/ Others may never feel tyrannic sway?" (p. 74). Besides toned-down diction, this passage alters statement to question and replaces "Britons" with the neutral "Others." The question suggests uncertainty, but it more probably reflects the author's polite deportment toward a London audience. In the earlier version, Wheatley believed Dartmouth to be sympathetic with her cause, so she had no reason to exercise deference toward him; she thought she could be frank. The shift from "Britons" to "Others" provokes a more compelling explanation. In the fall of 1772, Wheatley could still think of herself (or her owners, at least) as a British subject. But later, after rejoicing in the earl's administration had given way to restive disillusionment, perhaps the poet was less certain about her (or her owners') citizenry.

At any rate, the account of Wheatley's capture draws the picture of a bitter memory. The British threat of "tyrannic sway" nevertheless eclipses this first denial of her freedom. Three years after the publication of her 1773 volume,

Wheatley unabashedly celebrated the opposition to that "tyrannic sway" in "To His Excellency General Washington," newly appointed commander-in-chief of the Continental Army; the war of ideas had become one of arms. In this piece, which is more a paean to freedom than a eulogy to Washington, she describes freedom as "divinely fair,/ Olive and laurel bind her golden hair" (p. 145); yet "She flashes dreadful in refulgent arms" (p. 145). The poet accents this image of martial glory with an epic simile, comparing the American forces to the power of the fierce king of the winds:

> As when Eolus heaven's fair face deforms,
> Enwrapp'd in tempest and a night of storms;
> Astonish'd ocean feels the wild uproar,
> The refluent surges beat the sounding shore. (p. 145)

The rocking rhythm of this passage's last line echoes onomatopoeically the image the poet draws of the American armies' implacability in their determination to win freedom, making this line one of Wheatley's finest.

For the young poet, America—which she, probably for one of the first times in the history of American poetry, calls Columbia—is now "The land of freedom's heaven-defended race!" (p. 146). While the eyes of the world's nations are fixed "on the scales,/ For in their hopes Columbia's arm prevails" (p. 146), the poet records Britain's regret over her loss: "Ah! cruel blindness to Columbia's state!/ Lament thy thirst of boundless power too late" (p. 146). The temper of this couplet is in keeping with Wheatley's earlier attitudes toward oppression. The piece closes as the poet urges Washington on in his endeavor with the knowledge that virtue is on his side. If he allows the fair goddess Freedom to be his ide, Washington will surely emerge not only the leader of a victorious army but also the head of the newly established state.

Wheatley's political concerns in her poems were not always merely for the common good; on one particular occasion she clearly voices unmitigated concern for her people still in chains. Embedded within an elegy on General David Wooster, who died on May 2, 1777, from wounds received during Tryon's Danbury raid in April, is an impassioned plea that the colonies' quest for political freedom from Britain will be accompanied by political freedom for all black people as well. In the mouth of the deceased Wheatley places the following dramatic prayer:

> "But how, presumptuous shall we hope to find
> Divine acceptance with th' Almighty mind—
> While yet (O deed Ungenerous!) they disgrace
> And hold in bondage Afric's blameless race?
> Let Virtue reign—And thou accord our prayers
> Be victory our's, and generous freedom theirs." (pp. 149–50)

Within these lines Wheatley expresses the ironic contradiction between what Christianity professes (universal brotherhood of *all* men) and what Christians practice (the institution of slavery), echoing similar observations made in the earlier "On Being Brought from Africa to America." She takes bolder steps here than in the earlier poem; she unabashedly and directly labels all blacks the "blameless race," calls slavery a deed most "ungenerous," and maintains that, if virtue is allowed to take dominion, then an American military and political victory over Britain necessarily should indicate that blacks will subsequently and necessarily receive for themselves "generous freedom." Rather than complacently ignoring the question of her people's struggle for freedom, as several have stubbornly held,[11] this black woman poet courageously confronts slavery's assault on human dignity and wields her pen in the effort to bring about its cessation.

In Wheatley's last political poem, "freedom's heaven-defended race" has won its battle. Written in 1784, within a year after the Treaty of Paris, "Liberty and Peace" is a demonstrative celebration of American independence. The following lines, consistent with the poet's other criticisms of British domination, must have been particularly appealing to those Americans who purchased the poem, first published as a four-page pamphlet:

> Perish that Thirst of boundless Power, that drew
> On *Albion's* Head the Curse to Tyrants due.
> But thou appeas'd submit to Heaven's decree,
> That bids this Realm of Freedom rival thee! (p. 155)

British tyranny, the agent of American oppression, has now been taught to fear "americus," her child, "And new-born *Rome* shall give *Britannia* Law" (p. 154). This seat of new law, this "Realm of Freedom," (p. 155) is the "Progeny of Heaven" (p. 154) and therefore has, as so many other of history's martial conflicts have, divine sanction.

Wheatley concludes this piece with two pleasing couplets praising America's success, whose future is ensured by heaven's approval:

> Auspicious Heaven shall fill with fav'ring Gales,
> Where e'er *Columbia* spreads her swelling Sails:
> To every Realm shall *Peace* her Charms display,
> And Heavenly *Freedom* spread her golden Ray. (pp. 155–56)

Personified as Peace and Freedom, Columbia (America) will act as a world emissary, an emanating force like the rays of

the sun. In this last couplet, Wheatley has captured, perhaps
for the first time in poetry, America's ideal mission to the
rest of the world, a mission which the country pursues now
with the most profound sense of duty and urgency in its two
hundred years of participation in world affairs. This last image of freedom radiating from a heavenly sun also introduces
the second means by which Wheatley espouses the cause of
freedom in her work—the circular mandala archetype. But
before leaving Wheatley's treatment of political freedom, one
final observation presses itself on this discussion. Wheatley's
straightforward and forceful political poems chronicle with
dutiful loyalty important moments of the American Revolution and should grant her recognition as certainly the most
ardent female poet of the Revolution, if not, along with Philip
Freneau, as one of its two most prominent poetic defenders.

II

Wheatley's second means of advancing the cause of freedom
is temporal, as are her political poems, with one distinction.
Her political poems are, of course, fully conscious responses
to her country's overthrow of British oppression; but the
presence of the mandala archetype as the dominant image
pattern in her work suggests a partially unconscious response
to her personal predicament. The *mandala* (the Sanskrit word
for "circle"), Jung maintains, is an instrument of "meditation, concentration, and self-immersion, for the purpose of
realizing inner experience."[12] Jung further explains that "when
they appear in a series, they often follow chaotic, disordered
states marked by conflict and anxiety. They express the idea
of a safe refuge of inner reconciliation and wholeness."[13] In

Wheatley's poems and letters, the mandala archetype manifests itself in her preponderant solar imagery.

The word "sun" recurs with frequency in Wheatley's poetry, often connoting the traditional pun on the Son of God. In a letter describing the death of her beloved mistress, Susanna, Phillis illustrates her awareness of this play on words; it seems that Mrs. Wheatley has taken flight from this world of woes and now resides in "those blissful regions, which need not the light of any, but the sun of Righteousness" (p. 178). But the poet most often speaks of the sun in terms of classical nomenclature. The Latin name for the dawn, "Aurora," appears nine times in Wheatley's poetry; she repeats the Greek names for the sun, "Apollo" and "Phoebus," seven and twelve times, respectively, and uses the Latin "Sol" twice. The word "sun," a classical name for it, or such a phrase as "light of day" occurs in almost all of her fifty-five extant poems. Such regularity is certainly unusual if not unique in the work of poets from any age. How did Wheatley become so preoccupied with solar imagery? One obvious explanation has already been suggested; her intense devotion to New England Congregationalism is well known and partially accounts for her references to the Son-sun. But in Wheatley's case further explanation is demanded.

Phillis Wheatley arrived in colonial New England in the year 1761 with nothing more than a scrap "of dirty carpet" to conceal her nakedness. She was believed to have been "about seven years old, at this time, from the circumstance of shedding her front teeth." All that she is known to have recalled to her white captors about her native land is the fact that *"her mother poured out water before the sun at his rising"* (italics in original).[14] Such a ritual strongly suggests that Wheatley's parents were sun worshipers. The practice of sun worship combines the two primitive religions of animism and fetish-ism. Animism constitutes a belief in expired souls and their probable interaction with and influence on events of the natural world; fetishism belongs to "the doctrine of spirits embodied in, or attached to, or conveying influence through certain material objects."[15] The animistic emphasis on death among the people of her native Africa may help to explain Wheatley's celebration of death in her numerous elegies (a consideration reserved for the next section). But the fetishistic emphasis on material objects—where in the case of sun worshipers the focal point is, of course, the object worshiped—may have so pressed itself upon Wheatley's memory as never to have been far beneath her conscious mind; this memory may indeed have served her as a powerful source of consolation.

In her poetry, then, Wheatley has syncretized the memory of her mother's sun worship with Christianity. Because of the pun on sun and Son, the blend is an easy one to have made. In a letter to the black slave Obour Tanner, her most frequent correspondent, the poet speaks of God in fetishistic language: "But O that I could dwell on & delight in him alone above every other object!" (p. 181). One of her most philosophical poems, "Thoughts on the Works of Providence," identifies the sun as the supreme symbol of divine wisdom: "That *Wisdom*, which attends *Jehovah's* ways,/ Shines most conspicuous in the solar rays" (p. 44). In this meditation on God's creation of nature, the poet recommends, "when from balmy sleep thou op'st thine eyes,/ Let thy first thoughts be praises to the skies" (p. 48), as were her mother's. An elegy, "On the Death of the Rev. Mr. George Whitefield," characterizes the death of the most powerful voice of the Great Awakening in Colonial America as "the setting sun" (p. 22).

"An Hymn to the Morning" celebrates "bright Aurora" and "all the thousands dies,/ Which deck thy progress through the vaulted skies" (p. 56).

In each of these cases, the image Wheatley draws of the sun is that of a divine and serene instrument of order. Jung observes that the recurrence of the mandala figure often indicates a response to "chaotic, disordered states marked by conflict and anxiety." One need look no further than the fact that this young poet was a slave and a black woman to discover sources of intense conflict. In stark contrast to the cold, condescending stares and abuse she must have had to endure wherever she moved in Boston, her poems contain numerous images of the heavenly sun's soothing warmth. The poem about Dartmouth combines the abstract theme of freedom and the concrete spectacle of the dawn into a single image, "smiling like the morn,/ Fair *Freedom* rose" (p. 73), and therefore defines the mandala figure as a medium through which she (and her readers) may achieve freedom. Although this last poem expresses hope for freedom not delivered, it resembles the other poems mentioned above by showing that Wheatley never relinquished that hope.

Another feature of the mandala archetype which underscores Wheatley's attempt to maintain a sense of order and peace of mind occurs in her much less frequent lunar imagery. The cool moon, "Phoebe" or "Cynthia," twice complements the sun's quality of warm radiance. In the poem "Atheism," the persona instructs the reader to

> Mark rising Phoebus when he spreads his ray
> And his commission for to guide the day
> At night keep watch, and see a Cynthia bright
> And her commission for to guide the night (p. 131)

The persona of "On Recollection" extols the dark realm of "nocturnal visions" where Phoebe, "fair regent of the night," rules a bottomless well of poetic images from which the thoughtful poet draws. In such a curious dual mandala figure, Jung would identify the cooperation of conscious and unconscious acting to produce a fuller archetype of wholeness. Jung remarks, "It is . . . not unusual for individual mandalas to display a division into a light and a dark half, together with their typical symbols."[16]

The most exalted form the mandala assumes is " 'the squaring of the circle' . . . one of the many archetypal motifs which form the basic patterns of our dreams and fantasies." This quaternity is "the schema for all images of God, as depicted in the visions of Ezekiel, Daniel and Enoch, and as the representation of Horus with his four sons also shows."[17] Wheatley's "To the University of Cambridge, in New-England" displays this squaring. The poem's persona first admonishes the students of Cambridge (now Harvard) "to traverse ["contemplate" in earlier versions] the ethereal space,/ And mark the systems of revolving worlds" (p. 15); then she encourages them to meditate upon the crucifixion of Jesus of Nazareth: "See him with hands out-stretcht upon the cross;/ Immense compassion in his bosom glows" (p. 15). In this single image shines Wheatley's sun, the Son of God; the four corners of the cross, from whose center God's love emanates, crystallize her most inspired mandala figure. Such contemplation, she continues, permits all believers to "share with him [Jesus] in the sublimest skies,/ Life without death, and glory without end" (p. 16).

When Wheatley exhorts the young scholars of Cambridge to contemplate the possibility of total freedom through commitment to God, she urges upon them a means toward spiritual release. This sort of exhortation differs from her earlier ones which enthusiastically recommend the adoration of God's works in the world of nature. It approaches the kind of spirituality which characterizes her elegies and looks even farther ahead to her treatment of the imagination and the sublime. The undeniable presence of Jung's mandala archetype in Wheatley's work confirms her inner disquietude and disaffection with the world of human conflict which both enslaved and shunned her.[18] This imaginative mandala figure acts as her central image of freedom and finally directs her reader's attention away from worldly strife toward a realm "Where grief subsides, where changes are no more,/ And life's tumultuous billows cease to roar" (p. 99).

III

Commenting in another letter to her friend and confidante, Obour Tanner, Wheatley relates that from the beginning of the Revolutionary War to the letter's date of May 29, 1778, events in this world have convinced her "of the uncertain duration of all things temporal." The "proper result" of such uncertainty, continues the poet, stirs her desire to prepare ardently for "a state and enjoyments which are more suitable to the immortal mind" (p. 185). Her elegies most observably portray this desire and preparation for death. Sometimes written at the request of Bostonians whom the Wheatleys knew but probably as often prompted by her own response to those she herself knew, these poems fall into the tradition of meditation whose ultimate objective is personal knowledge of God. It is characteristic of Wheatley's elegies that she explores in them her own quest for enlightenment concerning her idea of God. As Abbie Findlay Potts puts it so well, "the characteristic drive of elegiac meditation [is] toward always better things—better men, better states, better hypotheses, truer truth."[19] Certainly in Wheatley's case, the goal of her elegiac meditations was to discover a realm wherein men did not enslave their black brothers and sisters; in other words, she sought better men and a better state or condition of being.

Comprising her most recurrent poetic form, eighteen of Wheatley's fifty-five extant poems are elegies. By choosing to devote nearly a third of her poetic energies to the explication of the impact and importance of death, she has carried out one of the central means of animistic worship, thereby recalling her African heritage. Expectedly, her elegies resemble the Puritan funeral elegy. This poetic form contains first a portrait or biography of the deceased, whose life is divided into three stages: vocation or conversion, sanctification or evidence of good works, and glorification or treatment of the deceased's joyous reception into heavenly reward. The second section of the Puritan funeral elegy, called exhortation, urges the living to put off mourning and to concentrate on earning for themselves a reward similar to that of the deceased.[20]

Wheatley's elegies generally concentrate more on exhortation of the living than on portraiture of the deceased. All glorify the dead and display the first two stages of portraiture, vocation, and sanctification. "On the Death of the Rev. Dr. Sewell" characterizes the minister's vocation (conversion) in the following pair of couplets:

"He sought the paths of piety and truth,
By these made happy from his early youth!
In blooming years that grace divine he felt,
Which rescues sinners from the chains of guilt." (p. 21)

Evidence of Sewall's sanctification is given in the couplets
"How oft for us the holy prophet pray'd!/ How oft to us the
Word of Life convey'd" (p. 20) and "Mourn him, ye youth,
to whom he oft has told/ God's gracious wonders from the
times of old" (p. 21). In the famous elegy on George Whitefield, the "Great Awakener," Wheatley speaks of both his
conversion and his sanctification in these lines:

> That Savior, which his soul did first receive,
> The greatest gift that ev'n a God can give,
> He freely offer'd to the num'rous throng,
> That on his lips with list'ning pleasure hung. (p. 23)

The third stage of biography, glorification, the young poet
celebrates in all of her elegies. C.E., an infant, "Through
airy roads . . . wings his instant flight" (p. 69); a clergyman's departed spouse dramatically "leans downward from
th' empyreal sky" and bids her husband to join " 'Our bliss
divine to mortals . . . unknown' " (p. 54); a child of five
discovers after her death that "Seraphic pow'rs" of angelic
song combine with the voices of saints (those among the deceased elected to salvation) and create joyful music of praise,
"their grateful voices raise,/ And saints and angels join their
songs of praise" (p. 26); and both Sewall and Whitefield in
their happy deaths "arriv'd th' immortal shore" (p. 19) and
achieved "thine immortal throne" (p. 22), each within the
first three lines of their respective elegies.[21] These fervent
illustrations of immortal bliss and apotheosis reflect the sort
of emotionalism which John W. Draper has observed marks
the contribution of the Methodist funeral elegy to English
romanticism.[22] More to the point of this discussion, however, these passages reflect the poet's conviction that the next
world holds far greater appeal than the present.

The structure of the Puritan funeral elegy easily accommodates Wheatley's temporary escape to a more satisfactory heavenly world. It provides her with the opportunity to reject the less satisfactory life on the horizontal earth and to long for the eternal life of happiness she believes is promised her in the Christian heaven poetically above her. Death's inevitability and the deceased's reluctance to return to an essentially evil world, full of misfortunes and anxieties,[23] are two themes which dramatically illustrate this horizontal-vertical tension. A clear image of death's inevitability occurs in "To a Lady on the Death of Her Husband," which opens rather bleakly but later encourages the bereaved mourner, Mrs. Leonard, to yearn toward her husband's reward of pleasures given to "th' immortal mind" (p. 30). The first ten lines are an extended apostrophe to death, the "Grim monarch!" Such alliterating phrases as "dusty death" and "dire dart" lend gravity to Wheatley's address, in which she laments the recognition that "Nor youth, nor science, nor the ties of love,/ Nor ought on earth thy flinty heart can move" (p. 29; note the curious mixture here of rhetoric from the Petrarchan tradition and the elegiac mode). But she refuses to indulge this morbid attitude; indeed, she instructs the lady to prepare herself "to pass the vale of night/ To join for ever on the hills of light" her husband's "joyful spirit" (p. 30).

Death, then, should not be viewed as final destruction but as a release from this horizontal world's "iron hand of pain" (p. 25; note the implication of shackles here); it frees one "from a world of sin, and snares, and pain" (p. 26). In another elegy, "From bondage freed, the exulting spirit flies/ Beyond *Olympus*, and these starry skies (p. 51). The changes which occur in Wheatley's horizontal world usually portend misfortune; in one elegy she speaks of "mortality's sad scenes"

(p. 83), while in another she rejoices in the promise of an immortality "where changes are no more,/ And life's tumultuous billows cease to roar" (p. 99). Her last published elegy, which appeared in 1784 only four months before her own pitiable death in a state of abject poverty, presents this world as "Oppress'd with woes, a painful endless train" (p. 152). This effusion marks her most negative renunciation of life on earth.

This world is to be understood in Wheatley's elegies as a repugnant state from which death opens the door to escape. Death becomes the great liberator and the subject of celebration. Trapped for the present in the horizontal world of "woes, a painful endless train," the poet requires a momentary means of escape, which she finds in contemplative action of the mind. "Ascend the sacred mount, in thought arise" (p. 52), she recommends to a woman who has just lost three of her relatives. In one of the most mature representations among her elegies of the power of the mind, "To a Clergyman on the Death of His Lady," the poet reassures the Reverend Pitkin that his departed wife now resides "Amid the seats of heav'n," where "a place is free" (p. 53). She also identifies this realm of freedom as the source "Where contemplation finds her sacred spring" (p. 53). Wheatley's intimate knowledge of ancient mythology enables her to draw this parallel between the Castalian fount, source of poetic inspiration, and heaven as infinite well of divine inspiration. An intimate knowledge of ancient mythology, however, does not describe the extent of the poet's knowledge of the classical world. In identifying the elegiac mode as that poetic form instrumental toward realizing the mind's contemplative action, Wheatley reveals to her readers a sophistication which exceeds the practice in this mode among such contemporaries as Mather Byles, Benjamin Church, and Charles Wesley; none of these elegists displays a disposition toward drawing concrete ties between their performances and classical paganism.

Wesley's 536-line elegy on Whitefield, for example, is studious not to associate the portrait of the deceased with any pagan reference, while Wheatley in hers on the same subject unabashedly asserts "Unhappy we the setting sun deplore,/ So glorious once, but ah! it shines no more" (p. 22)—unmistakably comparing Whitefield to an Apollo now deceased. In his 1761 elegy on the death of George II, Benjamin Church does obeisance to the tradition of pastoral elegy, yet in the later 1766 elegy on the American pastor Jonathan Mayhew, Church rejects the pagan muse in lieu of "the chaste Muse."[24] Mather Byles, one of Wheatley's literary mentors,[25] is careful in his poetry never to incur the charge of being a Ciceronian; his elegies read more like Christian prayers than they display a discernible relationship to their classical origins. I do not intend, of course, to suggest that Byles, Church, and Wesley were unaware or even unfamiliar with the classical tradition; to be sure, each was university trained and therefore could not have avoided an intimate acquaintance with classical learning. Nevertheless, it is Wheatley, not they, who often chooses to display in her elegies a conscious use of her classical knowledge.

In no other elegy does Wheatley demonstrate a greater indebtedness to classicism than in what may very well have been the last poem to come from her pen, the recently recovered "An Elegy on Leaving————[Poetry?]." Published in the Methodist vehicle, the *Arminian*, in July 1784, five months before Wheatley's death, the poem opens with this arresting pair of lines: "FAREWEL! ye friendly bow'rs, ye streams adieu,/ I leave with sorrow each sequester'd seat" (p.

156). Here the poet is exploring, in the words of Potts, "Light and its shadows, life and its shadow—death or whatever is deadly or about to die—change, transience, evanescence: these . . . constitute the theme of elegiac poetry, what it is about."[26] It is clear that Wheatley grasps the larger theme of the elegiac mode whose origins reside in a classical tradition; for, once "Rapt with the melody of Cynthio's [i.e., Apollo's] strain," now the poet, her poetry "about to die," has arrived at the negative revelation that "No more my hand shall wake the warbling lyre" (p. 156). Implicit behind this last line, the bleakest in Wheatley's extant canon, is the recognition, the anagnorisis, that the elegist now faces her own mortality. Even in such a dark state, the poet determines to rally; indeed, she invokes "sweet Hope" to "Bring calm Content to gild my gloomy seat,/ And cheer my bosom with her heav'nly ray" (p. 157). Still in her darkest hour, Wheatley looks upward for the gilding light of heaven's rays to restore her. Just as poetry and contemplation enable the bereaved Reverend Pitkin to "rise sublime, to equal bliss [of his departed spouse] aspire" (p. 54), so Wheatley's exploration of the tension between horizontal and vertical worlds empowers her with a temporary means of removing her mind, at least, from an oppressive present. Potts asserts that the form of the elegy "always suggests vertical power; for its spatial characteristics and its frame of direction it assumes an outer pattern of downward and upward tendencies and tensions."[27]

Wheatley avowedly hopes in her elegies to raise the souls of her readers (and finally her own) to empyreal bliss; in an elegy addressed to Andrew Oliver, lieutenant governor of the Massachusetts colony who had lost his wife in the spring of the year in which Wheatley's volume appeared, she explains that she "fain thy soul to heav'nly scenes would raise." Rather than dwelling upon his wife's death, he should not let his "wishes be to earth confin'd,/ But soaring high pursue th' unbodied mind" (p. 118). Like his deceased spouse, he can, for a brief time, unbody his own mind and participate with his wife in her achievement of joyous freedom. The means to do so is, of course, contemplative action of the mind. In her elegies, then, Wheatley observes that all temporal events are of "uncertain duration" and that, as a result, the living should desire death, "a state and enjoyments . . . more suitable to the immortal mind." In short, looking back to medieval monasticism but more precisely anticipating the thanatos-eros motif of romanticism, Wheatley rejects transitory life on earth and longs for escape through death.

IV

Just as Wheatley's elegies illustrate her struggle for spiritual freedom, those poems in which the imagination and the sublime dominate reinforce that same struggle. The emphasis she has placed in her elegies upon the action of the mind suggests the importance to her poetics of these two aesthetic ideas. Predictably, Wheatley's understanding of the imagination resembles that of Addison and Akenside, and her grasp of the sublime approximates that of Dennis, Addison (again), and Kames. But more significantly, her poetics of the imagination and the sublime strikingly anticipates Kant's "Analytic of the Sublime" in *The Critique of Judgment* (1790) and Coleridge's analysis of the imagination in *Biographia Literaria* (1817). Since Kant's systematic "Analytic" sanctioned the enthusiastic passions for nineteenth-century romanticism and since Coleridge's treatment of the imagination represents one of the highest achievements of romantic literary theory, any demonstration of Wheatley's application of these aesthetic ideas must point out parallels to Kant and Coleridge where they occur. To be sure, all three—Kant, Coleridge, and, most particularly herein, Wheatley—were profoundly concerned to determine the degree of freedom that aesthetic experience could provide.

To the young black poet, the imagination was sufficiently important to demand from her pen a fifty-three-line poem entitled simply "On Imagination." The piece opens with this four-line apostrophe:

> Thy various works, imperial queen, we see,
> How bright their forms! how deck'd with pomp by thee!
> Thy wond'rous acts in beauteous order stand,
> And all attest how potent is thine hand. (p. 65)

Clearly, Wheatley's imagination is a regal presence in full control of her poetic world, a world in which her "wond'rous acts" of creation stand in harmony, capturing a "beauteous order." These acts themselves give testimony to the queen's creative power. But, following a four-line invocation to the Muse, the poet distinguishes the imagination from its subordinate, the fancy:

> Now here, now there, the roving *Fancy* flies,
> Till some lov'd object strikes her wand'ring eyes,
> Whose silken fetters all the senses bind,
> And soft captivity involves the mind. (p. 65)

Unlike the controlled, harmonious imagination, the subordinate fancy flies about here and there, searching for some appropriate and desired object worthy of setting into motion the creative powers of her superior.

In another poem, "Thoughts on the Works of Providence," Wheatley describes the psychology of sleep in similar fashion. Having entered the world of dreams, the mind discovers a realm where "ideas range/ Licentious and unbounded o'er the plains/ Where *Fancy's* queen in giddy triumph reigns" (p. 47). Predicting Freudian dream analysis, Wheatley maintains that in sleep the imagination, once again *"Fancy's* queen," creates worlds which lack the "beauteous order" of the poet sitting before a writing desk; nevertheless these dream worlds provoke memorable images. In "On Recollection," Wheatley describes the memory as the repository on which the mind draws to create its dreams. What may be "long-forgotten," the memory "calls from night" and "plays before the *fancy's* sight." By analogy, Wheatley maintains, the memory provides the poet "ample treasure" from her "secret stores" to create poetry:

> . . . in her pomp of images display'd,
> To the high-raptur'd poet gives her aid. (p. 62)

"On Recollection" asserts a strong affinity between the poet's memory, analogous to the world of dreams, and the fancy, the associative faculty subordinate to the imagination. Recollection for Wheatley functions as the poet's storehouse of images; the fancy channels the force of the imagination through its associative powers. Both the memory and the fancy, then, serve the imagination.

Wheatley's description of fancy and memory departs markedly from what eighteenth-century aestheticians, including Locke and Addison, generally understood as the imagination.[28] The faculty of mind which they thought identified the imagination Wheatley relegates to recollection (memory) and fancy. Her description of recollection and fancy closely parallels Coleridge's in the famous thirteenth chapter of *Biographia Literaria,* where he states that fancy "is indeed no other than a mode of Memory emancipated from the order of time and space." Wheatley's identification of the fancy as roving "Now here, now there" whose movement is analogous to the dream state, where "ideas range/ Licentious and unbounded," certainly frees it from the limits of time and space. Coleridge further limits the fancy to the capacity of choice. "But equally with the ordinary memory," he insists, "the Fancy must receive all its materials ready made from the law of association."[29] Like Coleridge's, Wheatley's fancy exercises choice by association as it finally settles upon "some lov'd object."

If fancy and memory are the imagination's subordinates, then how does the imagination function in the poet's creative process? Following her description of fancy in "On Imagination," Wheatley details the role the imagination plays in her poetry. According to her, the power of the imagination enables her to soar "through air to find the bright abode,/ Th' empyreal palace of the thund'ring God" (p. 66). As in her elegies, the central focus of her poetry remains contemplation of God. Foreshadowing Wordsworth's "winds that will be howling at all hours," Wheatley exclaims that on the wings of the imagination she "can surpass the wind,/ And leave the rolling universe behind" (p. 66). Or, in the realm of the imagination, the poet can "with new worlds amaze th' unbounded soul" (p. 66).

Immediately following this arresting line, Wheatley illustrates in a ten-line stanza the power of the imagination to create new worlds. Even though winter and the "frozen deeps" prevail in the real world, the imagination can take one out of unpleasant reality and can build a pleasant, mythic world of fragrant flowers and verdant groves where "Fair *Flora*" spreads "her fragrant reign" and Sylvanus crowns the forest with leaves, and where "Show'rs may descend, and dews their gems disclose,/ And nectar sparkle on the blooming rose." Such is the power of imagination to promote poetic creation and to release one from an unsatisfactory world. But like reality's painful intrusion upon the delicate, unsustainable song of Keats's immortal bird, gelid winter and its severe "northern tempests damp the rising fire," cut short the indulgence of her poetic world and lamentably force Wheatley to end her short-lived lyric: "Cease then, my song, cease the unequal lay" (p. 68). Her lyric must end because no poet can indefinitely sustain a mythic world.

In her use of the imagination to create "new worlds," Wheatley's departure from eighteenth-century theories of this faculty is radical and once again points toward Coleridge. Although she does not distinguish between primary and secondary imagination as he does, Wheatley constructs a theory which approaches Coleridge's theory of secondary imagination. According to Coleridge, the secondary imagination, which attends the creative faculty, intensifies primary imagination common to all men. Coleridge describes how the secondary imagination operates in this well-known passage:

> It dissolves, diffuses, dissipates,
> in order to recreate; or where this
> process is rendered impossible,
> yet still at all events it
> struggles to idealize and to unify.[30]

Although Wheatley's attempt to dissolve, diffuse, and dissipate is assuredly more modest than Coleridge's "swift half-intermitted burst" in "Kubla Khan," she does nevertheless, like the apocalyptic romantics, idealize, unify, and shape a mythopoeic world. Proceeding in a systematic fashion, she first constructs a theory of a mental faculty which, when assisted by the associative fancy, then builds, out of an act of the mind, a new world which does indeed stand in "beauteous order." Wheatley uses this faculty, which she identifies as the imagination,[31] as a tool to achieve freedom, however momentary.

Wheatley does not derive her aesthetic of the sublime systematically in a single poem; rather, she develops this aesthetic idea in a variety of poems. She shows a broad familiarity with the tenets of the sublime as it was understood in her own time. But her grasp of the possibility of using the sublime as a principle of freedom exceeds that of her predecessors and anticipates Kant, English romanticism, and American transcendentalism. In one of her earliest poems, composed when she was only fourteen, she writes that while others sing of "gay *Elysian* scenes" and "balmy zephyrs," her song "more happy speaks a greater name,/ Feels higher motives and nobler flame." Her objective in composition, even at this early age, is to mount "sublime above inferior things" (p. 88). Although this poem, "To a Gentleman on His Voyage to Great-Britain for the Recovery of His Health," is an unlikely place for such a declaration, she seizes the occasion to address the sea with this vast, pictorial apostrophe: "O thou stupendous, earth-enclosing main" (p. 89).

What Wheatley appears to be doing here is adopting the grand style of Milton, one of her favorite poets and the only English poet she names in her extant verse.[32] Milton, whose grand style eighteenth-century aestheticians proclaimed as the

epitome of the sublime achievement, afforded the young poet
the finest example of poetic sublimity. The composition of
two epyllia, or short epics, vividly illustrates Wheatley's aspiration to mount "sublime above superior things." Both pieces
contain more than two hundred lines and represent her long-
est poems. The first, "Goliath of Gath," is much more than
a biblical paraphrase, a popular form of the time. This poem
is replete with two interpolations of thirty and twelve lines,
Christian machines, and an elaborate eight-line invocation to
the Muse. The other epyllion, "Niobe in Distress for Her
Children Slain by Apollo," contains a ten-line invocation,
long speeches, epic similes, and several interpolations of Ovid's
text. Both poems confirm Wheatley's ambition as a poet and
attest the "intrinsic ardor" (p. 15) which she avowed compelled her to write.

In "Isaiah LXIII. 1–8," another piece which far exceeds
paraphrase, Wheatley presents a more mature understanding
of the sublime than that which appeared in "To a Gentleman." Here Wheatley powerfully and successfully conveys
the enthusiastic passions in compressed and immediate images. The poem opens with a syncretistic invocation: "Say,
heav'nly muse, what king, or mighty God,/ That moves sublime from *Idumea's* road?" (p. 60). While the King James
Bible describes him as "glorious in his apparel, travelling in
the greatness of his strength" without benefit of any muse,
the young poet depicts the stranger as a "king" or "mighty
God" who "moves sublime." He does not simply walk as an
ordinary man; he moves not along but "from" the road. The
phrase "moves sublime from *Idumea's* road" suggests a tension between horizontal human movement and vertical
semidivine motion. This image prepares the reader for
Wheatley's interpretation of the stranger in the remainder of

the thirty-line poem as the Son of God, "th' Almighty Saviour."[33]

Wheatley's Saviour appears in complete battle array:

> . . . with maritial glories join'd,
> His purple vesture waves upon the wind.
> Why thus enrob'd delights he to appear
> In the dread image of the *Pow'r* of war? (p. 60)

The biblical version mentions nothing about war per se, although there the traveler's statement implies battle: "the day
of vengeance is in mine heart." In both versions, next follows the well-known metaphor of the winepress, which ty-
pologists have long maintained foretells Revelation 14:19: "the
great winepress of the wrath of God." This metaphor occurs
in Isaiah within the traveler's speech, which fills the remain-
ing six verses of the biblical passage the poet has elected to
explicate. Wheatley contracts these six verses into a single
couplet: "Compress'd in wrath the swelling wine-press groan'd,/
It bled, and pour'd the gushing purple round" (p. 60).

After having condensed the eight verses (thirty-two lines)
from Isaiah into the poem's first eight lines, Wheatley deliv-
ers a twenty-two-line typology of the entire passage, in which
she dramatizes the "savior" named in Isaiah 63:8 as Christ
speaking from the cross and then concludes the poem with a
commentary on the speech. The most significant interpretation Wheatley gives here occurs in this succinct line spoken
by her Saviour: "For man's release [I] sustain'd the pon-
d'rous load" (p. 60). Unmistakably, the source of sublimity
for this poem comes from the poet's belief that "th' Almighty
Saviour" can bring not only man's but her own release from
an unhappy existence in this world. The intensity and
compression she shows in this piece capture the same spirit

of eschatological desire she displays in her elegies and demonstrates what a recent critic has identified as the religious
sublime.[34]

Again showing her interest in the religious possibilities of
the sublime, Wheatley describes an image which Longinus
thought embodied overwhelming sublimity, the first light of
creation as presented in Genesis 1:3: "And God said, Let
there be light, and there was Light."[35] In "Thoughts on the
Works of Providence" the young poet renders this affective
moment in these fine couplets:

> "Let there be light," he said: from his profound
> Old *Chaos* heard, and trembled at the sound:
> Swift as the word, inspir'd by pow'r divine,
> Behold the light around its maker shine,
> The first fair product of th' omnific God,
> And now through all his works diffus'd abroad. (p. 47)

This paean to holy light, which, according to Wheatley,
"Shines most conspicuous in the solar rays," adds detail to
the immediate image of Genesis by emphasizing the grandeur of God's voice and by underscoring the pristine penetration of his light. The feeling pervading this passage resembles that of Jonathan Edwards expressed in the *Narrative
of His Conversion:*

> I have many times had a sense of
> the glory of the third person in the
> Trinity . . .
> as an infinite fountain of divine
> glory . . . like the sun in its
> glory, sweetly and pleasantly
> diffusing light and life.[36]

Other manifestations of the enthusiastic passions in Wheatley's poetry look back to her predecessors,[37] but of much

greater interest are those conceptions of the sublime which look ahead to Kant. Each perceives the feeling of the sublime to be the quintessential human expression of freedom. It is this particular correspondence of thought which provokes the present examination. The intention of this discussion is not in any way to imply influence but rather to trace resemblances and parallels. Although Kant's *Critique of Judgment* (1790) appeared six years after Wheatley's death in 1784, it is unlikely that a copy of *Poems on Various Subjects, Religious and Moral* could have come into the hands of the little scholar at Konigsberg. To be sure, many of the ideas expressed in the *Critique* were formed long before its publication.

Rather than having arrived at her views on the sublime from a long and full lifetime of reflection as did Kant, Wheatley displays in her poetic representation of the sublime the spontaneity of youth. "Thoughts on the Works of Providence" sets forth this spontaneous representation in its exuberant celebration of the heavens. As in "To a Gentleman," where she pictured the vastness of the ocean, the poet again portrays immensity. But here she strives to construct an indication of infinity, a quantity so grand that the human mind, though it can conceive it, finally fails to comprehend it by means of the senses alone. Wheatley's objective in "Thoughts" is to obtain knowledge, however meager, of God through contemplation of his works in nature, symbolized most fully in her recurring mandala archetype. Her sun, "monarch of the earth and skies" (p. 43), moves in time as well as in limitless space, as the sun "round its centre moves the rolling year" (p. 43). The ultimate goal of her contemplation is to reach the power "Which round the sun revolves this vast machine [the earth]" and "whirls surrounding spheres" but who finally remains "the God unseen" (p. 43).

Concentrating on the sun, "peerless monarch of th' ethereal train," Wheatley enumerates the vast distance between it and the poet in contemplation: "Of miles twice forty millions is his height." In establishing this distance (even though inaccurately), the poet has swiftly shifted the center of focus eighty million miles from "mighty Sol" to her own world on earth:

> And yet his radiance dazzles mortal sight
> So far beneath—from him th' extended earth
> Vigour derives, and ev'ry flow'ry birth. (p. 44)

Here enjambment, a rarity in Wheatley's verse, contributes to the image of rapid travel over great distance and emphasizes the energy of this mental movement. Then Wheatley abruptly shifts the focus back to the sun:

> Vast through her orb she [the earth] moves with easy grace
> Around her *Phoebus* in unbounded space;
> True to her course th' impetuous storm derides,
> Triumphant o'er the winds, and surging tides. (p. 44)

Once again the imaginations of poet and reader soar to the heavens. The pattern established here resembles Kant's illustration of the mind "set in motion in the representation of the sublime in nature." "This movement," Kant continues, "especially in its inception, may be compared with a vibration, i.e., with a rapidly alternating repulsion and attraction produced by one and the same Object."[38] Herein lies the sublime's negative pleasure, that pleasure which can not be completely realized. When the imagination is raised high, it can sustain itself only briefly before falling into failure. Wheatley's energic illustration of the alternate rise and fall of attention from sun to poet and back again depicts Kant's vibration.

Having represented boundless imagination, Wheatley devotes the remainder of "Thoughts" to a tabulation of God's goodness and wisdom as they affect the immediate world of man and nature. "Thoughts" concludes with a philosophical dialectic between Reason and Love in which Reason discovers the solution to the question, " 'What most the image of th' Eternal shows?' " (p. 48). Wheatley resolves the problem of this dialectic by asserting that "Infinite *Love*" appears "where'er we turn our eyes" (p. 49). Contemplation of the deity has taught her to discover a benevolent totality and design in the adored "God unseen." According to Kant, contemplating the sublimity of the universe causes "our imagination in all its boundlessness, and with it nature," to sink "into insignificance before the ideas of reason once their adequate presentation in poetry, e.g., is attempted."[39] This sort of sublime feeling, which Kant calls the mathematical (quantitative) sublime, obtains in "Thoughts."

Since it is the imagination which acts as mediator between poet and the absolute totality of God, a brief examination of how this mental faculty functions in representing the sublime feeling, both in Wheatley and in Kant, is in order. In "On Imagination," Wheatley identified the imagination as that faculty of mind which could allow both poet and reader to "surpass the wind,/ And leave the rolling universe behind." As such, this mental faculty mediates between the poet in contemplation, where she is confined by human limitations to a world of sensibility (perception) and understanding (abstract conceptualization), and the totality she struggles to reach. Wheatley understood early on the inevitable failure of attempting to constrain God within any poetic representation; at the age of sixteen, in the elegy "On the Death of the Rev. Dr. Sewell," she describes God as "incomprehensible, unknown/ By sense" (p. 20). The imagination nevertheless enables the mind to transcend the limitations of the human senses and permits one to contemplate an absolute totality.

Wheatley's grasp of the imagination as mediator closely parallels Kant's analysis of that faculty which sets into motion the response to the sublime object. In describing the sublime feeling, Kant submits that before any object can please, it must suggest a totality (noumenon). In the case of judging the beautiful, the mental process is based on perceivable finite objects. But in the case of the sublime, judgment is not based on sensory experience since it allows only for a subjective idea of totality. The faculty which grasps both the beautiful and the sublime is imagination; it is passive with the beautiful but active or "set in motion" with the sublime.[40] Wheatley's imagination is certainly active, and she shows practically no concern in her poetry for the aesthetic category of beautiful. One distinction between poet and philosopher must be made. Wheatley's "Great God, incomprehensible, unknown/ By sense" is no necessary hypothesis of absolute totality as in Kant; He is actual Being having both finite and infinite existence. Poet and philosopher nevertheless conceive a totality that is finally "knowable" only through subjective and nonsensuous intuition.

The climax of subjective and nonsensuous sublimity comes in what Kant terms the dynamic sublime. Whereas the mathematical sublime was a function of cognition or of the will, the dynamic sublime is seated in desire. In Wheatley, the distinction becomes apparent in her expression of the quantitative passion operating as a force of will in these lines from "Thoughts" prefacing her depiction of the solar system: "Arise, my soul, on wings enraptur'd, rise/ To praise the monarch of the earth and skies" (p. 43). Sheer force of will motivates her to contemplate "the God unseen/ Which round the sun revolves this vast machine." In her intense desire for union with God, however, she represents dynamic sublimity. Whereas God was the implicit goal of the quantitative sublime, he is the explicit end of the dynamic sublime.

Kant concedes that freedom is the final end of sublime feeling. He arrives at this judgment by identifying freedom as that expression which most compels the mind but which brings about the least success in attempts to represent it. As Kant himself states, *"The inscrutability of the idea of freedom precludes all positive representation."*[41] So artists such as Wheatley must be content with negative representations. Here one may recall her letter to the Indian evangelist Samson Occom in which she writes that all men, including her enslaved black brethren, possess an intense "Love of Freedom" which "is impatient of Oppression and pants for Deliverance." Her "Love of Freedom" reaches far beyond the political freedom hoped for in such poems as "Liberty and Peace" and "To His Excellency General Washington"; rather, she most fervently and most consistently seeks the "beatitude beyond the skies" (p. 85).

All of Wheatley's elegies convey this expression of dynamic sublimity, but perhaps one achieves its poetic representation best. "An Elegy . . . on the Death of . . . John Moorhead" describes the confessed sinner's contemplation of the sun as symbolic not simply of God's benevolence but even of his anger: "JEHOVAH'S Wrath revolving, he [the confessed sinner] surveys,/ The Fancy's terror and the Soul's amaze" (p. 138). Kant insisted that the dynamic sublime "must be represented as a source of fear"[42] which creates awe and astonishment. He further maintained that such fear can incite the feeling of sublimity only in the most moral, since "the righteous man fears God without being afraid of Him, because he regards the case of his wishing to resist God and His commandments as one which need cause *him* no anxiety."[43] In the elegy honoring John Moorhead, as is indeed the case in all her elegies, Wheatley clearly agrees with Kant; only the virtuous and exemplary, such as George Whitefield and Joseph Sewall, as well as John Moorhead, receive the reward of union with God.

Like Kant's righteous man, Wheatley's confessed sinner fears the potential anger of Jehovah, as seen in the fancy's association of the sun with God's might. But at the same time, this image of power transcends the sensible world, thereby creating a negative presentation which, according to Kant, "expands the soul"[44] or, in Wheatley's words, produces "the Soul's amaze." Such an experience of the sublime inevitably results in a response of humility, for both poet and philosopher. Wheatley's most piquant expression of humility comes when, in "On Imagination," painful reality intrudes upon her mythical realm, its "mountains tipt with radiant gold."[45] She continues with painful resignation, "But I reluctant leave the pleasing views" because *"Winter* austere forbids me to aspire,/ And northern tempests damp the rising fire" (p. 68). In her attempt to seek momentary release from the temporal world, "Oppress'd with woes, a painful endless train," she has endured what Kant calls "the pain of remorse."[46]

Although her demonstration of the sublime feeling is not systematic, Wheatley does demonstrate a grasp of this aesthetic idea which points directly toward Kant. Like the philosopher, she identifies the imagination as the means toward grasping partial knowledge of the deity; she employs imagery of the solar system as the most exalted symbol of God in nature, illustrating the mathematical sublime; her passionate desire to ascend toward heavenly and absolute freedom represents the dynamic sublime; and, finally, her demonstration of humility epitomizes the sublime as a negative pleasure. In addition, her modest analysis of the imagination prefigures Coleridge's compelling analysis in *Biographia Literaria*. Despite Wheatley's stubborn attachment to the heroic couplet,[47] a touchstone of neoclassicism (save Byron!), a great deal of the content of her poetry is consanguineous to romanticism.

CONCLUDING REMARKS

Phillis Wheatley is not a great poet, but she is a good one. For too long she has served merely as a pawn in various socioanthropological arguments. Few have taken the time or made the effort to read her poetry seriously. In 1773, many reviews of her only published book appeared in London. The following passage, taken from one of those reviews, captures the attitude of disdain in which her poetry has generally been held from the date of its publication:

> The poems written by this young negro bear no endemial marks of solar fire or spirit. They are merely imitative; and, indeed, most of those people have a turn for imitation, though they have little or none for invention.[48]

This reviewer has missed completely Wheatley's reliance upon her mother's sun; indeed, the "solar fire" burns in Wheatley's poetry with unmistakable resplendence. In a letter to John Thornton, the English philanthropist, Wheatley herself recognized that she and her race were "despised on earth on account of our colour" (p. 174). Yet such recognition did not prevent her from celebrating her country's quest for political freedom in poems filled with impassioned fervor. This same recognition did nevertheless leave its indelible mark on her poetry, as evidenced by her recurrent mandala archetype.

Failing to find fulfillment in the hostile, temporal world, Wheatley understandably turned toward the spiritual. Under the guise of providing comfort for the relatives of deceased persons (not to imply that her efforts to this end were insincere), she wrote elegy after elegy, poignantly mapping her struggle to obtain a glimpse of the happiness she indefatigably believed awaited her in the hereafter. This ardent belief in a better world, wholly separate from the unreceptive and unhappy one she knew, moved her to develop theories of the imagination and the sublime which were ahead of her time. It is true that in America only three years before her "On Imagination" appeared in the 1773 volume, Philip Freneau had written a poem entitled "Power of Fancy," three times as long as Wheatley's. Written while he was an undergraduate at Princeton, Freneau's poem, however, relies upon the eighteenth century's common grasp of the imagination as an associative function of the memory, as these lines illustrate:

> Fancy, thou the muses' pride,
> In thy painted realms reside
> Endless images of things,
> Fluttering each on golden wings,
> Ideal objects, such a store,
> The universe could hold no more.[49]

Even when one grants Freneau the advantage of his university training, which doubtless taught him Plato's theory of ideal forms made manifest in the above passage, Wheatley's use of the imagination as a means to transcend an unacceptable present and even to construct "new worlds [to] amaze th' unbounded soul" places her in a tradition which begins with Edwards and passes through Emerson and Whitman. It also aligns her with the mythopoeic romantics of America and Europe. Her grasp of the sublime and its approximation to Kant's "Analytic of the Sublime" only underscores her relationship to the nineteenth-century romantics.[50] Wheatley was indeed an imitator, but what writer, what literate human being, is not, to a marked degree, a product of his or her reading? Wheatley was an innovator as well, who also used old ideas in new and powerful ways. One must concede, then, that the nature of Wheatley's imitation was not external and derivative but internal and recreative.

When evaluating her work, one must also recall that Wheatley was only about twenty years old when she produced the bulk of her extant work. "On Imagination," "On Recollection," "Thoughts on the Works of Providence," the elegies on Sewall and Whitefield (among many others), and her two epyllia all appeared in the 1773 volume. When one reflects that no less a great poet than John Keats produced before the age of twenty such unpromising lines as "And all around it dipp'd luxuriously/ Slopings of verdure through the glossy tide,"[51] Wheatley's achievement is remarkable. However, she should not be judged simply on the basis of her precocity. Nor should she be considered merely in terms of a socioanthropological phenomenon.

Wheatley is a preromantic, not merely because of the fact that she was an historical precursor of Wordsworth and Coleridge. She is a preromantic because she actively contributed to the development of aesthetic theories which paved the way for the romantic movement. She wrote during the pre-Revolutionary and Revolutionary War era in America, a pe-

riod in which little poetry of great merit was produced. Such
lean achievement is understandable; people fighting battles
and struggling for survival have little time for poetry. But
Phillis Wheatley, laboring under the disadvantages of being
not only a black slave but also a woman, did find the time to
depict that political struggle for freedom and to trace her
personal battle for release. If one makes the effort to see
beyond the limitations of her sincere piety and her frequent
dependence on what Wordsworth called poetic diction, one
is sure to discover in her works a fine mind notably engaged
in creating some of the best early American poetry.

NOTES

ABBREVIATIONS

AL	*American Literature.*
AWB 1800	*American Writers before 1800: A Biographical and Critical Dictionary*, 3 vols., ed. James A. Levernier and Douglas R. Wilmes (Westport, Conn.: Greenwood Press, 1983).
CLA	*College Language Association Journal*
DAB	*Dictionary of American Biography*, 20 vols., ed. Allen Johnson and Dumas Malone (New York: Charles Scribner's Sons, 1928–37; Seven Supplements, 1944–65).
Deane	Charles Deane, ed., *Letters of Phillis Wheatley* (Boston: privately printed, 1864).
DNB	*Dictionary of National Biography*, 21 vols., 1 supplement, ed. Leslie Stephen and Sidney Lee (London: Oxford University Press, 1882–1900; Seven Supplements, 1901–70).
EAL	*Early American Literature.*
Jackson	Sara Dunlap Jackson, "Letters of Phillis Wheatley and Susanna Wheatley," *Journal of Negro History* 57, no. 2 (April 1972): 211–15.
Kuncio	Robert C. Kuncio, "Some Unpublished Poems of Phillis Wheatley," *New England Quarterly* 43 (June 1970): 287–97.
Mason	Julian D. Mason, Jr., ed., *The Poems of Phillis Wheatley* (Chapel Hill: University of North Carolina Press, 1966).
NEQ	*New England Quarterly.*

Robinson   William H. Robinson, ed., *Phillis Wheatley and Her Writings* (New York: Garland, 1984).

Sibley and   John L. Sibley and Clifford K. Shipton, *Biographi-*
Shipton   *cal Sketches of Those Who Attended Harvard College* (Vols. 1–3: 1642–89, Boston: Massachusetts Historical Society, 1873; Vols. 4–17: 1690–1771, Boston: Massachusetts Historical Society, 1933–75).

Silverman   Kenneth Silverman, "Four New Letters by Phillis Wheatley," *Early American Literature* 8, no. 3 (Winter 1974): 257–71.

POEMS ON VARIOUS SUBJECTS, RELIGIOUS AND MORAL (1773)

Frontispiece or Portrait Page

The significance of this portrait of Wheatley is difficult to overemphasize. In *The Journey Back: Issues in Black Literature and Criticism* (Chicago: University of Chicago Press, 1980), Houston A. Baker, Jr., observes that the portrait "strikes the informed consciousness as a singular—and almost revolutionary—signature on the scroll of American history." Then he explains that "the implements at Wheatley's table and her earnest concentration give the lie to that frequently repeated notion that all blacks (and especially those as far back in time as the eighteenth century) have perpetually spent their days in gross manual labor and their nights shuffling to the sound of exotic banjos" (p. 6). The only emendation I would make in this judicious passage is to alter "almost revolutionary" to read simply "revolutionary." Just a year before publication of this collection in 1773, Wheatley's proposal for another volume had been rejected by the Boston public for what are now understood to have been racist reasons; in Great Britain women authors of this period often adopted male noms de plume in order to attract an audience. For Wheatley to announce to the world in so dramatic a fashion both her African-ness and her sex was revolutionary indeed. When one acknowledges two additional factors—first, that Wheatley was the first black American author to publish a book and, second, that her publication venture was supported, both financially and intellectually, almost exclusively by other women—then this portrait of a literate, con-templative, black slave woman author increases in revolutionary im-portance. For not only was Wheatley a literate black slave, but she was a woman writer whose publications would probably never have seen the light of day were it not for the supportive efforts of her mistress, Susanna Wheatley, who encouraged her and praised her works, and Selina Hastings, Countess of Huntingdon, who backed the 1773 *Poems* with sufficient monies to see the volume through the press. With increasing frequency, Phillis Wheatley is justly being called the mother of black American literature. She may as well be considered the mother of American women writers; for, unlike those of her predecessor, Anne Bradstreet, whose poems were first seen through the press by male backers and exhorters, Wheatley's pub-lication ventures were rendered possible almost totally by the mach-inations of other women.

Title Page

The phrase, "NEGRO SERVANT to Mr. JOHN WHEATLEY" declares the poet's Africanness, underscoring the statement made by the portrait. In addition, however, the word "SERVANT," at the very least, implies the condition of her servitude. In 1772, the British judge Lord Mansfield handed down a decision regarding the case of a black man named Somerset which effectively freed all slaves in Great Britain. The decision was widely understood in the following terms: "as soon as a slave set his foot on the soil of the British islands he became free." See Harold J. Schultz, *History of England,* 2d ed. (New York: Harper and Row, 1971), p. 181, and David B. Davis' detailed discussion of the case in his *The Problem of Slavery in the Age of Revolution: 1770–1823* (Ithaca: Cornell University Press, 1975), pp. 479–84. When Wheatley arrived in

London on June 17, 1773, then, technically she became free, certainly while she remained in Britain. She would have to wait, however, until shortly before October 18, 1773, to be freed on the other side of the Atlantic in her "adoptive" Boston. The irony this phrase conjured in the minds of both Wheatley and apparently her master's son, Nathaniel, in whose charge Wheatley was placed during her London voyage, is suggested by the uncomfortable circumstance of Benjamin Franklin's calling on Phillis to offer "her any Services I could do her. Before I left the house, I understood her Master was there and had sent her to me but did not come into the room himself, and I thought was not pleased with the visit. I should, perhaps have enquired first for him; but I had heard nothing of him. And I have heard nothing since of her" (*The Papers of Benjamin Franklin*, ed. W. B. Willcox et al. [New Haven: Yale University Press, 1976], Vol. 20, pp. 291–92). The editors speculate that the Somerset case was the reason for the discomfiture (p. 292).

Dedication

Wheatley dedicated her *Poems* to Selina Hastings, Countess of Huntingdon, without whose financial backing this volume would probably never have appeared.

Preface

Wheatley asserts, "The following Poems were written originally for the Amusement of the Author." If we take this assertion as a sincere attempt to describe the provenance of her poetry, then we must assume that she wrote no poems simply "on demand" but exercised free choice, both of each poem's subject and of its mode or form.

John Wheatley's Letter

While this "Letter" describes carefully the conditions under which Wheatley came to speak and read English ("by only what she was taught in the Family, she, in sixteen Months Time from her Arrival [in Boston], attained the English Language"), it states that her capacity to write was prompted by an insatiable curiosity and that she had "a great Inclination to learn the Latin Tongue." We are led to conclude, therefore, that, although family members taught her to speak and read English, she must have gone outside the family circle to pursue her studies in Latin. Perhaps Mather Byles or Samuel Cooper, ministers whose counsel she sought regarding her poems, tutored her in Latin as well. Or perhaps one of the several itinerant foreign-language tutors in the Boston area during this time was enlisted to assist her. Given the quickness of her mind, she would not have required extensive attention toward attaining a substantial knowledge of this language. William Robinson may well have given us the name of this tutor, a certain Mr. Delile, who "wished to commemorate the publication" of the 1773 *Poems* by placing a Latin epitaph beneath the portrait (Robinson, p. 42).

To the Publick

Wheatley's so-called letter of attestation as to the authenticity of her authorship of *Poems* has received much attention in both Mason and Robinson. The names included on this attestation constitute an inventory of Boston's intellectual and economic elite. Much information may be found in *AWB 1800* on James Bowdoin, Mather Byles, Charles Chauncy, Samuel Cooper, Andrew Eliot, Joseph Green, Thomas Hutchinson, Samuel Mather, and Ebenezer Pemberton. The *DAB* may be consulted for John Hancock (signer of the Declaration of Independence) and Andrew Oliver; the *National Cyclopaedia of American Biography* (Vol. 31, p. 345) has information on John Erving. As Robinson points out, many of these most prominent members of Boston's citizenry were interconnected by both blood and marriage. Samuel Cooper, Joseph Green, and Mather Byles were all well-known amateur poets. Both Cooper and Byles served Wheatley as literary tutors and/or counselors. Cooper, Bowdoin, Hancock, and others eventually were to become American patriots; Hutchinson, Oliver, Gray, Green, Byles, and John Wheatley, among others, all became staunch loyalists. For instance, as late as 1775, Harrison Gray (c. 1711–1794), although an abolitionist, published a twenty-page pamphlet, "A Few Remarks upon

Some of the Votes and Resolutions of the Continental Congress," in which he calls the colonial opposition to British control a *"horrible rebellion"* whose *"ringleaders . . . may meet with the punishment that their crimes do justly deserve."* Subsequently, he pleads that all who support this *"horrible rebellion"* should seek the forgiveness of a "kind" monarch (p. 20). Wheatley disagreed with Gray, of course, though they were in accord regarding the slavery issue. She wrote elegies or occasional verse on or about Bowdoin, Cooper, Hubbard, Moorhead, and Oliver. Perhaps her "To Maecenas" is at least in part addressed to Mather Byles.

To Maecenas

Title. This poem does not number among those of Wheatley's early 1772 first proposal for a volume. One of the better performances of the 1773 *Poems*, this piece was probably composed between April 1772 (the month of the third and last advertisement for the 1772 volume) and early September 1773, when her volume was published in London. It is one among several others whose titles also do not appear in the 1772 proposals, including "Thoughts on the Works of Providence," "On Imagination," "To S.M. a Young African Painter," and "Niobe in Distress." Each of these poems is particularly polished and sophisticated, suggesting that the year preceding the appearance of her *Poems* was indeed a productive and creative one, marked by maturation of poetic theory and praxis. Several have tried to identify Wheatley's Maecenas, an allusion to the well-known Roman statesman and patron of the arts who contributed to the poetic efforts of Horace and Vergil. Wheatley's title is adapted directly from Horace's first "Ode" (Book I), wherein the Roman poet records his devotion to the art of poetry as well as to his patron. Wheatley pens more than her devotion to art and patron; indeed, she seizes this opportunity to display her power over the arrangement of words to create a desired effect and dramatically to announce her race to the world, for she, like Terence, was an African by birth. But who is Wheatley's Maecenas? In his 1966 edition of *The Poems of Phillis Wheatley*, Mason suggests that Maecenas is her master, John Wheatley (p. 3). Robinson, in his 1984 *Phillis Wheatley and Her Writings*, points to the poem itself as referring "to a much admired contemporary poet" (p. 217). While both Mason and Robinson agree that she must be referring to a living person, Robinson, I submit, is correct. But I further submit that Mather Byles, that irascible, cantankerous, but nonetheless likable Puritan divine and poet, may be Wheatley's Maecenas, or at least a part of that Maecenas. See my "Phillis Wheatley and Mather Byles: A Study in Literary Relationship," *CLA* 23, no. 4 (June 1980): 377–90. As succeeding lines, moreover, draw consciously from Alexander Pope's poems, it is most likely that the figure of Maecenas is here a conflation of both Byles and Pope. Pope was confessedly Byles's favorite British poet—one with whom the colonial poet had corresponded early in his poetic career. See Agnes Sibley, *Alexander Pope's Prestige in America 1725–1835* (New York: Columbia University Press, 1949), pp. 12–16. If Byles did indeed serve Wheatley as her tutor, he doubtless shared his enthusiasm for Pope with her. While certain passages in the poem do unquestionably make obeisance to the famous Augustan poet, whom both Wheatley and Byles admired, the line "Not you, *my friend* [italics added], these plaintive strains become" does seem to address someone quite familiar to the young poet. Maecenas may be best understood as Byles-Pope.

Line 7: "Homer." It is worth observing that Pope, in his *Essay on Criticism*, counsels critics and/or poets to "know well each ANCIENT proper *character*" (l. 119), then names Homer, Greek poet of the *Iliad* and the *Odyssey*, first among his slate of ancients (l. 124) and subsequently names Vergil, Roman author of the *Aeneid*, as his second ancient author to be emulated. Wheatley follows this order, naming Homer first and then calling Vergil *"Maro"* in l. 21 as Pope does in l. 130 of his *Essay*.

15–16. These slow-moving lines and those faster, more dynamic ones immediately above appear to be a demonstration of Pope's justly famous dictum, "The *Sound* must seem an *Eccho* to the *Sense*," l. 365 of *An Essay on Criticism*, quoted from *Poetry and Prose of Alexander Pope*, ed. Aubrey Williams (New York: Houghton Mifflin, 1969). In this couplet Wheatley adopts the sort of diction Pope employs to illustrate his dictum; Wheatley's "length'ning," "languishing," and "along" echo the liquid l's of Pope's "length along" (l. 357) and "languishingly" (l. 359).

17–20. This incident detailing Patroclus's plea to Achilles that he be allowed to go to the aid of the Greeks wearing Achilles' armor Wheatley almost certainly takes from the opening lines of the sixteenth book of Pope's translation of the *Iliad.* I quote from the Twickenham edition of the poems of Alexander Pope, *The Iliad of Homer: Books X–XXIV,* ed. Maynard Mack (New Haven: Yale University Press, 1967), pp. 233–34, ll. 3–8:

> Meantime *Patrochus* to *Achilles* flies;
> The streaming Tears fall copious from his Eyes;
> Not faster, trickling to the Plains below,
> From the tall Rock the sable Waters flow.
> Divine *Pelides,* with Compassion mov'd,
> Thus spoke, indulgent to his best belov'd.

19: "Prone." Here used poetically to indicate a leaning forward, not a lying down of the body with face turned downward.

20: "Pelides." This word is one of several epithets used throughout the *Iliad* for Achilles and identifies this Greek hero of the Trojan War as the son of Peleus, king of Phthia. Wheatley demonstrates her grasp of the epithet as applied to the names of epic heroes in her two epyllia (short epics), "Goliath of Gath" and "Niobe in Distress."

22: "The Nine." Here Wheatley employs the first of countless references throughout her poetry to the Muses, nine daughters of Mnemosyne (Memory) and Zeus (king of the gods) whose responsibilities were to serve the arts and literature. One of their most frequented, sacred residences, according to ancient mythology, was Helicon, named in l. 33 below. On Helicon, a mountain of ancient Boeotia, sprang the sacred fountains of Hippocrene and Aganippe, emblems of surging creativity in the minds of human artists. Indeed, the mystery of the creative process fascinated Wheatley throughout her poetic career, provoking the composition of such poems as "On Recollection," "Thoughts on the Works of Providence," and "On Imagination." Perhaps all of "To Maecenas" constitutes her invocation to the muse to bring inspiration to the whole of her volume.

37: "happier Terence." Of course, Terence was "happier" than Wheatley, who is "less happy" (l. 35) because she feels she "cannot raise the song" of musical poetry. However, Terence, Roman author of comedies (more refined than his predecessor Plautus) and, as Wheatley notes, "an *African* by birth," had been long a slave but had been freed by the fruits of his pen. Wheatley's affinity for the Roman playwright is particularly poignant, for perhaps she, a slave at the publication of her 1773 volume and hence "less happy," will achieve freedom by means of her pen and also become "happier." Worthy of observing here is the parallel between Wheatley's self-deprecating aspiration to write musical poetry ("The fault'ring music dies upon my tongue," l. 36) and Pope's acknowledgment in *An Essay on Criticism* that "Musick resembles *Poetry*, in each/ Are *nameless Graces* which no Methods teach,/ And which a *Master-Hand* alone can reach" (ll. 143–45).

46: "I'll snatch a laurel from thine honour'd head." This line may owe something to Pope's famous description in *An Essay on Man* of the creative mind of genius which occasionally breaks the rules but nevertheless manages to "*snatch* a *Grace* beyond the Reach of Art" (l. 155).

49: "Naiads." These mythological figures were female personifications of rivers, springs, mountains, streams, or even trees, who were supposedly beautiful, youthful revelers of music and the dance.

50: "Phoebus." Greek god of the sun, often called Phoebus Apollo. Wheatley refers to this god more frequently than to any other from mythology. Interestingly, solar imagery in general, of which her allusions to Apollo comprise a major manifestation, constitutes the most frequent, recurrent image pattern in her entire body of poetry.

53: "Parnassus."   Another Greek mountain, higher in elevation than Helicon, not far from Delphi, site of a shrine especially sacred to Apollo. On Parnassus is located the Castalian fountain, sacred both to the Muses and to Apollo.

On Virtue

Written 1766; published 1773.

This poem announces the theme of morality named in the collection's title. Not only is the idea of virtue not Christian in origin, but it is a distinctly classical concept having its roots in Greek and Roman Stoicism. Wheatley's dependence on virtue as that internalized, wholly positive mode of behavior whose practice will enable her to avoid despair (see l. 6) and to achieve a measure of goodness while also capturing a glimpse of eternality curiously approaches the understanding of this concept as articulated by the French *philosophes* Diderot and d'Alembert in their *Encyclopédie*. See the excellent discussion, *"Virtù* in and since the Renaissance," by Jerrold E. Seigel in the *Dictionary of the History of Ideas: Studies of Selected Pivotal Ideas*, gen. ed. Philip P. Wiener (New York: Scribner's, 1973), Vol. IV, pp. 476–86. While the maturity of vision in "On Virtue" may surprise today's readers—Wheatley was only about twelve when she composed the first version—we should reasonably expect the poet to have revised this poem, perhaps several times, before its publication in this volume. Even so, she was only nineteen or twenty at the time of the poem's publication.

To the University of Cambridge, in New-England

Written 1767; published 1773.

During the seventeenth and eighteenth centuries, Harvard College, located in Cambridge (a suburb of Boston), was often referred to simply as Cambridge. Wheatley was only about thirteen when she penned the first version of this poem. Comparison of this text with the earlier version given below in "Variant Poems and Letters" suggests that, at least in this case, Wheatley made few major alterations.

To the King's Most Excellent Majesty. 1768.
Written 1768; published 1773.
 See "Variant Poems and Letters," below, for an earlier version.

On Being Brought from Africa to America
Written 1768; published 1773.
 This poem is listed in the 1772 "Proposals" as "Thoughts on being brought from Africa to America." So what we have in the 1773 *Poems* is very likely a revision of an earlier poem. For intelligent discussions of this poem, perhaps Wheatley's best-known and at the same time her most controversial work, see James A. Levernier, "Wheatley's On Being Brought from Africa to America," *The Explicator* 40, no. 1 (Fall 1981): 25–26; and Sondra O'Neale, "A Slave's Subtle War: Phillis Wheatley's Use of Biblical Myth," *EAL* 21, no. 2 (Fall 1986): 144–65, especially pp. 147–52.

On the Death of the Rev. Dr. Sewell. 1769.
Written 1769; published 1773.
 The spelling of Sewall's name here is not incorrect; it merely indicates a variation (variations in spellings were frequent before 1800 and even before publication of Noah Webster's *American Dictionary of the English Language* in 1828. Sewall, son of diarist and Chief Justice Samuel Sewall (who also wrote one of the earliest antislavery tracts in the colonies, "The Selling of Joseph," in 1700), was principal minister of the famous Old South Church of Boston, which the Wheatley family attended—hence the poet's identification of him as "my monitor" (l. 49). For additional information on Joseph Sewall and his more famous father, see *AWB 1800*. The earlier, manuscript version of this elegy is in "Variant Poems and Letters," below.

On the Death of the
Rev. Mr. George Whitefield. 1770.

Written 1770; published 1770.

For other versions of this poem, see "Variant Poems and Letters," below. It is no exaggeration to submit that this single poem was the most pivotal publication of Wheatley's career. George Whitefield (1714–1770), who was known to colonial Americans as "the Voice of the Great Awakening" and as "the Great Awakener," was personal chaplain to the Countess of Huntingdon (later to be Wheatley's patron) and sometime friend of John and Charles Wesley (the founders of Methodism). During his spectacular career as Christian evangelist, Whitefield made seven journeys to America, dying there in Newburyport, Massachusetts, on September 30, 1770. The week before his death, Whitefield is known to have preached in Boston; and, given the fact that the Wheatley family carried on an active correspondence with the countess, he may well have resided briefly at the Wheatley mansion. Wheatley's vivid portrait of the minister may well have resulted from a personal encounter. This elegy almost certainly accompanied the news of Whitefield's death on the vessel carrying that news to England. Whitefield was an extremely popular figure on both sides of the Atlantic, and his death made provocative copy and created an enthusiastic market for Wheatley's commemoration. Her poem on Whitefield was widely reprinted in both England and America and is the very poem which first elicited the countess's sympathetic attention.

To a Lady on the Death of Her Husband

Written 1771; published 1771.

For another version of this poem, see "Variant Poems and Letters," below.

Goliath of Gath

Written 1772?; published 1773.

Wheatley names this poem in her 1772 proposals. She may have undertaken the composition of this biblical paraphrase-epyllion after

Mather Byles's example in his 1744 *Poems on Several Occasions,* wherein he includes "Goliah's *[sic]* Defeat," which he claims is written "In the Manner of Lucan." Although Byles says his poem is cast after the mode of the Roman poet's unfinished epic, *Pharsalia,* his seventy-eight-line paraphrase seldom departs from I Samuel 17. In stark contrast, Wheatley's "Goliath of Gath" incorporates Christian machines, interpolations of long speeches, and an eight-line invocation to the muse, none of which is present in the Bible or in Byles. Wheatley adapts to her epyllion several other epic characteristics not present in Byles or in Samuel. For discussion of other differences between the versions by Wheatley and Byles, see "Phillis Wheatley and Mather Byles: A Study in Literary Relationship," *CLA* 23, no. 4 (June 1980): 377–90. For treatment of additional epic elements in this poem, see "Phillis Wheatley's Use of Classicism," *AL* 52, no. 1 (1980): 97–111.

76: "*Eliab.*"   David's eldest brother.

204: "*the son of Ner.*"   Abner, Saul's cousin and general.

Thoughts on the Works of Providence

Written 1772 or early 1773; published 1773.

This is one of Wheatley's most self-consciously meditative poems and displays a debt to the meditative tradition which stretches all the way from the ancient practice of the *meditatio* in Greek and Roman literature. Discovering a *locus* (place) evocative of contemplation in her beloved Sun (Sol, Phoebus, or Apollo), the poet's memory conjures up various elements for extending the solar imagery into realms of thought wherein her understanding interacts with these images in an effort to grasp the implicit meaning of God's wonder-working acts in nature. Eventually, the operation of the understanding brings about the poet's grasp of the intelligent entity behind the wonder-working acts (Providence), leading to her challenge to her readers to allow their wills to enact a similar understanding and appreciation of the providential God. What takes place in this poem is, then, the praxis of the *meditatio* in which the mind of the meditator establishes a *locus* evocative of memory on which the understanding operates to bring about a resolve of the will. See discussions of this process within the mental faculties in Louis Martz, *The Poetry of Meditation* (New Haven: Yale University Press, 1954); and Charles E. Hambrick-Stowe, *The Practice of Piety: Puritan Devotional Disciplines in Seventeenth-Century New England* (Chapel Hill: University of North Carolina Press, 1982).

9–13. The images here of flight and of viewing the earth from the vantage point of God parallel a passage in Thomas Burnet, *The Sacred Theory of the Earth* (London: R. Norton, 1691): "Those who would have a true contempt of this world [i.e., those who would strive to achieve a condition of pious contemplation of God], must suffer the Soul to be sometimes upon the Wing, and to raise her self above the sight of this little dark Point, which we now inhabit. Give her a large and free prospect of the immensity of God's works, and of his inexhausted wisdom and goodness" (pp. 316–17). Wheatley's God is also one of wisdom and goodness: "what *Wisdom*, and what *Goodness* shine" (l. 26).

82: light "*through all his works diffus'd abroad.*"   Burnet speaks of a "mighty Mind" which can "diffuse/ All that's her own to others use" (p. 317). A passage from Jonathan Edwards's *Narrative of His Conversion* (1740) even more closely parallels Wheatley's sun-diffusing idea of God; the minister of the Great Awakening "many times had a sense of the glory of the third person in the Trinity . . . like the sun in its glory, sweetly and pleasantly diffusing light and life." Quoted in Herbert W. Schneider, "Religious Enlightenment in American Thought," *Dictionary of the History of Ideas*, gen. ed. Philip P. Wiener (New York: Scribner's, 1973), Vol. IV, p. 110.

88: "*Fancy's queen in giddy triumph reigns.*"   In *The Pleasures of the Imagination* (1744), Mark Akenside describes the fancy's realm in similar terms as "her giddy empire" (Book III, l. 70). It is worth observing that the fancy is never described as "giddy" in any of the works of Shakespeare, Milton, or Pope, nor do the words "giddy" or "fancy" ever appear in the King James Bible.

To a Clergyman on the Death of His Lady

Written 1772; published 1772.

For another version, see "Variant Poems and Letters," below.

An Hymn to the Morning

This paean to the dawn, or to Aurora (Latin name for the goddess of the dawn), recalls Wheatley's memory of her mother pouring out *"water before the sun at his rising"* (from Margaretta M. Oddell's "Memoir" prefacing the 1838 reprinting of Wheatley's 1773 *Poems* in Boston, p. 12) and may well recall a measure of her African heritage.

13: "Calliope." The name of the muse of epic poetry, sometimes evoked as personification of poetic afflatus or inspiration.

Isaiah LXIII. 1–8.

2: "Idumea's road." Idumea is a synonym for Edom, the direction from which the traveler comes.

3: "Bozrah's dies." Bozrah, a practically impregnable fortress, was Edom's chief city.

On Recollection

Written late 1771; published 1772.

For another version of this poem, see "Variant Poems and Letters," below.

1: "Mneme." This word may simply be a shortened form of Mnemosyne, Greek goddess of memory and mother of the muses, as Robinson suggests (p. 272). Sometimes in Greek mythology, however, three older Muses were cited: Melete (meditation), Aoide (song), and Mneme (remembrance). Wheatley may have in mind this older distinction.

12: "Phoebe's realms." The realms of the moon goddess or Artemis, sister of Phoebus Apollo, god of the sun. Both were twin children of Zeus and Leto, or Latona, who play a significant role in Wheatley's epyllion "Niobe in Distress."

32: "round the central sun."   This phrase appears in Byles's *Poems on Several Occasions* (1744, p. 89), but it does not appear in Milton or in Pope.

On Imagination

11: "silken fetters."   This phrase also appears in Akenside's *Pleasures of the Imagination,* in the line "The silken fetters of delicious ease" (Book II, l. 562), but not in Shakespeare, Milton, Pope, or the King James Bible.

21: "There in one view we grasp the mighty whole."   In Book IX of *The Complaint or Night Thoughts,* Edward Young writes of the overwhelming effect of God's creation on the heart even of the undevout; for "matter's grandeur" provokes him to "grasp creation with a single thought." (From *The Poetical Works of Edward Young* [Westport, Conn.: Greenwood Press, 1970], Vol. I, p. 284). Succeeding lines from the same passage parallel additional movement of the mind in Wheatley's poem:

> And if man hears obedient, soon he'll soar
> Superior heights, and on his purple wing,
> His purple wing bedropp'd with eyes of gold,
> Rising, where thought is now denied to rise,
> Look down triumphant on these dazzling spheres.

27: "Fair Flora."   Roman goddess of the spring and of flowers.

29: "Sylvanus."   Roman god presiding over forest glades and plowed fields.

43: "Tithon's bed."   This shortened form of Tithonus identifies the once mortal lover of Aurora.

To Captain H——d, of the 65th Regiment

Robinson has concluded that "Captain H————d" was Captain John Hanfield, attached to the British regiment enlisted from the latter part of 1769 to quell the growing anti-British sentiment expressed by Boston patriots (p. 273). Whether or not Wheatley omitted this poem from her 1772 proposal for a volume to be published in Boston because of a desire not to offend American patriots, as Robinson goes on to speculate, is probably not crucial to a reading of the poem. As a political piece, it is relatively innocuous. The poem does reveal Wheatley's persistent concern to identify and to record the qualities of heroic behavior.

To the Right Honourable William, Earl of Dartmouth

Written 1772; published 1773.

William Legge (1731–1801) was Second Earl of Dartmouth, appointed secretary of state for the American colonies and president of the Board of Trade and Foreign Plantations. He remained in these offices until November 1775. Dartmouth was sympathetic with the Methodist movement in England and was a friend to the Countess of Huntingdon. Wheatley, therefore, had some reason to be jubilant upon his appointment, for she thought he would also be a friend to the colonial quest for less restrictions from the crown. For another version of this poem, see "Variant Poems and Letters," below. For more information on Dartmouth, see the *DNB*.

40: "heav'ns refulgent fane." This phrase may be paraphrased as "shimmering temple of heaven."

Ode to Neptune

While Mason (p. 35) concludes this essentially Horatian ode refers to a voyage undertaken by Susanna Wheatley, the poet's mistress, Robinson (p. 273) maintains that Mrs. Wheatley never sailed to London (certainly not in 1772 or 1773), but rather the poem appears to be dedicated to a Mrs. Susanna Wright, an artist celebrated for her work in wax. At any rate, this poem shows that Wheatley could experiment with other poetic forms besides heroic couplets, as she had done in the blank-verse poems "On Virtue" and "To the University of Cambridge, in New-England." The poem is arranged in three stanzas; the meter of the first four lines of each is iambic tetrameter; all three stanzas conclude with an iambic pentameter couplet. The rhyme scheme of the first two stanzas is aabbcc; the third stanza varies this pattern as ababcc.

2: "Ae'lus."   Aeolus, god of the winds.

To a Lady on Her Remarkable Preservation in an Hurricane

5: "Boreas."   The North Wind.

6: "Nereids."   These mythological nymphs were daughters of Nereus, who was, according to Homer, the "Old Man" of the sea.

To a Lady and Her Children, on the Death of Her Son and Their Brother

Written c. 1772; published 1773.

In the proposals of 1772, Wheatley lists this title as "To Mrs. Boylston and Children on the Death of Her Son and Their Brother."

To a Gentleman and Lady on the Death of the Lady's Brother and Sister, and a Child of the Name Avis, Aged One Year

Written c. 1772; published 1773.

In the 1772 proposals, Wheatley lists this title as "To *James Sullivan*, Esq; and Lady on the Death of Her Brother and Sister, and a Child *Avis*, Aged 12 Months."

5: "the offspring of six thousand years."   At least for the duration of this poem, Wheatley here subscribes to the dating for the earth's creation espoused by James Ussher, archbishop of Armagh (1581–1656), who calculated from literal biblical data that God had created the earth in 4004 B.C., or some six thousand years before 1772.

7–12.   These lines present a description of death's domain which is distinctly chthonic in nature (i.e., similar to the ancient Greek understanding of the underworld). Wheatley describes the afterlife in such chthonic terms in several of her elegies.

On the Death of Dr. Samuel Marshall. 1771.

Written 1771; published 1771.

For another version, see "Variant Poems and Letters," below. As in the preceding elegy, the chthonic again plays a dominant role. One could argue convincingly that this poem is thoroughly pagan. Dr. Marshall, who was a relative of Susanna Wheatley, had probably attended the Wheatley family—hence the "we" of ll. 17 and 25. For more information about Marshall, see Sibley and Shipton.

13: "on Tyler's soul." Lucy Tyler, the physician's wife.

19: "our Aesculapius." Aesculapius (Latin) or Asclepius (Greek) was the Greek god of medicine who was, according to some accounts, a son of the god of healing, Apollo.

To a Gentleman on His Voyage to Great-Britain for the Recovery of His Health

Written c. 1767; published 1773.

According to Mason (p. 41), "this poem is addressed to Joseph Rotch, a brother of William Rotch, Sr., both members of the prominent merchant family of the same name of New Bedford and Nantucket." Wheatley's wish for his recovery was not granted, however; young Rotch died shortly after reaching his destination, reportedly in 1767. As one of her earliest poems, therefore, this work is of particular interest because of its proclamation of "higher motives and a nobler flame" (l. 4), apparently higher and nobler than those motives associated with the pastoral tradition, which she rejects in the poem's first two lines. The poet's objective, then, appears to reside in a concern to express the "motives" of the epic or of heroic verse.

1: "gay Elysian scenes." Those scenes associated with Elysium, which, according to Homer, was a beautiful meadowlike paradise, a retreat for deceased heroes, located in later times in the underworld.

To the Rev. Dr. Thomas Amory
on Reading His Sermons . . .

Written 1772; published 1773.

According to Robinson (p. 273–74), Thomas Amory's *Daily Devotions Assisted and Recommended in Four Sermons,* 2d ed. (London, 1770; reprint Boston, 1772), was a gift to Wheatley from the Reverend Charles Chauncy (1705–1787), one of Boston's most distinguished clergy and a signer of the 1773 volume's letter of attestation to the authenticity of Wheatley's authorship. The drawing out of the value of sermons had been pursued by another woman poet of colonial Boston only the year before. In 1771, Jane Dunlap's *Poems Upon Several Sermons Preached by the Rev'd and Renowned George Whitefield While in Boston* appeared, in which Dunlap makes mention of Wheatley's elegy on Whitefield (on p. 4 she cites "a young Afric damsel's virgin tongue").

An Hymn to Humanity. To S.P.G. Esq.

Mason (p. 45) speculates that "S.P.G." may be Samuel P. Gardner, whose name suggests his renown for his elaborate garden.

15–17. These lines appear to be a thinly veiled plea for tolerance. Wheatley dramatically places within God's own voice the commission to his Son-sun to "Each human heart inspire:/ To act in bounties unconfin'd [by prejudice, e.g.]/ Enlarge the close contracted [again, by prejudice] mind."

To the Honourable T.H. Esq;
on the Death of His Daughter

For another version of this poem, see "Variant Poems and Letters," below. "T.H." is Thomas Hubbard (1702–1773), a prominent merchant of Boston, who also served as Harvard's treasurer for some twenty years. Hubbard lived long enough to sign Wheatley's attestation letter. The deceased of this elegy is Thankfull Hubbard Leonard, to whom the poet had earlier addressed an elegy, "To Mrs. Leonard on the Death of Her Husband." See "To a Lady on the Death of Her Husband" in *Poems* and another version in "Variant Poems and Letters," below.

Niobe in Distress for Her Children Slain by Apollo, from Ovid's *Metamorphoses*, Book VI. And from a View of the Painting of Mr. Richard Wilson

Title. Wheatley takes the story of Niobe from ll. 148–312 of the sixth book of Ovid's *Metamorphoses*. She seldom departs from Ovid's version, but she does frequently interpolate passages into her translation-adaptation (e.g., her ten-line invocation to the Muse and her four-line speech [ll. 165–68] made by Niobe, an indignant response, still haughty after having lost several of her fourteen children to Apollo's "feather'd vengeance"). The Welsh painter Richard Wilson (1714–1782) is most famous for his landscape paintings influenced by the "classical" landscapes of Gaspard Poussin and Claude Lorrain. The Victorian master of prose and critic of art John Ruskin has written in *Modern Painters* that with Wilson's name "the history of sincere landscape art founded on a meditative love of nature begins in England"—and, of course, it reaches its zenith in the rural landscapes of John Constable and in the magnificent romantic-impressionistic seascapes of Joseph Turner. It is known that Wilson painted at least three different renditions of Ovid's Niobe episode. Robinson says that Wilson "painted several landscapes for Lord Dartmouth and rendered his 'Niobe' three times" (p. 274). Since it is known that Wheatley visited Lord Dartmouth during her sojourn to England in the summer before publication of her 1773 *Poems,* she may have viewed all three of Wilson's Niobes while visiting Dartmouth. Yet I can find no record of Dartmouth's having owned any of the Niobe renditions. Rather, according to W. G. Constable in *Richard Wilson* (London: Routledge & Kegan Paul, 1953), the three paintings are, first, the "Destruction of Niobe's Children," owned before 1792 by Sir George Beaumont and destroyed by enemy action during World War II, which did not contain the figure of Niobe; second, the "Destruction of Niobe's Children," owned originally by the Earl of Ellesmere and containing the figure of Niobe; and, third, "A Large Landskip with the Story of Niobe," acquired shortly after exhibit in 1760 by William Augustus, Duke of Cumberland. While Constable (W. G., not John) lists many Wilsons among paintings owned by the earls of Dartmouth, none is a version of the Niobe episode. The Cumberland picture, which has now disappeared, was engraved by William Woollett in 1761 and published by Boydell. As late as 1779, Boydell's catalog describes this engraving "as from the collection of the late Duke of Cumberland" (W. G. Constable, p. 161). Among the three paintings named above, only the Cumberland Niobe pictures all of the following: Niobe surrounded by her dying or expired children, Apollo shadowed by his sister Phoebe (or Diana), and most significantly only this Apollo holding a clearly visible bow in one hand while drawing taut the bow string poised with arrow in the other. The other paintings do contain Apollo and Phoebe, but their instruments of vengeance are not so clearly visible. Based on the poem's fine line describing Apollo ready to loose another arrow—"The feather'd vengeance quiv'ring in his hands" (l. 108)— I submit that the Wilson Wheatley has in mind is either the Cumberland Niobe or the Woollett engraving based on the Cumberland version. Another source for this line (celebrated by the Duyckinck brothers in their popular 1866 *Cyclopaedia of American Literature* as "not a translation of anything in Ovid, for that writer has neglected so striking a position for his Deity" [I, 368]—though, of course, Wilson has given Apollo exactly this position in the Cumberland Niobe) may have come to Wheatley's attention from her reading of sermons. In Jonathan Edwards's famous "Sinners in the Hands of an Angry God," the minister of the Great Awakening speaks of "the floods of God's vengeance" made manifest in the following vivid description: "The bow of God's wrath is bent, and the arrow made ready on the string, and justice bends the arrow at your heart and strains the bow" (*Anthology of American Literature*, 2d ed., gen. ed. George McMichael [New York: Macmillan, 1980], Vol. I, p. 241). For details taken from W. G. Constable's *Richard Wilson*, see pp. 70–75, 86–87, and 160–63; and see plates 19a, 19b, 20a, 20b, 21a, and 21b. The Dartmouth paintings by Wilson are indicated on pp. 282–83. See also the comprehensive discussion of Wilson's contribution to English painting in William Gaunt's *A Concise His-*

tory of English Painting (New York: Frederick A. Praeger, 1964), pp. 83–88.

11: "Maeonia."   Lydia, in Asia Minor.

14: "Tantalus."   He is a son of Zeus, hence Niobe could claim a sort of marginal deity. But Tantalus was consigned to punishment in Tartarus (place of torture in the underworld) for attempting to deceive the gods into eating his own son (as roasted flesh), brother of Niobe. So the strain of haughtiness was shared between father and daughter.

15: "Dodonean Jove."   Jove, or Jupiter in Latin and Zeus in Greek, was the king of the gods. Dodona was the ancient seat of Zeus's oracle and was the greatest early oracle of all, later eclipsed by the oracle at Delphi.

37: "Manto."   Daughter of Tiresias; both were renowned for their abilities to prophesy.

43: "great Latona's will."   Leto, or Latona, was daughter of the Titan Coeus (l. 67) and the moon goddess, Phoebe, according to older accounts. More recently, she becomes Zeus's mistress, by whom she gave birth to Apollo the sun and Artemis (Phoebe) the moon. She was often worshiped by the ancients in conjunction with her better-known twins.

58: "Like heav'nly Venus."   Goddess of love and beauty. Here Wheatley interpolates or adds to Ovid, who does not mention Venus in his Niobe episode. Significantly, Niobe is only "Like" the goddess Venus, not herself a goddess.

71: "Cadmus palace."   Cadmus, mythological founder of Thebes, built for the city the stronghold Cadmes before he went on to carry out other deeds in other lands.

78: "pitying Delos."   This figure of speech constitutes a vivid example of metonymy, wherein the poet has substituted the name of a residence, in this case the central island of the group Cyclades located in the eastern Mediterranean Sea, which was, as birthplace to Apollo and Artemis (or Diana, or Phoebe), especially sacred to Artemis, to represent her. Ovid also uses this figure.

90: "Cynthus' summit."   Mount Cynthus was located on the

isle of Delos and was also closely associated with Artemis, or Phoebe, the goddess of the moon.

166: "the Delian god." Here, in naming the masculine "god," Wheatley refers to Apollo, who has, just a few lines earlier, mortally wounded Ilioneus (l. 159).

213–24. Robinson (p. 274) asserts that these lines, "the work of another Hand," were "probably the work of Mary Wheatley, Phillis' tutor in English and Latin." While Mary Wheatley, whose twin was Nathaniel, most probably did assist Wheatley, initially, with her learning of English, "to read any, the most difficult Parts" of the Bible, it is less likely that Mary served as the poet's "tutor in . . . Latin." I find no evidence that Mary Wheatley knew Latin well enough to assist Wheatley with a translation of anything in Ovid, or even that Mary ever studied Latin herself. As for Nathaniel Wheatley, it is most probable that, given the wealth and status of the Wheatley family, he attended the Boston Latin School through the sixth form, in which case he would have parsed Vergil (entire), would have memorized major portions of the *Aeneid*, and would have even learned some Greek (I have not been able to establish that he ever matriculated with Harvard College). If he did not attend the Boston Latin School or some other comparable grammar school, he may well have enjoyed the benefit of a private tutor, in which case the poet may have been allowed some instruction. Wheatley may have received some assistance with her Latin studies from any one or all of her literary and/or spiritual mentors—Joseph Sewall, Samuel Cooper, and Mather Byles—all of whom were Harvard graduates. For information regarding educational opportunities in colonial Boston, see Kenneth B. Murdock's still useful "The Teaching of Latin and Greek at the Boston Latin School in 1712," *Publications of the Colonial Society of Massachusetts* 27 (March 1927): 21–29; and Lawrence A. Cremin's substantial (if more recent) *American Education: The Colonial Experience, 1607–1783* (New York: Harper and Row, 1970). The most comprehensive examination of educational opportunities for slaves in colonial New England remains Lorenzo Johnston Greene, *The Negro in Colonial New England* (New York: Columbia University Press, 1942), pp. 237–45.

To S.M. a Young African Painter, on Seeing His Works

Both Mason (p. 54) and Robinson (pp. 274–75) identify "S.M." as Scipio Moorhead, black slave of the Reverend John Moorhead, on whose death Wheatley wrote an elegy addressed to Moorhead's daughter Mary (see "Extant Poems Not Included in 1773 *Poems*," below). Robinson also suggests that the black painter may have executed the engraving of Wheatley's portrait for the 1773 *Poems* frontispiece.

18: "Celestial Salem."   This phrase constitutes an idealization of Jerusalem as the heavenly city, a common practice of the time.

29: "Damon's tender sighs."   The poem may be alluding to the immortalized friendship of Damon and Pythias (actually Phintias in history—see *The Oxford Classical Dictionary*, 2d ed., ed. N. G. L. Hammond and H. H. Scullard [London: Oxford University Press, 1970], p. 311). Given Wheatley's frequent references to the tradition of the classical pastoral, however, it is probably more likely (since the subject of friendship seems not to be the point of emphasis here—though Wheatley does often treat this subject) that the poet here makes reference to the pastoral's Damon as idealized rustic and singer of love themes (see, e.g., Vergil's eighth "Eclogue").

To His Honour the Lieutenant-Governor, on the Death of His Lady. March 24, 1773.

The "Lieutenant-Governor" named in this title was Andrew Oliver (1731–1799), one of the signers of the letter of attestation.

9: "the refulgent car."   For a close parallel, observe the following passage from Akenside's *Pleasures of the Imagination* ". . . as Venus, when she stood/ Effulgent on the pearly car" (Book I, ll. 329–30).

24: "While heav'n's high concave."   In the *Sacred Theory of the Earth*, Burnet speaks of "the great concave of the Heavens" (p. 109) and identifies such appearances of the infinite God as "too big for our comprehension[;] they fill and over-bear the mind with their Excess, and cast it into a pleasing kind of stupor and admiration" (p. 110). Here Burnet essentially defines the feeling of the sublime, one of the major aesthetic categories with which artists of the eighteenth century were preoccupied and one with which Wheatley was particularly concerned. See the second half of the essay, "Phillis Wheatley's Struggle for Freedom in Her Poetry and Letters," above, for a discussion of how the poet expressed her great concern to depict this aesthetic category.

A Farewel to America. To Mrs. S.W.

For two variant versions of this poem, see "Variant Poems and Letters," below.

S.W. is surely "Susanna" Wheatley, mistress of the poet. Note Wheatley's use here of ballad stanza (alternating lines of iambic tetrameter and trimeter rhyming abcb).

30: "Hebe's mantle." As Greek goddess of eternal youth, Hebe may have represented to Wheatley the hope of health restored; one of her avowed reasons for voyaging to England was in the interest of restoring her health. According to some ancient traditions, Hebe was identified as freeing men from bondage and chains, her rites being observed by celebrations of unrestraint. Wheatley's intrinsic interest in these attributes of Hebe needs little comment.

A Rebus, by I.B.

Both Mason (p. 59) and Robinson (p. 275) suggest that "I.B." is James Bowdoin, founder of Bowdoin College, governor of Massachusetts (1785–1789), founder of the American Academy of Arts and Sciences, and a signer of the letter of attestation authenticating Wheatley's authorship of her 1773 *Poems*. For additional information regarding this significant early American, see the *DAB*, Sibley and Shipton, and *AWB 1800*. Wheatley included this poem, of course, because it gave her the opportunity to solve this riddle (or rebus) in the following, final poem of the volume.

An Answer to the Rebus, by the Author of These Poems

Wheatley's responses to the rebus include *"Quail"* (of l. 3), *"Unicorn"* (l. 6), *"Emerald"* (l. 7), *"Boston's"* (l. 9), *"Euphorbus"* (l. 13), and "*C———m,*" for William Pitt, First Earl of Chatham (1708–1778) who often spoke sympathetically in Parliament regarding the colonies. Of course, the first letters of each of the responses spell "*Quebec*" (of l. 17), the summary "Answer to the Rebus."

13:"*Euphorbus of the Dardan line.*"   After Patroclus persuades Achilles to allow him to wear Achilles' armor into the battle between the Greeks and the Trojans (Book XVI of the *Iliad;* see also Wheatley's affective rendering of this scene in ll. 17–20 of "To Maecenas"), Patroclus succeeds for a time in routing the Trojans. With the help of Apollo, however, who "taps" Patroclus, causing Achilles' armor to fall away from Patroclus's body, Patroclus is wounded by the Dardanian Euphorbus, but it is Hector who subsequently deals the death blow, not Euphorbus.

EXTANT POEMS NOT INCLUDED IN THE 1773 *POEMS*

Atheism

This text is based on Kuncio. See "Variant Poems and Letters," below, for two other versions.

11: "preterperfect."   More than perfect.

44: "Minerva."   Roman goddess of invention, meditation, and the intellect, who eventually became identified with the Greek goddess Pallas Athene, whose attributes were comparable.

45: "Pluto."   Roman god of the underworld.

55: "Cynthia."   A synonym for Diana or Phoebe, goddess of the moon.

An Address to the Deist

This text is based on that of Robinson (pp. 133–34). I suspect the other version in Phil Lapsansky's "*Deism*—An Unpublished Poem by Phillis Wheatley," *NEQ* 50, no. 3 (September 1977): 517–20, is, though perhaps an earlier version, not the author's preferred, partially corrected version given here.

25: "Who trod the wine-press of Jehovah's wrath?"

Wheatley has in mind here Isaiah 63: 1–81 (or, more specifically, verse 3). Note that the 1773 volume would later contain a thirty-line poem treating this passage—"Isaiah LXIII. 1–8."

On Messrs. Hussey and Coffin

This text is based on that of Carl Bridenbaugh given in "The Earliest Published Poem of Phillis Wheatley," *NEQ* 42, no. 4 (December 1969): 583–84. Prefacing the poem, Bridenbaugh also includes the following matter, which accompanied its printing:

> [*Newport Mercury*, December 21, 1767]
> To the PRINTER.
>
> *Please to insert the following Lines, composed by a Negro Girl (belonging to one Mr. Wheatley of Boston) on the following Occasion, viz. Messrs Hussey and Coffin, as undermentioned, belonging to Nantucket, being bound from thence to Boston, narrowly escaped being cast away on Cape Cod, in one of the late Storms; upon their Arrival, being at Mr. Wheatley's, and, while at Dinner, told of their narrow Escape, this Negro Girl at the same Time 'tending Table, heard the Relation, from which she composed the following Verses.*

America

This text is taken from Kuncio, p. 293.

To the Honble. Commodore Hood on His Pardoning a Deserter

This text is based on Robinson, p. 138. If Robinson is correct that this poem derives from the events given in a notice in the *London Gentleman's Magazine and Historical Chronicle* 39 (February 1769): 105—namely the pardoning of one of two sailors under Hood's command, one of whom was to be flogged and the other to be executed (it is this later sailor who was pardoned)—then, since the date of these actions is given as "Dec. 2," this poem must have preceded composition of "On Friendship" (July 15, 1769). Hence the order given here. The commodore was Samuel Hood (1724–1816), who was commander of the North American station from 1767 to 1770; eventually he was made a lord of the admiralty (1788–1793) and finally Viscount Hood and governor of Greenwich (1796). See the *DNB*.

On Friendship

This text is taken from Robinson's *Early Black American Poets* (Dubuque, Iowa: William C. Brown, 1969), pp. 111–12.

1: "Amicitia." The poet's use of the Latin noun for friendship indicates two patterns which were quickly beginning to characterize her works: her high regard for the institution of friendship (not feigned or polite, but *real* friendship, the kind that does not see color!) and her enthusiasm for classicism.

4: "Amor." Latin for "love." It is worthy of note that Burnet in *The Sacred Theory of the Earth* observes, "the Ancient Philosophers, or at least the best of them, to give them their due, always brought Mens [i.e., the notion of the creative principle] or *Amor*, as a Supernatural principle to unite and consociate the parts of the Chaos" (p. 64). In l. 6 of this same poem, Wheatley speaks of "Mental imaginations" as bringing joy to the process of meditation. The poet's world of slavery versus British tyranny masked as freedom must surely have struck her as chaotic. In other words, the temper of mind here both of Wheatley and of Burnet appears to move along parallel planes.

On the Death of Mr. Snider Murder'd by Richardson

This poem numbers among those listed in Wheatley's 1772 Boston proposal for a volume; her decision to drop it from the 1773 London volume was doubtless a political one. For the identification of the conditions which precipitated the actions described here, see the portion of the essay "Phillis Wheatley's Struggle for Freedom in Her Poetry and Prose," above, devoted to her political poems. The text for this poem derives from Kuncio, p. 297.

4: "Achilles." The Greek hero of Homer's immortal epic, the *Iliad*. Note the poet's celebration of heroic acts in epic terms both here and elsewhere, a practice she repeats frequently.

An Elegy to Miss Mary Moorhead, on the Death of Her Father, the Rev. Mr. John Moorhead

This text is based on that given by Mason (pp. 79–81). At the end of the broadside printing of this elegy appeared the following information: "Printed from the Original Manuscript, and Sold by WILLIAM M'ALPINE, at his shop in *Marlborough-Street*, 1773." John Moorhead (1703–1773), pastor of the Scotch Presbyterian Church (from 1730 throughout his adult life) located on Long Lane (today Boston's Federal Street), was the head of the Moorhead family to whom Wheatley addressed several poems, including "To S.M. a Young *African* Painter," that is, Scipio Moorhead, black servant to the Moorheads. It is worth noting that Sarah Parsons Moorhead, Mary's mother, was herself a published poet (see Pattie Cowell, *Women Poets in Pre-Revolutionary America: 1650–1775* [Troy, N.Y.: Whitston, 1981], pp. 269–71, 349, and 366; see also her critical assessment in *AWB 1800*); hence Wheatley's affinity for this family is not difficult to determine.

5: "Shade." Reference to departed spirits as shades probably derives from Wheatley's recurrently manifested interest in the chthonic, or the ancient Greek attitudes and depictions of the underworld as realm of the afterlife.

41: "Tremendous Doom!" In this phrase, "Doom" carries its now somewhat archaic meaning of judgment. To be sure, the poet intends with this phrase to underscore "the final Judgment" of two lines above.

42: "Tophet." The poet probably has in mind the Tophet of Isaiah 30:33—burning "like a stream of brimstone"; according to G. A. Barrois, the word "Tophet" (or Topheth), which derives from Aramaic, was given the vowels of *bōsheth* by the Masoretes, which means in Hebrew "shameful thing," "on account of the shocking associations of the place" (from *The Interpreter's Dictionary of the Bible,* gen. ed. George A. Buttrick, vol. IV [Nashville: Abingdon, 1962], p. 673). The language throughout this passage (ll. 31–56) resembles that of Burnet in a chapter from *The Sacred Theory of the Earth* entitled "An Imperfect Description of the Coming of Our Saviour, and of the World on Fire" (pp. 299–306); Burnet speaks of "Earth-quakes [which] are the Sons of Fire [and which] . . . will tear the body and bowels of the Earth" (p. 305). He continues by calling up various images of smoke and fire, all of which constitute "a lively representation of *Hell* itself. For, Fire and darkness are the two chief things by which that state, or that place, uses *[sic]* to be describ'd: and they are both here mingled together: with all other ingredients that make that Tophet that is prepar'd of old" (p. 305). Wheatley describes what the mind of the sinner sees in Hell in similar language: "Trembling he sees the horrid Gulf appear,/ Creation quakes, and no Deliverer near" (ll. 45–46).

51–52: "He [Moorhead] points the trembling Mountain, and the Tree,/ Which bent beneath th' incarnate Deity." Earlier in the same chapter on "the World on Fire," amidst all the earthquakes, Burnet muses, "Then look down upon the Earth, and see a naked Body hanging upon a cursed Tree in *Golgotha*" (p. 303). Both Wheatley and Burnet are describing in quite similar language the crucifixion in the middle of their respective depictions of Judgment Day.

58: "Like MOSES' Serpent in the Desert wild." The reference here is to the "Brazen Serpent" shaped by Moses (Numbers 21:8–9) while the Hebrews wandered in the wilderness, this particular case occurring as a consequence of many Hebrews having been bitten by fiery snakes. In this instance, this otherwise symbol of evil and destruction represents healing properties (cf. the caduceus of Mercury, symbol of physicians even today) and brings about the healing of those bitten.

66: "To Him whose Spirit had inspir'd his Lays." Apparently, Moorhead was himself at least a part-time poet.

To a Gentleman of the Navy

This poem by Wheatley appeared first in the "Poetical Essays" section (a commonly occurring, even expected magazine feature in those
days of superior literacy) of the *Royal American Magazine* 1 (December 1774): 473–74, with the following headnote:

> *By particular request we insert the following Poem addressed, by*
> *Philis, (a young* Affrican, *of surprising genius) to a gentleman*
> *of the navy, with his reply.*
>
> *By this single instance may be seen, the importance of educa-*
> *tion.—Uncultivated nature is much the same in every part of*
> *the globe. It is probable* Europe *and* Affrica *would be alike*
> *savage or polite in the same circumstances; though, it may be*
> *questioned, whether men who have no* artificial *wants, are ca-*
> *pable of becoming so ferocious as those, who, by faring* sump-
> *tuously every day, are reduced to a habit of thinking it necessary*
> *to* their *happiness, to plunder the whole human race.*

This poem was followed in the same issue by the next poem printed
in this edition, this one not by Wheatley but by an admirer who
was more than likely the "Rockfort" of l. 3 of this poem. The next
issue (January 1775) of the *Royal American* printed Wheatley's re-
joinder. I include the poem "The Answer" in the present volume
simply because Wheatley's "Reply to the Answer" does not make
sense without the middle poem in this sequence of three. Both Mason (p. 82) and Robinson (p. 282) identify "Greaves" (l. 3) as
member of a family of seafarers whose name was Graves. "Rockfort" has not been identified. But Robinson provocatively submits
that "both Rockfort and Graves may have been billeted in John
Wheatley's King Street mansion by virtue of the expansion of the
1765 British Quartering Act."

11: "Achaian." The shore of Greece; the Greeks sought to
reclaim Helen, wife of Menelaus, king of Sparta, from Paris, who,
while enjoying the hospitality of Menelaus, had abducted her. This

precipitated the event which provoked the Trojan War, or Greece's War with Illion (l. 10) or Troy.

19: "Albion." Deriving from the Celtic root *alb-*, meaning "high," this word has come to represent, in a literary sense, all of Britain.

33: "Cerulean." This word derives from Latin *caeruleus*, meaning "dark blue" or "azure," which is itself finally derived from Latin *caelum* for "sky"—hence the application here, sky-blue, probably a reference to the color of those naval officers' uniforms.

The Answer [By the Gentleman of the Navy]

33: "great Sir Isaac." Sir Isaac Newton, British scientist, philosopher, and mathematician, whose most noted work included the invention of differential calculus, theories of color, treatises on astronomy, and confirmation of universal gravitation (based on the limited knowledge of his day of astrophysics and higher math).

42: "The pristine state of paradise." This reference to the condition of paradise describes, in terms of Judeo-Christian mythology, Adam's perception of it before his loss of that realm; hence the reference is actually to *Paradise Lost* by John Milton ("nature's bard" of l. 41).

Phillis's Reply to the Answer

16: "At British Homer's and Sir Isaac's feet." At the feet of Milton and Newton.

22: "pleasing Gambia on my soul returns." Mason (p. 87) cautions that the poet's reference here to Gambia as her native land "may be a poetic pose." Robinson (p. 286), however, speculates that Wheatley could well have consulted Timothy Fitch, wealthy slave merchant of Boston and owner of the vessel which "brought [the poet] from Africa to America," or she may have sought information from Captain Peter Gwin, commander of Fitch's *Phillis*, in both instances to discover descriptions of her homeland. I submit that a young girl of seven or eight with Wheatley's intelligence would hardly require information from her captors regarding her home-land. Robinson goes on to observe that "Fitch repeatedly ordered Gwin to get slaves from the coasts of Senegal and Gambia." See the tract published by a close relation of Boston's Fitch family for *The Anti-Slavery Record* 11, no. 5 (May 1836): 7–8, and reproduced by Robinson (pp. 458–59); here is told an anecdote about the poet's visit (by invitation) to Timothy Fitch's wife, Eunice Brown Fitch (1731–1799), and her daughters for the purpose of describing her summer journey to London. Quite significantly, "the young ladies became delighted with Phillis . . . and found that with all their wealth and advantages she knew more than they did" (p. 459). Robinson concludes his discussion of the poet's reference to Gambia with this pertinent observation: "Whether she is being poetically extravagant or defensive or indeed autobiographical in this poem, Phillis is the first black American poet to rhapsodize about black Africa" (p. 286). For a detailed investigation of Wheatley's connections to her homeland, see the chapter "African Origins" in my forthcoming *Phillis Wheatley's Poetics of Liberation*.

To His Excellency General Washington

Wheatley's letter to George Washington appears in the section on her prose under the entry of October 26, 1775. Washington's reply to her appears below:

> Miss Phillis, Your favor of the 26th of October did not reach my hands, till the middle of December. Time enough, you will say, to have given an answer ere this. Granted. But a variety of important occurrences, continually interposing to distract the mind and withdraw the attention, I hope will apologize for the delay, and plead my excuse for the seeming but not real neglect. I thank you most sincerely for your polite notice of me, in the elegant lines you enclosed; and however undeserving I may be of such encomium and panegyric, the style and manner exhibit a striking proof of your poetical talents; in honor of which, and as a tribute justly due

to you, I would have published the poem, had I not been apprehensive, that, while I only meant to give the world this new instance of your genius, I might have incurred the imputation of vanity. This, and nothing else, determined me not to give it place in the public prints.

If you should ever come to Cambridge, or near headquarters, I shall be happy to see a person so favored by the Muses, and to whom nature has been so liberal and beneficent in her dispensations. I am, with great respect, your obedient humble servant.

Washington passed along the poet's paean to a former secretary, Colonel Joseph Reed, with a missive dated February 10, 1776, from Cambridge; the matter pertaining to Wheatley is as follows:

I recollect nothing else worth giving you the trouble of, unless you can be amused by reading a letter and poem addressed to me by Miss Phillis Wheatley. In searching over a parcel of papers the other day, in order to destroy such as were useless, I brought it to light again. At first, with a view of doing justice to her poetical genius, I had a great mind to publish the poem; but not knowing whether it might not be considered rather as a mark of my own vanity, than a compliment to her, I laid it aside, till I came across it again in the manner just mentioned.

These two selections from Washington's letters may be found in *The Writings of George Washington*, ed. Jared Sparks (Boston: Russell, Odiorne, and Metcalf, 1834), Vol. III, pp. 297–98, 288. Reed seems to have forwarded Wheatley's letter and poem to John Dixon and William Hunter, editors of the *Virginia Gazette*, where both were published on March 20, 1776—all apparently without Washington's permission. Thomas Paine reprinted the poem and letter in *The Pennsylvania Magazine* or *American Monthly Museum* for the April 1776 number. In the concluding moments of the second, two-hour segment of a recent television biography of Washington (CBS's three-part miniseries, "George Washington," which first aired on the evenings of April 8, 10, and 11, 1984), John Adams (Hal Holbrook) quoted to Washington (Barry Bostwick) the final couplet of a poem—"A crown, a mansion, and a throne that shine,/ With gold unfading WASHINGTON! be thine"—curiously without attribution. This miniseries was avowedly based on James T. Flexner's four-volume biography, *George Washington* (Boston: Little, Brown, 1969–72). Flexner mentions Wheatley's correspondence with the general and quotes the two lines given above, with attribution. Perhaps Flexner's condescending attitude toward the author of these lines suggested to producers of the miniseries that to acknowledge Wheatley's authorship would serve a bootless purpose. About Washington's concern with Wheatley and her poem to him, Flexner concludes: "Washington would have liked to give to the press, 'as a compliment' to the poetess, an ode to him by the colored versifier Phillis Wheatley, but he decided it was wiser to suppress the effusion" (Vol. III, p. 63). For Washington's attitude toward slavery in general, Flexner's discussion in the fourth volume of the biography (pp. 112–25) is instructive, though certainly not definitive.

   2: "Columbia's scenes of glorious toils."   The scenes of the recent American victories over Great Britain. For the most current discussion of Wheatley's use of the poetic "Columbia" to represent America, see Thomas J. Steele, "The Figure of Columbia: Phillis Wheatley Plus George Washington," *NEQ* 54, no. 2 (June 1981): 264–66. Steele offers the comprehensive observation that "The name 'Columbia' was used as early as 1761 to designate English America as opposed to 'Britannia,' but earlier uses of the word are not fully developed personifications" (p. 264).

   30: "Gallic powers."   Here the poet refers to the French military and economic support of the American patriots during the Revolutionary War.

On the Capture of General Lee

Written late 1776; published 1863.

The first printing of this poem occurred in the October 1863 issue of the *Proceedings of the Massachusetts Historical Society* 7 (1863–64): 165–67. Preceding the body of the poem are the following introductory lines by Wheatley:

> The following thoughts on his Excellency Major General Lee being betray'd into the hands of the Enemy by the treachery of a pretended Friend: To the Honourable James Bowdoin Esqr. are most respectfully Inscrib'd, By his most obedient and devoted humble servant,
>
> Phillis Wheatley

Much has been made of the fact that the subject of this poem, General Charles Lee, wanted to replace Washington as commander-in-chief. This fact, however, was unknown to Wheatley at the time she wrote this poem. It should finally be read, in any event, only on its own merits; note the poet's continued emphasis on the epic associations of American heroism in America's struggle against British tyranny.

On the Death of General Wooster

The text of this poem is based on that given by Mukhtar Ali Isani in " 'On the Death of General Wooster': An Unpublished Poem by Phillis Wheatley," *Modern Philology*, 77, no. 3 (February 1980), 306–9. The letter in which the poem was embedded is given in the section on Wheatley's prose, below.

To Mr. and Mrs. ———, on the Death of Their Infant Son

Written c. 1779; published 1784.

Although the printing of this poem (in *The Boston Magazine* for September 1784 on p. 488 in an editorial note describing Wheatley's final 1784 attempt to publish a second volume, where it is offered "as a Specimen of her Work," p. 462) and its relatively bleak tone concur with the cruel decline in her fortunes which resulted in her death on December 5, 1784, I submit, given her former practice of altering titles between the 1772 proposals and the 1773 *Poems,* that this poem is probably the same one she names in the 1779 proposals as "To P.N.S. & Lady on the death of their infant son." See the section on Wheatley's prose, below. Therefore, this poem could likely date from at least as early as 1779.

An Elegy Sacred to the Memory of . . . Dr. Samuel Cooper

This elegy was published as an eight-page pamphlet, the title page of which, following Dr. Samuel Cooper's name in the title, read:

Who departed this life December 29, 1783,
AETATIS 59.
BY PHILLIS PETERS.
BOSTON: Printed and Sold by E. Russell,
in Essex-Street, near Liberty-Pole,
M, DCC, LXXXIV.
To the CHURCH and CONGREGATION
assembling in Brattle-Street, the following
ELEGY,
Sacred to the MEMORY of their late
Reverend and worthy PASTOR, Dr.
SAMUEL COOPER, is, with
the greatest Sympathy, most respectfully
inscribed by their Obedient,
Humble Servant,
Phillis Peters

This pamphlet also included (on pp. 7–8) "Words for a Funeral Anthem" by William Billings, America's first full-time composer-musician. For more information concerning Wheatley's relationship to this early American musician and conductor of singing schools for young ladies, see the chapter "The Poet as Sound Technician" in my forthcoming *Phillis Wheatley's Poetics of Liberation;* in Billings's *New England Psalm-Singer* (1770), his first book-length publication, there appears a hymn entitled "Africa," perhaps composed with Wheatley in mind. See *The Complete Works of William Billings,* ed. Karl Kroeger (Charlottesville: University of Virginia Press, 1977), Vol. I, pp. 88–89. *William Billings of Boston: Eighteenth-Century Composer,* by David P. McKay and Richard Crawford (Princeton: Princeton University Press, 1975), is the standard biography. This same Samuel Cooper is the minister who baptized the poet on August 18, 1771; according to her own testimony in this elegy, Cooper also served as one of Wheatley's literary mentors (see ll. 43–44). The standard biography is Charles W. Akers' *The Divine Politician: Samuel Cooper and the American Revolution in Boston* (Boston: Northeastern University Press, 1982).

Liberty and Peace

In its first publication in 1784 as a four-page pamphlet, this poem's title was followed by this information: *"By Phillis Peters. Boston: Printed by WARDEN and RUSSELL, At Their Office in Marlborough-Street. M, DCC, LXXXIV."*

37: "Hibernia." The Latin and poetic name for Ireland.

An Elegy on Leaving ———

This text is taken from that given by Mukhtar Ali Isani in " 'An Elegy on Leaving ———': A New Poem by Phillis Wheatley," *AL* 58, no. 4 (December 1986): 609–13.

17: "Cynthio." Both Apollo and his twin, Artemis (or the moon), were born on Mount Cynthus on the isle of Delos. Ordinarily one would expect to find the feminine form of Cynthus, "Cynthia," which is used as a synonym for Artemis. It is clear in this case, however, that since the poet speaks in the preceding line of passing "in grateful solitude the day," she intends to make reference to Artemis's twin, Apollo, god of the sun—hence the less commonly occurring masculine spelling, "Cynthio."

PROSE

Letters will be identified by date.

October 25, 1770
(to the Countess of Huntingdon)

This text is based on that given in Jackson (p. 212).

November or December 1771 (to Abigail May?)

This text may be found in *The London Magazine: Or, Gentleman's Monthly Intelligencer* 41 (March 1772): 134–35 (in the "Poetical Essays" feature). The major object of communication here was, of course, Wheatley's poem "Recollection." Mason (p. 73) speculates that the "Madam" of the latter may be Abigail May, who joined the Old South Church of Boston during the same year in which Samuel Cooper baptized Wheatley (on August 18, 1771). Preceding both the letter and a poem (both by Wheatley) is an editorial introduction by a citizen known here only as "L."; the text is as follows:

To the Author of the
London Magazine

Boston, in New-England, Jan. 1, 1772

Sir,

As your Magazine is a proper repository for any thing valuable or curious, I hope you will excuse the communicating the following by one of your subscribers.

L.

There is in this town a young *Negro woman,* who left *her* country at ten years of age, and has been in *this* eight years. She is a compleat sempstress, an accomplished mistress of her pen, and discovers a most surprising genius. Some of her productions have seen the light, among which is a poem on the death of the Rev. Mr. George Whitefield.—The following was occasioned by her being in company with some young ladies of family, when one of them said she did not remember, among all the poetical pieces she had seen, ever to have met with a poem upon RECOLLECTION. The *African* (so let me call her, for so in fact she is) took the hint, went home to her master's, and soon sent what follows.

April 21, 1772 (to John Thornton)

The text is taken from Silverman, pp. 263–64. John Thornton (1720–1790) was a wealthy British merchant whose philanthropic activities included strong support of the first generation of British "Evangelicals" through contributing large sums toward the circulation of bibles and so on. He was a member of the circle which embraced George Whitefield, Samson Occom (with whom Wheatley also corresponded), and the Countess of Huntingdon. See the *DNB*.

The virgules (slashes) which appear in this letter and in the three other letters to Thornton are Silverman's way of distinguishing in the transcripts of the letters careted matter appearing above lines.

May 19, 1772 (to Obour or Abour Tanner)

This letter to Obour Tanner of Newport, Rhode Island, is taken from Deane, pp. 12–13.

July 19, 1772 (to Arbour Tanner)

This letter is from Deane, pp. 13–14.

October 10, 1772 [to the Earl of Dartmouth]

This letter's text derives from that of Mason, pp. 110–11. According to Robinson (p. 316), the letter was Addressed "To The Right Hon'ble The Earl of Dartmouth & & & pr. favour of Mr. Wooldridge." Thomas Wooldridge (fl. 1770–1780) was apparently a subordinate to the earl and kept him apprised of developments in the American colonies. Dartmouth is, of course, the same British figure who moved in the circle of the Countess of Huntingdon and whose monies helped to establish Dartmouth College in Hanover,

New Hampshire. The "Joyful occasion" of which Wheatley speaks refers to Dartmouth's appointment in August 1772 to the position of secretary of state for North America. This occasion was a happy one for many colonists who recalled the earl's recent assistance toward repeal of the despised Stamp Act. Wooldridge reported, along with observations regarding the earl's speculations toward the purchase of land in Florida, the following information concerning Wheatley, about whom the earl was apparently curious:

> While in Boston, I heard of a very extraordinary female slave, who had made some verses on our mutually dear deceased Friend; I visited her mistress, and found by conversing with the African, that she was no Impostor: I asked if she could write on any Subject; she said Yes; we had just heard of your Lordship's appointment; I gave her your name, which she was acquainted with. She immediately wrote a rough Copy of the inclosed Adress & Letter, which I promised to convey or deliver. I was astonish'd, and could hardly believe my own Eyes. I was present while she wrote and can attest that it is her own production; she shew'd me her Letter to Lady Huntingdon, which I daresay, Your Lordship has seen; I send you an account signed by her master of her Importation, Education &c. they are all wrote in her own hand. Pardon the account I have given you of this poor untotor'd slave, when, possibly, your precious time may be very ill bestowed in reading my scrawls . . .

In the phrase "the late unhappy Disturbances" in Wheatley's letter to the earl, she makes reference, of course, to such incidents of opposition to British tyranny as the Boston Massacre, about which the poet wrote "On the Affray in King-Street, on the Evening of the 5th of March [1770]." This poem is no longer extant, but see Robinson, p. 455, for what he maintains may be a twelve-line selection from this poem.

June 27, 1773 (to the Countess of Huntingdon)

This text is based on Jackson, pp. 214—15. The Richard Carey (1717—1790) named in this letter's first paragraph is one of those who signed the letter of attestation to Wheatley's authenticity as composer of the 1773 *Poems*. For correspondence between Carey (whose letter of introduction to the countess Wheatley took with her to London) and Selina Hastings, Countess of Huntingdon, see Robinson, p. 318.

July 17, 1773 (to the Countess of Huntingdon)

This text is taken from Jackson, p. 215. Note that both this and the preceding letter were written during Wheatley's six-week stay in London. The phrase "that Friend of Mental Felicity" is worthy of comment; it quite simply indicates a consistent pattern of mind which obtains throughout this black slave poet's work—that of discovering moments of true happiness, not in this world of bondage's vicissitudes but in the realm of the mind, in the world of the poet's imagination as she analyzes it in "On Imagination" (in the 1773 *Poems*).

October 18, 1773 (to David Wooster)

This text is taken from that given by Mukhtar Ali Isani in "Phillis Wheatley in London: An Unpublished Letter to David Wooster," *AL* 51, no. 2 (May 1979): 253—60. Isani provides a thorough discussion of the several dignitaries Wheatley names. But the letter is not merely important because of its catalog of cultural activities in which the poet engaged during her London visit (her schedule sounds exhausting); it is of particular interest because it narrows the moment of her manumission. We can say with certainty now that Wheatley had been given her freedom by mid-October 1773. Practically all the dignitaries she names may be found listed in the *DNB*. It is nonetheless evident, despite Wheatley's humility in providing the information, that the black poet was held in no little esteem by the elite of London's citizenry. The fact that Wheatley observes of

Thomas Gibbons (1720–1785) that he was a professor of rhetoric signals more than a casual intellectual connection between them. A dissenting minister and composer of hymns and devotional verse, he too had penned a poem on the death of George Whitefield, an epitaph in Latin. Granville Sharp (1735–1813), Wheatley's escort on tours of the Tower of London, the Horse Armoury, and so on, was an advocate of the cause of the American colonies, founded a British society for the abolition of slavery in 1787, and was instrumental in securing the outcome of the famous Somerset decision of 1772 which maintained that "as soon as any slave sets foot upon English territory he becomes free." The set of Pope's *Works*, each volume of which is signed by Wheatley (who bought it with the gift of five guineas from Dartmouth), is now held in the Rare Book Room of the library of the University of North Carolina at Charlotte. The folio edition of Milton's *Paradise Lost* is housed in Harvard's Houghton Library. The Schomburg Center for Research in Black Culture in The New York Public Library contains the edition of *Don Quixote* inscribed to Wheatley by the Earl of Dartmouth, as well as the second and third volumes of William Shenstone's *Complete Works in Verse and Prose*, 3d ed., 4 vols. (London, 1773), with the inscription "Mary Everleigh to Phillis Wheatley, Sept. 24, 1774"—these last two volumes obviously given after Wheatley's return to Boston. Shenstone (1714–1763), who attended Pembroke College, Oxford, while Samuel Johnson was there, was an author of elegies, odes, songs, ballads, and literary essays, all influenced by a penchant for the pastoral tradition of Vergil and by a reaction to symmetrical gardening; his "natural" garden on his estate at the Leasowes, not far from Halesowen, was famous throughout the eighteenth century.

October 30, 1773 (to Obour Tanner)

Based on Deane, pp. 14–15, the "young man" named in the post scriptum was probably John Peters, who would later become Wheatley's husband.

December 1, 1773 (to John Thornton)

This text derives from Silverman, pp. 264–65.

February 9, 1774 (to Samuel Hopkins)

This text is based on that given in the *Pennsylvania Freeman* for May 9, 1839. This abolitionist weekly newspaper was edited by John Greenleaf Whittier, ardent abolitionist and well-known poet, from March 1838 to February 1840. The "two negro men" Wheatley names have been identified by Robinson (p. 329) as Bristol Yamma (1744?–1793) and John Quamine (1743?–1799). For the Reverend Samuel Hopkins's role in the movement to Christianize Africa, see Lorenzo J. Greene, *The Negro in Colonial New England* (New York: Columbia University Press, 1942), pp. 277–79. The "precious crumbs" passage, of course, refers to Matthew 15:27; the specific Psalm referred to is 68 (see v. 31).

February 11, 1774 (to Samson Occom)

Based on the text given in *The Massachusetts Spy* for March 24, 1774, according to Robinson (p. 332), this letter, Wheatley's most eloquent and emphatic condemnation of slavery, appeared first in the *Connecticut Gazette* for March 11, 1774. *The Massachusetts Gazette and Boston Post Boy and Advertiser* for March 21, 1774, carried with it the following headnote: "The following is an Extract of a letter from Phillis, a Negro Girl of Mr. Wheatley's of this Town, to the Rev. Samson Occom, which we are desired to insert as a specimen of her Ingenuity. It is dated February 11, 1774" (from Robinson's *Phillis Wheatley: A Bio-Bibliography* [Boston: G. K. Hall, 1981], p. 26). Robinson (p. 332) observes that this exquisite prose tract, Wheatley's finest, was reprinted "in almost a dozen New England newspapers."

March 21, 1774 (to Obour Tanner)

The text is from Deane, pp. 16–17.

March 29, 1774 (to John Thornton)

This text is from Silverman, pp. 265–67.

May 6, 1774 (to Obour Tanner)

The text is based on that given by Deane, p. 18. Note Wheatley's keen attention to the details of the sales of her 1773 *Poems*.

May 6, 1774 (to Samuel Hopkins)

The text here is based on that given by Carter G. Woodson, ed., *The Mind of the Negro as Reflected in Letters Written during the Crisis 1800–1860* (Washington, D.C.: Association for the Study of Negro Life and History, 1926), pp. xvi–xvii. Notice how, once again and on the same day, Wheatley is actively engaged in the enterprise of distributing her 1773 *Poems* to a receptive market.

October 30, 1774 (to John Thornton)

Based on Silverman, pp. 267–68, this letter constitutes a flat rejection of Thornton as a religious guide, a declaration of her temporal (and spiritual?) freedom, and a refusal to serve in any capacity the movement to Christianize Africa. The subtle diplomacy with which Wheatley issues these three injunctions displays her intelligence, her sparkling wit, and her eloquent command over words. The reference to "the language of the Anamaboe" identifies a region in Africa (today a part of Ghana) from which came John Quamine, one of the two black missionaries Wheatley names in the February 9, 1774, letter to Samuel Hopkins.

October 26, 1775 (to George Washington)

This text is based on that of the *Virginia Gazette* for March 20, 1776, p. 1A.

May 29, 1778 (to Obour Tanner)

Based on Deane, pp. 18–19. If the author is to be believed and this "scrawl" was indeed "hasty," this letter is no small illustration of Wheatley's judicious spontaneity with the use of words.

July 15, 1778 (to Mary Wooster)

Taken from the text given by Mukhtar Ali Isani in " 'On the Death of General Wooster': An Unpublished Poem by Phillis Wheatley,"

Modern Philology 77, no. 3 (February 1980): 306–9, this letter embraced the text of Wheatley's elegy on the death of David Wooster, Mary's husband. The poem comes immediately after the dash following the phrase "the Cause of Freedom—" and immediately precedes the phrase "you will do me a great favour."

May 10, 1779 (to Obour Tanner)

The text of this last letter to Obour, Wheatley's close black friend ("sister") and her possible cohabitor on the ship during the terrible Middle Passage from Africa to America, is based on Deane, p. 19. It is one of her shortest extant letters, and she may well have found the vicissitudes of the Revolution comprising the "variety of hindrances" which had prevented her correspondence.

Proposals for Printing by Subscription

These 1772 proposals were, according to Robinson (p. 309), printed in the *Boston Censor* for February 29 (p. 3), March 14 (p. 3), and April 18 (p. 3). As Robinson has done, I have added the bracketed numbers for the convenience of reference. Based on the fact that this volume's design would have included many of Wheatley's political, anti-British poems—such as "On America," "On the King," "On the Death of Master Seider," "On the Affray in King-Street" (about the Boston Massacre), and "To Samuel Quincy, Esq; a Panegyrick" (who prosecuted the British soldiers who fired on the American colonists in the massacre)—this volume, perhaps to be entitled *A Collection of Poems,* could well have been considered the first poetic tribute to the Revolutionary War.

Proposals

The text of these proposals appeared in Boston in the *Evening Post and General Advertiser* for October 30, November 6 and 27, and December 4, 11, and 18—all in 1779. This volume never appeared. Notice, however, the poet's continued interest in classical subjects, especially the pastoral, in such titles as "A Complaint," "To Philandra an Elegy," "Chloe to Calliope," and "To Musidora on Florello."

Wheatley's Final Proposal

This final proposal for a volume, apparently to have been virtually the same collection proposed in 1779, appeared in *The Boston Magazine* on p. 462 of the September number of 1784. The poem referred to in this proposal as appearing on p. 488 of this journal is presented in the section "Extant Poems Not Included in the 1773 *Poems*," above. Entitled "To Mr. and Mrs. ———, On the Death of Their Infant Son" in *The Boston Magazine*, this is probably the same poem called "To P.N.S. & Lady on the death of their infant son" in the 1779 proposals.

Sabbath—June 13, 1779

Diana Lachatanere of the Schomburg Center for Research in Black Culture of The New York Public Library has graciously provided the transcription of the badly damaged manuscript on which this text is based.

VARIANT POEMS AND LETTERS

To the University of Cambridge, Wrote in 1767

This text is taken from Mason, pp. 63–64.

On Atheism [Variant I]

The text here is taken from Kuncio, pp. 294–96.

On Atheism [Variant II]

This third version is that given by Robinson, pp. 356–57.

Deism

This version is probably the older though not preferred rendering; the later version in "Extant Poems Not Included in the 1773 *Poems*," above, contains fewer misspellings and better grammatical constructions. This text, based on that given by Phil Lapsansky in *"Deism—An Unpublished Poem by Phillis Wheatley," NEQ* 50, no. 3 (September 1977): 517–20, provides an opportunity to observe a work evolving. Note that the author has dropped the prose prayer of ll. 41–49, as well as the concluding couplet.

To the King's Most Excellent Majesty on His Repealing the American Stamp Act

The text here is that of Kuncio, p. 292.

On the Death of the Rev'd Dr. Sewall, 1769

The text is that of Mason, pp. 64–66.

31: "(The rocks responsive to the voice, reply'd.)" Here Wheatley attempts a rare (for her) use of the "echo device," whereby the auditory image she calls up describes the sounds of grief echoing off the stones of Sewall's Old South Church. She dropped this line, among several others, for the 1773 *Poems*.

To Mrs. Leonard, on the Death of Her Husband

This poem's text is taken from the broadside version.

An Elegiac Poem on the Death of . . . George Whitefield [Variant I]

This text was published as a broadside in Boston. In the title to this poem, following George Whitefield's name, the text reads:

Chaplain to the Right Honourable the Countess of Huntingdon, &c. &c.
Who made his Exit from this transitory
State, to dwell in the celestial Realms of Bliss, on LORD's Day 30th of September, 1770, when he was seiz'd with a Fit of the Asthma, at NEWBURYPORT, near BOSTON, in NEW ENGLAND. In which is a Condolatory Address to His truly noble Benefactress the worthy and pious Lady HUNTINGDON,—and the Orphan-Children in GEOR-GIA; who, with many Thousands, are left, by the Death of

this great Man, to Lament the Loss of a Father, Friend, and Benefactor.

By PHILLIS, a Servant Girl of 17 Years of Age, Belonging to Mr. J. WHEATLEY, of Boston:—And has been but 9 Years in this Country from Africa.

Following the poem, the text continues: "Sold by EZEKIAL RUSSELL, in Queen-Street, and JOHN BOYLES, in Marlboro-Street."

An Ode of Verses on the Much-Lamented Death of the Rev. Mr. George Whitefield [Variant II]

This version of Wheatley's elegy on Whitefield is a broadside variant which circulated in London. Following George Whitefield's name in the title and preceding the actual poem, the text reads:

> Late Chaplain to the Countess of *Huntingdon*; Who departed this Life, at *Newberry* near *Boston* in *New England*, on the Thirtieth of *September*, 1770, in the Fifty-seventh Year of his Age. Compos'd in America by a Negro Girl Seventeen Years of Age, and sent over to a Gentleman of Character in *London*.

The poem itself contains several unusual lines, such as the bold phrasing in l. 44 spoken by the Voice of the Great Awakening about those blacks who convert: "He'll [Jesus will] make you free, and Kings, and Priests to God." Additionally, since the final fourteen lines of this version do not appear either in the American or in the 1773 *Poems* versions and since the anapests of ll. 51–58 are unique in Wheatley's poetry, these final lines are probably by another writer. Following the poem, the text reads: "Printed and sold for the Benefit of a poor Family burnt out a few Weeks since near Shoreditch Church, that lost all they possessed, having nothing insur'd. Price a Penny apiece, or 5 s. a Hundred to those that sell them again."

On the Death of Doctor Samuel Marshall

The text here is that of Mukhtar Ali Isani, "The Original Version of Wheatley's 'On the Death of Dr. Samuel Marshall,' " *Studies in Black Literature* 7, no. 3 (Autumn 1976): 20.

Recollection, to Miss A——, M——

As indicated, this text is taken from *The London Magazine: Or Gentleman's Monthly Intelligencer* for March 1772.

28: "Menellian strains."   An unusual spelling, this word is possibly a reference to Mt. Maenalus in Arcadia, sacred to Pan. See Vergil's eighth Eclogue, where "Macnalios" is repeated as a refrain. In the 1773 *Poems*, Wheatley renders this phrase somewhat more dryly as "entertaining strains."

To the Rev. Mr. Pitkin, on the Death of His Lady

This poem first appeared as a broadside, a photocopy of which has been included in C. F. Heartman, *Phillis Wheatley (Phillis Peters): A Critical Attempt and a Bibliography of Her Writings* (New York, 1915). In the 1773 *Poems*, this poem is revised and entitled "To a Clergyman on the Death of His Lady."

To the Hon'ble Thomas Hubbard, Esq; On the Death of Mrs. Thankfull Leonard

Based on a broadside of the date indicated, this poem's lines 19 and 20, deleted in the 1773 *Poems* version (where the title is "To the Honourable T.H. Esq; on the Death of His Daughter"), depict a clear example of Wheatley's practice of syncretizing ancient classicism with Christianity. The "unreluctant" (l. 17) deceased flies to her heavenly reward, where her "bless'd eyes salute the op'ning morn" (l. 20)—the poet's beloved Aurora, goddess of the dawn.

To the Right Honourable William Legge, Earl of Dartmouth

This early version of the Dartmouth poem, which appears in the 1773 *Poems* under the more formal title "To the Right Honourable

William, Earl of Dartmouth," was printed in the *New York Journal* for June 3, 1773. Mukhtar Ali Isani reprints it along with a version of the poet's accompanying letter (see below) in "Early Versions of Some Works of Phillis Wheatley," *EAL* 14, no. 2 (Fall 1979): 149–55.

To the Empire of America
. . . Farewell . . . . [Variant I]

Taken from *The Massachusetts Gazette and Boston Post-Boy and Advertiser* for May 10, 1773, this version of the poem appeared in Boston only two days after Wheatley's departure for London. This version contains several lines which are deleted in the 1773 *Poems* version. See the recent reprinting of this version in Mukhtar Ali Isani, "Wheatley's Departure for London and Her 'Farewel to America,' " *South Atlantic Bulletin* 42, no. 4 (November 1977): 123–29.

Farewell to America [Variant II]

The Massachusetts Gazette and Boston Weekly News Letter for May 13, 1773, also printed a version of "Farewell to America" with the following headnote: "Boston, May 10, 1773, Saturday last Capt. Calef sailed for London, in whom went Passengers Mr. Nathaniel Wheatley, Merchant; also, Phillis, the extraordinary Negro Poet, Servant to Mr. John Wheatley." For a recent reprinting of this version, see Robinson, pp. 392–93.

An Elegy Sacred to the Memory of the
Rev'd Samuel Cooper, D.D.

This variant's text is the editor's transcription of the original manuscript (in Wheatley's own hand) now housed at the Massachusetts Historical Society.

43: "indulgent rays."   In the printed, broadside version of the elegy, this phrase is rendered "indulgent grace," losing altogether the extension of the "radient [*sic*] lamp" metaphor of l. 24. Earlier, Wheatley had referred to Whitefield as "the setting sun" (l. 9 of the

1773 *Poems* version) and to Sewall as having "brighter lustre than the sun" (l. 35 of the 1773 *Poems* version). Surely the printer (and/or typesetter) of the broadside version, in canceling the perfectly rhyming "rays" in favor of the slant-rhyming "grace," has tampered with the poet's original intentions.

On the Death of J.C. an Infant

Based on the anonymous version printed in the *Methodist Magazine* (Philadelphia) in the September issue of 1797, this version has been recently reprinted by Mukhtar Ali Isani in "Early Versions of Some Works of Phillis Wheatley," *EAL* 14, no. 2 (Fall 1979): 154. For more information concerning Wheatley's Methodist connections, see Isani's article devoted entirely to this topic: "The Methodist Connection: New Variants of Some Phillis Wheatley Poems," *EAL* 22, no. 1 (Spring 1987): 108–13.

October 25, 1770 (to the Countess of Huntingdon)

This text is a transcription of the manuscript version in Wheatley's handwriting, apparently made as a copy of the version given by Jackson (p. 212). A facsimile of this letter is reproduced by Robinson (p. 399). The papers of the Countess of Huntingdon are housed by the Cheshunt Foundation in Cambridge University, England.

June 3, 1773 (to the Earl of Dartmouth; another version of the letter dated October 10, 1772)

Recently reprinted by Isani in "Early Versions of Some Works," the text of this version first appeared in the *New-York Journal* for June 3, 1773, followed by a version of "To the . . . Earl of Dartmouth" and preceded by this headnote:

> *We have had several Specimens of the poetical Genius of an African Negro Girl, belonging to Mr. Wheatley of Boston, in New England, who was Authoress of the following Epistle and Verses, addressed to Lord Dartmouth—They were written, we are told on the following Occasion, viz[:] A Gentleman who*

had seen several of the Pieces ascribed to her, thought them so much superior to her Situation, and Opportunities of Knowledge, that he doubted their being genuine—And in order to be satisfied, went to her Master's House, told his Doubts, and to remove them, desired that she would write something before him. She told him she was then busy and engaged for the Day, but if he would propose a Subject, and call in the Morning, she would endeavour to satisfy him. Accordingly, he gave for a Subject, The Earl of Dartmouth, *and calling the next Morning, she wrote in his Presence, as follows.*

PHILLIS WHEATLEY'S STRUGGLE FOR FREEDOM IN HER POETRY AND PROSE

1. A variety of biographical sources about Wheatley are available; for the most up-to-date information on her London activities, see William H. Robinson, "Phillis Wheatley in London," *CLA Journal* 21, no. 2 (1977): 187–201; James A. Rawley, "The World of Phillis Wheatley," *New England Quarterly* 50, no. 4 (December 1977): 666–77; Mukhtar Ali Isani's extremely useful "The British Reception of Wheatley's *Poems on Various Subjects*," *Journal of Negro History* 66, no. 2 (Summer 1981): 144–49; William J. Scheick, "Phillis Wheatley and Oliver Goldsmith: A Fugitive Satire," *Early American Literature* 19, no. 1 (Spring 1984): 82–84; and Wheatley's informative letter to David Wooster detailing her activities, pp. 169–71 in this volume. Sidney Kaplan has included a photocopy of Jones's letter mentioning Wheatley in *The Black Presence in the Era of the American Revolution: 1777–1800* (Greenwich, Conn.: New York Graphic Society, 1973), p. 161. For severely censuring opinions of Wheatley's work, see especially J. Saunders Redding, *To Make a Poet Black* (Chapel Hill: University of North Carolina Press, 1939), pp. 9–11; and Martha Bacon, *Puritan Promenade* (Boston: Houghton Mifflin, 1964), p. 38. Recently many critics have risen to Wheatley's defense; an especially intelligent and judi-

cious example of the positive approach is Sondra O'Neale, "A Slave's Subtle War: Phillis Wheatley's Use of Biblical Myth and Symbol," *EAL* 21, no. 2 (Fall 1986): 144–65.

2. For the establishment of the period of Wheatley's manumission, see Mukhtar Ali Isani, "Phillis Wheatley in London: An Unpublished Letter to David Wooster," *American Literature* 51, no. 2 (May 1979): 255–60.

3. I refer to the title given in the poem's manuscript version, which was first published in Robert Kuncio's "Some Unpublished Poems of Phillis Wheatley," *New England Quarterly* 43 (June 1970): 292.

4. Ibid., p. 297.

5. In Vol. III of *The History of the Colony and Province of Massachusetts Bay*, ed. Lawrence S. Mayo (Cambridge, Mass.: Harvard University Press, 1936), Thomas Hutchinson, governor of the colony and one of the signatories of the letter of attestation which prefaced Wheatley's 1773 volume, records that before the assault on Richardson's house, Richardson had objected to the mob's gathering outside the home of one of four persons who had recently been denounced publicly as enemies of the colony (i.e., as British sympathizers). It was as a consequence of Richardson's objection that he was pursued to his own home (pp. 193–94). During the trial, "the whole court was clear in opinion, that the evidence against Richardson, at most, amounted to manslaughter; and one or more declared the homicide excusable. . . . But party prejudices in times of civil dissension in England, had often prevailed more with juries than all other considerations." So the court officially found him guilty of murder (p. 206). But at length, "the prisoner having been brought into court early in a morning, when scarce any persons except the officers of the court, were present, pleaded his majesty's pardon, and was discharged and immediately absconded" (p. 207n). Wheatley and her compatriots had good reason to be resentful. For another account of this incident, see Arthur M. Schlesinger, *The Colonial Merchants and the American Revolution 1763–1776* (New York: Columbia University Press, 1918), pp. 179–80.

6. For this title and Wheatley's first proposal, consult William H. Robinson, *Black New England Letters* (Boston: Boston Public Library, 1977), pp. 50–51; and Mukhtar Ali Isani, "The First Proposed Edition of *Poems on Various Subjects* and the Phillis Wheatley Canon," *American Literature* 49, no. 1 (March 1977): 97–103. Robinson discusses the racial issue which prevented publication of the first volume; Isani emphasizes the dating and the subjects of the poems listed.

7. Samuel Eliot Morison, *The Oxford History of the American People* (New York: Oxford University Press, 1965), pp. 199–200. Morison writes that "two more were mortally wounded," leaving a total of five dead. Morison describes the black man, Attucks, as "the most aggressive member of the mob." It is noteworthy that Morison also pays tribute to Wheatley in his volume. He calls her the girl wonder of the revolutionary age and quotes four lines from her "Liberty and Peace" (p. 289).

8. Robinson, in *Black New England Letters*, pp. 27–62, explains in detail the Boston prejudice toward publication of Wheatley's first book.

9. The Earl of Dartmouth belonged to a circle of Calvinistic Methodists headed by Selina Hastings, Countess of Huntingdon, to whom Wheatley's 1773 volume is dedicated (Hastings lent her financial support to the enterprise), and included George Whitefield, the well-known evangelist of the Great Awakening who had been entertained by the Wheatleys and whose death Wheatley celebrated in a widely published elegy; Samson Occom, an American Indian evangelist with whom Wheatley corresponded; and John Thornton, an evangelistic philanthropist who contributed a tidy sum to the founding of Dartmouth College and with whom Wheatley also corresponded. See Rawley, "The World of Phillis Wheatley," pp. 666–77, which intelligently and comprehensively draws a portrait of Wheatley's relation to this circle.

10. All nine of the British reviews of Wheatley's 1773 *Poems* have been reprinted in Isani, "The British Reception of Wheatley's *Poems.*"

11. Three particularly harsh recent assessments are those by Donald B. Gibson in *Encyclopedia of Black America*, ed. W. A. Low and Virgil A. Clift (New York: McGraw-Hill, 1981), p. 519; S. E. Ogude in "Slavery and the African Imagination: A Critical Perspective," *World Literature Today* 55, no. 1 (Winter 1981): 21–25; and J. Saunders Redding in *Dictionary of American Negro Biography*, ed. R. W. Logan and M. R. Winston (New York: Norton, 1982), pp. 640–42.

12. C. G. Jung, *The Archetypes and the Collective Unconscious*, trans. R. F. C. Hull (New York: Pantheon, 1959), pp. 383–84.

13. Ibid., p. 384.

14. Margaretta Odell, *Memoir and Poems of Phillis Wheatley: A Native African and a Slave. Also, Poems by a Slave* (3d ed., 1838; reprint Miami, Fla.: Mnemosyne, 1969), p. 12.

15. E. B. Tylor, *Religion in Primitive Culture* (New York: Harper and Row, 1958), pp. 11, 230. It is generally held today that animistic and fetishistic practices are not learned until adolescence (perhaps even late adolescence), but I am assuming that Wheatley was too sensitive an individual not to have retained a measure of her African religious heritage. See my chapter on "Phillis Wheatley's African Origins" in the forthcoming *Phillis Wheatley's Poetics of Liberation*.

16. Jung, *The Archetypes*, p. 389.

17. Ibid., p. 388.

18. Some have charged that Wheatley was a petted slave and therefore immune to the wounds of prejudice. In *Black New England Letters*, Robinson's discussion of the problems with prejudice that Wheatley encountered when she tried to publish a volume of her poetry in Boston in 1772 proves this charge vacuous. Odell, in *Memoir and Poems of Phillis Wheatley*, documents Wheatley's deference to the elite of Boston and the major problems with survival she encountered after her marriage to a black man, John Peters. This move away from the protection of sympathetic whites, probably forced by the deaths of her mistress, her master, and their son all within a very short time, and only exacerbated by the war, sub-

sequently brought about the deaths of her three children and her own death in abject poverty at the early age of thirty-one.

19. Abbie Findlay Potts, *The Elegiac Mode: Poetic Form in Wordsworth and Other Elegists* (Ithaca: Cornell University Press, 1967), pp. 44–45.

20. Robert Henson, "Form and Content of the Puritan Funeral Elegy," *American Literature* 32, no. 1 (1970): 12.

21. Gregory Rigsby, in "Form and Content in Phillis Wheatley's Elegies," *CLA Journal* 19, no. 2 (1975), acknowledges the presence of the elements of portraiture and exhortation in Wheatley's elegies, but then he contradicts himself when he insists that the breakdown of portraiture into the steps of vocation, sanctification, and glorification "are never used by Miss Wheatley" (p. 249).

22. Wheatley had met Whitefield shortly before his death, and she dedicated her 1773 volume to Selina Hastings, Countess of Huntingdon and Whitefield's patron. Both these figures were loud voices in the Methodist movement in England; their influence on Wheatley is thoroughly probable. John W. Draper, in *The Funeral Elegy and the Rise of English Romanticism* (1929; reprint New York: Phaeton Press, 1967), gives a seven-page discussion of the effect of Methodism on the elegy in England (pp. 286–92). He suggests that it shifted the onus of salvation from the Puritan church: "Salvation by the power of the Church had, in Calvinistic theology, given way to Salvation by the Grace of God, and in Wesleyan teaching to Salvation by emotional uplift. Emotional uplift was the immediate purpose and effect of the sermons of John Wesley and of Whitefield" (p. 287). Draper maintains that the elegies that Methodism produced all had one unvaried theme, "the extasy of heaven" (p. 288). Wheatley's starting her poems on Whitefield and Sewall with their apotheoses suggests another affinity with the Methodist elegies. "The Methodists," states Draper, "instead of reserving the apotheosis for the climax of the elegy commonly state it boldly at the start." Then Draper quotes as an example Charles Wesley's "elegy" on Whitefield (1771) which begins in much the same spirit as Wheatley's (hers preceding his by a year): "And is my Whitefield

entered into rest,/ With sudden death, with sudden glory blest?" (p. 288).

23. At this point, Wheatley espouses ideas which characterize the personal elegy of the English Renaissance. A. L. Bennett, in "The Principle Rhetorical Conventions in the Renaissance Personal Elegy," *Studies in Philology* 51, no. 2 (1954), observes that these elegies speak of the dead as having endured the inevitable (p. 117) and extend "the classical argument that the deceased would not return to this world of evil, misfortune, and anxiety even if he could" (p. 121).

24. Jeffrey B. Walker, "The Devil Undone: The Life of Benjamin Church (1734–1778) to which is added, An Edition of His Complete Poetry," dissertation, Pennsylvania State University, 1977, p. 182.

25. John C. Shields, "Phillis Wheatley and Mather Byles: A Study in Literary Relationship," *College Language Association Journal* 23, no. 4 (June 1980): 377–90.

26. Potts, *The Elegiac Mode*, pp. 97–98. Other places where one may find discussions of Wheatley' classicism include John C. Shields, "Phillis Wheatley's Use of Classicism," *American Literature* 52, no. 1 (1980): 97–111; and the chapter on classicism in my forthcoming *Phillis Wheatley's Poetics of Liberation*.

27. Potts, *The Elegiac Mode*, pp. 44–45.

28. In "The Neoclassical Psychology of the Imagination," *Journal of Literary History* 4 (1937), Donald F. Bond insists that most of the aestheticians in the eighteenth century, Locke and Addison included, thought the imagination was "a means of simple apprehension, the collecting of phantasms or sense impressions, which are stored up for the scrutiny of reason and making of abstract conceptions" (p. 246).

29. Samuel Taylor Coleridge, *Biographia Literaria*, ed. James Engall and W. Jackson Bate (Princeton: Princeton University Press, 1983), p. 305.

30. Ibid., p. 304.

31. Additional observations concerning Wheatley's use of the

imagination as a means of ascent shed light on how her conception
of the imagination derives from eighteenth-century aesthetics. The
phrase "the mental train" occurs in "Thoughts" (p. 48) and in "On
Imagination" (p. 67). Both times, it refers to a sequence of thoughts
which the reason, the ordering principle of imagination (at least in
Wheatley's conception), structures. This idea probably derives from
the Hobbesian notion of a "Trayne of Thoughts" *(Leviathan, 1651,*
ch. 8) described by Bond as "a lively interest in the freedom of the
imagination to associate ideas . . . and to supply wit with its quickness in tracing resemblances" ("The Neoclassical Psychology of the
Imagination," p. 258). Hobbes's "Trayne of Thoughts" resembles
what Wheatley describes as the movement of the fancy through the
memory prior to the act of creating a poem. In *Elements of Criticism,* an extremely popular eighteenth-century treatise on taste and
aesthetics (first published 1762; 6th ed., 1785), Henry Home, Lord
Kames, observes in a chapter on uniformity and variety, "The pleasure that arises from a *train of connected ideas,* is remarkable in a
reverie" (Vol. I, p. 315; italics added). It is also worth observing
that during the seventeenth century "thoughts" and "imaginations"
were often synonyms (see the *O.E.D.).* Kames was read by many
Americans such as Jonathan Edwards, Thomas Jefferson, Joel Bar-
low, Timothy Dwight, and Benjamin Franklin. It is within reason
to hypothesize that Wheatley herself may have read *Elements of
Criticism.* See the substantial discussion of Kames's American influence by Liza Dant, "Henry Home, Lord Kames," in *Dictionary of
Literary Biography: American Colonial Writers, 1735–1781,* Vol. 31,
ed. Emory Elliott (Detroit: Bruccoli Clark, 1984), pp. 322–28.

Wheatley's own idea of the imagination (different from Hobbes's) displays a marked similarity to that of Addison. In *The Spectator* 411 (June 21, 1712), Addison wrote:

> We cannot indeed have a single Image in the Fancy that did
> not make its first Entrance through the Sight: but we have
> the Power of retaining, altering, and compounding those
> Images, which we have once received, into all the varieties

of Picture and Vision that are most agreeable to the Imagination: for by this Faculty a Man in a Dungeon is capable
of entertaining himself with Scenes and Landscapes more
beautiful than any that can be found in the whole Compass
of Nature." (Donald F. Bond, ed., *The Complete Works of
Joseph Addison*, Vol. III [London: Oxford University Press,
1965], p. 537)

In a note to the phrase, "the Power of retaining, altering, and
compounding," Bond observes, "These activities of the imagination
had long been recognized; as the century progresses, critics come to
be increasingly impressed by the liveliness with which the imagination performs these functions." In his *The Imagination as a Means
of Grace: Locke and the Aesthetics of Romanticism* (Berkeley: University of California Press, 1960), Ernest Tuveson expresses the opinion that "The imagination, for Addison, reconciles man with his
spiritual needs and his desire to belong to a living universe of purpose and values with a cosmos that begins to appear alien, imper-
sonal, remote, and menacing" (p. 97). This same grasp of imagination and its potentially spiritual function is also present in Wheatley's
poetics, except that she moves beyond Addison. In her poetry, "all
the senses" are bound, not just the sight. She makes a clear distinction between the fancy and the imagination, whereas Addison's the-
sis is to allay confusion that early-eighteenth-century critics made in
using the two terms by explaining that the words are synonymous.
But most important is Wheatley's belief that the imagination recre-
ates and builds "new worlds to amaze th' unbounded soul" (p. 66).
Such understanding, potentially present in Addison, is alive in
Wheatley's rendering of "Thy won'drous acts" and points directly
toward the "romanticism" of the early nineteenth century in England and America.
A last affinity which Wheatley shows for eighteenth-century ideas
may be more than coincidental. Some phrases that describe her idea
of fancy are apparently borrowed from Mark Akenside's *The Pleasures of the Imagination* (1744). This blank-verse poem was im-

mensely popular throughout most of the late 1700s and should have been readily available to Wheatley. Specifically, I have in mind Wheatley's phrases "silken fetters" ("On Imagination," p. 65) and *"Fancy's* queen in giddy triumph" ("Thoughts," p. 47), and the corresponding phrases in Akenside's *Pleasures:* "The silken fetters of delicious ease" (Book II, 1.562) and "her giddy empire" (Book III, 1.70). It is worth observing that the phrase "silken fetters" does not occur in Shakespeare, Milton, Pope, or the King James Bible and that the fancy is never described as "giddy" in any of these works. Nor do the words "giddy" or "fancy" ever appear in the King James Bible.

32. Wheatley's phrase describing Milton as the "British Homer" appears on p. 143, l. 16.

33. Here Wheatley follows a long tradition. James Muilenbaum, one of the principal editors of *The Interpreter's Bible,* gen. ed. George A. Buttrick, Vol. V (Nashville: Abingdon Press, 1965), p. 726, observes about this passage from Isaiah:

> Church fathers like Tertullian, Origen, Jerome and their successors have interpreted it messianically. Theology and poetry have joined in recasting and reinterpreting the thought in ways which, while foreign to the original meaning, have nevertheless done some justice to its sublimity.

34. David B. Morris, *The Religious Sublime: Christian Poetry and Critical Tradition in 18th-Century England* (Lexington: University of Kentucky Press, 1972), pp. 98–103. According to Morris, four poetic forms characterized the religious sublime: the biblical paraphrase, the eschatological poem, poems on the attributes of God, and poems which celebrate imaginative devotion (Addison's phrase). Wheatley composed poems which fit each category.

35. See Samuel Holt Monk, *The Sublime: A Study of Critical Theories in XVIII-Century England,* 2d. ed. (Ann Arbor: University of Michigan Press, 1960), pp. 31–32, for a discussion of how Boileau deduced that this suggestion from Longinus's *Peri Hupsous*

that God's creation of light demonstrates sublimity is actually the epitome and the zenith of the sublime image in literature.

36. From a passage in Edwards's *Narrative of His Conversion* which appears in Herbert W. Schneider, "Religious Enlightenment in American Thought," *Dictionary of the History of Ideas*, gen. ed. Philip P. Wiener (New York: Scribner's, 1973), Vol. IV, p. 110.

37. Other manifestations of the sublime in Wheatley include John Dennis's angry god—see *The Critical Works of John Dennis*, ed. Edward N. Hooker (Baltimore: Johns Hopkins University Press, 1939), Vol. I, p. 356—who in Wheatley appears as Jehovah in "Goliath of Gath" and many other poems and as Apollo in "Niobe in Distress"; Joseph Addison's imaginative devotion *(Spectator* 412), which is evident in almost every one of Wheatley's poems; Edmund Burke's "ideas of pain"—see his *Philosophical Inquiry into the Origin of Our Ideas of the Sublime and Beautiful*, ed. J. T. Boulton (New York: Columbia University Press, 1958), 39—which Wheatley derives from her desire to escape temporal "woes, a painful endless train," from her depiction of the wrath of angry gods, and from her aching reluctance to surrender her poetic world as in "On Imagination"; and finally Lord Kames's solar system—see *Elements of Criticism*, 6th ed. (1785; reprint New York: Garland, 1973), Vol. I, p. 256—which Wheatley dramatically represents in "Thoughts." The point here is not that Wheatley consulted any of these critics' works but that she participated actively in the shaping of an aesthetic idea which permeated the air.

38. Immanuel Kant, *Critique of Aesthetic Judgment*, ed. and trans. James C. Meredith (Oxford: Clarendon Press, 1911), p. 107. In *Elements of Criticism*, Kames speaks of "the vibration of mind between two opposite passions directed to the same object" (vol. I, p. 145).

39. Kant, *Critique*, p. 105. Such contemplation precedes Wheatley and Kant by some twenty-five hundred years. At least from the time of Pythagoras and his musical harmony of the spheres, man has looked at the stars as a macrocosm of universal harmony. For further information, see *The Dictionary of the History of Ideas*, es-

pecially Gretchen L. Finney's "Harmony or Rapture in Music" (Vol. II, pp. 388–95) and George Boas's "Macrocosm and Microcosm" (Vol. III, pp. 126–31). Two further observations concerning the thought of Wheatley and Kant should be made. Reason, for Kant, enables one to conceive *a priori* the ideas of noumena or theoretical objects or powers (totalities such as absolute mass, space, or truth) which at last transcend human experience; the only totality that concerns Wheatley is, of course, her idea of God. But both Kant and Wheatley agree that finally the feeling of the sublime does not reside, as Kant writes, "in any of the things of nature, but only in our own mind" (p. 114). To both, the sublime feeling, then, never occurs in objects themselves but always results from a mental response to contemplation of them. In *Elements*, Kames speaks of contemplation of the planetary system as provocative of the most exalted sublimity: "if we could comprehend the whole ~~ .... [of planets] at one view, the activity and irresistible force of these immense bodies would fill us with amazement: nature cannot furnish another scene so grand" (Vol. I, p. 256).

40. Kant, *Critique,* pp. 94, 107.

41. Ibid., p. 128.

42. Ibid., p. 109. The importance of fear as an incitement to sublimity is also articulated by Dennis, *Critical Works,* and Burke, *Philosophical Inquiry.*

43. Kant, *Critique,* p. 110.

44. Ibid., p. 127.

45. Kant expresses a similar view when he details his description of the moral man. The moral man, says Kant, is capable of the affection of *"astonishment* amounting almost to terror, the awe and thrill of devout feeling, that takes hold of one when gazing upon the prospect of mountains ascending to heaven, deep ravines and torrents raging there, and deep-shadowed solitudes that invite to brooding melancholy" *(Critique,* pp. 120–21). The spirits of *Sturm und Drang* and nineteenth-century romanticism gather here.

46. Ibid., p. 114.

47. Wheatley does not always depend on the heroic couplet; two

of her poems are written in hymn stanza, a third is written in blank verse (suggesting Milton), and a fourth is a Horatian ode. Her last poem, "An Elegy on Leaving_____," is cast in elegiac stanzas.

48. Isani, "The British Reception of Wheatley's *Poems*," p. 147.

49. Philip Freneau, *The Poems of Philip Freneau*, ed. Fred L. Pattee (New York: Russell and Russell, 1902), Vol. I, p. 39. In all fairness to Freneau (one of my favorite American poets), however, several lines from this piece coincide with the enthusiasm Wheatley shows, as in the following: "Ah! What is all this mighty whole,/ These suns and stars that round us roll!" (Freneau, p. 35), and:

> What is this globe, these lands, and seas,
> And heat, and cold, and flowers, and trees,
> And life, and death, and beast, and man,
> And time—that with the sun began—
> But thoughts on reason's scale combin'd,
> Ideas of the Almighty mind! (p. 35)

This last passage predicts in a small way Whitman's technique of cataloging.

50. Other characteristics of Wheatley's poetry which extend her alignment to the romantics are the spontaneity of her compositional process (see Odell, *Memoir and Poems*, p. 18); her frequent celebration of nature, as in "Thoughts," "An Hymn to the Morning," and "An Hymn to the Evening"; her tendency toward mysticism, as shown at several points in the above discussion; and the recurrent lyric quality of her verse, as in her hymns and "On Imagination." It is also pertinent to point out that her poems held almost as much interest for the English as for Americans before the 1830s. Between the years of 1773 and 1820, five new editions of her *Poems* appeared in England, and in America the book was published seven times. In 1805, a printer in Halifax, Yorkshire, not too far from the Lake District, saw fit to bring out an eight-page duodecimo pamphlet of "Thoughts." Joseph Sabin et al., *A Dictionary of Books Relating to*

America (New York: Bibliographical Society of America, 1936), Vol. XXVIII, pp. 168–73.

51. John Keats: *Complete Poems and Selected Letters*, Clarence P. Thorpe ed. (New York: Odyssey Press, 1935), pp. 4, 11, 28–29.

CHRONOLOGY

1619	First blacks "Brought from Africa to America."
1727–1755	Public poetic career of Mather Byles, nephew of Cotton Mather and one of Wheatley's literary advisors; subsequently Byles renounced his public career as poet to pursue his ministry of Hollis Street Church in Boston, until his removal in 1776. He died in Boston in 1788.
1753	Birth of Phillis Wheatley, perhaps along the Gambia River, Africa.
1761	Publication of *Pietas et Gratulatio*, which contained two poems by Samuel Cooper, one containing the line "Imagination! heaven-born maid!" Cooper would later become another of Wheatley's literary mentors.
1761, July 11	Wheatley herself "Brought from Africa to America." She arrives in Boston Harbor aboard the slave schooner *Phillis* and is bought shortly thereafter by John and Susanna Wheatley "for a trifle" and apparently named for the vessel which had transported her.
1765	Wheatley's first known writing, an undated letter (nonextant) to Samson Occom, the Mohegan Indian minister.
1767, December 21	Wheatley's first published writing, the

	poem "On Messrs. Hussey and Coffin." The poet's age is about fourteen.
1769	Death of Joseph Sewall, son of diarist Samuel Sewall and Wheatley's most trusted spiritual counselor; publication of Wheatley's elegy on Sewall's death.
1770, February	"On the Death of Mr. Snider Murder'd by Richardson" celebrates the first martyr of the Revolutionary War.
1770, March	"On the Affray in King-Street, on the Evening of the 5th of March," Wheatley's commemoration of the Boston Massacre. The Wheatley mansion was located on the corner of King Street and Mackerel Lane.
1770, October 2	"On the Death of the Rev. George Whitefield," when published shortly after in London, makes Wheatley an author of international distinction.
1771, August 18	Wheatley baptized by Samuel Cooper, subsequently one of her spiritual and literary advisors.
1772, February 29	Publication of Wheatley's first proposals for a volume of poems, rejected by the Boston public largely for racist reasons.
1773, May 8	Wheatley sets sail for London, accompanied by Nathaniel Wheatley, son of John and Susanna Wheatley, Phillis's owners. She arrives in London on June 17; avowedly this journey is for her health, though she will, while in London, prepare her *Poems* for the press.
1773, July 26	After a six-week stay in England, Wheatley embarks for Boston to take her place at

	the bedside of her dying mistress, Susanna.
1773, August 6	First announcement of the publication of *Poems on Various Subjects, Religious and Moral,* made by A. Bell, Wheatley's London publisher. The volume does not actually appear until early September.
1773, October 18	Wheatley writes David Wooster announcing details of her recent manumission.
1774, March 3	Susanna Wheatley dies. Phillis's fortunes begin to decline shortly after this time.
1778, April 1	Wheatley marries John Peters.
1779, October 30	First publication of Wheatley's final proposals for yet another volume of poems, this book to contain thirteen letters as well as thirty-three poems, none of which was included in the 1772 proposals or in the 1773 *Poems.* Most of these poems and letters remain lost.
1784, December 5	Phillis Wheatley, formerly renowned internationally for the products of her pen, dies in poverty, largely forgotten.
1786	First American printing of Wheatley's *Poems,* at Philadelphia.